GW00802180

THE COWBOY AND THE COSSACK

Merline Lovelace

Harlequin
Mills & Boon

⚜ THE ULTIMATE COLLECTION ⚜

First Published 1995
Second Australian Paperback Edition 2005
ISBN 0 733 55761 9

THE COWBOY AND THE COSSACK © 1995 by Merline Lovelace
Philippine Copyright 1995
Australian Copyright 1995
New Zealand Copyright 1995

Published by
Harlequin Mills & Boon
3 Gibbes Street
CHATSWOOD NSW 2067
AUSTRALIA

Printed and bound in Australia by
McPherson's Printing Group

Prologue

"*There is only you.*"

The low voice, made harsh by the rasp of pain, tore at Alexandra's soul. She leaned over the recumbent figure. "Don't ask this of me."

Gnarled fingers tightened around hers. "I must."

"No. I'm not the one to lead these people."

"You're of my blood, the only one of my blood I can entrust them to. They are your people, too."

"But I'm not of their world."

In the dimness of the shadow-filled tent, she saw bitterness flare in the golden eyes staring up at her. A hawk's eyes, mesmerizing even in the thin, ravaged face. Fierce, proud eyes that proved Alexandra's lineage more surely than the goatskin scrolls used to record the tribe's births. And the deaths. So many deaths.

"Don't fool yourself," the old man went on, his voice grating. *"Although your father, damn his soul, took you away, the steppes are in your heart."* Hatred long held and little lessened by imminent death gave strength to the clawlike hold on her hand. For a moment, the fierce Cossack chieftain of Alexandra's youth glared up at her.

"Grandfather..." she whispered.

His burst of emotion faded. He fell back against the woven blanket, gasping. A ripple of frightened murmurs undulated the circle of women surrounding the aged warrior, tearing Alex from her personal, private battle with the old man. She glanced up and saw the stark fear on their faces.

He was right, she thought in despair. There was no one else. Certainly no one in this huddle of black-clad widows and young girls. Nor among the crippled old men, as war-scarred and ancient as her grandfather, who sat cross-legged on the far side of the smoldering peat fire. They were so old, these men, and so few. Alex felt a stab of pain for her lost uncles and cousins, men she vaguely remembered from her youth. Bearded, muscled warriors who'd flown across the windswept steppes on their shaggy mounts, at one with their horses. They were gone now. All that remained were these women. A few children. The old men. And her.

"We...we wrested back our land when the Soviet bear fell," her grandfather gasped. *"We cannot lose it to the wolves who would devour it now that I...that I..."*

A low rattle sounded, deep in his throat. One of the women moaned and buried her face in her hands, rocking back and forth.

"Prom—promise me!" he gasped, clutching at Alex's hand. His lips curled back in a rictus of effort. *"Promise me you'll hold against—aaah!"*

"Grandfather!"

The golden eyes glazed, then rolled back in their sockets. Alex sat back on her heels, ignoring the ache in her fingers from his agonizing hold, unmindful of the fact that she hadn't eaten or slept in two days of hard traveling to reach his side. She wanted to scream at him not to leave her, not to desert these people who needed him so desperately. She wanted to run out of the smothering black tent and fly back to Philadelphia, to her own world and all that was familiar. But she did none of these things. With the stoicism he himself had taught her, Alexandra watched her grandfather die.

Later, she stood alone under the star-studded sky. The distant sound of women keening vied with the ever-present whistle of the wind across the steppes. Low in the distant sky, the aurora borealis shimmered like an ancient dowager's diamond necklace.

Slowly, Alex lifted her hand. Unclenching her fingers, she stared at the two objects her grandfather had passed to her. A silver bridle bit, used by a fourteenth-century Cossack chieftain, the host's most sacred relic of their past. And a small, palm-size black box, a piece of twentieth-century technology that would ensure her people's future—or spell their doom.

Curling her fist around the two objects, she lifted her face to the velvet sky.

Chapter 1

On a quiet side street just off Massachusetts Avenue, in the heart of Washington's embassy district, hazy September sunlight glinted on the tall windows of an elegant Federal-style town house. Casual passersby who took the time to read the discreet bronze plaque beside the front door would learn that the tree-shaded building housed the offices of the president's special envoy. That wouldn't tell them much.

Most Washington insiders believed the special envoy's position was another of those meaningless but important-sounding titles established a few administrations ago to reward some wealthy campaign contributor. Only a handful of senior cabinet officials were aware that the special envoy performed a function other than his well-publicized, if mostly ceremonial, duties.

From a specially shielded high-tech control center on the third floor of the town house, he directed a covert agency. An agency whose initials comprised the last letter of the Greek alphabet, OMEGA. An agency that, as its name implied, was activated as a last resort—when other, more established organizations such as the CIA, the FBI, the State Department or the military couldn't respond for legal or political reasons.

OMEGA's director alone had the authority to send its agents into the field. He was about to do so now.

"Karistan?"

Perched on one corner of a mahogany conference table, Special Agent Maggie Sinclair swung a burgundy suede boot back and forth. Brows several shades darker than her glossy, shoulder-length brown hair drew together in a puzzled frown. She threw a questioning glance at the other agent who'd been called in with her.

Sprawled with his usual loose-limbed ease in a wing-back chair, Nate Sloan shrugged. "Never heard of the place, unless it's where those fancy rugs come from. You know, the thick, fuzzy kind you can't even walk across without getting your spurs all tangled up in." His hazel eyes gleamed behind a screen of sun-tipped lashes. "That happened to Wily Willie once, with the most embarrassin' results."

Maggie swallowed the impulse to ask just what those results were. No one at OMEGA had ever met Wily Willie Sloan, but Nate's irreverent tales about the man who'd raised him had made the old reprobate a living legend.

She'd have to get the details of this particular incident later, though. The call summoning her and Nate to the director's office had contained a secret code word that signaled the highest national urgency. She turned her attention back to the dark-haired man seated behind a massive mahogany desk.

"Karistan is a new nation," Adam Ridgeway informed

them in the cool, precise voice, which carried only a trace of his Boston origins. "Less than two months old, as a matter of fact, although its people have been struggling to regain their independence for centuries."

He pressed a hidden button, and the wood panels behind his desk slid apart noiselessly to reveal a floor to ceiling opaque screen. Within seconds, a detailed global map painted across the screen, its land masses and seas depicted in vivid, breathtaking colors. Several more clicks of the button reduced the area depicted to the juncture of Europe and Russia. Adam nodded toward a tiny, irregular shape outlined in brilliant orange.

"That's Karistan. I'm not surprised you haven't heard of it. Neither the State Department nor the media took any special note when it emerged as a separate entity a few months ago. Part of the country is barren, mountainous terrain, the rest is high, desolate steppe. It's sparsely populated by a nomadic people, has no industry other than cattle, and possesses no natural resources of any value."

"It has something we want, though," Maggie commented shrewdly.

"We think it does," Adam admitted. "The president is hoping it does."

She leaned forward, tucking a thick fall of hair behind one ear. The tingling excitement that always gripped her at the start of a mission began to fizz in her veins. Adam's next words upped that fizz factor considerably.

"The borders of the new nation run right through a missile field."

"Missile?" Maggie asked, frowning. "Like in nukes?"

Adam nodded. "SS-18s, to be exact."

Nate Sloan's slow drawl broke the ensuing silence.

"Best I recall, the Soviets scheduled the SS-18s for dismantling under the Strategic Arms Reduction Treaty. They're pretty ancient.''

''Ancient and unstable,'' Adam confirmed. ''Which is why the Soviets offered them up so readily under the treaty. Many of the SS-18 missiles have already been dismantled.''

''But not the ones in Karistan.''

''Not the ones in Karistan. When the U.S.S.R. fell apart, the resulting instability in that area derailed all efforts to implement the treaty. Only recently did things settle down enough for a UN inspection team to visit the site.''

Adam paused, then glanced at each of them in turn. ''A U.S. scientist was on the team. What he saw worried him enough for him to pay a personal and very secret visit to the Security Council as soon as he got home.''

Here it comes, Maggie thought, her every sense sharpening. She hunched forward, unconsciously digging her nails into the edge of the conference table.

''According to this scientist, the device that cycles the warhead's arming codes is missing.''

Nate whistled, low and long.

''Exactly,'' Adam responded, his voice even. ''Whoever holds this decoder can arm the warheads. Supposedly, the missiles can't be launched without central verification, but with the former Soviet missile command in shambles, no one knows for sure.''

For a few moments, a strange silence snaked through the director's office, like a finger of damp fog creeping and curling its way across the room. Maggie felt goose bumps prickle along her arms. It was as though some insidious presence from the fifties had drifted in—a nebulous ghost of the doomsday era, when the massive buildup of nuclear weapons had dominated international politics and school children had practiced crouching under their desks during nuclear-survival drills. She swallowed, re-calling how she'd recently chuckled her way through a replay of the old movie *Dr. Strangelove,* starring Peter Sellers. She didn't find it quite so amusing now.

Crossing her arms, Maggie rubbed her hands up and down her silky sleeves. "So the agent you're sending into the field is supposed to find this missing device? This de-coder?"

"As quickly as possible. Intelligence believes it's in the possession of either the Karistanis or their neighbors in Balminsk. The two peoples have been feuding for centu-ries. They're currently holding to a shaky cease-fire, but it could shatter at any moment. There's no telling what might happen if either side felt threatened by the other."

"Great," Maggie muttered, her gaze drawn to the post-age-stamp-size nation outlined in orange.

"Which is why OMEGA's going in. Immediately."

Her attention snapped back to the director. Since both she and Nate had been called in, Maggie knew one of them would man the control center at the headquarters while the other was in the field. Although the controller's position was vital during an operation, she, like the dozen or so other handpicked OMEGA agents, far preferred being in the middle of the action.

Nibbling on her lower lip, she rapidly assessed her strengths and weaknesses for this particular mission. On the minus side, her technical knowledge of nuclear mis-siles was limited to the fact that they were long and pointy. She'd be the first to admit she didn't know plutonium from Pluto.

But she enjoyed an advantage in the field that none of the other OMEGA agents could lay claim to—an incred-ible gift for languages. Having traveled with her Oklahoma "tool pusher" father to oil-rich sites all over the world, she could chatter away in any one of four languages before she learned to read or write.

With formal study, that number had grown considerably, and her natural ability had become her profession. Until two years ago, she'd chaired the foreign language department of a small midwestern college. A broken engagement, a growing restlessness and a late-night phone call from a strange little man her father had once helped escape from a Middle Eastern sheikhdom had culminated in her recruitment by OMEGA.

Given Karistan's location, Maggie suspected its dialect was a mixture of Russian, Ukrainian and possibly Romanian. She could communicate at the basic level in any of those languages. With a day of intensive audio-lingual immersion, she could do better than just communicate. Her speech patterns, idioms and intonation would let her pass for a native.

Adam's deep voice interrupted her swift catalog of her skills. "The mission is a bit more complex than just finding the decoder. The old Karistani headman, the one who allowed in the UN team, died a few weeks ago. The president wants us to deliver a gift to the new ruler, something he hopes will cement relations and get the nuclear-reduction efforts back on track."

"What kind of gift?" Nate asked. "Something along the lines of a blank check written on the U.S. Treasury?"

"Not exactly. The Karistanis are descendants of the Cossacks who used to roam the steppes. They're fiercely proud, and stubbornly independent. They fought a bitter war for their country, and now guard it fiercely. The new ruler flatly refused the economic aid package the State Department put together, saying it had too many strings attached. Which it did," Adam added dryly.

He paused, glancing down at the notepad beside his

phone. "This time the president is sending something more personal. We're to deliver a horse called Three Bars Red. He's a—"

"Whooo-eee!"

Nate's exultant whoop made Maggie jump.

Adam gave a small smile, as if he'd expected just such a reaction from a man whose background had earned him the OMEGA code name Cowboy. A former air force test pilot with skin weathered to a deep and seemingly permanent bronze by his native Wyoming's sun, Nate had won a rodeo scholarship to UW at seventeen, and still worked a small spread north of Cheyenne when he wasn't in the field for OMEGA.

"Three Bars Red's a short-backed, deep-barreled chestnut who happens to possess some of the greatest genes in American quarter horse history," Nate exclaimed, no trace of a drawl in his voice now. "He's a 'dogger right off the range. Only did fair to middling on the money circuit but darned if he didn't surprise himself and everyone else by siring two triple As and eight Superiors."

As Cowboy rattled off more incomprehensible details about this creature named Three Bars Red, Maggie realized that her extensive repertoire of languages had one or two serious gaps. Somehow, she'd missed acquiring horsese, at least the version Nate was speaking.

"I'm not sure of the exact count," he continued, raking a hand through his short, sun-streaked blond hair, "but I know over two hundred of Ole Red's offspring have won racing and performance Register of Merits."

Maggie's mouth sagged. "Two hundred?"

"It may be closer to three hundred by now. I haven't read up on him in a while."

"Three hundred?" she echoed weakly. "This horse has sired three *hundred* offspring?"

''He's produced three hundred *winners*,'' Nate said with a grin. ''And a whole bunch more who haven't placed that high in the money.''

''Which is why the president convinced his owner to part with him in the interests of national defense,'' Adam interjected, his blue eyes gleaming at Maggie's stunned expression. ''Our chief executive is as enthusiastic about the animal as Nate appears to be.''

Cowboy's grin took on a lopsided curve. ''Well, hell! If I'd known he was so horse-savvy, I might have voted for the guy. Sending Ole Red to Karistan is one smart move. A quarter horse is the perfect complement to the tough little mounts they have in that part of the world. He'll breed some size and speed into their lines. I hope the new headman appreciates the gift he's getting.''

''I'm sure she does.''

Nate arched a brow. ''She?''

''She. The granddaughter of the old headman, and now leader of the tribe, or host, as they call it. Alexandra Jordan. Interestingly enough, she carries dual citizenship. Her mother was Russian, her father a U.S. citizen who—''

This time it was Maggie who gave a startled yelp. ''*That* Alexandra Jordan?''

''Do you know her?''

''I know *of* her. She's one of the hottest fashion designers on either side of the Atlantic right now. As a matter of fact, this belt is one of her designs.''

Planting the toe of one of her suede boots in the plush carpet, Maggie performed a graceful pirouette. The movement showed off the exotic combination of tassels, colored yarn and gold-toned bits of metal encircling the waist of her matching calf-length suede skirt.

''These are genuine horsetail,'' she explained, fingering one of the tassels. ''They're Alexandra Jordan's signature.

She uses them in most of her designs. Now that I know about her Cossack heritage, I can understand why. Isn't this belt gorgeous? It's the only item I could afford from her fall collection.''

The two men exchanged a quick glance. Suave, diplomatic Adam merely smiled, but Nate snorted.

Maggie pursed her lips, debating whether to ignore these two fashion Philistines or set them straight about the Russian-born designer's impact on the international scene.

Nate gave her a placating grin. ''Maggie, sweetheart, you can't expect a cowhand to appreciate the subtleties of a fashion statement made by something that rightfully belongs on the back end of a horse. Besides, that little doo-dad could be dangerous.''

At her skeptical look, he raised a palm. ''It's true. Wily Willie once got bucked backward off an ornery, stiff-legged buckskin. He took a hunk of the bronc's tail with him when he went flying, then decided to weave it into a hatband. As sort of a trophy, you understand, since he was out of the money on that ride.''

Despite herself, Maggie couldn't resist asking. ''And?''

''And the other horses got wind of it whenever Willie strolled by. After being kicked halfway across Saturday by a mare in season who, ah…mistook him for an uninvited suitor, Willie was forced to burn that hatband. And his best black Resistol with it.''

''I'll try to avoid mares in season when I'm wearing this belt,'' Maggie promised dryly.

Nate winked at her, then turned his attention to the director again. ''So who's going in, Adam?''

''And when?'' she added.

''You both are. Immediately. Because of the remoteness of the area and the lack of any organized host-country resources to draw on, you'll back each other up in the field. Nate will deliver the president's gift to the new Karistani ruler, and Maggie…'' Adam's blue eyes rested on her face for a moment. ''You'll go into neighboring Balminsk.''

Maggie was still trying to understand exactly why that brief glance should make her skin tingle when the director rose, tucking the end of his crimson-and-blue-striped Harvard tie into his navy blazer.

''David Jensen's flying in from San Diego to act as controller. He should be here in a couple of hours.''

''Doc?''

Maggie felt a spear of relief that the cool, methodical engineer would be calling the shots at HQ during this operation. His steady head and brilliant analytical capabilities had proved perfect complements to her own gut-level instincts in the past.

''Your mission briefings start immediately, and will run around the clock. An air force transport is en route to pick up Three Bars Red, and will touch down here at 0600 tomorrow to take Nate on board. Maggie, you have an extra day before you join the team.''

''Team?''

''The UN is pulling together another group of experts to continue the inspections. You'll go into Balminsk undercover with them. Experts from the Nuclear Regulatory Agency and the Pentagon are standing by to brief you.''

Maggie swallowed an involuntary groan. She understood the urgency of the mission, and was far too dedicated to protest. But she couldn't help feeling a flicker of regret that she'd be spending her time in the field with a clutch of scientists instead of the brilliant international designer whose work she so admired.

* * *

The next ten hours passed in a blur of mission briefings and intense planning sessions.

The initial area familiarization that Maggie and Nate received focused on topography, climate, the turbulent history of the nomadic peoples who inhabited the target area, and the disorder that had resulted from the disintegration of the Soviet political system.

Maggie hunched forward, chin propped in one hand, brown eyes intent on the flashing screen. Her pointed questions sent the briefer digging through his stack of classified documents more than once. Nate sprawled in his leather chair, his hands linked across his stomach, saying little, but Maggie knew he absorbed every word. The only time he stirred was when a head-and-shoulders shot of Karistan's new ruler flashed up on the briefing screen.

"This is a blowup of Alexandra Jordan's latest passport photo," the briefer intoned. "We've computer-imaged the photo to match her coloring, but it doesn't really do her justice."

"Looks damn good to me," Nate murmured.

"They all look good to you," Maggie replied, laughing.

Not taking his eyes from the screen, he slanted her an unrepentant grin. "True."

With his easy smile, rangy body and weathered Marlboro-man handsomeness, Nate never lacked for feminine companionship. Despite the very attractive and very determined women who pursued him, however, Cowboy made it a point to keep his relationships light and unencumbered. As he reminded Maggie whenever she teased him about his slipperiness, in his line of business a man had to keep his saddlebags packed and his pistol primed.

Once or twice Maggie had caught herself wondering if his refusal to allow any serious relationship to develop had something to do with the disastrous mission a few years ago that had left a beautiful Irish terrorist dead and Nate with a bullet through his right lung. No one except Adam Ridgeway knew the full details of what had happened that cold, foggy morning in Belfast, but ever since, no woman had seemed to spark more than a passing interest in Cowboy's eyes.

Which made his intense scrutiny of the face on the screen all the more interesting.

Studying Alexandra Jordan's image, Maggie had to admit that she appeared to be the kind of woman who would prime any man's pistol. Her features were striking, rather than beautiful, dominated by slanting, wide-spaced golden eyes and high cheekbones Maggie would have killed for. A thin, aristocratic nose and a full mouth added even more character. Long hair flowed from a slightly off-center widow's peak and tumbled over her shoulders in a cloud of dark sable.

All that and talent, too, Maggie thought, repressing a sigh. Some things in life just weren't fair.

"Alexandra Danilova Jordan," the briefer intoned, in his clipped, didactic manner. "'Danilova' is a patronymic meaning 'daughter of Daniel,' as I'm sure you're aware. Born twenty-nine years ago in what is now Karistan. Father an economist with World Bank. Mother a student at the Kiev Agricultural Institute when she met Daniel Jordan."

The thin, balding researcher referred to the notes clutched in his hand. Maggie knew he'd had only a few hours to put together this briefing, but if there was any facet of Alexandra Jordan's life or personality that would impact this mission, he would've dug it up. The OMEGA agents didn't refer to him privately as the Mole without cause. Of course, the man's narrow face and long nose might have had something to do with his nickname.

"Ms. Jordan spent a good part of her youth on the steppes, although her father insisted she attend school in the States. Evidently this decision severely strained relations between Daniel Jordan and the old Karistani chieftain, to the point that the headman..."

The Mole frowned and squinted at his notes. "To the point that the headman once threatened to skin his son-in-law alive. Ms. Jordan herself held the chieftain off. With a rifle."

"Well, well..." Nate murmured. "Sounds like a woman after Wily Willie's heart."

When David Jensen arrived a short time later, the pace of the mission preparation intensified even more. With his engineer's passion for detail, Doc helped put together a contingency plan based on the situation in Karistan as it was currently known. True to his reputation within OMEGA as a problem-solver, he swiftly worked up the emergency codes for the operation and defined a series of possible parameters for mission termination.

Around midnight, the chief of the special devices lab arrived with the equipment Maggie and Nate would take to the field. After checking out an assortment of high-tech wizardry, the agents sat through another round of briefings. Just before dawn, the last briefer fed his notes into the shredder and left. Nate packed his personal gear, kept in readiness in the crew room lockers, and had a final consultation with Doc.

The long night of intense concentration showed in Maggie's tired smile as she walked him to the control center's security checkpoint.

"See you on the steppes, Cowboy."

The tanned skin at the corners of Nate's eyes crinkled. "Will I recognize you when I see you?"

"*I* probably won't even recognize me."

Maggie had earned her code name, Chameleon, by her ability to alter her appearance for whatever role the mission required. This skill, combined with her linguistic talents, had enabled her to penetrate areas no other agent could get into—or out of—alive. Still, she couldn't help eyeing Nate's well-worn boots, snug jeans and faded denim jacket with a touch of envy. She doubted her own working uniform would be nearly as comfortable.

"I can just imagine what the field dress unit has come up with for a scientist traveling to a remote, isolated site. Clunky, uncomfortable, and Dull City!"

"Maybe you can talk them into including some of Alexandra Jordan's horsetail jobbies in your kit," Nate replied with a grin. "Just to liven it up a bit."

"Right."

"I'd wear some myself, just to get on the woman's good side, you understand, but the champion stud I'm delivering from the president might mistake me for the competition and try to take me out."

"I suspect that if you show up in Karistan wearing tassels, Alexandra Jordan will take you out herself."

"Might be interesting if she tried." Nate's grin softened into a smile of genuine affection. "It's going to be wild out there. And dangerous. Be careful, Chameleon."

"You too, Cowboy."

Settling a black Denver Broncos ball cap over his blond head, he swung his gear bag over one shoulder and pressed a hand to a concealed wall sensor. After the few seconds it took to process his palm print, the heavy, titanium-shielded oak door hummed open. Fluorescent lights illuminated a flight of stairs that led to the lower floors and a secret, underground exit.

Nate tipped two fingers to the brim of his ball cap. "Be talkin' to you, sweetheart."

When the door slid shut behind his tall, broad-shouldered form, Maggie brushed off her weariness. Squaring her shoulders, she headed for the room where the field dress experts waited. She had a few ideas of her own about her disguise for this particular mission.

Chapter 2

Nate was driven to Andrews Air Force Base, just outside Washington, D.C. After showing a pass that gave him unescorted entry to the flight line, he walked across the concrete parking apron to the specially outfitted jet transport and met his charge for the first time.

Three Bars Red was everything Nate had expected, and then some. A compact, muscular animal, with a strong neck set on powerful, sloping shoulders, a deep chest and massive rounded hindquarters, he stood about fifteen and a half hands. Liquid brown eyes showed a range-smart intelligence in their depths as they returned Nate's assessing look. After a long moment, the reddish brown chestnut chuffed softly and allowed the agent to approach.

Nate ran a palm down the animal's sleek neck. "Well, old boy, you ready to go meet some of those pretty little Karistani fillies?"

At that particular moment, Ole Red seemed more interested in immediate gratification than in the promise of future delights. He nosed the slight bulge in Nate's shirt pocket, then clomped hairy lips over both the pocket and the pack of chewing gum it contained.

Nate stepped back, grinning. "Like sugar, do you?"

"Like it?" The handler who'd flown in with Red grunted. "He's a guldurned addict. You can't leave a lunch bucket or a jacket around the barns, or he'll be in it, digging for sweets."

Nate took in the innocent expression on Ole Red's face. "Guess I'd better lay in a supply of candy bars before we leave."

"Just make sure you don't set them down within sniffing distance," the man advised, "or you'll have twelve hundred pounds of horseflesh in your lap, trying to get to them."

The aircraft's crew chief good-naturedly offered to procure a supply of candy bars, which were duly stored in the aft cargo hold, while Nate conferred with the trainer on Ole Red's more mundane needs. Just moments after the man deplaned, the pilot announced their imminent departure.

The stallion didn't bat an eyelash when the high-pitched whine of the engines escalated into an ear-splitting roar and the big cargo plane rumbled down the runway. Once they were airborne, Nate made sure his charge was comfortable and had plenty of water. Then he stretched out in a rack of web seats, pulled his ball cap down over his eyes and caught up on missed sleep.

After a late-night stop at Ramstein Air Force Base in Germany to refuel and allow their distinguished passenger some exercise, the crew set the transport down the following noon at a small airport in the Ukraine, about fifty miles from the Karistani border. As had been prearranged, a driver waited with a truck and horse van to transport them to the border.

Two hours later, the truck wheezed to a stop at the entrance to the gorge guarding the western access to the new nation. Nate backed Red out of the trailer, smiling at the stud's easygoing nature. Quarter horses were famed for their calm dispositions, but Red had to be the most laid-back stallion Nate had ever worked with. He stood patiently while the foam stockings strapped to his hocks to prevent injury during travel were removed, then ambled along at an easy pace to work out the kinks from the long ride. He was rewarded with an unwrapped candy bar that Nate allowed him to dig out of a back pocket. Big yellow teeth crunched once, twice, and the candy was gone.

Red whickered, either in appreciation of the treat or in demand for more, then suddenly lifted his head. His ears swiveled to the side, then back to the front, trying to distinguish the sound that had alerted him. He gave a warning snort just as a mounted figure rode out of the gorge.

"Your guide comes," the driver informed Nate unnecessarily.

"So I see." Hooking his thumbs in his belt, Nate eyed the approaching rider.

Slumped low in a wooden saddle, his knees raised high by shortened stirrups, the Karistani looked as though he'd just ridden out of the previous century. Gray-haired and bushy bearded, he wore a moth-eaten frock coat that brushed his boot tops and a tall, black sheepskin cap with a red bag and ragged tassel hanging down the side. An old-fashioned bandolier crossed his chest in one direction, the strap of a rifle in the other.

With his creased leather face and I-don't-give-two-hoots-what-you-think air, he reminded Nate instantly of Wily Willie. Of course, Willie wouldn't be caught dead with a gold ring in his left ear, but then, this scraggly bearded horseman probably wouldn't strut around in a gaudy silver bolo tie set with a chunk of turquoise the size of an egg, either.

The newcomer reined to a halt some yards away and crossed his wrists on the wooden tree that served him as a saddle horn. His rheumy eyes looked Nate over from ball cap to boot tip. After several long moments, he rasped something in an unfamiliar dialect. The driver tried to answer in Russian, then Ukranian.

The guide turned his head and spit. Disdaining to reply in either of those languages, he jerked his beard at Nate. "I have few English. You, horse, come."

With the ease of long practice, Nate outfitted Ole Red with the Western-style tack that had been shipped with the stud. After strapping his gear bag behind the cantle, he slipped the driver a wad of colorful paper money, mounted, and turned Red toward the gorge.

As they stepped onto the ledge hacked out of the cliff's side, Nate felt a stab of relief that he was riding a seasoned trail horse instead of some high-stepping, nose-in-the-air Thoroughbred. The chestnut kept his head down and picked his way cautiously, allowing his rider a good view of what lay ahead.

The view was spectacular, but not one Nate particularly enjoyed. Except for the narrow ledge of stone that served as a precarious track, the gorge was perfectly perpendicular. Wind whistled along its sheer thousand-foot walls, while far below, silvery water rushed and tumbled over a rocky riverbed.

A gut-wrenching half hour later, they scrambled up the last treacherous grade and emerged onto a high, windswept plain. Rugged mountains spiked the skies behind them, but ahead stretched a vast, rolling sea of fescue and feather grass. The knee-high stalks rippled and bowed in the wind, like football fans doing the wave. Karistan's endless stretch of sky didn't have quite the lucid blue quality of Wyoming's, but it was close enough to make Nate feel instantly at home.

"There," the old man announced, pointing north. "We ride." Slumping even lower over his mount's withers, he flicked it with the short whip dangling from his wrist.

After thirty-eight hours of travel and a half hour of sheer, unrelenting tension on that narrow ledge, Nate was content to amble alongside his uncommunicative host. The wind whistled endlessly across the high plains, with a bite that chilled his skin below the rolled-up sleeves of his denim jacket, but he barely noticed. With every plop of Ole Red's hooves, Nate felt the power of the vast, empty steppes.

Aside from some darting prairie squirrels and a high, circling hawk, they encountered few other living creatures and even fewer signs of human habitation. At one point Nate spied a rusted truck of indeterminate vintage, stripped of all removeable parts and lying on its side. Later Red picked his way over the remains of a railroad track that ended abruptly in the middle of nowhere.

After an hour or so, they rode up a long, sloping rise and reined in.

"Karistani cattle," the guide said succinctly, jerking his beard toward the strung-out herd below, tended by a lone rider.

Nate rested a forearm on the pommel and ran a knowing eye over the shaggy-coated stock. A cross between Hereford and an indigenous breed, he guessed, with the lean, muscled hardiness necessary to survive on the open range.

At that moment, a couple of cows broke from the pack and skittered north. The lone hand jerked his horse around and took off in pursuit. Almost immediately, a white-faced red steer darted out of the herd. This one decided to head south—straight for the edge of a deep ravine.

The guide grunted at about the same moment the powerful muscles in Red's shoulders rippled under Nate's thighs. He glanced down to see the stallion eyeing the runaway steer intently. Red's ears were pricked forward and his nostrils were flaring, his inbred herding instincts obviously on full alert.

"So you think we ought to stop that dumb slab of beef before it runs right into the ravine?" Nate gave the stallion's dusty neck a pat. "Me too, fella."

He unhooked the rope attached to the saddle and worked out a small loop. "I haven't done this in a while, but what the hell, let's go get that critter."

Bred originally for quick starts and blinding speed over a quarter-mile track, a quarter horse can leap from a stand into a gallop at the kick of a spur. True to his breeding, Red lunged forward at the touch of his rider's heels, stretched out low, and charged down the slope.

Nate ignored the guide's startled shout, focusing all his concentration on the animal running hell-bent for disaster.

Ole Red closed the distance none too soon. The ravine loomed only fifty yards ahead when he raced up behind the now galloping steer. Nate circled his right arm in the air, his wrist rotating, then swept it forward. The rope dropped over the right horn and undulated wildly a few precious seconds before settling over the left.

Red held his position just behind the charging steer as Nate leaned half out of the saddle. With a twist of his wrist, he slipped the line down the animal's side and under its belly. Then he reined Red to the right, and the horse took off.

When he hit the end of the line, Three Bars Red showed

his stuff. He never flinched, never skittered off course. His massive hindquarters bunching, he leaned into the breast harness with every ounce of power he possessed. At the other end of the rope, the cow's momentum dragged its head down toward its belly. In the blink of an eye, a half ton of beef somersaulted through the air and slammed into the earth.

Fierce satisfaction surged through Nate. It was a neat takedown, one of the best he'd ever made, and far safer for the charging animal than simply roping it and risking a broken neck when it was jerked to a halt.

He dismounted and moved toward the downed steer, planning to signal Red forward and loosen the tension on the rope when it stopped its wild thrashing. Intent on the indignant, bawling animal, he paid no attention to the thunder of hooves behind him.

But there was no way he could ignore the sharp, painful jab of a rifle barrel between his shoulder blades.

"Nyet!"

The single explosive syllable was followed by a low, deadly command that sliced through the steer's bellows. Although he didn't understand the dialect, Nate had no difficulty interpreting the gist of the woman's words.

He raised his arms and turned slowly.

Squinting against the sun's glare, he found the business end of a British Enfield bolt-action rifle pointed right at his throat—and the golden eyes that had so fascinated him during his mission briefings glittering with fury.

On the screen, Alexandra Jordan had stirred Nate's interest. In the flesh, she rocked him right back on his heels.

Narrowing his eyes, he tried to decide why. An impartial observer might have said she was a tad on the skinny side. Her slender body certainly lacked the comfortable curves Nate usually enjoyed snuggling up against.

But long sable hair, so rich and dark it appeared almost black, whipped against creamy skin tinted to a soft gold by the wind and the sun. Thick lashes framed tawny eyes that reminded Nate forcibly of the mountain cats he'd hunted in his youth. In high leather boots, baggy trousers and a loose white smock belted at the waist, Alexandra Jordan looked as wild and untamed as the steppes themselves.

Wild and untamed and downright inhospitable. The rifle didn't waver as she rapped out a staccato string of phrases.

"Sorry, ma'am," Nate drawled, "I don't par-lay the language."

Her remarkable eyes narrowed to gleaming slits and raked him from head to foot. "You're the American! The one I sent Dimitri to meet!"

Nate lowered his hands and hooked his thumbs on his belt. "That's me, the American."

"You fool! You damned idiot!"

With a smooth, coordinated movement that told Nate she'd done it a few times before, she slid the rifle into a stitch-decorated, tasseled case.

"Don't you know better than to come charging down out of nowhere like that? I thought you were raiding the herd. I was about to put a bullet through you."

"You were about to try," he said genially.

The laconic response made her mouth tighten. "Be careful," she warned. "You're very close to learning how to dance, Cossack-style. If this steer has been lamed, you might yet!"

She swung out of the saddle and stalked toward the downed bovine. Pulling a lethal-looking knife from a sheath inside her boot, she sawed through the taut rope tethering it to Red. The animal scrambled to its feet, gave an indignant bellow, then took off.

"Hey!"

Nate jumped back just as it dashed by, its horns scraping the air inches from his stomach. His jaw squared, he turned back to face the woman.

"Look, lady, you might at least show a little appreciation for the fact that I kept that hunk of untenderized meat from running headfirst into that ravine."

"That ravine is where it's *supposed* to go," she informed him, scorn dripping from every word. "There's water at the bottom."

Nate glanced sideways, just in time to catch the irritated flick of a tail as the shaggy-haired beast stepped into what looked like thin air. Instead of plunging into oblivion, however, he stomped down a steep, hidden incline and disappeared, pound by angry pound. Almost immediately, Nate heard the slow rumble of hooves as the rest of the herd moved to follow.

"Well, I'll be—" He broke off, a rueful grin tugging at his lips.

One dark eyebrow notched upward in a sarcastic query. "Yes?"

Still grinning, Nate tipped a finger to the brim of his ball cap. "Nate Sloan, at your service. Out of Wolf Creek, Wyoming. I run a few head there myself, when I'm not delivering stock for the president of the United States."

All of which was true, and would be verified by even the most diligent inquiry into his background. What wouldn't be verified was any link between Nate Sloan, former AF test pilot turned small-time rancher, and OMEGA.

She glanced over his shoulder at Three Bars Red. "And that, I take it, is the horse I was told about."

"Not just the *horse*," Nate told her, offended on Ole Red's behalf by her slighting tone. "The sire of champions."

He turned and whistled between his teeth. Red ambled forward and plopped his head lazily on Nate's denim-covered shoulder.

As Alexandra eyed the dusty face, with its white blaze and its wiry gray whiskers sprouting from the velvet muzzle, the ghost of a smile softened her face, easing the lines on either side of her mouth.

"This is the sire of champions?"

"World-class," Nate assured her. He rubbed his knuckles along Red's smooth, satiny cheek, while his senses absorbed the impact of that almost-smile. "I've got his papers in my gear bag, but you'll see the real evidence for yourself come spring."

The hint of softness around her mouth disappeared so fast it might never have been. "I may see the evidence," she replied stiffly, "*if* I decide to accept this gift."

Nate's knuckles slowed. "Why wouldn't you accept him?"

Her chin angled. "The people of this area have an old saying, Mr. Sloan. 'When you take a glass of vodka from a stranger, you must offer two in return.' I've made it clear that I'm not prepared to offer anything, to anyone, at this point."

Well, that settled the question of whether Alexandra Jordan might hand over the decoder if asked quietly through diplomatic channels…assuming she had it in her possession, that was.

Tipping the ball cap to the back of his head, Nate leaned against the chestnut's shoulder.

"There aren't any strings attached to this gift," he told

her evenly, "except the one you just hacked up with that Texas-size toothpick of yours."

"I'm not a fool, Mr. Sloan. I've learned the hard way that you don't get something for nothing in this world, or any other. Karistan is in too precarious a position right now to—" She broke off at the sound of approaching hooves.

When the guide drew up alongside, she held a brief exchange in the flowing, incomprehensible Karistani dialect. After a few moments, Alexandra gave a small shrug. *"Da, Dimitri."*

She turned back to Nate, her eyes cool. "Dimitri Kirov, my grandfather's lieutenant and now mine, reminds me that it is not the way of the steppes to keep travelers standing in the wind, offering neither food nor shelter."

If he hadn't been briefed on Alexandra Jordan's cultural diversity, her formal, almost stilted phrasing might have struck Nate as odd, coming from a woman who'd graduated from Temple University's school of design and maintained a condo in Philadelphia when she wasn't holed up in her Manhattan studio. Here on the steppes, Alexandra's Karistani heritage obviously altered both her speech and her attitude toward a fellow American.

"You'll come to our camp and take bread with us," she told him, "until I make up my mind whether to accept this gift."

It was more order than invitation, and a grudging one at that, but it served Nate's purpose.

"Ole Red and I appreciate the generous offer of hospitality, ma'am."

Her golden eyes flashed at the gentle mockery in his voice, but she turned without another word. She headed for her mount, holding herself so rigid she reminded Nate of a skinned-cypress fence pole…until a fresh gust of wind flattened her baggy trousers against her frame.

A bolt of sheer masculine appreciation shot through Cowboy. Damned if the woman didn't have the trimmest, sweetest curving posterior he'd been privileged to observe on any female in a long, long time.

Too bad she didn't have the disposition to go with it, he thought, eyeing that shapely bottom with some regret. He generally made it a point to steer clear of prickly-tempered females. There were enough easy-natured ones to fill his days and occasional nights when he wasn't in the field.

Although… For a fleeting moment, when she eyed Ole Red, Nate had caught a hint of another woman buried under Alexandra Jordan's hard exterior. One who tantalized him with her elusiveness and made him wonder what it would take to coax her out of the shell she'd built around herself.

Shaking his head at his own foolishness, he gathered Red's reins. Although OMEGA agents exercised considerable discretion in the field, Nate was careful not to mix business with pleasure. He'd learned the hard way it could have disastrous results.

As he pulled Red around, he glanced across a few yards of windswept grass to find Dimitri combing two arthritic fingers through his scraggly beard, his cloudy eyes watching Nate intently.

"I stay, cattle. You ride." The aged warrior's chin jerked toward the mounted woman. "With *ataman*."

Ataman. Nate chewed on the word as he rode out. It meant "headman," or so he'd been briefed. Absolute ruler of the host. Although the Karistanis practiced a rough form of democracy based on the old Cossack system of one man, one vote, they left it to their leader's discretion to call for that vote. Thus their "elected" rulers exercised almost unchallenged authority, and had through the centuries, despite the efforts of various czars and dictators to bend them to their will.

Red's longer stride closed the distance easily. As Nate drew alongside the new Karistani leader, he found himself wondering how a woman coped with being the absolute leader of a people descended from the fierce, warlike Cossacks...the legendary raiders who had made travel across the vast plains so hazardous that the Russian czars at last gave up all attempts to subdue them and gradually incorporated them into their ranks. The famed horsemen whose cavalry units had formed the backbone of Catherine the Great's armies. The boisterous warriors who swilled incredible amounts of vodka, performed energetic leg kicks from a low squat, and dazzled visitors and enemies alike with their athletic displays of horsemanship.

Having seen the way Alexandra Jordan handled both the raw-boned gray gelding she rode and that old-fashioned but lethal Enfield rife, Nate didn't make the mistake of underestimating her physical qualifications for her role. But he had more questions than answers about her ability to lead this minuscule country into the twentieth century. Why had she refused all offers of aid? What was causing those worry lines at the corners of her eyes? And where the hell was that decoder?

Nate had the rest of the day and most of tomorrow to find some answers to those questions, before Maggie arrived in the area. He ought to have the situation pretty well scoped by then. Maybe he'd even get lucky and find the decoder right away, saving Maggie at least a part of the long trip.

He slanted the woman beside him another glance.

Then again, maybe he wouldn't.

* * *

Alex ignored the man beside her and kept her eyes on the far horizon.

Damn! As if she didn't have enough to worry about without some long-legged, slow-talking *cowboy* from the States charging down out of nowhere, almost scaring the wits out of her with his rodeo stunts! Every time Alex thought about how close she'd come to putting a bullet through him, her heart thudded against her breastbone.

She had to stop jumping at every shadow. Despite the garbled message old Gregor had received a couple days ago over his ancient, wheezing transmitter, there'd been no sign of any raiding party from Balminsk. In two days of hard riding, the patrols she'd led out hadn't found any trace of them. It was just another rumor, another deliberate scare tactic from that wild-eyed bastard to the east.

The old wolf was trying to keep her off-balance, and he was succeeding. He wanted to goad her into some action, some incident that would shatter the shaky cease-fire between Balminsk and Karistan and give the outside world the excuse it was waiting for to intervene. And once the outside powers came in, they would never leave. Karistan's centuries-long battle with the Russians had taught them that.

Even her own country, Alex thought bitterly. Even the U.S. Her hands tightened on the reins as she recalled the conditions the State Department representative had laid out as part of the aid package he presented. If she'd agreed to those conditions, which included immediate dismantling of the missiles on Karistan's border, her tiny country would've lost its only bargaining power in the international arena. It would've become little more than a satellite, totally dependent on the vagaries of U.S. foreign policy to guarantee its future.

The sick feeling that curled in Alex's stomach whenever

she thought of those missiles returned. Swallowing, she gripped the reins even tighter to keep her hands from trembling. She still couldn't believe she was responsible for such awesome, destructive power.

Dear God, how had her life changed so dramatically in three short weeks? How had she been transformed overnight from the latest rag queen, as the trade publications had labeled her, to a head of state with absolute powers any dictator might have envied? How was she—?

"This country's a lot like Wyoming," the man beside her commented, his deep voice carrying easily over the rhythmic thud of hooves against soft earth. "It's so big and empty, it makes a man want to rein in and breathe the quiet."

"It's quiet now," Alex replied. But it wouldn't be for long, she thought, if she didn't find a way to walk the tightrope stretching before her.

As if reading her mind, the stranger nodded. "I heard about Karistan's troubles."

"I'm surprised." Alex was careful to keep the bitterness out of her voice. "Most of the press didn't consider my grandfather's struggle for independence front-page material."

His lips curved. "Well, there wasn't much coverage in the *Wolf Creek Gazette,* you understand, but I generally make it a point to do a little scouting before I ride over unfamiliar territory."

Alex frowned, not at all pleased with the way his crooked grin sent a flutter of awareness along her nerve endings. Good Lord, the last thing she needed right now was a distraction, especially one in the form of a broad-shouldered, lean-hipped man! Particularly one with a gleam in his eyes that told her he knew very well his impact on the opposite sex.

She almost groaned aloud, thinking of the problems his presence was going to generate in a camp whose population consisted primarily of ancient, war-scarred veterans, a handful of children, and a clutch of widows and young women. As if she didn't have enough to worry about.

"You want to tell me about it?" His deep voice snagged her attention. "Karistan's struggle for independence, I mean?"

For a crazy moment, Alexandra actually toyed with the idea of opening up, of sharing the staggering burden that was Karistan with someone else. Almost as quickly as the idea arose, she discarded it. The responsibility she carried was hers and hers alone. Even if she'd wanted to, she couldn't risk sharing anything with a man who was delivering a gift that, despite any claim to the contrary, came with obligations she wasn't ready to accept.

"No, Mr. Sloan, I don't care to tell you about it," she replied after a moment. "It's not something you need to be concerned with."

His brown-flecked agate eyes narrowed a bit under the brim of his hat, but he evidently decided not to push the issue.

"Might as well call me Nate," he offered, in that slow, deliberate drawl that was beginning to rasp on Alex's taut nerves. "Seeing as how we're going to be sharing a campfire for a while."

She gave a curt nod and kneed her horse into a loping trot that effectively cut off all conversation.

Drawing in a slow breath, Cowboy tugged his hat lower on his forehead and set Red to the same pace. Alexandra Jordan was one stiff-necked woman.

He suspected he had his work cut out for him if he was going to have anything significant to report to Maggie when she arrived in the area.

Chapter 3

At that moment, Maggie wasn't sure if she was ever going to get to her target area.

She dropped a clunky metal suitcase containing her personal gear and a stack of scientific tomes on the second-floor landing of OMEGA's headquarters and scanned the flickering closed-circuit TV screen overhead. Verifying that the director's outer office was clear, she palmed the sensor.

"Is he in?" she asked the receptionist breathlessly.

Gray-haired Elizabeth Wells glanced up from the Queen Anne-style cabinet she was locking. Her hands stilled, and a look of uncertainty crossed her usually serene features. "Maggie? Is that you?"

Maggie reached up to whip off glasses as round and thick as the bottom of a Coke bottle. Her spontaneous grin slipped into a grimace as her scraped-back hair tugged against her scalp.

"Yes, Elizabeth. Unfortunately."

"Good heavens, dear. I doubt if even your own father would recognize you."

Maggie hitched one hand on a hip in an exaggerated pose. "Amazing what a pair of brogans, a plaid shirt and a plastic pocket pack full of pens can do for a woman's image, isn't it?"

"But...but your face! What did you do to it?"

"A slather of bone white makeup, some gray shadow under my eyes, and a heavy hand with an eyebrow pencil." She waggled thick black brows Groucho Marx would have envied. "Good, huh?"

"Well..." Elizabeth's worried gaze flitted to the dark blemish of the left side of her jaw.

Maggie fingered the kidney-shaped mark, pleased that it had drawn Elizabeth's notice. The unsightly blemish should draw everyone else's attention, as well. Maybe, just maybe, the distraction would give Maggie the half second's edge that sometimes meant the difference between life and death in the field.

"Don't worry," she assured the receptionist. "The guys in Field Dress assured me they didn't use *exactly* the same technique as a tattoo. They have some formula that dissolves the ink under my skin when I get back."

"I hope so, dear," Elizabeth said faintly.

Maggie clumped toward the hallway leading to the director's inner office. "Is the boss in? I need to see him right away."

"You just caught him." The receptionist pressed the hidden electronic signal that alerted Adam Ridgeway to a visit from an OMEGA operative. "He wanted to be sure you were on your way before he left for the ambassador's dinner."

Maggie hurried down the short corridor to the director's inner office, not the least worried that her dramatically altered appearance might trip one of the lethal devices the security folks euphemistically termed "stoppers." The pulsing X-ray and infrared sensors hidden behind the wood-paneled walls didn't rely on anything as unsophisticated as physical identification. Operating at mind-boggling speed, they scanned her body-heat signature, matched it to that in the OMEGA computer, and deactivated the security devices.

Maggie stopped on the threshold to the director's office, searching the dimly lighted room. She caught sight of Adam's lean silhouette in front of the tall, darkening windows, and drew in a sharp breath.

Adam Ridgeway in a business suit or expertly tailored blazer had stopped more than one woman in her tracks on D.C.'s busy streets.

In white tie and tails, he was enough to make Maggie's heart slam sideways against her rib cage and her lungs forget to function.

Damn, she thought as she fought for breath. No man should be allowed to possess such a potent combination of self-assurance and riveting good looks. Not for the first time, she decided that the president couldn't have chosen a more distinguished special envoy than Adam Ridgeway. In his public persona, at least, he epitomized the wealthy, cultured jet-setter dabbling in politics that most of the world believed him to be.

The dozen or so OMEGA agents he directed, however, could attest to the cool, ruthless mind behind the director's impenetrable facade. None of them were privy to the full details of Adam's past activities in service to his country, but they knew enough to trust him with their lives. What was more, he possessed knife-edged instincts, and a legendary discipline during crises.

Only Maggie had been known to shake him out of his rigid control on occasion. She cherished those moments.

Evidently this wasn't one of them. Adam lifted one dark brow in cool, unruffled inquiry. "A last-minute glitch, Chameleon?"

Folding her arms across her plaid-shirted chest, Maggie peered at him over the rims of the thick glasses. "Didn't I disconcert you? Even for a moment?"

After a hesitation so slight she was sure she'd imagined it, his mouth curved in a wry smile. "You disconcert me on a regular and frequent basis."

She would've loved to explore that interesting remark, but a driver was waiting for her downstairs. "Uh, Adam, I have a small problem. The sitter I had lined up for Terence just backed out. Would you keep him while I'm gone?"

"No."

The flat, unequivocal refusal didn't surprise her. "Adam…"

"Save your breath, Maggie. I will not keep that monster from hell. In fact, if he ever crosses my path again, I'll likely strangle him with my bare hands."

She tugged off the glasses. "Oh, for heaven's sakes! What happened last time was as much your fault as his. You shouldn't have left that rare edition on your desk. I told you he likes to eat paper."

"So you did. You failed, however, to mention that he also likes to creep up behind women and poke his head up their skirts."

Maggie concealed a fierce rush of satisfaction at the thought of the dramatic encounter between the scaly, bug-eyed blue-and-orange iguana she'd acquired as a gift from a Central American colonel and Adam's sophisticated sometime companion. By all accounts, Terence had thoroughly shaken the flame-haired congresswoman from Connecticut and sent her rushing from Adam's Georgetown residence. The redhead couldn't know, of course, that the German shepherd-size reptile was as harmless as it was ugly. Nor had Maggie felt the least urge to correct the mistaken impression when she called to apologize.

As much as that incident had secretly delighted Maggie, however, it had drawn her boss's wrath down on her unattractive pet. She tried once again to smooth things over.

"Terence was only feeling playful. He's really—"

"No."

"Please. For me?"

Adam's eyes held hers for a few, fleeting seconds. Maggie felt her pulse skip once or twice, then jolt into an irregular rhythm.

"I can't," he said at last. "The Swedish ambassador and his wife are staying with me while their official quarters are under repair. Ingrid's a good sport, but I don't think Börg would appreciate your repulsive pet's habit of flicking out his yardlong tongue to plant kisses on unsuspecting victims."

Having been subjected to a number of those startling kisses herself, Maggie conceded defeat.

Adam held himself still as her sigh drifted across the office. Over the years, he'd mastered the art of controlling his emotions. His position required him to weigh risks and make a calculated decision as to whether to put his agents in harm's way. There was little room for personal considerations or emotions in such deadly business.

Yet the distracted look in Maggie's huge brown eyes affected him more than he would admit, even to himself.

"You might try Elizabeth," he suggested after a moment.

"I tried her before I hired the sitter. She still hasn't

forgiven Terence for devouring the African water lilies she spent six years cultivating. In fact,'' Maggie added glumly, ''she threatened to shoot him on sight if he ever came within range.''

It wasn't an idle threat, Adam knew. The grandmotherly receptionist requalified every year at the expert level on the 9 mm Sig Sauer handgun she kept in her desk drawer. She'd only fired it once other than on the firing range— with lethal results.

Watching Maggie chew the inside of one cheek, Adam refrained from suggesting the obvious solution. She wouldn't appreciate the reminder that lizard meat had a light, tasty succulence when seared over an open fire. Instead, Adam pushed his conscience aside and offered up OMEGA's senior communications technician as a victim.

''Perhaps Joe Sammuels could take care of…it for you. He returned last night from his satellite-communications conference in the U.K.''

''He did? Great!'' Maggie jammed her glasses back on, wincing as the handles forced a path through the tight hair at her temples. ''Joe owes me, big-time! I kept the twins for a whole week while he and Barb went skiing.''

Adam's lips twisted. ''He'll repay that debt several times over if he takes in your walking trash compactor.''

Behind the thick lenses, Maggie's eyes now sparkled with laughter. ''Joe won't mind. He knows how much the twins enjoy taking Terence out for a walk on his leash. They think it's totally rad when everyone freaks out as they stroll by.''

''They would.''

''I'll go call Joe. I can leave a key to my condo for him with Elizabeth. Thanks, Adam.'' She started for the door, throwing him a dazzling smile over her shoulder. ''See you…whenever.''

"Maggie."

The quiet call caught her in midstride. She turned back, lowering her chin to peer at him over the black rims. "Yes?"

"Be careful."

She nodded. "Will do."

A small silence descended between them, rare and strangely intense. Adam broke it with a final instruction.

"Try not to bring home any more exotic gifts from the admirers you seem to collect in the field. Customs just sent the State Department another scathing letter about the unidentified government employee who brought a certain reptile into the country without authorization."

Wisely, Maggie decided to ignore Adam's reference to what had somehow become a heated issue between several high-ranking bureaucrats. Instead, she plucked at the sturdy twill pants bagging her hips and waggled her black eyebrows. "Admirers? In this getup? You've got to be kidding!"

She gave a cheerful wave and was gone.

Adam stood unmoving until the last thump of her boots had faded in the corridor outside his office.

"No," he murmured. "I'm not."

He flicked his tuxedo sleeves down over pristine white cuffs, then patted his breast pocket to make sure it held his onyx pen. The microchip signaling device implanted in the pen's cap emitted no sound, only a slight, intermittent pulse of heat.

Adam never went anywhere without it.

Not when he had agents in the field.

After a quick flight from Washington to Dover Air Force Base in Delaware, Maggie jumped out of the flight-line taxi and lugged her heavy suitcase across the concrete parking apron. The huge silver-skinned stretch C-141 that would transport the UN inspection team crouched on the runway like a mammoth eagle guarding its nest. Its rear doors yawned open to the night.

"Be with you in a minute, ma'am," the loadmaster called from inside the cavernous cargo bay.

Maggie nodded and waited patiently at the side hatch while the harried sergeant directed the placement of the pallets being loaded into the hold. A quick glance at the stenciling on the crates told Maggie that about half contained supplies for the twelve-person UN team, and half were stamped FRAGILE—SCIENTIFIC EQUIPMENT.

Racks of floodlights bathed the plane in a yellow glare and heated the cool September night air. Maggie stood just outside the illuminated area, in the shadow of the wing, content to have a few moments to herself before she met her fellow team members for the first time. Now that she was within minutes of the actual start of her mission, she wanted to savor her tingling sense of anticipation.

The accumulated stress from almost twenty hours of intense mission preparation lay behind her.

The racing adrenaline, mounting tension and cold, wrenching fear that came with every mission waited ahead.

For now, there was only the gathering excitement that arced along her nerves like lightning slicing across a heated summer sky.

She breathed in the cool air, enjoying this interlude of dim, shadowed privacy. In a few minutes, she'd be another person, speak with another voice. For now, though, she—

The attack came with only a split second's warning.

She heard a thud. A startled grunt. The loud rattle of her metal suitcase as it clattered on the concrete.

Maggie whirled, squinting against the floodlights' glare.

If the lights hadn't blinded her, she might have had a chance.

Before she could even throw up her hands to shade her eyes, a dark silhouette careened into her.

Maggie and her attacker went down with a crash.

She hit the unyielding concrete with enough force to drive most of the air from her lungs. What little she had left whooshed away when a bony hipbone slammed into her stomach.

An equally bony forehead cracked against hers, adding more black spots to those the blinding lights had produced. Fisting her fingers, Maggie prepared to smash the soft cartilage in the nose hovering just inches above her own.

"Oh, my— Oh, my God! I'm—I'm sorry!"

The horrified exclamation began in something resembling a male bass and ended on a high soprano squeak. Maggie's hand halted in midswing.

Almost instantly, she regretted not taking out the man sprawled across her body. As he tried to push himself up, he inadvertently jammed a knee into a rather sensitive area of her female anatomy.

At her involuntary recoil, he stammered another, even more appalled apology. "Oh! Oh, I'm sorry! I'll just… Let me just…"

He lifted his knee in an attempt to plant it on less intimate ground. He missed, and ground it into Maggie's already aching stomach instead. She stilled his jerky movements with a death grip on his jacket sleeves.

He swallowed noisily as he peered down at her. With the lights glaring from behind his head, Maggie couldn't make out any facial features.

"Are…are you all right?"

"I might be," she said through tight jaws, remembering just in time to clip her words and adopt the slightly nasal tone she'd perfected for this role. "If you'd stop trying to grind my liver into pâté."

"I'm...I'm sorry."

"So you've said. Several times. Look, just lift your knee. Carefully!"

Once freed of his weight, Maggie rolled, catlike, to her feet. Taking a couple of quick breaths to test her aching stomach muscles, she decided she'd live. Barely.

Turning so that the spotlight no longer blinded her, she shoved the glasses dangling from one ear back onto her nose. The black spots faded enough for her to see her attacker's features at last.

The man—no, the boy, she corrected, running a quick searching glance over his anxious face and gangly frame— tugged his zippered jacket down from where it had tangled under his armpits.

"I'm sorry," he repeated miserably. "Your suitcase... I, uh, tripped. I didn't mean to..."

"It's okay," she managed. "I think my digestive system's intact, and I'm getting close to the end of my child-bearing years, anyway."

Actually, at thirty-two, she still had plans for several children sometime in the future. She'd only meant to lighten the atmosphere a little, but she saw at once her joke had backfired. The boy's face flamed an even brighter shade of red, and he stammered another string of apologies.

"I'm fine," she interjected, her irritation easing at his obvious mortification. "Really. I was just teasing."

He stared at her doubtfully. "You were?"

"Couldn't you tell?"

"No. No one ever teases me."

Maggie didn't see how this clumsy young man could possibly avoid being the butt of all kinds of jokes. He was all legs and arms, a walking, talking safety hazard. Which made her distinctly nervous on this busy flight line.

"Look, are you supposed to be out here? This is a restricted area."

"I'm…I'm traveling on this plane." He glanced up at the huge silver C-141, frowning. "At least, I think this is the plane. The sergeant who dropped me off here said it was."

Maggie's eyes narrowed, causing a painful tug at her temples. She grimaced, vowing silently to get rid of the tight bun at the back of her neck at the first possible moment, while her mind raced through the descriptions of the various team members she'd been given. None of them correlated with this awkward individual. For a heart-stopping moment, she wondered if her mission had been compromised, if an impostor—other than Maggie herself—was trying to infiltrate the team.

Apparently thinking her grimace had been directed at him, he hastened to reassure her. "Yes, I'm sure this is the right plane. I recognize the crates of equipment being loaded."

"Who *are* you?" she asked, cutting right to the heart of the matter.

"Richard. Richard Worthington."

With the velocity and force of an Oklahoma twister, Maggie's suspicion spiraled. "Richard Worthington?"

He blinked at the sharp challenge in her voice. "Uh, the Second."

The tornado slowed its deadly whirl. Drawing in a deep breath, Maggie studied the young man's worried face. Now that she had some clue to his identity, she thought she detected a faint resemblance to the scientist who would head their team. Not that she could have sworn to it. Even the Mole had been able to produce only sketchy background details and a blurred photo of the brilliant, reclusive physicist. Taken about a year ago, the picture showed a hazy profile almost obliterated by a bushy beard.

"I didn't realize Dr. Worthington had a son," she said slowly. "Or that he was bringing you along on this trip."

"He's not. Er, I'm not. That is, I'm Dr. Worthington."

Right, and she was Wernher von Braun!

Maggie wanted to reject his ridiculous claim instantly, but the keen mind that had helped her work through some rather improbable situations in the past three years suggested it *could* be possible. This earnest, anxious young man *could* be Dr. Worthington. The Mole had indicated that Worthington had gained international renown at an early age. But this early?

"You don't look like the Dr. Richard Worthington I was told to expect," Maggie challenged, still suspicious.

A bewildered look crossed his face for a moment, then dissolved into a sheepish grin. "Oh, you mean my beard? I just grew it because my mother didn't want—that is, I decided to experiment." Lifting a hand, he rubbed it across his smooth, square chin. "But the silly thing itched too much. I shaved it off for this trip."

Maggie might have questioned his ingenious story if not for two startling details. His reference to his mother caught her attention like a waving flag. The intelligence briefing had disclosed that Dr. Worthington's iron-willed mother guarded the genius she'd given birth to with all the determination of a Valkyrie protecting the gates of Valhalla.

With good reason. At the age of six, her famous child prodigy had been kidnapped and held for ransom. His kidnappers had sent his distracted mother the tip of one small finger as proof of their seriousness. The hand this young man now rubbed across his chin showed a pinkie finger missing a good inch of its tip.

Despite the conclusive evidence, Maggie didn't derive a whole lot of satisfaction from ascertaining that the individual facing her was in fact Dr. Richard Worthington. With a sinking feeling, she realized she was about to take off for the backside of beyond, where she'd proceed to climb down into silos filled with temperamental, possibly unstable, nuclear missiles, alongside a clumsy boy... man...

"Just how old are you?" she asked abruptly.

"Twenty-three."

Twenty-three! Maggie swallowed, hard.

"You're *sure* you're the Dr. Richard Worthington who possesses two doctorates, one in engineering and one in nuclear physics?"

His eyes widened at the hint of desperation in her voice. "Well, actually..."

Wild hope pumped through Maggie's heart.

"Actually, I was just awarded a third. In molecular chemistry. I didn't apply for it," he added, when she gave a small groan. "MIT presented it after I did some research for them in my lab."

"Yes, well..." With a mental shrug, Maggie accepted her fate. "Congratulations."

She'd been in worse situations during her years with OMEGA, she reminded herself. A lot worse. She could handle this one. Pulling her new identity around her like a cloak, she squared her shoulders and held out a hand.

"I'm Megan St. Clare, Dr. Worthington. A last-minute addition to your team."

Maggie had constructed a name and identity for this mission close enough to her own that she could remember them, even under extreme duress. A minor but important point, she'd discovered early in her OMEGA career.

Worthington's fingers folded around hers. "Could you call me Richard? I'm a bit awkward with titles."

Was there anything he wasn't awkward with? "Richard. Right. I believe the UN nuclear facilities chairman faxed you my credentials?"

"Well, yes, he did. Although I must say I was surprised he decided to add a geologist to the team at the last moment."

Maggie could've told him that the chairman had decided—with a little help from the U.S. government—to add a geologist because she'd known she could never pass herself off as an expert on nuclear matters with this group of world-renowned scientists for more than thirty seconds. But she'd absorbed enough knowledge of geological formations from her oil-rigger father to hold her own with anyone who wasn't fully trained in the field.

She started to launch into her carefully rehearsed speech about the need to assess the soil around the missile site for possible deep-strata permeation of radioactive materials, but Worthington forestalled her with another one of his shy smiles.

"Please don't think I meant to impugn your credentials. This is my first time as part of a UN team...or any other team, for that matter. I'm sure I'll appreciate your input when we arrive on-site."

Maggie stared at him for a long, silent moment. "Your first time?"

A gleam of amusement replaced the uncertainty in his eyes, making him seem more mature. "There weren't all that many physicists clamoring for the job. I'm looking forward to it."

At that particular moment, Maggie couldn't say the same. She stared at him for a long moment, then shrugged.

''Well, I suppose we should get this...expedition under way.''

She bent to pick up her suitcase, only to knock heads with Worthington as he reached for it at the same moment.

He reached out one hand to steady her and rubbed his forehead with the other. ''Oh, no! I'm sorry! Are you hurt, Miss St. Clare? Uh, Dr. St—?''

Maggie snatched her arm out of his grip and blinked away bright-colored stars. ''Call...me ...Megan...and... bring...the—''

Just in time, she cut off the colorful, earthy adjective she'd picked up from the rowdy oil riggers she'd grown up with.

''Bring the suitcase,'' she finished through set jaws.

Stalking to the side hatch, she clambered aboard the cargo plane and forced herself to take a deep, calming breath. Her mission was about to get under way. She couldn't let the fact that she was saddled with a bumbling team leader distract her at this critical point.

She'd just have to turn his inexperience to her own advantage, Maggie decided, buckling herself in beside a gently snoring woman with iron gray hair and a rather startling fuchsia windbreaker folded across her lap. Worthington's clumsiness would center the other team members' attention on him as much as his reputed brilliance. Which would make it easier for her to search for the decoder and slip away when she needed to contact Cowboy.

Maggie glanced down at her digital watch. Calculating the time difference, she estimated that Nate should be arriving at the Karistani camp about now.

Sternly she repressed a fervent wish that she could exchange places with him right now.

Chapter 4

As Nate rode beside Alexandra into the sprawling city of black goathair tents that constituted Karistan's movable capital, he decided that the average age of the male half of the population must hover around sixty. Or higher.

Eyes narrowed, he skimmed the crowd gathering in the camp to greet their leader. It seemed to consist mostly of bent, scarred veterans even more ancient than Dimitri. Only after they'd drawn nearer did Nate see a scattering of children and women among the men.

Most of the women wore ankle-length black robes and dark shawls draped over their heads. A few were in the embroidered blouses and bright, colorful skirts Nate associated with the traditional dress in this part of the world. Whatever their age or dress, however, the women all seemed to greet his arrival with startled surprise and a flurry of whispered comments behind raised hands.

As the riders approached, one of the women stepped out of the crowd and sauntered forward. Although shorter and far more generously endowed than Alexandra, the girl had a dramatic widow's peak and confident air that told Nate the two women had to be related.

Alexandra drew to a halt a few yards from the younger woman and swung out of the saddle. Nate followed suit, hiding his quick stab of amusement as the girl looked him over from head to toe with the thoroughness of a bull rider checking out his draw before he climbed into the chute.

She asked a question that made Alexandra's lips tighten. Flashing the girl a warning look, the older woman indicated Nate with a little nod.

"Out of courtesy to our guest, you must use the English you learned during your year at the university, Katerina. This is Mr. Sloan…"

"Nate," he reminded her lazily.

Alexandra wasn't too pleased with the idea of his getting on a first-name basis with Katerina, if her quick frown was any indication, but she didn't make an issue of it.

"He brings the horse we were told of," she continued, "the one from the president of the United States. He only visits with us for a *short* time."

The well-rounded beauty's brows rose at the unmistakable emphasis. "Do we… Do we…"

She paused, searching what Nate guessed was a limited and long-unused English vocabulary. Triumph sparkled in her dark eyes when she found the words she sought.

"Do we…give him much comfort, my cousin, per-perhaps he will visit longer."

Comfort sounded more like *koom-foot,* and Nate had to struggle a bit with *wheez-it,* but he caught her drift. Seeing as how she tossed in a curving, seductive smile for good measure, he could hardly miss it. His answering grin made Alexandra's sable brows snap into a straight line.

Katerina sashayed forward, ignoring her cousin's frown.

"Come, *Amerikanski*, I will—how you say?—take you the camp."

Nate was tempted. Lord, he was tempted. The little baggage had the most inviting eyes and beguiling lips he'd stumbled across in many a day. As accommodating as she appeared to be, he figured it would take him about three minutes, max, to extract whatever she knew of the decoder. Among other things.

Too bad he hadn't yet reached the point of seducing young women to accomplish his mission, he thought with a flicker of regret. Still, he wasn't about to let a potential source like Katerina slip through his fingers entirely.

"That's real friendly of you, miss," he replied, smiling down at her. "Maybe you can, ah, take me the camp later. Right now, I'd better see that Three Bars Red here gets tended to."

Her full lips pursed in a pretty fair imitation of a pout. "The men, they can do this."

"I'm sure they can," Nate replied easily, "but I don't plan to let them. I'm responsible for this animal...until your *ataman* decides if she's going to accept him."

Alexandra's eyes narrowed at his use of her title, but she said nothing. Katerina, on the other hand, didn't bother to hide her displeasure at coming in second to a horse.

"So! Perhaps do I take you the camp later. Perhaps do I not." Tossing her head, she walked off.

Yep, the two women were definitely related, Nate decided.

At her cousin's abrupt departure, Alexandra gestured one of the watching men forward.

"This is Petr Borodín."

The way she pronounced the name, *Pey-tar Bor-o-deen,* with a little drumroll at the end, sounded to Nate like a sort of musical poetry.

"He is a mighty warrior of the steppes who served in two wars," she added.

Nate didn't doubt it for an instant. This bald scarecrow of a man with baggy pouches under his eyes and an empty, pinned-up left sleeve sported three rows of tarnished medals on his thin chest. Among them were the French Croix de Guerre and the World War II medal the U.S. had struck to honor an elite multinational corps of saboteurs. These fearless sappers had destroyed vital enemy supply depots and, incidentally, guided over a hundred downed U.S. airmen to safety.

"Petr will show you where you will stay," Alexandra continued, in the rolling, formal phrases that intrigued Nate so. "And where you may take the horse."

He thought he saw a shadow of a smile in the glance she gave Ole Red, who was watching the proceedings with sleepy-eyed interest. A sudden, inexplicable desire to keep that smile on her face for longer than a tenth of a second curled through Nate.

Surprised by the sensation, he tucked it away for further examination and stood quietly while Alexandra issued quick instructions to this Petr fellow. When she finished, he gave her a nod and gathered Red's reins.

"I've never been in these parts before," he offered as he fell in beside his new guide, testing the man's English and value as a possible information source. "What say we take a ride after I drop off my gear, and you show me the lay of the land?"

"No!"

Alexandra's sharp exclamation halted both men in their tracks. She stepped forward as they swung around, and shot a quick order to the Karistani before facing Nate.

"The steppes can be treacherous, if you don't know them. You mustn't leave this camp, except as I direct."

Nate let his gaze drift over her face. "Guess we'd better talk about that a bit. Much as I wouldn't mind lazing around for a few days, Ole Red here will need exercise."

"You'll stay in camp unless I say otherwise," she snapped. "And even in camp, you will stay with your escort. Our ways are different. You may give offense without knowing it, or…" She circled a hand in the air. "Or go where you're not permitted."

Nate didn't so much as blink, but the pulse in the side of his neck began a slow tattoo. "So you're saying certain parts of the camp are off-limits? You want to be more specific? Just so I don't give offense, you understand."

Her chin lifted at his sarcasm. "To be specific, I suggest you stay away from the women's quarters, and from Katerina."

Now that was hitting just a little below the belt. Nate hadn't exactly invited the girl to swish her skirts at him the way she had. What was more, he fully intended to enter the women's quarters at the first opportunity. At the moment, though, the thought of searching Alexandra's belongings didn't hold nearly as much appeal as the thought of searching Alexandra herself. The unfriendlier the woman got, the more Nate found himself wanting to pierce her hard shell.

"Do you hold all men in such low regard?" he drawled. "Or maybe just me in particular?"

She sent him an icy stare. "That, Mr. Sloan, is none…"

"Nate."

"…of your business. All you need to know is that I'm responsible for what happens in this camp. Everything that happens. For your own safety, I won't have you wandering around unescorted. As long as you're here, you'll respect my wishes in this and in all other matters."

Not quite all, Nate amended silently as she spun on one

heel. He had a few wishes of his own to consider. One had to do with a certain decoder. Another, he decided, watching her trim bottom as she walked away, just might have to do with discovering Alexandra Jordan's answer to the second part of his question.

Petr Borodín took his chief's orders to heart and stuck to Nate like cockleburs to a saddle blanket for the rest of the afternoon. After showing the *Amerikanski* to a tent where he could dump his gear, the aged warrior helped unsaddle and curry Red with a skill that belied his lack of one arm. That done, he led the way to the pasturage.

A dozen or so geldings and a shaggy roan that Nate guessed was the band's alpha mare were hobbled in a stretch of prairie at the rear of the camp. Another dozen mares, and several yearlings, grazed around them. Evidently none of the females were in season, since neither Red nor the feisty little stallion tethered some distance away showed much interest in them. They did, however, take immediate exception to each other. For all his gregarious nature and easy disposition, Red recognized the competition when he saw it.

After a prolonged display of flat ears, snaked necks and pawed ground, Nate decided to keep the quarter horse away from the band until Alexandra made up her mind about him. No use letting Red chase off the smaller stallion if he wasn't going to be allowed to claim the mares.

Peter the Great, as Nate christened the veteran—much to his delight when he understood the reference—tethered Red to the side of their tent. Once fed a mixture of prairie grass and the oats Nate had brought along to help him adjust to the change in his diet, the stallion was once again his usual placid self.

Placid, at least, until he got a whiff of the candy bar

Nate stuck in his shirt pocket before he scooped a bucket of water from the sluggish stream behind the camp. By the time Red had satisfied his sweet tooth, both man and horse were soaked.

Ducking under the tent flap to change his shirt, Nate surveyed the dim interior. Dust pushed under the sides by the wind drifted on air scented by old boots, musty furs, and a faint, lingering hint of incense. The tent's interior was larger than some of the crew quarters Nate had occupied in the air force, and a good deal cleaner than some of the dives he'd shared while riding the rodeo circuit.

While Nate sat on a low, ingeniously constructed folding cot piled high with rough blankets and a thick, shaggy wolf pelt to strip off his shirt, Peter the Great rummaged through a low chest.

"*Wodka!*" he announced, holding up a bottle half filled with cloudy liquid.

Nate answered the man's gap-toothed grin with one of his own. "Well, now, I don't mind if I do."

A stiff drink would be more than welcome after the chill of his unexpected bath. And, he reasoned, it just might loosen up his appointed guardian enough to allow some serious intelligence-gathering.

Several hours later, Nate leaned back against a high, sheepskin-covered saddle. Smoke from a half-dozen campfires curled into the star-studded sky and competed with the lingering aroma of the beef slathered in garlic that had constituted the main course at the evening meal. In the background, the small portable gas generators that provided the camp with electricity hummed. It was a foreign sound in a night that belonged to flickering fires and a star-filled sky.

Low murmurs and laughter from the men beside Nate

told him they were engaged in the age-old pastime of cowboys around the world—sharing exaggerated tales of their
prowess in the saddle. Or out of it. He smiled as one mus-
tachioed individual in a yellowed sheepskin hat broke into
a deep, raucous belly laugh. Pushing his impatience to the
back of his mind, Nate took a cautious sip of vodka.

So he hadn't been able to shake Peter the Great this
afternoon, not even for a trip to the communal latrine that
served the camp. So Dimitri, when he took over guard
duty from his cohort, had shrugged off all but the most
casual questions. The afternoon still hadn't been a total
loss. In the preceding hours, Nate had memorized the layout of the camp, cataloged in exact detail the Karistani's
eclectic collection of weapons, and done an exterior surveillance of the tent Alexandra and the other unattached
women slept in.

Nate was turning over in his mind several possible sce-
narios for gaining access to that tent, some of which involved Alex's cooperation, some of which didn't, when
the rustle of heavy skirts stirred the air behind him.

Katerina plopped down beside him, a hand-thrown pot-
tery jug in hand. Nate could tell by the sultry smile on her
full lips that she'd decided to forgive him for declining
her invitation this afternoon.

"You wish...more *wodka?*"

He glanced down at the tin cup in his hand. It was still
full of the throat-searing liquid, which the little minx could
see as plain as tar paper. His lips curved as he tipped some
of the potent mixture into the dirt and held up his cup.

"Sure."

With a look of pure mischief on her face, Katerina
leaned forward to refill his cup. The cloaklike red wrap
she'd donned against the night air gaped open, revealing

full breasts that spilled just about clear out of her low-necked blouse.

Nate imagined Alex's reaction if she knew her cousin was pressing those generous breasts against his arm right now. He considered the implications of said reaction to his mission. He even reminded himself that Katerina looked to become something of a problem if he didn't rein her in soon. All the while, of course, he enjoyed the view.

Not that he could've avoided it, even if he'd wanted to. Katerina made sure of that. She dipped even lower to set the jug on the ground beside him, and Nate's brow skittered upward.

"Are you...cowboy?" Katerina asked softly.

The hairs on the back of Nate's neck rose. Years of intense survival training and his own iron control kept his muscles from coiling as she leaned even closer.

"Cowboy, like in films I see at university?" she cooed. "Like the men of the steppes?"

Air snuck back into Nate's lungs. "Sort of."

"So do I think." A smug little smile traced her mouth. "You walk, you ride the same. Like all this, you own."

Her sweeping gesture encompassed the vast, rolling prairie, the inky black sky, and the waterfall of stars tumbling out of the heavens. From that gesture, Nate gathered that the men of the steppes swaggered a bit when they walked, and rode as though they and their ponies were alone in the universe. Much like their Wyoming counterparts, he decided with an inner smile.

"Do you have the land, in *Amerika?*"

"A little."

She slid one hand up his arm, then edged it toward his chest. "How much it is, this little?"

Grinning, Nate caught her hand before her fingers slipped inside his denim jacket. "Where I come from, a lady doesn't ask a man the size of his spread. It tends to get him real nervous…or real interested.''

Keeping her wrist in a light hold, he rose and pulled her up with him. ''Being of the nervous type myself, I'd better walk you back to your campfire.''

Clearly, Katerina had no idea what he was talking about, but she didn't seem the least averse to taking a stroll with him. She tucked her hand in his arm and tipped him a look that warned Nate he'd better keep to the well-lighted areas.

''Have you the woman in *Amerika?* The…um…wife?''

On reflection, Nate decided that handling Katerina might just be a bit trickier than he'd anticipated. The girl had the tenacity of a bull terrier and the subtlety of the rodeo clowns who whacked a rampaging bull up side the head to get its attention.

''No, no wife,'' he answered, then firmly shifted the conversation to what he hoped might eventually lead to little black boxes. ''So, what about you? Have you always lived here, on the steppes?''

''Always.'' The single word held a wealth of emotion. Pride. Bitterness. Frustration. ''Except for the year I go to university, always do I live here.''

''What university?''

She gave a little shrug. ''The institute of technology. In Lvov. My grandfather wished for me to learn the science.''

''That so? What kind of science?''

''Pah! You would not believe! Such courses he wished me to take. The…the *mathematik.* The *physik.* I have perhaps the head, but not the heart for such—''

''Katerina!''

At the sharp admonition, the girl whipped her hand free of Nate's arm and spun around. He turned more leisurely, his senses leaping at the sight of the woman who strode toward them.

A long khaki coat covered her from shoulder to boot top. One of her own designs, Nate guessed. Only someone as talented as Maggie said Alexandra Jordan was could've fashioned that particular model. Similar to the long, open-fronted frock coats favored by the men of the camp, the semifitted military-style garment showed off her slender figure to perfection and swirled about her ankles seductively when she walked. With some interest, Nate noted the tassels banded in colored yarn that decorated the yoke of the garment.

Damned if those horsetail thingamabobs weren't starting to strike his fancy.

What didn't strike any fancy, however, was the braided horsetail whip looped about Alexandra's wrist. It cracked ominously against her boot top with each step.

Katerina's lower lip jutted out as her cousin strode toward them. Obviously deciding to take the offensive, she rattled off something in Karistani that earned a sharp retort.

The two women faced each other, one softly rounded and flushed, the other rigid and unyielding in her authority. After a short, terse exchange, Katerina evidently came out the loser. Her eyes snapping, she faced Nate.

"God keep you until the dawn," she muttered. She flounced away, then added defiantly over her shoulder, "I will see you then."

Alexandra's whip snapped several more times against her leather boot, and she gave Nate a look that would've made bear bait out of a less seasoned hand.

"I want to talk to you." She threw a quick glance at the circle of interested faces watching from around the campfire. "Privately."

She whirled and strode toward the far perimeter, only to stop when she noticed he wasn't following.

Having made his point, Nate nodded. "I guess maybe it is time we had a little chat."

Her mind seething with a jumble of emotions, Alex led the way toward the outskirts of the camp. She didn't understand what it was about this unwanted visitor that had set her teeth on edge from the first moment of their meeting.

He was handsome enough, in his rangy, loose-limbed way, she admitted. If one cared for sun-streaked blond hair, a square jaw, and skin tanned to the sheen of fine oak, that is.

Who was she kidding? she thought testily. Sloan made the models she'd hired last spring for the premiere of her Elegance line of men's evening wear look as though they hadn't gone through puberty yet.

All right, it wasn't his appearance that irritated her, Alex decided with a fresh spurt of annoyance. It was his attitude. His deliberately provocative manner. The way he drew out his words until they grated on her ears. The way his hazel eyes seemed to brim with some lazy private amusement when they looked at her and issued a challenge only she seemed to see.

Alex wasn't used to being challenged.

By anyone.

Even before she assumed leadership of the host, the men of the steppes had always accorded her the deference due the headman's granddaughter. In the business world, her associates had given her respect she'd earned by her success in an industry that regularly devoured its own.

Even the few men in her life with whom she'd developed anything more than a business relationship hadn't affected her equilibrium the way Sloan did. Not one of them had let his gaze slide from her lips to her throat so slowly that she felt her very skin burn in anticipation of its touch. None had drawn out each move, each touch, each murmured word, until she wanted to scream…

Alex pulled herself up short, not quite believing the direction her mind had taken. She was getting as bad as Katerina, she thought grimly, her worry coming full circle.

She halted abruptly beside the wood-framed trailer that was used to transport the tents. Its high sides afforded a modicum of privacy in a city without walls. Wasting no time on preliminaries, Alex plunged to the heart of the matter.

"Look, Mr.— Look, Nate. You're only going to be here for a short time. I don't want you to encourage Katerina."

Sloan leaned an arm against the side of the wagon and let his shadowed gaze drift over her face. "Seems like you've got a long list of things you don't want me to do while I'm here, *ataman.*"

"And that's another item to add to the list," Alex snapped. "I don't want you to call me by that title. It's one the elders gave me, but I've not yet earned."

His head cocked. "That so?"

"That's so."

"And just what do you have to do to earn it… Alexandra?"

He drew her name out in that deep, slow way of his, until it assumed a consistency similar to the thick, creamy yogurt the women made from mare's milk. The suspicion that he did it deliberately tightened Alexandra's mouth.

"That's not something that concerns you. What *should* concern you, however, is the fact that many of the people of this country cling to the old ways." She tilted her head, eyeing him through the screen of her lashes. "Do you have any idea how Cossacks of old dealt with those who transgressed their laws?"

His eyes glinted in the moonlight. "No, but I suspect I'm about to find out."

She held up her short braided whip. "This is called a *nagaika.* The horsemen of the steppes use this instead of spurs to control their mounts. They also use it to strip the flesh from anyone who dishonors a woman of the host."

He didn't appear overly impressed. "Aren't you getting your feathers all ruffled up unnecessarily? Where I come from, a man doesn't exactly dishonor a woman by taking her for a stroll through a crowded camp."

"You're not where you come from," she reminded him, emphasizing her words with a crack of the whip. "You're in Karistan. I told you, our ways are different."

He glanced down at the braided flail. When his eyes met hers again, they held a glint she couldn't quite interpret.

"Not that different, sweetheart."

Before she could protest this rapid progression from a respectful title to casual familiarity, he straightened and took a step forward.

"Now, maybe if I'd invited your cousin to stroll out here in the darkness the way you invited me, Alexandra, you might've had reason to be suspicious."

The low, husky quality of his voice took Alex by surprise. Good Lord, surely the man didn't think she'd brought him out here for any other reason than to...

"And maybe if I'd let that pie-plate moon stir my blood," he continued, closing the distance, "you might've had cause to flick that little horsetail flyswatter of yours against your boots."

His voice retained its easy, mocking modulation, but as he moved toward her Alex was suddenly and disturbingly aware of the breadth of his shoulders and the leashed power in his long body.

"But you wouldn't have had any real cause to be concerned…"

Her breath caught as he planted both hands on wood planking, caging her in the circle of his arms.

"Sloan! What—?"

"…unless I'd done something like this."

Sheer astonishment held her immobile as he brushed his mouth across hers, once, twice.

For a moment, when he loomed over her, Alex had felt a flutter of trepidation, as though she'd wakened a sleeping beast she wasn't sure she could control. But the soft, unthreatening touch of his lips told her how ridiculous that fear was. Imperceptibly she relaxed her rigid stance.

As if he'd been waiting for just such a reaction, he slanted his head and deepened the kiss. Wrapping one arm about her waist, he pulled her up against his unyielding body.

Stunned at the swift, confident move, Alexandra yielded her lips to a skilled assault. Disconcerted, unable to move, she clutched at his tough denim jacket.

A deep, hidden part of her leaped in response to his rough possession. The part of her with roots fed by women of the steppes, women who celebrated victories with their men in wild abandon. For a fleeting moment, Alexandra tested his strength, tasted his lips, and took a swift, fierce satisfaction in the uncompromising masculinity of the body pressed against hers.

It was only after he raised his head and she drew in a slow, unsteady breath that Alex realized he'd proved his point.

If he'd brought Katerina out here under the dark skies and ignited her senses like that, she certainly would've had cause to worry. More cause to worry.

Gathering the shreds of her dignity, she met his shadowed gaze. "If you touch me again without my permission," she said quietly, "I'll use this whip you dismiss so contemptuously."

He stared at her for a long moment, and then his mouth twisted into a rueful grin. "If I do, and if you did, you'd be in the right of it."

The apology—if it was one—surprised her. Alex frowned up at him, as confused by the way her heart refused to cease its wild pumping as by the way he lifted one hand to rub his thumb gently along her brow.

"Oh, hell, I didn't mean to put that crease back in your forehead," he murmured, half under his breath. "Wily Willie would have my hide for that."

"Who?" she asked, pulling back from his touch, confused by her reaction to this man.

"Wily Willie Sloan. He always warned me never to put a frown on a pretty girl's face—especially one as handy with a gun or a knife as you are. I figured he knew what he was talking about, since I once saw the sweetest, most demure little strawberry blonde west of the Mississippi pepper his backside with buckshot for doing what I just did."

Alex shook her head. "Is this...is this your father you're talking about?"

Sloan's grin widened. "Well, he never actually admitted to it. Except once when I was about six, and got a little too close to an edgy jenny mule. She darn near kicked me into the next county. Willie dusted me off and bragged that I must have inherited my hardheadedness from him, but he was pretty drunk at the time, so I didn't put any stock in it."

Alex stared at him, her mind whirling. She didn't understand how Sloan had managed to defuse what only a few moments ago had been an explosive situation. For her, at least. But the shattering tension between them had somehow softened, mellowed.

It was that damned grin, she thought with a wave of self-disgust. The gleam in his eyes as he spun his tales of this Willie character.

"Look, I—"

She broke off as a scream shattered the night.

Without thought, without hesitation, Alex whirled.

Her booted feet flew across the stubble as she raced toward the sound of muffled shouts. Cursing herself for having left her rifle at her tent, she bent down on the run and drew her knife from the leather sheath strapped just inside her boot top.

Sloan appeared beside her, as swift as she was, and far more silent. Alex barely spared him a glance, but she caught the glint of moonlight on the gun in his hand. She'd assumed he was armed. Anyone who traveled to such a remote part of the world without protection was a fool, and she was fast coming to the realization that, whatever else he was, Sloan was no fool.

As another high-pitched shriek sounded, Alex dodged through the rows of tents. She gathered a following of grim-faced armed men as she ran. No one spoke, no one questioned. As silent as death, the warriors of the steppes raced toward the unknown danger.

Chapter 5

Alex dodged the dark shape of a tent, then skidded to a halt. Her heart pounding, she stared at the chaotic scene before her.

Half the ropes mooring the tent she shared with Katerina and the other unmarried women had been pulled loose. The heavy goathide had partially collapsed, and was now draped over several thrashing figures of indistinct shape and size.

As she watched, a muffled shriek sounded from under the smothering material, and the pole supporting the peaked roof was knocked aside. The entire structure tumbled down. Various articles of clothing, several brass cooking pots and the white fur pelt that ordinarily covered her bed lay exposed to the night as those trapped inside dragged the heavy black hide this way and that.

Her knife held low for a slashing attack, Alex stalked toward the heaving mass. She sensed, rather than saw, Dimitri and Sloan a half pace behind her, while the others fanned out to encircle the collapsed structure. Whoever battled within would not escape.

At that moment, an edge of the hide lifted and a dark shape tumbled out.

"Katerina!" Alex bent and grasped her cousin's arm, helping her to rise. "Are you all right?"

The young woman lifted a shaky hand and shoved her hair out of her eyes. "Y-yes," she gasped.

"What happened?"

"That…that beast…came into the tent."

"Beast!" Releasing Katerina's arm, Alex whirled. "Give me your rifle!"

Without a word, Dimitri passed her the weapon. Holding the Enfield at waist level, she spun back to face the tent and snapped the bolt.

"No, cousin!" Katerina screeched.

At the same instant, a dark figure stepped in front of her and grabbed the rifle barrel. In a swift, powerful movement, Sloan pushed it toward the sky.

"I'm not sure what you think is under that tent, but the—"

"Release my rifle."

"But the shape looks a bit familiar. I'd appreciate you not putting a bullet through it just yet."

"Release my weapon."

The command was low, intense and deadly. After a long, silent moment, Sloan complied. To Alex's consternation, he also turned and strode toward the tent, his broad shoulders blocking her line of fire. When he stooped and heaved the hide upward, she gripped the rifle in tight hands and moved forward.

It would serve the fool right if she let him be savaged by whatever was trapped beneath the hide, Alex thought furiously. He couldn't know about the wolves that roamed the steppes, or the vicious wild dogs that could bring down even full-grown cattle.

It wasn't a wolf or a dog that finally emerged from under the edge of the hide, however. Her mouth sagging, Alex stared at the apparition before her.

"Dammit, Red!" Sloan snarled. "What the hell did you get into?"

Goathair, Alex thought wildly. He'd gotten into the long, fleecy angora hair one of her aunts spun into mohair yarns. Huge clumps of the stuff decorated the chestnut's face, while more long, fuzzy strands hung from his chin. What looked like Katerina's best silk blouse was draped over one twitching ear, and the copper pot Ivana used to collect wild honey was stuck on his muzzle.

With a low, colorful curse, Sloan stepped through the scattered debris toward his charge.

Chuffing softly, the stud tossed his head up, then from side to side. At first Alex thought he was trying to shake the copper pot loose, but she soon realized he was draining the last of Ivana's honey and licking the inside of the vessel.

"You lop-eared hunk of crow bait, get your head down."

Sloan yanked at the rope dangling from the animal's halter, then flung up an arm as Red obeyed his terse command. The copper pot whacked against his upraised forearm.

"Christ!" he muttered.

Alex bit down on her lower lip.

Treating Three Bars Red to a version of his ancestry that Alex suspected didn't appear anywhere in his papers, Sloan worked the honey pot off the stallion's muzzle. Once free, Red licked his lips to catch the last drops of honey. He also caught a mouthful of fuzzy angora hair, which he promptly spit out.

Swearing once more, Sloan swiped at the sticky glob decorating his jacket front.

Alex's teeth clamped down harder on her lip.

The honey pot empty, Three Bars Red had no objection to departing the scene of his crime. Responding to the jerk on his halter, he picked his way through the scattered debris with all the aplomb of a gentleman out for an evening stroll.

Nate led his charge toward the waiting woman, his jaws tight. In the dim light, he couldn't see the look in Alexandra's eyes, but he had a pretty good idea of what must be running through her mind. His supposed attentions to Katerina a while earlier had earned him a casual threat of being skinned alive. He could just imagine what this disaster might warrant.

Grimly he eyed the men ranged on either side of their leader. He wondered if he'd have to knock a few heads together to keep Ole Red—and perhaps himself—from joining the ranks of the geldings.

"You—" Alexandra cut off whatever she was going to say.

"Yeah?" Nate growled. "I what?"

"You—" She swallowed. "You have goat's hair hanging from your chin."

Glowering, he ran his free hand across his chin. It came away with a sticky mass attached.

Alex gave a hiccuping little gasp.

When Nate tried to shake the mess from his fingers, the gasp became a gurgle, then spilled over into helpless giggles.

Nate stopped in midshake, transfixed by the sight of Alexandra with the lines smoothed from her brow. Her generous mouth curved in a delighted smile, and her eyes sparkled in the dim light. This vibrant, laughing woman was all that he'd sensed she'd be, and then some.

Desire, heavy and swift, stirred in his belly. Not the casual, rippling kind of desire that streaks through a man when the woman he's taken an interest in unexpectedly pleasures him with a certain look, or a smile, or a come-hither hitch of her shoulder. This was a gut-twisting, wrenching sort of need that Nate had absolutely no business feeling for a woman who was his target.

For the second time in less than an hour, the urge to kiss Alex gripped Nate. This time, he rigidly controlled it.

"Take this..." She flapped one hand in his general direction. "Take this marauder away. Then you can come back and help repair the damage he's done."

As he led the animal back through the camp, any lingering exasperation Nate might have felt over the stallion's antics vanished. With a wry grin, he realized that Ole Red had accomplished two of the objectives he himself had been wrestling with all evening.

He'd handed Nate the perfect excuse to go nosing around Alexandra's tent.

And he'd brought a smile to her face that just about blinded them both with its candlepower.

Of course, Nate reflected, he'd accomplished the third objective on his own. He'd discovered that Alexandra wasn't averse to all men. In fact, for a few moments out there beside the wagon, he'd gotten the feeling maybe she wasn't even as averse to him as she let on.

Tying the halter lead more securely to a tent rope, Nate pulled a wad of fleecy hair from above Red's left eye.

"I guess we both got a taste of something sweet tonight, fella. I'm afraid it's gonna have to last us awhile."

Leaving Red to think about that, Nate rejoined the crew
gathered at the scene of the disaster.

It took less than fifteen minutes to raise the heavy black
goathide tent.

The women untangled the ropes and stakes with smooth
efficiency, while Sloan and several Karistani men rolled
out the hide and raised the poles.

Since Alex had spent most of her summers riding the
steppes beside her grandfather, she was less skilled in
these domestic matters. The thick, oiled ropes felt awkward and uncooperative in her fingers, the stakes shaky.
One of her aunts by marriage, a gentle, doe-eyed woman
closer to Alex's own age than to the tall, mustached man
she'd married and subsequently buried some years ago,
edged her aside. Giving Alex a small smile, Anya secured
the anchoring line with competent hands.

"Your mother always claimed you were better with the
horses than with the tents and cook fires," she said, in her
soft, pretty voice.

Alex sat back on her heels. "So she did."

The older woman glanced sideways as she gave the rope
a final twist. "It was a matter of much pride to her that
your grandfather favored you. And much worry."

"I know."

Her aunt's words echoed in Alex's mind a short time
later, as she knelt among her scattered possessions. She
righted a small bird cage-shaped chest, her heart aching at
the painful memories it brought. Her mother had laughed
and hidden little treasures for a young, curious Alex in the
chest's many small drawers. It seemed so long ago, so
many tears ago, that Alex had last heard her mother laugh.

Even now, five years after Elena Jordan's death, Alex
still carried the scars left by the complex relationship be-

tween the hawk-eyed chieftain and the daughter who'd defied him to wed where she would. For as long as Alex could remember, the three people she'd loved most in the world had been pulled in opposite directions. Her grandfather by tradition and his responsibilities. Her mother by her love for the outsider she'd married. Her father by his refusal to believe guns were the solution to Karistan's problems.

During her visits to Karistan, Elena had pleaded with the old chieftain to understand that violence and bloodshed were not her husband's way. Daniel Jordan was an economist, a man of learning, wise in the ways of the outside world. Although he chose words over weapons, he wasn't the weak half man the headman believed him to be. In disgust, the Karistani chieftain had tolerated the outsider only for his daughter's sake.

The tension between the two strong-willed people had grown with each passing year, however, until at last Elena had stopped returning to the steppes altogether. She'd sent Alex back each summer, refusing to deny her her heritage.

Ultimately, her grandfather's unceasing hostility toward Daniel Jordan had driven Alexandra away, as well. Fiercely loyal to the man whose gentleness had often been her refuge, Alex had sprung to her father's defense whenever the chieftain's hatred spilled over into some vitriolic remark. The summer she turned seventeen, the *ataman* had made one scathing comment too many. The final quarrel between them had shaken the entire camp with its fury. That had been the last summer Alexandra had spent on the steppes.

She'd been back only once since. After her parents' deaths. After the fall of the Soviet Union, when reports of the violence between Karistan and Balminsk had begun to filter out to the rest of the world.

She'd been appalled at the devastation she found during that brief visit. And hurt as she'd never been hurt before. Her grandfather had told her brutally that she was of no use to him unless she wrung all trace of Daniel Jordan from her soul and stayed to fight by his side. She must choose, once and for all, between her two worlds.

Alexandra had refused to deny the father she loved, and the hawk-eyed chieftain had turned away in silent fury.

He hadn't spoken to her when she left, or during the years that followed. He must have known she'd funneled every penny of profit she earned from her designs into Karistan through Dimitri, but the headman had never acknowledged it. He hadn't relented, hadn't ever forgiven her for not choosing him over her father's memory.

In the end, he'd taken the choice out of her hands.

She was here. And she was *ataman.* Now she carried the burden he had shouldered for so long.

"This yours?"

Alex glanced up to see the American standing over her, a gold satin bra trimmed with ecru lace in his hand and a wicked gleam in his eyes. She pushed the painful memories aside and reached for the filmy undergarment.

"It is."

"I thought so. From the color," he added, when she flashed him a quick look. "It's the same as your eyes— sort of halfway between honey and hardtack."

Alexandra snatched the lacy confection from his hand. "Thank you...I think!"

What was it with this man? Despite her best efforts to keep him in his place, Sloan simply wouldn't stay there. In the short hours since he'd arrived, he and his grin and his blasted horse had literally turned the camp upside down. Stuffing the bra into one of the mother-of-pearl boxes, Alex tried again to assert her authority.

''I told you a half hour ago, we don't need your help any longer. We'll take care of the rest.''

''Now, that wouldn't be right, Alexandra, seeing as how Ole Red caused this havoc in the first place.''

He rolled her name in his slow, teasing way that caused Alex to grit her teeth and Katerina to send him a sharp look. Across the width of the tent, the younger woman's eyes narrowed with suspicion and instant jealousy.

Alex suppressed a sigh. Things were bad enough between her and her cousin without this man's presence exacerbating them further. An ancient Cossack saying, one passed from mother to daughter over the centuries, rose in her mind. Men were ever the burden women must bear in life—one could not live with them, nor cook them in oil rendered from yak grease, as they generally deserved.

Unaware of the fate she contemplated for him, Sloan hunkered down beside her and picked up one of the odd-shaped drawers. ''Do all these little jobbers go in that chest?''

''Yes, but I'll put them away.''

Ignoring her protest, he angled the box to fit into an empty slot. In the process, he also spilled its entire contents. Childhood trinkets, her mother's hand-carved ebony comb, her pens and the few sketches Alex had found time to do since returning to Karistan tumbled out onto the patterned carpet.

His big hands shuffled through the loose papers, adding to their general disorder and Alex's exasperation. Tilting them up to the light provided by the overhead bulb, he studied the top sketch.

Alex glanced at the drawing. It showed her cousin standing at the edge of the steppes, her head thrown back and her hair whipping in the wind. She wore the traditional calf-length skirt and belted tunic of Karistan, to which

Alex had added rows of piping in an intricate, exotic mo-
tif. Both the skirt and the tunic shirt were smoother,
sleeker versions of the traditional dress, and allowed the
ease of movement and tailored comfort the women who
could afford Alex's designs preferred.

The overall effect was one of East meeting West. A
blending of cultures and continents. A harmony that Alex
could express in her designs, but had yet to find in herself.

When Sloan gave a low, appreciative murmur, however,
Alex was sure he wasn't admiring her design or her
cousin. Irritation spurted through her, and something else
that she refused to identify. She tugged the sketches out
of his hand.

"I'll put those away. Go join the men!"

He quirked an eyebrow at her tone, then pivoted on one
heel and swept the tent with an assessing glance. When
he swung back to face her, his knee brushed against her
thigh with a sudden, startling intimacy.

"It's still the far side of disaster in here. Sure you don't
want me to—?"

"No! Yes! I'm sure." Alex edged her leg away from
his. "Just go."

He rose, dusting his hands on his jeans, then stared
down at her for a moment. "God keep you until the dawn,
Alexandra Danilova Jordan."

She blinked, surprised at how comforting the traditional
blessing sounded in his deep voice.

"And...and you."

The tent's flap had barely dropped behind his broad-
shouldered silhouette before Katerina made her way across
the tent.

"How is it the *Amerikanski* calls you by name? You
don't permit the men of our host to do so!"

Alex crammed the last of her belongings into the chest

and rose. She was too tired for another bout with her cousin, but from long experience she knew Katerina wouldn't be put off when she wore that surly expression.

"It's not that I don't permit them to call me by name. They choose not to, out of respect." As they always did when she spoke Karistani, her dialogue and thoughts alike took on a more formal, stylized structure.

"So he does not respect you, this countryman of yours?" Katerina's upper lip curled. "Just what did you do after you sent me back to my tent like a child tonight, that caused him to lose respect for you?"

"Cousin!"

Katerina placed both hands on her full hips. "What, *Alexandra?*"

Alex bit back a sharp rebuke. As much as the younger woman had strained her patience these past weeks, she disliked arguing with her in front of the others.

"We will not discuss the matter now."

"Yes, we will."

"Katerina, I don't wish us to argue like this, in front of the others."

The women watching the scene from the far end of the tent stirred. Ivana of the honey pot set down the skirts she'd been folding. "We'll go, *ataman.*"

Alex shook her head. "No, there's no need."

Her face pale against the black kerchief covering her hair, the young widow glanced at the others. Evidently, what Ivana saw in their faces gave her the courage to speak.

"There is need. You must talk with Katerina. Listen to her. She…she echoes many of our thoughts."

A familiar sense of frustration rose in Alexandra's chest as the other women filed out. She was their leader, yet they would not confide in her. She was of their blood, yet different from them in so many ways.

Suppressing the feeling with an effort of will, she faced her cousin. From the set, angry expression on Katerina's face, Alex knew she'd have to take the first step to heal the breach.

"I'm sorry if I embarrassed you tonight. I should have used more tact."

"Yes, you should have."

"And you, my cousin, perhaps you should have shown more restraint."

"More restraint?" Katerina's voice rose. "More restraint?"

"You were draped over Sloan like a blanket," Alex reminded her. "Such forwardness is not our way."

A long-held bitterness flared in her cousin's dark eyes. "What do you know of our ways? What can you possibly know? You've passed your life in America, enjoying your pretty clothes and your fancy apartment and your lovers."

"Katerina!"

"It's true. You may have spent long-ago summers on the steppes, but you're not really one of us. You weren't here in the winters, when the cattle froze and we ate the flesh of horses to survive. You weren't here during the years of war, when our men died, one after another."

Stunned by the vicious attack, Alex could only stare at her.

"And even when you were young," Katerina rushed on, as though a dam had broken inside her, "our grandfather set you apart. You rode, while the rest of us walked. You sat with him and listened to his tales of forgotten glory while we labored at the cooking pots. He petted and protected you even then."

Alex's pride wouldn't allow her to point out that grueling fourteen-hour days in the saddle hardly constituted petting and protecting. "I but followed his will," she answered through stiff lips.

"Just as you followed his will when you assumed leadership of this host, *Alexandra?* You, a woman! An outsider!"

"I'm of his blood, as are you."

"Yet he chose you over me."

Now they came down to it...the hurt that had festered between them for weeks.

"Yes, he chose me. I didn't want this, Katerina! You know I never intended to stay when I came back. But I gave my promise."

The girl bent forward, her eyes glittering. "Do you know why our grandfather called you back, cousin? Do you?"

Her heart twisting at the irony, Alex nodded. "Yes, I do. As much as he hated my other life, he came to realize it gave me knowledge of the outside world. Knowledge necessary to deal with the vultures he knew would descend on Karistan with his death."

"So you may think!" Katerina retorted. "So you may tell yourself! But it was not your knowledge of the outside world that made him choose you. It was your hardness! Your coldness!"

"What are you saying?"

"Do you think our grandfather mourned your absence all these years? Pah! He reveled in it. He boasted that it proved you as strong and proud as he himself. So proud you couldn't refuse the title when he passed it to you. So strong you would never be swayed by your heart, like the other women of this host."

Alex reeled backward, wanting desperately to deny the stinging charges. Yet in a dark, secret corner of her mind she knew Katerina was right. Her grandfather had possessed a strength of will that was both his blessing and his curse.

As it was hers.

The two women faced each other, one breathing fast and hard with the force of her anger, the other rigid and unmoving. Then, slowly, like rainwater seeping into the steppes after a pelting storm, the bitterness drained from Katerina's face.

"Don't you see, cousin? Our grandfather gave you leadership of the host because you alone have the strength to hold Karistan together, as I...as the others...could not. Only you would ensure that our people don't scatter to the winds."

Under her embroidered blouse, Katerina's shoulders slumped. "But perhaps only by scattering, by leaving this bloodstained land, will we find peace."

Her heart aching at the bleakness on her cousin's face, Alex reached out to grasp her hand.

"Katrushka..." she began, using the pet name of their childhood in a desperate attempt to bridge the gap between them. "You must give me time. A little time."

"Too much time has been lost already. Too much blood spilled, and too many tears shed." The younger woman sighed. "Only the old ones are left now, 'Zandra, and the women. We...the women...we talk of leaving. Of going to the lowlands."

"You can't leave. Not yet."

"Don't you understand? We want husbands, men to warm our beds and our hearts. Children to bring us joy. We won't find them here."

Alex gripped her fingers. "You mustn't leave here. This is your home. Just give me a little time. I...I have a plan. Not one I can speak of yet, because it may not work. But someone comes, someone who can help us, if we just hold out a little longer.''

The two women searched each other's eyes.

"I'm sorry," Katerina said at last. "I but add to your burdens. I don't mean to, cousin.''

Alex forced a small smile. "I know.''

"I...I shouldn't have become so angry when you took me to task tonight.''

"And I shouldn't have taken you to task so clumsily."

Katerina hesitated, then gave Alex's hand a little squeeze. "I know you think me overbold, 'Zandra, but I'm not like you. None of us here are. We don't think as you do. We believe a woman is not a woman unless she has a man to warm her bed.''

Well, she was right there, Alex thought. In that, at least, she and her cousin were worlds apart.

"I... We... We want a man," Katerina said simply. "Someone like this *Amerikanski*.''

"*What?*" Alex jerked her hand free.

"Someone young and strong, with laughter in his eyes instead of hate. Someone whose blood runs hot on a cold night and whose arms were made to hold a woman.''

"Katerina!''

"Why do you sound so shocked? He's much a man, this one. Any woman would be happy to take him to her bed.''

"For heaven's sake, he's only been in camp for a few hours! You know nothing about him. He could be an...an ax murderer! Or have a wife and six children waiting for him in America.''

If he did, Alex thought, remembering their searing kiss, she pitied the woman.

Some of the lingering hurt between the two women faded as Katerina flipped her hair to one side and essayed a small, brave grin. "Pah! Do you think I waste my time? I learned all I need to know of him in less time than it takes to thread the needle. He has no wife, although many pursue him, I would guess. One has only to see the gleam in his eyes to know he has the way with women."

He had that. He certainly had that, Alex agreed silently.

"He's an outsider," she protested aloud.

"He may be an outsider, but he has the wind and the open skies in his blood. He owns only a small piece of land in America, not enough to hold him, or he would not wander as he does, delivering horses to strange countries."

Surprised at her cousin's shrewd character assessment, Alex stared at her.

"He's like the men of the steppes used to be," Katerina finished on a dreamy note. "Strong and well muscled. He would give a woman tall, healthy children. Smiling daughters and hearty sons."

The guilt, worry and resentment that had been building within Alex since the night of her grandfather's death threatened to spill over.

"Perhaps we should consider putting the man instead of the horse to stud," she snapped.

"Perhaps we should," Katerina agreed, laughing.

Alex shook her head. This was all too much. "I…I need to think!"

Now that she'd said her piece, Katerina's earlier animosity was gone. "Go. Take the air, and do your thinking. I'll finish here and brew us some tea. Go!"

Grabbing the coat she'd tossed down earlier, Alex lifted the tent flap. Once outside, she sucked in deep, rasping gulps of the cold night air.

With all her heart, she longed to saddle her gelding and head north for the ice cave her grandfather had shown her as a child. It had been her special place, her retreat whenever they clashed over his unceasing hostility toward her father. Since her return, it had become the only place she could really be alone in a land with few walls and little privacy. The only place she could find the quiet to sort through the worries that weighed on her.

But she didn't dare ride out at night unescorted. Not with the ever-present threat of raiders from Balminsk. Not with Nate Sloan in camp. She couldn't take the chance that he might stumble over something he wouldn't understand.

Damn it all to hell!

Simmering with frustration and confusion, Alex threw her cloak over her shoulders and stalked to the outskirts of the camp.

What in the world was she doing here?

Why had she abandoned her business, her scattering of friends, her on-again-off-again fiancé, to come back to Karistan?

Why, after all those years of unrelenting silence, had she answered her grandfather's stark three-word message?

"I die," the telegram had read. "Come."

So she had come. And been forced into the leadership of a people she barely knew anymore. She'd promised, and on the steppes, a promise made was a promise kept.

Although she felt trapped by this unfamiliar role, there was no one to pass it to. Katerina herself admitted she didn't have the strength; nor did the other women still left of her grandfather's line. Although one of her aunts was an artist of great skill, and another cousin a gifted healer who'd studied at the Kiev Medical Institute, the women of Karistan hadn't been trained for leadership. Nor did they want it.

With a small groan, Alex tried to come to grips with what they did want.

Her mind whirling, she tucked her chin into the folds of her coat. Gradually, the ordinary, familiar sounds of the camp settling down for the night penetrated her chaotic thoughts.

A man's low, gruff laugh.

The whinny of a horse in the distance.

The plink of a three-stringed balalaika picking out an ancient melody.

Alex tilted her head, straining to catch the faint, lilting notes. Like the wipe of a cool cloth across fever-burned skin, the music of the steppes eased the tight band around her heart.

Soothed by the haunting tune, she shrugged off her doubts and feelings of inadequacy. Whatever the reasons her grandfather had had for summoning her, she was here. Whether she wanted it or not, she carried the burden of this small country until she could pass it to someone else and get on with her life.

As the balalaika poured its liquid, silvery notes into the night, Alex felt a gathering sense of purpose.

She had to hold off the wolf from Balminsk.

She had to keep her disintegrating host together.

For a few more days. A week at most. Just until the man she'd sent for arrived and told her whether she could barter death for life.

Drawing in a deep, resolute breath, Alex turned and strode back to the tent. When she entered, Ivana and the other women threw her tentative looks. Katerina came forward with a peace offering and a determined smile.

Alex accepted the steaming mug of tea. "Thank you, Katrushka. Now we must talk. All of us."

In the tent he shared with Dimitri and the others, Nate declined another glass of vodka and weaved his way through the scattered cots toward his own. After the long day and even longer evening, he was ready to pull off his boots and crawl into his bedroll.

One scuffed boot hit the faded carpet covering the earthen floor with a dull thud. Nate was tugging off the other when the sound of music drifted over the murmur of the other men. Resting his forearms across a bent leg, Nate tilted his head to catch the faint, distant tune.

Whoever was plucking at that sweet-sounding guitar could sure make it sing. The haunting notes seemed to capture the vastness of the steppes. Their loneliness. Their mystery.

When the song ended, Nate shook his head at his fancifulness and slipped his automatic under the folded sheepskin that served as a pillow. As he emptied his pockets, an old Case pocketknife with a worn handle clattered down beside a handful of oddly shaped coins.

Nate fingered the handle, imagining how surprised Wily Willie would be to know that the knife he'd won in a poker game all those years ago and given to Nate as a belated birthday gift now housed one of the world's most sophisticated metal detectors. So sophisticated that it would register the wire used to solder transistors to circuit boards. More specifically, the solder used on the circuits in the small black box that cycled the arming codes for 18 nuclear warheads. The wizards in OMEGA's special devices unit had rigged the pocketknife to vibrate silently if it was within twenty yards of the decoder Nate sought.

Hefting the knife in one hand, he scowled down at it. He wished the blasted thing had begun to vibrate in the women's tent tonight. Somehow his need to find the decoder had escalated subtly in the past ten hours. That black box was a major factor in the lines etched beside Alexandra's golden eyes, Nate was convinced.

Now that he'd caught a glimpse of those glorious eyes free of worry and sparkling with laughter, he couldn't seem to shake the need to keep them that way.

Chapter 6

"You wanted to speak with me, *ataman*."

"Yes, Dimitri. Will you take tea?"

When the gray beard bobbed in assent, Alex picked up a hammered tin mug and half filled it with steaming green tea from the samovar that was always kept heated just outside the women's tent. Adding thick, creamy milk from a small pitcher, and four heaping teaspoons of coarse sugar, Alex handed the mug to Dimitri. He cradled it in arthritic hands for a moment, letting the soothing heat counteract the chill of the early-morning air.

"Did the sentries note any unusual activity last night?" she asked when he'd taken a sip of the rich, warming brew.

Amusement flickered in his cloudy eyes. "Other than the attack on the honey pot?"

"Other than that."

He peered at her through the steam spiraling from the

mug. "There were no riders, if that's what you ask. No new tracks."

"That relieves me, Dimitri."

"Me, also, *ataman*."

"Nevertheless, I wish you to choose four of our best men to ride with me this afternoon," she instructed. "I would check our borders."

"It is done."

There were many aspects of life on the steppes that made Alex grit her teeth. The lack of privacy. The constant wind. The impermanence of a way of life built around grazing herds. This unquestioning obedience from subordinates, however, was one facet that definitely appealed to her. If only the dedicated but temperamental genius responsible for translating her designs into market-test garments was as cooperative as Dimitri, Alex thought wryly. She'd be spared the dramatic scenes that punctuated the last frantic weeks before a new line debuted. There'd be no bolts of fabric thrown across fitting rooms, no mannequins in tears, no strident demands to know just what in God's name Alex had been thinking of when she draped a bodice in such an impossible line!

Perhaps when she flew back to the States, she could convince Dimitri to come with her and impose some order on the chaos of her small but flourishing firm…assuming she had a firm left after she'd dumped the latest batch of designs in her assistant's hands and taken off as she had.

Deliberately Alex forced all thought of her other world from her mind. She wouldn't be flying anywhere, not for a while. Not until Karistan's future was assured. Which brought her to the point of her conversation with her lieutenant.

"There is another matter I would speak to you about," she said.

Weak early-morning sunlight glinted on the gold hoop in Dimitri's left ear as he cocked his head, waiting for her to continue.

"This man, Sloan, and the gift he brings. I've...I've given both much thought."

"That does not surprise me."

At her quick look, Dimitri shrugged. "Gregor saw you with him last night."

"Yes, well, I... That is, Katerina and the other women..."

"Yes, *ataman?*"

Alex squared her shoulders. She alone could take responsibility for this decision.

"I've decided we should accept the president's gift."

Nate chewed slowly, savoring the coarse bread covered with creamy, pungent cheese. As breakfasts went, this one was filling and tasty, but he would've traded just about anything he owned at that moment for a cup of black coffee. Controlling an instinctive grimace, he washed the bread down with a swallow of heavily sweetened tea.

Beside him, Peter the Great argued amiably with a sunken, hollow-cheeked man who looked like he'd last seen action in the Crimean War. While they bantered back and forth, Nate stole a quick look at his watch.

Two hours until his first scheduled contact with Maggie. She should be in Balminsk right about now. He was anxious to hear her assessment of the situation there, to see if it tallied with the bits of information he'd gleaned about its vitriolic, reactionary leader from the Karistanis.

He'd have to give his one-armed guardian the slip for a few moments to contact Maggie. Peter the Great hadn't relaxed his vigilance, but Nate knew his way around well enough now to put some tents between himself and the aged warrior when he was ready to.

At a sudden stirring among the men, he glanced over his shoulder and spied Alexandra crossing the open space in the center of camp. The sight of her caused his fingers to curl around the tin mug. He'd spent more hours last night than he wanted to admit imagining her long, slender body in that satin bra and not a whole lot more. But even his most vivid mental images didn't convey the vitality and sheer, stunning presence of the woman who walked toward him.

In her black boots and those baggy britches that shaped themselves to her hips with every shift in the contrary wind, she would have caught Nate's eye even if she wasn't wearing a belted tunic in the brightest shade of red he'd ever seen. Rows of gold frog fastenings marched down its front, reminding him of an eighteenth-century hussar's uniform. More gold embroidery embellished the cuffs, giving the illusion of an officer's rank.

Come to think of it, he decided with an inner grin, it wasn't an illusion.

Like a general at the head of her troops, Alex led a contingent of the camp's women. She was flanked on either side by Katerina, bright-eyed and pink-cheeked in the crisp air, and a pale, honey-haired widow Nate had heard referred to as Ivana. More women streamed along behind her, as well as a gathering trail of curious camp residents. Dimitri followed more slowly, his lined face impassive.

Tossing the rest of his tea to the ground, Nate set the tin mug aside and rose. Ole Red must have done more damage to the women's tent last night than he'd estimated to generate a turnout like this. Wondering just what he'd have to do to smooth over Karistani-American relations, he hooked his thumbs in his belt.

He didn't wonder long.

After a polite greeting and the hope that he'd slept well, Alexandra plunged right to the heart of things.

"I've given the matter that brought you to Karistan a great deal of thought."

"That so?"

"Yes, that's so. I...I have decided to accept the president's offer of a stud."

Nate wasn't sure exactly why, but the way she announced her decision didn't exactly overwhelm him on Ole Red's behalf. Maybe it was the strange, indecipherable glint in her eyes. Or the curious air that hung over the small crowd, watching and intent. Shrugging, he acknowledged her decision.

"You won't be sorry. He's one of the best in the business."

The glint in her eyes deepened, darkening them to a burnished bronze. "That remains to be seen. There are conditions, however."

"What kind of conditions?"

"He must prove himself."

"That shouldn't be difficult. Just turn him loose with the females."

Katerina gave a smothered laugh. Her dark eyes dancing, she treated the other women to what Nate guessed was an explicit translation of his words, since it drew a round of giggles. Alex quieted them with a wave of one hand.

"I meant that he must prove himself on the steppes. Show he has endurance and heart for this rugged land."

Nate could understand that. He wouldn't acquire a horse without seeing it put through its paces, either.

"Fair enough."

"We ride out this afternoon," she told him. "The ride will be long and grueling."

"Ole Red and I will manage to keep up somehow," he drawled. Relieved that one part of his mission, at least, was under control, Nate allowed himself a grin. "Trust me. Three Bars Red won't disappoint you. Or the fillies, when you put him to stud."

Drawing in a long, slow breath, Alex met his gaze with a steady one of her own. "I'm not talking about Three Bars Red, Sloan."

"Evidently I missed something vital in this little conversation. Just who *are* we talking about?"

"You."

Nate narrowed his eyes. "You want to run that one by me one more time?" he asked slowly, deliberately.

"It's very simple. The president was right, although he didn't know it. Karistan needs new blood. New life. But not..." She wet her lips. "Not just among our horses."

His first thought was that it was a joke. That Alex and the other women were paying him back, in spades, for the havoc Red had wrought last night.

His second, as he took in the determined lift to Alex's chin, and Katerina's eager expression, was that Maggie was never going to believe this.

As the dilapidated truck she was riding in hit another rut, Maggie braced both hands against the dash. She felt her bottom part company with the hard leather seat, then slam down again. Suppressing a groan, she glared at the driver.

"If you don't slow down," she warned him in swift, idiomatic Russian, "your mother will soon have a daughter instead of a son."

Shaking his head in admiration, the brawny driver

grinned at her. "How is it that you speak our language with such mastery?"

"I watched the Goodwill Games on TV. Hey, keep at least one eye on the road!"

Whipping the steering wheel around to avoid a pothole the size of the Grand Canyon, the driver sent the truck bouncing over a nest of rocks at the edge of the track. He spun back onto the road without once letting up on the gas pedal.

Maggie grabbed the dash again and hung on, swearing under her breath. After six hours in this doorless, springless vehicle, she felt even worse than she had after the first week of the grueling six-month training course OMEGA put her through.

The head training instructor, a steel-eyed agent whose code name, Jaguar, described both his personality and his method of operation in the field, had brushed aside Maggie's rather vocal comment about sadists. When he finished with her, he'd promised, she could hold her own in everything from hand-to-hand combat to a full-scale assault.

At this moment, she would've opted cheerfully for a full-scale assault. It had to be less dangerous than rattling along at sixty miles an hour down a road that existed only in some long-dead mapmaker's imagination! In a vehicle that had rolled off a World War II assembly line, no less.

Another wild swerve brought the other passenger in the open cab crashing into her side. Maggie held her breath until Richard Worthington righted himself, with only a single jab of his bony elbow in her ribs.

"Uh, sorry…" he yelled over the clatter of the crates in the truck bed.

"That's okay," Maggie shouted back. "What's one more bruise here and there?"

He grabbed at the frame to steady himself. "Will you ask the driver to pull over? I need to check the map. We should have passed that town by now, the one just over the Balminsk border."

"We did pass it, Richard. A half hour ago."

He stared at her blankly. "I don't remember seeing anything but a few houses and a barn."

"That was it. On the steppes, two houses and a barn constitute a town."

"But...but..."

"But what?" she yelled, struggling to keep the exasperation out of her voice. Two days of flying and six hours of driving with Dr. Richard Worthington, brilliant young physicist and klutz extraordinaire, had strained Maggie's patience to the limit.

"But that was where we were supposed to meet our escort."

"What?"

They bounced upward, then slammed downward, with the precision of synchronized swimmers.

"Uh, we'll have to go back."

Maggie closed her eyes and counted to ten.

They'd already lost almost half a day's travel time due to confusion among the airport officials when they landed and an extended search for the transit permits that Richard had, somehow, packed with his underwear. At this rate, they wouldn't make Balminsk's capital until late afternoon.

When Maggie opened her eyes again, Richard's earnest, apologetic face filled her dust-smeared lenses. Bracing one hand against the roof, she swiveled in her seat.

"Stop the truck, Vasili."

"No, no! She goes well. If we stop, she may not start again."

"We have to turn around and go back."

The broad-faced driver rolled his eyes toward Richard. "Do not tell me. This one lost another something."

"All right, I won't tell you. Just stop. We'll have to let the rest of the team know. When they catch up with us," Maggie added darkly.

Vasili's quick-silver grin flashed. Muttering something about old women in babushkas who should ride only bicycles, he swung the wheel with careless abandon. Maggie felt her kidneys slide sideways, and grabbed Richard's arm before the rest of her followed.

With dust swirling all around them, Vasili braked to a screeching halt and cut the engine. While it hacked and shuddered and wheezed, Richard climbed out of the high cab and turned to help Maggie down.

His hand felt surprisingly firm after the shaky, soul-shattering ride. They stood for a moment in unmoving relief, and then Richard lifted a hand to shade his eyes.

"How far back are the others, do you think?"

"A half hour as the crow flies. Or ten minutes as Vasili drives."

The smile that made him seem so much younger than his years lightened his face. "I have to admit, I hadn't anticipated quite this much excitement our first day in-country."

Maggie's irritation with him faded, as it always seemed to do when he turned that shy, hesitant look on her. He thought this was excitement? Well, maybe it was, compared to spending ten or twelve hours a day bent over a high-powered microscope, playing with protons and neutrons.

"I think I can do with a little less of Vasili's brand of thrills," she answered, smiling.

Rolling her shoulders in a vain attempt to ease the strain

of the past few hours, Maggie glanced at her watch. At least this unplanned stop would give her a chance to contact Nate during the time parameters they'd agreed on. She scanned the rolling countryside for a moment, then nodded toward a low, jagged line of rocks a hundred yards away.

"That looks like an ignimbrite formation. I'm going to go take a look."

"I'll come with you. Those rocks could be dangerous. You might trip."

Right. *She* might trip. "No, thanks, I don't need an escort."

"You could twist your ankle or fall." Richard assumed an air of authority. "I'm responsible for the team's well-being. I'd better come...."

"Richard, I have to go to the bathroom."

"Oh." He blinked several times. "Yes, of course."

Plucking her backpack out of the truck bed, Maggie trudged off toward the low-lying formation.

She really did have to go to the bathroom.

That basic need attended to, she examined the chronometer on her left wrist. With its black band, chrome face and series of buttons for setting the date, the time and the stopwatch function, it looked exactly like a runner's watch. It also contained a state-of-the-art miniaturized communications device that produced and received crystal-clear, instantaneous satellite transmissions. Scrambled incoming signals so that they couldn't be intercepted. Was shockproof. Radar-proof. Urine-proof.

Maggie chuckled, remembering the lab director's stunned reaction when she'd relayed the information that several orphans had piddled in Jaguar's boot during a mission in Central America and put the highly sophisticated unit concealed there out of commission. This new, improved version, he had solemnly assured her and Cowboy a few days ago, would not fail. She punched in a quick series of numbers on the calculator buttons.

A few nerve-racking minutes later, a flashing signal indicated that her transmission was being returned. Eagerly Maggie pressed the receive button.

"Chameleon here, Cowboy. Do you read me?"

"Loud and clear. Are you in place?"

"Well, almost." She gave him a succinct but descriptive rundown of the adventures attendant upon traveling with Dr. Worthington. "How's it going at your end? Have you located the boom box yet?"

"No."

The clipped response was so unlike Nate's usual style that Maggie instinctively tensed.

"There's been a slight change in the mission parameters," he supplied, confirming her suspicion that something was wrong.

"What kind of change?"

For several long moments, he didn't reply. When he did, it was in a low, acerbic tone.

"Alexandra Jordan has decided to accept the president's gift of a stud, but not the four-legged variety."

"Come again, Cowboy? I didn't quite catch that last transmission."

"She's suggesting that I stand in for Three Bars Red."

Frowning, Maggie shook her wrist. Despite the lab chief's assurances, the transmitter had to be malfunctioning. Either that, or Nate was using some kind of code. Maybe he was under observation, Maggie thought, her pulse tripping. Maybe he was under duress.

"I'm not sure I understand what you're trying to tell me," she replied, listening intently for a hidden message in his words.

"Dammit, I'm trying to tell you that she expects me to

single-handedly repopulate Karistan. Or at least a good portion of it.''

Nate was definitely under duress, Maggie decided. But not the kind that would cause her to open the crate marked Geological Survey Equipment and roll out the specially armed helicopter to rush to his assistance.

''I'm sorry I'm a bit slow on the uptake,'' she said, still not quite believing what she was hearing. ''Are you saying that she expects—? That you're supposed to—?''

''Yes, she does, and yes, I am.'' Nate gave an exasperated snort. ''At first I thought it was a joke, but apparently the entire unmarried female portion of the camp voted on the idea.''

''They…they did?''

He caught the unsteady waver in her voice. ''You won't think it's so funny when I tell you that I haven't had two seconds to myself in the last few hours. I can't even take a leak without some interested party showing up to inspect the plumbing. You wouldn't believe what I had to go through to slip away for this contact.''

''Try me,'' she suggested, her lips quivering.

''Chameleon,'' he warned, ''this is not— Oh, hell, here comes Ivana. Let Control know what's happened. I'll contact you later.''

The transmission terminated abruptly.

For several seconds, Maggie could only stare at the watch. Then a huge, delighted grin split her face.

Cowboy was about to give the term *deep cover* a whole new meaning!

This was priceless. When the small, select fraternity of OMEGA agents heard about this, they'd never let him live it down.

Poor Nate, she thought with a hiccup of laughter. The woman who'd snagged his attention and masculine interest during the mission prebrief had just offered him up as the jackpot in the Karistani version of lotto. No wonder he didn't view the situation with his characteristic easygoing sense of humor.

Still grinning, Maggie forced herself to consider the implications to their mission of what she'd just heard. She didn't believe for a moment that Nate would let this bizarre development impact his ability to accomplish his task. He was too good in the field, too experienced, to be distracted, even by a camp full of women who wanted to…to inspect his plumbing. If Alexandra Jordan or any of the other Karistanis had possession of the decoder, Nate would find it. But he'd sure have his hands full while he was looking for it.

Her eyes sparkling with delight, Maggie punched in another code and waited for her OMEGA controller to acknowledge her call. This contingency was definitely outside the range of possible parameters David Jensen had defined in such detail during their mission-planning session. She could visualize the pained expression his handsome, square-jawed face assumed whenever something occurred that he hadn't envisioned or planned for. That didn't happen very often, which was why Doc ranked as one of OMEGA's best agents.

What she couldn't visualize, however, was Adam Ridgeway's reaction when David relayed her report. That just might be one of those rare moments when even Adam's rigid control would slip. With all her heart, Maggie wished she could be there to see it.

Still chuckling, she made her way out of the rocks a little while later.

"Are you ready to go?" she called, rounding the end of the truck.

"Not…quite."

Richard's reply sounded indistinct and muffled. Which wasn't surprising, seeing as he was lying spread-eagled in the dirt, with a rifle barrel held to his head.

Chapter 7

Maggie peered over the tops of her dust-smeared glasses at the murderous-looking brigand holding the rifle to Richard's head.

"Who are you?"

"He...he is the son of the Wolf," Vasili gasped from his prone position a few yards away, then grunted when another bandit prodded him viciously in the back.

Maggie folded her arms across her chest. "No kidding?"

Her phrasing translated as something along the lines of "You do not speak the joke to me?"—but it was close enough. Either the words or the nonchalance with which she spoke them seemed to impress the dark-haired, menacing stranger. Without relieving the rifle's pressure on Richard's skull, he smiled.

It wasn't much of a smile, Maggie noted. More a twist of lips already pulled to one side by the raw, angry scar cutting across his left cheek. Now that, she thought, comparing the scar to her own semitattooed chin, was definitely an attention getter.

"No, he does not make the joke," the brigand responded. "Who are you?"

Under her folded arm, Maggie's fingers deftly extracted the small, pencil-thin canister sewn into her jacket's side seam.

"I'm Dr. St. Clare," she stated calmly. "I'm with the UN nuclear facilities site inspection team, as are my companions. We're traveling under international passports, with guarantees of safe passage through Balminsk."

She didn't really expect these men to be impressed with the thick sheaf of papers signed by a battery of clerks and stamped with seals in a dozen different languages. Assuming, of course, that Richard could produce them again. Still, the longer she delayed using deadly force, the better her chances were of getting Richard and Vasili out of harm's way.

"Forgive me, Dr. St. Clare."

Maggie's eyes widened at the smooth, lightly accented English. To her considerable surprise and Richard's audible relief, the man stepped back. A nod from him sent Vasili's guard back a step as well.

"We were told the UN team would be in convoy. When we saw this lone vehicle stopped along the road, naturally we came to check it out."

Maggie sent Vasili an evil glare, which he ignored as he scrambled to his feet.

"Is this how you check things out?" she asked the leader.

The faint smile edged farther to one side. "Not as a rule. But when your companion attacked, we responded in kind."

Maggie's incredulous gaze swung to the attacker in question.

"They, uh, came up so quietly," Richard explained, dusting off his jacket front. "When I turned around and saw them behind me, I sort of freaked out."

With great effort of will, Maggie managed not to freak out, as well.

The leader gazed at the young scientist with something that might have been amusement. With that scar, it was hard to tell.

"The way things are in this part of the world, we take no chances, you understand."

"I'm beginning to," Richard admitted, a touch of belligerence in his voice.

The stranger's black eyes went flat, and his face hard under its livid scar. "The least spark will ignite a conflagration between Balminsk and Karistan. Surely you were told of this before you ventured into this remote area?"

"Yes, we were," Richard replied. "But we weren't told exactly where you fit into all this, Mr....Wolf."

"My father is known as the White Wolf of Balminsk. I am Nikolas Cherkoff. Major Nikolas Cherkoff, formerly of the Soviet transcontinental command."

Cherkoff! The pieces fell into place instantly for Maggie. So this was the son of the wild-eyed radical, Boris Cherkoff, who ruled Balminsk. The man whose blood feud with Karistan had kept this corner of the world in turmoil for decades. She'd been briefed that Cherkoff's son was in the military, but intelligence reports had last placed him at the head of an elite, highly mobile combat unit, the Soviet version of the Rangers. She wondered what he was doing here, then decided that the rawness of the jagged wound on his cheek probably had something to do with the fact that he now wore civilian clothes instead of a uniform.

"Formerly?" Richard asked innocently, echoing her thoughts.

"There is no longer any Soviet Union," he replied, his tone dispassionate. "Nor am I any longer on active duty. I will escort you to my father."

Maggie slipped the tiny lethal canister back into the slit in her jacket sleeve. The special weapons folks had assured her that the biochemical agent it contained was extremely potent, but localized and temporary. She was just as happy not to have had to use it on this hard-eyed major. She had a feeling he would've been twice as tough to handle once he'd recovered from a "temporary" disabling.

Cherkoff, Jr., relegated Richard to the truck bed and took his place beside Maggie in the cab. Squeezed between his hard, unyielding body and Vasili's brawny one, she contemplated the interesting turn her mission had taken in the past few minutes. Now she had not only Dr. Richard Worthington and the unpredictable, warlike leader of Balminsk to deal with, she also had to factor his son into the equation.

She'd have to let Nate know about this new development as soon as possible—assuming he could manage to slip away from his bevy of potential brides to answer her call, Maggie thought with an inner grin.

Stifling a groan, Nate held up a hand. "No, thanks, Anya. No more."

The dainty, sloe-eyed woman smiled and pushed another plate piled high with steaming, dough-wrapped meat pastries across the folding table. Blushing, she said something in a soft, sweet voice that under any other circumstances would have completely delighted him.

"Anya speaks of an old...old...saying among the women here," Katerina translated, her forehead wrinkled with the effort to find the right words. "Keep the cooking pot full, and...and...even the stupidest of men will find his way home in the dark."

Despite himself, Nate laughed. "Sounds about right. I'd find my way through a blinding blizzard if I knew something like these dumplings were waiting at the other end. But I can't eat any more, Anya, I swear."

When Katerina relayed his words, the young widow cocked her head and looked him up and down. Her soft comment brought a burst of laughter from the group around Nate. He decided not to stick around for the translation this time. Ignoring a flutter of feminine protest, he eased through the circle.

"I'm riding out this afternoon, remember? I'd better go before I'm too heavy for Ole Red to carry."

As Nate made his way through the camp, the mingled irritation and embarrassment that had dogged him ever since Alex dropped her little bombshell earlier this morning returned full-force. He felt like a fat, grain-fed steer ambling down the chute toward the meat-processing plant. The men grinned as he passed, nudging each other in the ribs. The women chuckled and looked him over as though they were measuring him for the cooking pot Anya had mentioned.

It didn't help his mood any to see Alex waiting for him across the square, wearing her long, figure-flattering coat over her bright red shirt, an amused expression on her face. And to think he'd wanted to keep a smile on the woman's face, he thought in derision.

Nate knew his present disgruntled feeling had a lot to

do with the fact that she'd been discussing his merits as a possible breeder with all the other unmarried women in camp while he was weaving fantasies about her and her alone. Fantasies he had no business weaving. At least until this mission was over. But once it was…

Controlling with sheer willpower the sudden tightening in his loins at the thought of proving to Alexandra Jordan just how good a breeder he might be, Nate strolled across the dusty square.

"Been waiting long?"

"Only a few moments. I could see you were busy."

"Just finishing dinner." Nate kept his tone light and easy. He wasn't about to let on how disconcerting it was for a man to chew his food with half a dozen women watching every bite and swallow.

"Good," she responded. "You'll need your strength this afternoon to keep up with us."

Nate eyed the others who were drifting up beside her. Having learned from Wily Willie early on to measure a man by the size of his heart and not the length of his shadow, he didn't make the mistake of underestimating Dimitri or Petr or the big, beefy-faced man with jowls to match his sagging belly. Still, he had to have thirty, maybe forty, fewer years under his belt than any one of the Karistani men. He figured he'd keep up.

When they were all mounted, Alex swung her gray gelding around. "Are you ready to ride?"

Although her question was polite enough, there was no mistaking the challenge in her amber eyes. Or the amusement. Obviously she thought Nate's only alternative to this little excursion was to stay in camp and be force-fed more of Anya's dumplings.

She couldn't know that he wasn't about to let her out of his sight.

"Yes, ma'am, I surely am."

* * *

They rode at a steady jog across the high plains, dodging the ravines that scarred the steppes' surface at intermittent intervals. The morning sunshine faded slowly as clouds piled up, and a decided chill entered the air.

When Alex called a halt at a stream lined with feathery, silver-leafed Russian olive trees, Nate tipped his ball cap back and surveyed their small band. If any of the men slumped untidily in their saddles felt any strain from the long ride, they sure didn't show it. Nor did their shaggy, unshod mounts.

Sitting easy while Red watered, Nate eyed the Karistani's horses with new respect. Descendants of the tough little steppe ponies, that could gallop for an hour without stopping, last two days without food or water and remain impervious to the extremes of temperature that ravaged the steppes, the small, shaggy Dons weren't even blowing hard.

The beefy, red-faced rider caught Nate's appraising look and said something to Alex.

"Mikhail sees that you eye his mount," she translated. "He says it may be small compared to the red, but very agile."

"That so?"

"That is so. He wonders if you'd like to see what the Don can do. A small race, perhaps?"

Nate realized he was being given the first opportunity to "prove" himself.

"Mikhail much admires your hat," Alex added. "If you care to wager it, he'll wager his own in return."

That alone would have been enough to make Nate turn down the bet. He didn't particularly fancy the greasy black sheepskin hat the big, raw-boned man wore at a rakish angle. Nor was he in any particular hurry to play Alex's game. But he'd never been one to pass up a good race— or the challenge in a pair of gleaming golden eyes.

"Fine by me," he replied easily.

They used the stand of trees as a course for what turned out to be the Karistani version of a barrel race.

Weaving through the thicket with hooves pounding, Red stayed well out in front for the first few turns. A true cutting horse, he could wheel on a dime and give back nine cents change. He couldn't, however, duck under low-hanging branches and just about skin the bark from the tree trunks with every turn, as the smaller, nimble Don could. By the sixth turn, Red had lost the advantage of his size and speed. By the tenth, the Don held the lead.

Nate didn't begrudge Alex and Mikhail their grins when he crossed the finish line well behind the Karistani.

"That was some fine riding," he conceded.

Tugging off the ball cap, he tossed it to the victor. Mikhail stuffed his sheepskin hat in his pocket and donned his trophy.

Alex translated his laughing reply. "He says that all he knows of riding he learned from Petr Borodín."

Her casual tone didn't fool Nate for a moment. Sure enough, the balding, bag-eyed hero of the steppes was the next to suggest a little contest. It sounded simple enough. The first one to fill a pouch with the water trickling along the muddy bed and then return to the starting point would be the winner.

"Let me make sure I understand this. He wants to race to that little creek, fill one of these skins, and race back?"

Alex nodded. "That's it."

Nate glanced at the one-armed warrior, who winked and upped the stakes.

"He has a bottle of his best vodka in his bag," Alex commented. "He'll wager that against your watch."

"Make it my belt buckle, and he's on," Nate countered.

Red made it to the shallow ravine several lengths ahead of Petr's mouse-colored Don. Nate was out of the saddle and down on one knee in the muddy water before Red had come to a full stop. Glancing up at the sound of approaching hooves, he almost dropped the leather pouch.

While his mount galloped at full speed, Petr Borodín hung upside down from the saddle. Using only the strength of his thighs to hold him in place, he gripped the reins in his one hand and the strings of the pouch in his teeth. The leather sack trailed the water for a few seconds before Petr dragged himself upright. By the time Nate and Red had clambered up the shallow bank, their opponents were already back beside Alex.

Cowboy drew up beside them, shaking his head in genuine admiration. "I doubt if there are many two-armed rodeo trick riders who could do that."

"It's called the *djigitovka*," Alex explained, her eyes sparkling. "It's one of the many circus tricks the Cossacks of old used to perform to impress the Russians and other outsiders."

"Well, it sure impressed the hell out of me."

Grinning, Nate unhooked his belt and passed the silver buckle, with its brass stenciling, to Petr. The gap-toothed warrior promptly hung it from one of the frayed medals decorating his chest. Reining his mount around, he went over to display his trophy to the others.

"At this rate, I'll ride back into camp buck-naked."

Alex arched a brow. "Katerina and the others would certainly appreciate that."

"Think so, do you?"

A delicate wash of color painted her cheeks at his sar-

donic reply, but she let her glance roam over his body in
a slow, deliberate appraisal.

"Yes. I think so."

That little flush went a long way toward shooting out
the dents in Nate's ego. He felt a whole lot better knowing
he had somewhat of the same effect on Ms. Jordan as she
had on him. Crossing his wrists over the saddle horn, he
decided to get this thing out in the open.

"I guess this is as good a time as any to talk about your
little announcement this morning."

"There's nothing to talk about. My father would've defined it as a simple matter of supply and demand."

"They demand and I supply, is that it?"

The color crept higher in her cheeks, but she kept her
head high. "That's it."

"You want to tell me how I progressed overnight from
a potential rapist who had to be warned off with threats
of being flayed alive to the prize in the Crackerjack box?"

"As Katerina informed me, it was time to reassess
Karistan's needs. All of them."

"Come on, Alexandra. What's really behind all this
nonsense?"

"What makes you think it's nonsense?"

"Give me a break, lady. This is the twentieth century,
not the eighteenth. A woman today ought to be looking
for something more in a mate than mere availability."

Alex sat back in the saddle, thinking of all the responses
she could make to that statement.

She could tell Sloan that availability didn't rank quite
as high on his list of qualifications as the strong arms Ivana
had speculated about during breakfast this morning and
Alex herself had experienced last night.

That Anya, sweet, pale-haired Anya, had gotten up with
the dawn to light the cook fires, commenting on how much

pleasure it gave her to prepare delicacies for someone with such a long, lean body and flat belly.

That, despite herself, Alex was coming to agree with Katerina. A smile in a man's eyes went a long way toward countering any less desirable traits he might have.

Instead, she simply shrugged. ''Availability is as good a criterion as any other on the steppes. We have a saying here, that women must have the courage of the bear, the strength of the ox, and the blindness of the bat. Otherwise none would wed.''

Nate's bark of laughter had the other men swinging around to stare. ''For all that they're anxious to acquire husbands, seems to me that the women of Karistan don't hold men in very high regard.''

''Oh, we like men well enough,'' Alex returned. ''In their place.''

Leaving Nate to chew over that one, she signaled that it was time to move out.

Whatever other ''tests'' Alexandra had planned for him quickly got shoved to the back burner.

They'd ridden only a few miles when Dimitri, who was in the lead, suddenly pulled up and signaled her forward.

Sitting easy in the saddle, Nate watched the dark-haired woman confer with her lieutenant. When she called the rest of them forward, her eyes were flat, and tight lines bracketed either side of her mouth.

''Dimitri has found some tracks he does not recognize,'' she told Nate tersely. ''We will follow them.''

Picking up the pace, she led the small band farther and farther east. Nate didn't need to consult the compass built into his chronometer to know they were heading directly toward Balminsk. Lowering his chin against the gathering wind, he wondered just what the Karistanis intended to do if they caught up with the riders who'd made those tracks.

Given the shaky state of affairs between the two nations, he wouldn't be surprised to find himself in the middle of a firefight.

Nate glanced at Alex's back and felt a sudden clammy chill that had nothing to do with the wind. His jaw hardening, he battled memories of another cold, rainy day. A day when Belfast's streets had erupted with gunfire and a desperate, determined woman had died in his arms. Pushing that black memory back into the small, private corner of his soul where it permanently lodged, Nate edged Red up alongside Alex's gray.

A half hour later, the storm that had been threatening began pounding the plains ahead of them. Not long after that, Alex called a halt. Her mouth tight, she stared across the wide ravine that blocked their path. Although the stream that wandered through it was no doubt just a trickle ordinarily, now it was swollen and rushing with the rains that lashed the steppes.

When Dimitri called out a question, Alex eyed the far bank, then reluctantly shook her head.

Smart move, Nate acknowledged silently. He'd seen his share of bloated carcasses swept along on these gully-washers. While he didn't doubt Red's ability to swim the rushing torrent, he wasn't anxious to see Alex try it on her smaller mount.

When Dimitri rode back to confer with the others, Nate threw her a sidelong glance.

"You want to tell me just who we've been tracking these last few hours?"

She pulled her gaze from the black clouds scudding toward them and gave a little shrug.

"Whoever it was, we won't be able to track them any farther. Not with the storm washing the plains."

Her refusal to share even this bit of information with him didn't set well with Nate.

"You've all but invited me to become part of the family," he tossed at her. "Don't you think it's about time you tell me what the hell's putting that crease between your brows?"

She blinked at the uncharacteristic edge to his voice, but before she could reply, the first fat raindrops splattered on her shoulders.

"I don't think this is the time to talk about much of anything."

As if to punctuate her words, the storm erupted around them in awesome fury. Lightning snaked down and cracked against the earth, too close for Nate's comfort. The roiling black clouds spit out their contents, and the wind picked up with a vengeance, flinging the rain sideways, right into their faces.

The Karistanis, used to the violence of the steppes, buried their chins in the high protective collars of their greatcoats and slumped even lower in their saddles. Nate dragged on the yellow slicker that had seen him through similar Wyoming storms. He wished he had his ball cap to keep some of the pelting rain out of his eyes.

"We'll take shelter among those rocks till it passes," Alex called above the howl of the wind, pointing to a line of black basalt boulders thrusting up out of the plains some distance away.

Nate nodded as she turned her gray and kicked him into a gallop. With the ravine on their right, they raced toward the dark, towering shapes. Dimitri and the others pounded behind them.

They weren't the only ones headed for the rocks, they soon discovered. Over the rumble of thunder, Nate heard the sound of hoofbeats coming from their left. He pulled

his .38 out of the holster tucked under his armpit just as
Alex whipped her rifle out of its leather saddle case.

"They're ours," she shouted in relief a second later, as
a small band of riderless horses charged out of the rain.
"Usually they graze south of here. The storm must have
driven them across the steppes."

Within moments, the two bands had merged and were
flowing toward the rocks. They'd almost made it when
lightning arced to the earth just a short distance ahead of
them.

Even Red, as well trained as he was, shied.

Thighs gripping, body thrusting forward, Nate kept his
seat. The Karistanis, Alex included, did the same.

A quick glance over his shoulder showed Nate that the
blinding flash of light had panicked the other horses.
Manes whipping, tails streaming, they scattered in all directions. Through the sheeting rain, he saw a bay yearling
head right for the ravine's edge. It went over with a
whinny of sheer panic.

Nate whipped Red around. Following the rim, he
searched the rushing, muddy water for some sign of the
colt. A few moments later, its muzzle broke the surface.
Even from this distance, he could see its eyes rolling in
terror and its forelegs flailing uselessly as it was dragged
back under.

Nate yanked his rope free and followed the course of
the rim, waiting for the yearling to surface again. When it
did, it had been carried to the far side of the gorge, well
beyond his reach. Cursing, he watched the rushing water
slam the colt into a toppled, half-submerged satinwood
tree that was still tethered to the far bank by its long,
snakelike roots. Over the roar of the rain he heard the
animal's shrill cries, and then the brown water closed over
its head once more.

"Sloan! What is it? What are you doing?" Alex brought her gray to a dancing halt beside him.

"You've got a horse down!" he shouted. "There! He's caught in that tree."

Shoving her wet hair out of her eyes with one hand, Alex squinted along the line of his outstretched arm. "I see him!"

Standing up in the stirrups, Nate searched the ravine in both directions. "Any place I can get across?"

She shook her head. "Not for another twenty kilometers or so. We'll have to jump it."

"The hell *we* will!" he yelled. "Red can carry me across, but that little pony of yours won't make it."

"He'll make it. Either that, or he swims!"

"No! Dammit, Alex, wait!"

The wind tore the words away almost before Nate got them out. His heart crashed against his ribs as he saw her race the gelding toward the ravine's edge. She bent low over its neck, until the line between horse and rider blurred in the driving rain.

Cursing viciously, Nate sent Red in pursuit. There was only a slim chance the bigger, faster quarter horse could catch the smaller Don before it reached the rim, but Nate was damn well going to let him try.

Ears flat, neck stretched out, Red gave it everything he had. Throwing up clods of muddy grass with each pounding stride, he closed the short distance. But the gray's lead was a few whiskers too long. With a thrust of its muscled haunches, it launched itself across the raging torrent.

In the split second that followed, Nate had the choice of drawing rein or joining Alex in her attempt to bridge the dark, ragged chasm. Without conscious thought, he dropped the reins and gave Red his head. The chestnut's massive hindquarters corded. His rear hooves dug into the dirt. With a powerful lunge, he soared into the driving rain.

Chapter 8

The gray landed with inches to spare.

Red hit the grassy rim with a wider margin of safety and a whole lot more power. By the time Nate brought him around, Alex had already dismounted.

Swiftly she stripped off her heavy, swirling greatcoat and tossed it over her saddle before heading toward the edge. The rain immediately darkened her red shirt to a deep wine and molded it to her slender body in a way that would've closed Nate's throat if it wasn't already tight.

He ripped the rope from his saddle and threw a leg over the pommel. Catching up with her in a few long strides, he spun her around.

"Loop this around your waist," he barked, furious over the fear that had clawed at his chest when he saw her sail across that dark torrent.

She blinked at his tone, but saw at once the sense of an anchor line. While she fumbled with the thin, slippery hemp, Nate whipped the other end around one of the sat-

inwoods that were still firmly rooted on the bank. Shoving
the end through his belt, he tied it in a slipknot.

"Play the rope out with both hands as I go down," he
shouted.

"Wait, Sloan. I'll go. I'm smaller, lighter. Those roots
may not take your weight without giving way."

"They may not take either one of us. Just hold on to
the damn rope!"

She flung her head back, throwing the wet hair out of
her eyes. But either she decided not to waste precious
moments arguing or she realized that smaller and lighter
weren't real advantages when it came to wrestling a three-
hundred-pound animal from a nest of branches. Gripping
her end of the rope in both hands, she watched as he slid
down the bank on one heel and one knee.

With a grim eye on his footing, Nate worked his way
along the slippery, half-submerged trunk. The satinwood
strained and groaned as rushing brown water pulled at its
tenuous grip on the bank. The frantic, thrashing yearling,
its eyes rolled back in fright, added his cries to the chorus.

"Whoa, youngster. Hang on there."

A fresh torrent swept over the tree, forcing it and the
trapped animal under. Lunging forward, Nate grabbed a
fistful of black mane. His muscles straining against the
combined pull of the water and the colt's weight, he
dragged its head back above the surface. Balancing one
hip against a heavy branch, he held on to the plunging,
flailing creature with one hand and worked the slipknot
with the other. It took him a couple of tries, but he managed to get a loop over the horse's small head. That done,
he tore at the branches that caged it.

The water rushed over the tree with brutal force. The
branches sliced back and forth, slashing at Nate's arms
like sharp serrated knives. His slicker and the denim jacket

underneath protected him from the worst of the cuts, but he felt their lash against his neck and face. With each whip and tug of the muddy water, the tree fought its anchor in the bank.

The colt came free at last. While Alex used the fulcrum of the rope to swim it to shore, Nate fought his way back along the shuddering trunk. He was halfway to solid ground when the satinwood groaned and its roots began to give way with a sickening popping sound. Cursing, Nate dived for the bank. His hands dug into the slick earth just as the tree pulled free of its last fragile hold.

When it went, it took a good chunk of earth along with it. Before Alex could scramble backward to safety, the ground she was standing on crumbled beneath her feet. With a startled shout, she slid down the steep slope on her backside and tumbled into the rushing, muddy water.

Nate threw himself sideways and grabbed at the rope still tethering her to the colt. The hemp tore across his palms with a raw, searing heat before he could get a good grip on it. Looping the rope around his wrist, he pulled Alex out of the swirling water. She crawled up the slippery bank on all fours, coughing and spitting.

Nate traded his hold on the rope for one on her arm and dragged her to her feet. "You okay?"

"Except for swallowing half the steppes," she said, choking, "I'm fine."

"Then I suggest we get the hell out of here before we end up swallowing the rest."

With the palm of his hand against her rear, he boosted her up. Once back on solid ground, she wrapped the rope he passed her around her gray's saddle, then backed it up slowly to guide the shaky yearling. Nate followed a few seconds later.

With the rain sheeting down around them and the thunder still rolling across the sky, Alex took a moment to soothe the shivering colt. Nate wasn't sure when he'd seen a sorrier-looking pair. The wobbly legged youngster shuddered with every breath, his sides heaving under his drenched hide. Alex herself wasn't in much better shape. The brave red tunic that had so impressed Nate this morning with its gold frogging and braid was now a sodden, muddy brown. Her pants clung to her slender curves like the outer wrapping of a cheroot, and her once silky, shining mane was plastered to her head.

But when she lifted her wet face and gave Nate a wide-eyed, spike-lashed look of triumph over their shared victory, Nate was sure he'd never seen anything quite as beautiful in his life.

He forgot the cold. Forgot the mud seeping down along his instep. The need to sweep her into his arms and taste the rain on her lips crashed through him. The fact that another bolt of lightning slashed out of the sky at approximately the same moment was all that held him back.

At the sudden flash, Alex ducked and buried her face in the colt's wet, muddy side. By the time she recovered from her reflexive action, Nate had himself once more in hand.

"If I remember correctly," she shouted, rising, "there's a ledge of sorts a little farther south. It has an overhang wide enough to shelter us."

"Lead the way."

Alex felt a jumble of confused emotions as she grabbed the gray's reins and mounted. She was wet to the bone and colder than sin, but swept with an exhilaration at having wrested a victim from the violence of the storm. The stark, unguarded look she'd seen on Sloan's face for a brief instant added to her tumult, layered as it was on top of the wrenching fear that had sliced through her when the tree gave way and almost took him with it.

Stretching up in the stirrups, she waved to the men watching from the other side, signaling them to go on. Dimitri acknowledged her wave with a lift of his arm, then turned and led the others toward the jagged line of rocks, still some distance away. Tucking her chin down against the rain, Alex headed south. The colt, still tethered by the rope, trailed at Red's heels as Sloan followed suit.

Within minutes, she found the stone shelf carved high above the raging waters. It was wide enough to take the three horses without crowding, and deep enough to cut off the slanting, driving rain. Shoulders sagging in relief, Alex slid out of the saddle and leaned her forehead against the gray's neck for a few moments.

Sloan's voice filled the small space, carrying easily now over the rain's tattoo. "Looks like we might be here awhile."

Alex lifted her head and stared out at the gray, sheeting wall. "I've known these storms to last an hour...or a day." One shoulder lifted in a shrug that rippled into a shiver. "On the steppes, one never knows."

She turned away to loosen the gelding's girth. Although the Don was hardy and tough, Alex had learned early to put her mount's well-being before her own. Pulling a shaggy wool hat from the coat she'd tossed over the saddle earlier, she began to rub the gray down.

From the corner of one eye she saw Nate shrug out of his slicker and toss it over his saddle. Shaking his head like a big, well-muscled dog to rid it of the water, he lifted an elbow to wipe his face on his denim sleeve. That done, he moved to Alex's side and tugged the woolly hat out of her hands.

"I'll do that. You'd better go dry yourself off. You're

wetter than he is." His glinting gaze drifted down her front. "A whole sight wetter."

The gleam in his hazel eyes reinforced what Alex already knew. Her thin wool tunic, one of the hottest-selling items from her spring Militariana collection, clung to her skin like a wet leaf. She didn't need to glance down to know that her nipples were puckered with the cold and pushing against the thin lace of her bra.

"Go on," he instructed. "Your lips are turning purple, which makes an interesting combination with that chili-pepper shirt."

Alex might have hesitated if a violent shiver hadn't started at her shoulders and jiggled its way down her spine. It jiggled down her front, as well, and the gleam in Sloan's eyes deepened.

The fact that she was uncomfortable aside, Alex had been taught to respect the power of the elements. Only a fool would ride out into the snows that blanketed the steppes in winter without knowing where to find shelter for himself and his mount. Likewise, those who worked the herds in the cold, wet rains knew better than to risk pneumonia in a land where medicines were precious and physicians rare.

Snatching her greatcoat from the saddle, she moved to the back of the shallow cave. The high-collared calf-length coat was modeled after the *cherkessa* that had protected her ancestors from heat, wet and cold alike. Alex had executed her design in a tightly woven combination of wool and camel hair similar to the fabrics used a century ago. Although damp on the outside, the coat's inner lining was dry and warm.

Keeping an eye on Nate's back, she peeled off her wet, clammy tunic. Her boots gave her some trouble, but eventually yielded to determined tugging. Numb fingers fumbled with the buttons to her pants and finally pushed them down over her hips. The thick felt socks she wore under her boots soon joined the heap of sodden garments. With another quick glance at Sloan's back, she decided she could stand the dampness of her lacy underwear.

A few quick twists wrung most of the moisture out of her clothes. They'd still be clammy when she put them on again, of course, but not sopping-wet. Alex set them aside, thankful that she'd be dry and warm for the duration of the storm, at least.

Wrapping herself more snugly in the heavy coat, she leaned her shoulders against the stone wall and watched Sloan work. His broad shoulders, encased in weathered blue denim a few shades lighter than his worn jeans, strained at the jacket's seams with each sure stroke. The jacket rode up as he worked, giving Alex a glimpse of a narrow waist and lean flanks. Admiration sparked through her for the corded, rippling sinews of his thighs and the tight muscles of his buttocks. Her interest in his physique was purely objective, of course. Assessing the line and shape of the human body was part of the job for a woman in her profession.

He wiped the thick wool hat over the gelding with slow, sure strokes that told her he didn't consider tending to animals a chore. When he finished the gray, he nudged it aside with one shoulder and went to work on Three Bars Red.

They were a lot alike, Alex mused, this tall, broad-shouldered man and the well-muscled stallion. Both exhibited a lazy, easygoing nature, although she'd seen them move with blinding speed when the occasion warranted. Neither showed the least hint of softness or aristocratic pedigree in the raw power of his body. They were built for performance, not show, she decided.

The thought sent a spear of heat to her belly.

For the first time, the possibility occurred to her that Sloan might actually "perform" the role she'd assigned him. As Katerina would say, he was much a man, this compatriot of hers.

Alex had no doubt that Dimitri and the men would agree he had proven himself this afternoon. The games they'd played with him earlier had been just that, tests of his temper more than of his horsemanship. She knew his good-humored compliance with their wagers and his unstinting praise for their skill had impressed them far more than if he'd won the races himself.

But it was the way he'd pitted himself against the raging waters for a spindly-legged creature he had no responsibility for or claim on that would win their respect. Among the Karistani, bravery was valued not so much for its result as for the fact it shaped a man's soul and gave him character. Whatever else he might have, Alex thought wryly, Nate Sloan certainly had character.

So why did the realization that he might choose one of the women who fluttered around him like pigeons looking for a nest leave her feeling edgy? Why did the idea of Sloan performing with Katerina or Anya or Ivana of the honey pot make her fingers curl into the thick camel-hair fabric of her coat?

Damp, frigid air swirled around Alex's bare feet as she asked questions she wasn't ready to answer. Slowly she slid down the wall to a sitting position and tucked her cold toes under her.

A few moments later, Nate gave Red a final slap. "That ought to do you, fella."

The chestnut lowered his head and nuzzled his broad chest. Nate knuckled the white blaze.

"Sorry, big guy. I don't have anything on me but some chewing gum."

"For pity's sake, don't give him that!" Alex pleaded. "I don't want to think what he could do with gum in such close quarters."

Nate laughed and pushed Red's broad face away. Catching the rope still looped around the colt's neck, he tugged it toward Alex.

"Here, you work on this one while I dump the water out of my boots. I'm walking around in the half of the steppes you didn't swallow."

Glad to have something to take her mind from her chaotic thoughts, Alex took the soggy hat from him and rose up on her knees. Her hands moved in smooth, rhythmic motions over the shivering animal while she murmured meaningless nonsense in its ear.

Nate sat on the stone shelf, his back to the curving wall at a slight angle to hers and hooked a foot up on his knee. He grunted as he tugged at his worn boot. It came off with a whoosh, spilling a stream of muddy water. A second small cascade followed a few moments later.

Since the man had dragged her out of a raging torrent, Alex decided she could be magnanimous. "Use the skirt of my coat to dry your feet," she tossed over her shoulder.

"Thanks, but there's no sense muddying it up any more. I'll use my shirt to dry off with. It's already half soaked and sticking to me like feathers to tar."

He shrugged out of his jacket, and Alex noted the businesslike shoulder holster he wore under it. Despite her father's aversion to firearms, she was no stranger to them. During her summers on the steppes, she'd learned to handle them and respect them. Sloan unbuckled the weapon and set it aside, then unbuttoned his blue cotton shirt.

Resolutely Alex kept her attention fixed on her task,

ignoring the ripple of muscle and the slick sheen of his skin as he shook himself like a lean, graceful borzoi. He toweled his tawny hair, sending water droplets in all directions, then sat down again to tug off his socks.

By the time he tossed the shirt aside and pulled his jacket back on, Alex had finished with the colt. The animal whuffled softly and stuck its muzzle into her side, as if wanting to share her body heat. Evidently deciding she didn't have enough to spare, he ambled over to join the other horses. With a tired sigh, she sank back down.

Sloan's deep voice carried easily over the drumming rain. "Your turn."

"What?"

By way of response, he dug under her coat and located one icy foot. Grasping her heel firmly in one hand, he began to massage her numb toes with the other.

Alex jerked at the touch of his big, warm hands on her skin.

"Relax," he instructed. "I've had a lot of practice at this. From the time I was big enough to get my hands around a bottle of liniment, I'd work Wily Willie over after every rodeo."

He glanced up from his task, his mouth curving. "Willie generally collected a sight more bruises than he did prize money, you understand?"

"Mmm…"

That was the best Alex could manage, with all her attention focused on the warmth that was transferring itself from his hands to her chilled toes. He had working hands, she thought, feeling the ridges and calluses on his palms with each sure, gentle stroke. The kind of hands her grandfather had possessed.

"What did he do when he wasn't rodeoing?" she asked

after a few moments, more to distract herself from the feel of his flesh against hers than anything else.

"Willie?" The skin at the corner of Nate's eyes crinkled. "As little as possible, mostly. As long as he had enough money in his pocket for the entry fees at the next event and the gas to get us there, he was happy."

"And you? Were you happy?"

"What kid wouldn't be? I grew up around men who didn't pretend to be anything but what they were, which was mostly down-and-out cowhands. I was convinced that sleeping in the bed of a truck and feasting on cold beans out of the can was the only way to live."

"You slept in a truck?"

"When we had one," he replied, with a lift of one shoulder. "Willie was always selling it to raise the cash for entry fees. He and I were the only ones who knew how to wire the starter, though, so we always got it back at a reduced price when he was in the money again. Here, give me your other foot."

How strange, Alex thought, studying his face as he took her heel in his lap and worked her instep with his incredible, gentle hands. All the while he shared more stories of this character who had given him his name and his peculiar philosophy of life and not much more, apparently. Nate Sloan came from a background as nomadic as that of any Karistani, one he'd evidently enjoyed, despite the deprivations he made light of.

Alex hadn't thought about it before, but perhaps in every culture, on every continent, there were people who preferred change to stability, movement to security. People who felt restless when surrounded by walls, and crowded when within sight of a town.

With a grudging respect for Katerina's instincts, Alex admitted that her cousin had been right in her assessment of this man. Sloan seemed to possess many of the same characteristics as the Cossacks who had originally claimed the steppes—the stubbornly independent outcasts who'd fled Russian oppression and made the term *kazak* synonymous with ''adventurer'' or ''free man.''

This tall, self-assured man fit in here far more than she did herself, Alex thought, with a twist of the pain she'd always kept well buried. She was the product of two cultures, torn by her loyalties to both, at home in neither. Sloan was his own man, and would fit in anywhere.

''And now?'' Alex probed, wanting to understand more, to know more. ''Now that you say Willie's retired and settled on this bit of land you have in…''

''Wolf Creek.''

''In Wolf Creek. Do you always just pick up and travel halfway across the world as the mood or the opportunity strikes you?''

His hands shaped her arch, the thumbs warm and infinitely skilled as they massaged her toes. ''Pretty much.''

''You've never married? Never felt the need to stay in Wolf Creek?''

''No, ma'am,'' he drawled. ''I've never married. Why? Does it concern you? Are you worried that I might be woman-shy and upset this little scheme of yours?''

''I worry about a lot of things,'' she responded tartly. ''That's not one of them.''

He caught her glance with a sardonic one of his own. ''I might not have the experience Three Bars Red has, but I'll surely try to give satisfaction.''

At the sting in his voice, Alex hesitated. ''Look, Sloan, I know I may have pricked your ego a bit this morning by offering you up like a plate of pickled herring, but…but you don't understand the situation here.''

Strong, blunt-tipped fingers slid over her heel and moved up to knead her calf. "Try me."

Alex bit her lip. For a few seconds, she was tempted. With an intensity that surprised her, she wanted to confide in this man. Wanted to share the doubts and insecurities that plagued her. To test her half-formed plan for Karistan's future against the intelligence he disguised behind his lazy smile.

With a mental shake, Alex shrugged aside the notion. One of the painful lessons she'd learned in the past few weeks was that responsibility brought with it a frightening loneliness. She couldn't bring herself to trust him. To trust any outsider. Not yet. Not while there was still so much danger to her people and to Karistan. And not while Sloan had his own role to…to perform in the delicate balance she was trying to maintain for the next few days, a week at most.

While she debated within herself, his hands continued their smooth, sure strokes.

"You're using me as a diversionary tactic, aren't you, Alexandra?"

She shot him a quick, startled glance. Had the man read her mind?

His eyes locked with hers. "I'm supposed to draw the friendly fire, right? Keep Katerina and the others occupied until you resolve whatever's putting that crease in your brow? No, don't pull away. We can talk while I do this."

"Maybe you can," she retorted, tugging at her leg. "I can't."

Alex wasn't sure, but she thought his jaw hardened for an instant before he shrugged. "Okay, we'll talk later."

It wasn't the answer she'd expected, but then, Alex never knew quite what to expect of this man. Frowning, she tugged at her leg. "Look, maybe this isn't such a good idea."

He relaxed his hold until her calf rested lightly in his palm. "Why so skittish, Alexandra?" he taunted softly. "We established the ground rules last night, remember? I won't touch you...unless you want it. Or unless I want to risk getting my hide stripped by that short-tailed whisker brush you tote."

"I wouldn't be so quick to dismiss the *nagaika,* if I were you," she retorted. "The Cossacks of old could take out a gnat's eye with it...at full gallop."

A rueful gleam crept into his eyes. "After seeing Petr Borodín in action this afternoon, I don't doubt it."

Belatedly Alex realized that his hands had resumed their stroking during the short exchange. Had he taken her failure to withdraw from his hold as permission to continue? Or had she given it?

With brutal honesty, she acknowledged that she had. His touch was so gentle, so nonthreatening. So soothing. Slumping back against the wall, she gave herself up to the warmth he was pumping through her veins.

The minutes passed. Rain drummed on the stone roof above them. An occasional roll of thunder provided a distant counterpoint to the snuffling of the horses. The faint scent of wet wool and warm horseflesh filled Alex's nostrils.

Gradually it dawned on Alex that Sloan's gentleness was every bit as seductive as the raw strength she'd tasted in his arms last night. The slow, sure friction of his big hands generated more than just heat. Prickles of awareness followed every upstroke. Whispers of sensation came with each downward sweep. Telling herself that she was crazy to let him continue, Alex closed her eyes.

Only a few moments more, she promised herself. She'd

hold on to this strange, shimmering feeling that pushed her tension and her worry to a back corner of her mind for just a little longer.

Only a little while longer, Nate told himself. He'd only touch her a little while longer.

Although it was taking more and more effort to keep his hold light, he wasn't quite ready to let her go. He couldn't. Despite the heat that warmed his skin and the slow ache that curled in his belly.

When her dark lashes fluttered down against her cheeks, a tangle of emotions twisted inside Nate. Emotions he had no business feeling.

He should be using this enforced intimacy to draw some answers out of her, he reminded himself brutally. She still stubbornly refused to confide in him, but she was coming to trust him on the physical level, at least. It was a step. A first step. Something he could build on. Something his instincts told him he could take to the next, intimate level…if he was the kind of man she thought he was. If he was the stud she proclaimed him.

At that moment, he sure as hell felt like one. He'd spent enough of his life around animals to respect the breeding instinct that drove them. And to know the raw power of the desire that sliced through his groin as he stared at her shadowed face.

Fighting the ache that intensified with each pulse of the tiny blue vein at the side of her forehead, he stilled his movements.

"Alexandra?"

The dark lashes lifted.

"I think you ought to know that massaging Wily Willie's aches and pains never gave me a whole set of my own."

It didn't take her long to catch his meaning. Eyes wide, she tugged her leg out of his hold.

As her warm flesh slid from his palm, Nate cursed the sense of loss that shot through him. Settling back against the stone wall, he raised one leg to ease the tight constriction in his jeans and rested his arm across his knee.

With Alex watching him warily, he repeated a silent, savage litany.

This woman was his target.

She was the focus of his mission.

He was here to locate a small black box and extract it from her. Not the shuddering, shimmering surrender he was beginning to want with a need that was fast threatening to overwhelm both his common sense and his self-restraint.

Christ! He had to get himself under control.

Forcing his eyes and his thoughts away from the woman sitting two heartbeats away, he made himself focus on the mission. He'd made a little progress this morning, but not much. With Katerina and Anya and the others as willing, if unwitting, accomplices, he'd pretty well searched the entire camp. If Alex had the damn thing in her possession, he was willing to bet it wasn't hidden in any of the goat-hide tents.

A frustration he didn't allow to show grabbed at his gut. It was two parts physical and one part professional, with a whole lot of personal thrown in. The agent in him didn't like the fact that his progress was so slow. As a man, he was finding the fact that Alex couldn't bring herself to trust him harder and harder to deal with.

As he settled back against the stone wall, Nate hoped to hell Maggie wasn't running into as many complications on her end of this mission as he seemed to be.

Chapter 9

Oh, Lord, Maggie thought with an inner groan. As if this operation weren't complicated enough!

Reaching across the table, she eased a cloudy, half-full glass out of Richard's shaky grasp.

"But we're not fin… We haven't finush…" He blinked owlishly. "We're not done with the toasts."

"I'm sure President Cherkoff will understand if we don't salute the rest of the nations represented on the UN team. At least not until they arrive tomorrow."

She set the glass out of Richard's reach and glanced at the man with the shock of silver hair and the gray, almost opaque eyes. Those eyes had sent an inexplicable shiver along Maggie's nerves when the White Wolf of Balminsk received them a half hour ago.

"We've been traveling for three days," she offered as a polite excuse. "We haven't slept in anything other than a vertical position in all that time. We must seek out our beds."

President Cherkoff curled a lip in derision, as if in recognition of the fact that Dr. Richard Worthington would be horizontal soon enough, with or without the benefit of a bed.

Maggie stiffened at the look, although she had to admit, if only to herself, that Richard was rather the worse for wear. She hadn't needed his ingenious aside to know that he'd never tasted vodka before. When the first shot hit the back of his throat, his brown eyes had rounded until they resembled one of Vasili's threadbare truck tires. His Adam's apple had worked furiously, but, to give him his due, he'd swallowed the raw liquor with only a faint, gasping choke.

Unfortunately, with each of the interminable toasts their host insisted on, Richard had managed to get the vitriolic alcohol down a little more easily. In the process, he seemed to have lost the use of his vocal cords. Maggie should've had the foresight to warn him to sip the darn stuff instead of letting himself be pressured into following their host's example and throwing it down his throat.

"One last salute," Cherkoff ordered in heavily accented English. "Then my son will show you to your quarters."

It was a test. A crude one, admittedly, but a test nonetheless. Maggie recognized that fact as readily as Major Nikolas Cherkoff, who stood just behind his father. The livid scar slashing across the major's cheek twitched once, then was still.

Richard stretched across the table to retrieve his glass. The clear liquid sloshed over his shaky hand as he raised it shoulder-high.

"To the work that has brought you here," the White Wolf rasped. "May it achieve what we wish of it."

Since Cherkoff had made no secret of the fact that he bitterly resented the UN's interference in the affairs of

Balminsk, Maggie wondered exactly what results he
wished the team would achieve. She'd been briefed in detail about Cherkoff's reluctant compliance with the Strategic Arms Reduction Treaty. Only the fact that his country teetered on the brink of collapse had forced him to
comply with the START provisions at all.

Once part of the breadbasket of the Soviet Union,
Balminsk was now an *economic* basket case. During their
ride across the high, fertile plains, Maggie had learned
from Vasili that the huge combines that had once moved
through endless wheat fields in long, zigzagging rows had
fallen into disrepair, with no replacement parts to be had.
The rich black chernozem soil now lay fallow and un-
planted.

As they drove through the deserted, echoing capital,
Maggie had seen only empty store windows and equally
empty streets. A casual query to Major Cherkoff had elic-
ited the flat response that prices in this small country now
doubled every four weeks. A month's salary wouldn't
cover the cost of one winter boot…if there was one to be
bought.

From her briefings, Maggie knew most experts blamed
Balminsk's problems on President Cherkoff's mismanage-
ment and the unceasing war he'd conducted with his hated
enemy, the old headman of Karistan. Unlike Karistan,
however, Balminsk had at last ceded to economic pressures.

In return for promises of substantial aid, Cherkoff had
agreed to allow the UN to inspect and dismantle the missiles occupying the silos on the Balminsk side of the border. But the old hard-line Communist wasn't happy about
it. Not at all.

Even Richard sensed the hostility emanating from the

ramrod-stiff man across the table. Blinking to clear his glazed eyes, he lofted his glass higher.

"To...to the work that brought us here."

Throwing back his head, Richard tossed down the rest of the vodka. He swallowed with a gurgling sort of gasp, blinked rapidly several times, then turned to look at Maggie.

As did the White Wolf of Balminsk.

And Major Nikolas Cherkoff.

Suppressing a sigh, Maggie pushed her thick, black-framed lenses back up the bridge of her nose with one forefinger and lifted her half-full glass. She downed the colorless liquid in two swallows, set the glass back on the table and gave the president a polite smile.

Behind that smile, liquid fire scorched her throat, already searing from the cautious sips she'd taken after each toast. Raw heat shot from her stomach to her lungs to her eyelids and back again, while her nerve endings went up in flames. Yet Maggie's bland smile gave no hint of how desperately she wanted to grab the water carafe sitting beside the vodka bottle and pour its contents down her throat.

The White Wolf bared his teeth in response and waved a curt dismissal.

With Richard stumbling behind her, Maggie followed the major from the dank reception room. Once out of the president's line of sight, she slipped two fingers under her glasses to wipe away the moisture that had collected at the corners of her eyes. Dragging in quick, shallow breaths, she brought her rioting senses under control and began to take careful note of her surroundings.

From the outside, Balminsk's presidential palace had appeared a magical place of odd-shaped buildings, high turrets and colorful, onion-shaped domes. Inside, however,

long strips of paint peeled from the ceilings and brown
water stains discolored the walls. The cavernous reception
room they'd been shown into boasted ornate carved pillars
and moldings, but the gilt that had once decorated them
was chipped and more verdigris than gold. The empty
rooms they now walked through hadn't withstood the passage of time any better. Maggie's boots thumped against
bare, sadly damaged parquet floors and sent echoes down
the deserted corridors.

After a number of convoluted turns, the major stopped
in front of a set of doors guarded by an individual wearing
a motley assortment of uniform items and a lethal-looking
Uzi over one shoulder. At Cherkoff's nod, the guard threw
open the doors and stood to one side.

"It is not the St. Regis," Nikolas said, "but I hope you
will be comfortable here. There are enough rooms for the
rest of your team members when they arrive."

Richard mumbled something inaudible and tripped inside. Maggie paused on the threshold, tilting her head to
study the major's lean face. Just when had this enigmatic,
scarred man been inside that venerable landmark, the St.
Regis?

"I spent two years in New York City," he said in answer to her unspoken question. "As military *chargé* with
the Soviet consulate."

Before Maggie could comment on that interesting bit of
information, he bowed in an old-fashioned gesture totally
at odds with his rather sinister appearance.

"Sleep well, Dr. St. Clare."

Maggie stepped inside the suite of rooms. The door
closed behind her, and she heard the faint murmur of
voices as the major issued orders to the guard to stay at
his post.

Her eyes thoughtful, she strolled across a small vestibule lined with an array of doors. In the first room she peered into, a magnificent nineteenth-century sleigh bed in black walnut stood in solitary splendor in the middle of the floor. Her battered metal suitcase was set beside it. There wasn't another stick of furniture to be seen. No chair, no wardrobe, and nothing that even faintly resembled a sink. After a quick search through several other similarly sparse rooms, she finally located Richard.

He was standing in an odd, five-sided room, staring out a window that showed only the wall of an opposite wing and the gathering darkness.

Tugging off her heavy glasses, Maggie slipped them into her shirt pocket. "Richard, have you discovered the bathroom yet?"

"N-no."

Her heavily penciled brows drew together at his mumbled response. "Are you all right? Can I get you something? I think I have some Bromo-Seltzer in my bag."

He hunched his shoulders. "No. Thanks."

"Richard, if you're going to throw up, I wish you'd find the bathroom first."

"I—I'm not going to throw up."

Maggie sighed. Crossing the dusty parquet floor, she gave his shoulder a consoling pat.

"Look, you don't have to be embarrassed or macho about this. That was pretty potent stuff you chug-a-lugged back there. I'm not surprised it's making you sick."

"It...it's not making me sick...exactly."

"Then what?" Maggie tugged at his shoulder. "Richard, for heaven's sake, turn around. Let me look at you."

"No, I don't think I should."

"Why not?"

"It's...not...a good idea."

Alarmed at the low, almost panicky note in his voice,

Maggie took a firm grip on his arm and swung him around. He stood rigid and unmoving, his brown eyes pinned on the blank space just over her left shoulder.

Frowning, she searched his face. His dark hair straggled down over his forehead, and he was a little green about the gills, but he didn't look ill enough to explain his unnatural rigidity or the way he kept swallowing convulsively. Unless…unless the damned White Wolf of Balminsk had slipped something other than vodka into his glass.

"Richard, what's the matter?" Maggie asked sharply. "What's wrong with you?"

"It's not an unexpected physiological reaction," he said through stiff lips.

"What is?" She shook his arm. "Tell me what you're feeling!"

"In…in clinical terms?"

"In any terms!" she shouted.

He swallowed again, then forced himself to meet her eyes. "I—I'm aroused."

"You're *what?*" Involuntarily, Maggie stepped back. Her gaze dropped, and then her jaw.

Dr. Richard Worthington was most definitely aroused. To a rather astonishing degree.

"I'm sorry…" His handsome young face was flaming. "It's the vodka. Apparently alcohol has a stimulating and quite unexpected effect on my endocrine system."

Maggie dragged her stunned gaze away from his runaway endocrines. Wetting her lips, she tried to ease his embarrassment with a smile.

"Gee, thanks. And here I thought it might have been this road-dust cologne I've been wearing for the last six hours."

His agonized expression deepened. "Actually, you have

a very delicate scent, one that agitates my olfactory sense.''

''Richard, I was kidding!''

''I'm not. I find you very excitatory. Sexually speaking, that is. Er, all of you.''

Maggie gaped at him. She was wearing boots that gave her the grace and resonance of a bull moose making his way through the north woods. Her pants were so stiff and baggy, not even the roughnecks on her father's crew would have pulled them on to wade through an oil spill. The heavy, figure-flattening T-shirt under her scratchy wool shirt just about zeroed out her natural attributes, and there was enough charcoal on her eyebrows to start a good-size campfire. Yet this young man was staring at her with a slowly gathering masculine warmth in his brown eyes that made her feel as though the artists at Glamour Shots had just worked their magic with her.

It was Maggie's turn to swallow. ''I think we need to talk about this.''

''Not if it makes you feel uncomfortable,'' Richard replied with a quiet dignity.

It wasn't making *her* feel uncomfortable, Maggie thought wryly. She wasn't the one with a bead of sweat trickling down the side of her neck and the endocrine system working double overtime.

Although it obviously took some effort, he managed a small, tight smile. ''You don't have to worry. I won't attempt anything Neanderthal. But you must know how I feel about you.''

Astounded at his mastery over a vodka-filled stomach and rampaging hormones, Maggie shook her head.

''Well, no, as a matter of fact. I don't.''

He lifted one hand and traced the line of her cheek with

a gentle finger, gliding over the semitattoo on the side of her jaw.

"I think you shine with an inner beauty few women possess, Dr. St. Clare…Megan. A beauty that comes from the heart. I've seen you swallow your impatience with me time and again these last few days. You've never once undermined my authority with the team, or let the delays and inconveniences bother you. I've heard you laugh in that delightful way you have when the others were simmering with irritation, and seen your eyes sparkle with a joy of life that makes my breath catch. You're a kind person, Megan, and a very beautiful woman. And I'm sure you're a most proficient geologist," he tacked on.

Kindness wasn't exactly high on the list of most desired qualities in an OMEGA agent. And, in Richard's case, at least, beauty was definitely in the eye of the beholder.

But Maggie sighed and let her chin rest in his warm palm. That was the longest, most coherent string of sentences she'd heard the young physicist put together at one time, and probably the sweetest compliment she'd ever receive in her life.

"Just how many women have you really known, Richard?" she asked softly. "Outside the laboratory, I mean?"

The shy smile that made him seem so much younger than his years tugged at his lips. "Aside from my mother? One, really. And I didn't particularly impress her, either. In fact, I've only heard from her once in the three years since we met. But that doesn't mean I don't fully appreciate what I feel for you."

Maggie didn't make the mistake of dismissing his emotions lightly. For all his seeming ineptitude, Richard was a highly intelligent man. And one whose self-restraint she had to admire. She doubted she'd exhibit the same rigid control after several glasses of potent vodka if she was locked in a room with, say…

Unbidden, Adam Ridgeway's slate blue eyes and lean, aristocratic face filled her mind. Maggie pulled her chin free of Richard's light hold, frowning at the sudden wild leaping of her pulse. She must have been more affected by that one glass of raw alcohol than she'd thought.

"We'll talk about this tomorrow, after the vodka has worked its way through your, ah, system."

"Megan…"

"Get some sleep, Richard. The rest of the team should arrive early in the morning. When they do, you'll want to update them on your meeting with Cherkoff and review the schedule for our first day on-site."

He accepted her reminder of his responsibilities with good grace and stood quietly as she left.

With a silent shake of her head, Maggie made her way to her own room. Good grief. She'd better make sure Richard avoided any more ceremonial toasts. That rather spectacular display of his endocrine system would definitely rank among the more vivid memories she'd take away from this particular mission, but it wasn't one she wanted him to repeat on a frequent basis. Not when she needed to focus all her concentration on nuclear missiles and hostile, hungry wolves.

Maggie stopped just inside the threshold to her room and eyed the thick, feather-filled comforter piled atop the curved bed. Imagining how wonderful it would be to sink down into that fluffy mound, she sighed. Later, she promised herself. Later, she would strip down to her T-shirt and panties and lose herself in that cloud of softness.

Right now, however, she had a mission to conduct.

Closing the door to her room, she sat on the edge of the bed and punched Cowboy's code into her wristwatch.

While she waited for him to respond, she opened the suitcase and rummaged through her possessions. By the time
she'd tugged off the plaid shirt and bulky pants and pulled
on a black turtleneck and slacks, Nate still hadn't returned
her signal. Grinning, Maggie wondered if he was having
difficulty slipping away from a potential bride who wanted
to inspect his plumbing.

David Jensen, on the other hand, responded immediately.

"OMEGA Control. Go ahead, Chameleon."

"Just wanted to confirm that I'm in place, Doc."

"I've been tracking you. You made good time, despite
the initial delays."

Maggie's grin widened. She would've bet her last pair
of clean socks David had plotted the digitized satellite signals to know exactly when she'd arrived in Balminsk's
capital. With his engineer's passion for detail, he wouldn't
let her and Cowboy out of his sight for a second. His
precision in the control center certainly gave Maggie a
sense of comfort.

In response to his comment, she dismissed the hair-
raising, heart-stopping hours in Vasili's truck with a light
laugh. "Our driver is in training for the first Russian
Grand Prix. He made up for lost time. I couldn't raise
Cowboy, Doc. Have you heard from him?"

"One brief transmission, several hours ago. He said
something about losing a race to a one-armed acrobat and
heading toward Balminsk."

"He's heading here?" Maggie's heavy brows drew together.

"He was. I now show him stopped 27.3 miles from the
border. He's been at that position for several hours. There
are satellite reports of heavy weather in the area, which
may explain why he's holding in place."

"Well, the weather's fine here," Maggie replied. "I'm going out to reconnoiter."

"Roger, Chameleon. Good hunting."

"Thanks, Doc."

Maggie knelt on one knee, surveying the contents of her open suitcase. She didn't need to scan it with the infrared sensor concealed in the handle to know the various objects inside had been handled by someone with a different body-heat signature from hers. If the White Wolf hadn't thought to order a search, his son would have. Unless the searchers were a whole bunch more imaginative than OMEGA's special devices unit, though, they wouldn't have found anything except some plain cotton underwear, thick socks, another plaid shirt or two, some essential feminine supplies, a Sony Walkman with a few tapes, and the geological books and equipment Maggie had considered necessary for her role.

Pursing her lips, she studied the various items, trying to decide which had the most value in a country whose economy was in such shambles that black-marketing and barter were the only means of commodity exchange.

A few moments later, she opened the door to the suite. The guard pushed his shoulders off the opposite wall, his bushy brows lowering in a suspicious scowl.

"Good evening, my friend," Maggie said in the Russian dialect predominantly used in Balminsk. "Does your wife have a fondness for perfumed body lotion, perhaps?"

Okay, Maggie thought as the guard sniffed the small black-and-white plastic squeeze tube, so some people might not consider Chanel No. 5 Body Creme an essential feminine supply. She did. But she'd decided not to risk agitating Richard's olfactory sense any further.

Three hours later, Maggie and the guard wound their way back through the dark, deserted corridors of the presidential palace. Her mind whirled with the bits and pieces of information she'd managed to collect.

She hadn't expected the few residents of Balminsk she'd encountered to open up to an outsider, and they hadn't. Exactly. But a few country-and-western tapes, a confident smile and her ease with their language had helped overcome their surly suspicion to a certain degree.

At her request, the guard had taken her to what passed for a restaurant in Balminsk. He'd explained to the proprietor of a tiny kitchen-café that the *Amerikanski* was with the UN team and wished to sample some local fare after her long trip. The ruddy-faced cook had shrugged and shown her to the only table in the room. The other customers, all two of them, had crowded to the far end of the table and shot Maggie frowning glances over their bowls of potato soup.

The soup was thin and watery and deliciously flavored. Maggie followed the other patrons' example and sopped up every drop from the bottom of her bowl with a chunk of crusty black bread. Her first bite of a spicy, meat-filled cabbage roll had her taste buds clamoring for more, but the empty pot on the table indicated that she'd exhausted the café's supply of menu items. Luckily, the light, crispy strips of fried dough drenched in honey that the cook served for dessert satisfied the rest of her hunger. So much so that she had to force down a minuscule cup of heavily sweetened tea.

The patrons of the tiny café mumbled into their cups in answer to her casual questions. When she inquired as to their occupations, they responded with a shrug. It was only through skillful questioning and even more skillful listening that Maggie learned anything useful. Like the fact that the brawny, muscled man in blue cotton work pants and a sweatshirt proclaiming the benefits of one of the Crimea's better known health spas was a modern-day cattle rustler. It slipped out when the cook made a comment about needing more Karistani beef for the *peroshki*.

The low-voiced discussion that followed gave Maggie a grim idea of how desperate Balminsk's economic situation really was. With so many other hot spots in the world demanding the West's attention, it was entirely possible the economic aid package Balminsk had been promised might arrive too late to prevent widespread starvation during the coming winter. Unless the men of this country took action of their own to prevent it. If that action resulted in a renewal of the hostilities that had ravaged Balminsk and Karistan for centuries, so be it.

From what Maggie could glean, that action would come soon.

As she followed the guard back through the palace, she knew she needed to talk to Cowboy, fast. Slipping her escort a Randy Travis cassette for his troubles, she lifted the latch on the door to the team's suite and eased inside. Richard's room was bathed in dark stillness, punctuated at regular intervals by a hiccuping snore. Smiling, Maggie opened her own door.

She'd taken only two steps inside when a hard hand slapped over her mouth. In a fraction of a heartbeat, her training kicked in, and she reacted with an instinctive sureness that would've made even the steely-eyed Jaguar proud.

Her right elbow jabbed back with every ounce of force she could muster. Her left ankle wrapped around one behind her. As her attacker went down, Maggie twisted to face him.

A single chop to the side of the neck sent him crumpling to the floor.

Chapter 10

Maggie made herself comfortable on the sleigh bed while she waited for Nikolas Cherkoff to recover consciousness. Holding her .22-caliber Smith and Wesson automatic in her left hand, she used the other to break off bits of the crispy dough strip she'd brought back as a late-night snack.

As she nibbled on the savory sweet, she kept a close watch on the major. She had far too much experience in the field to take her eyes off a target, even an unconscious one, which was probably what saved her life a few moments later.

Cherkoff, Sr., might be known as the White Wolf, but Cherkoff, Jr., possessed a few animal traits all his own. His lids flew up, and his black eyes focused with the speed of an eagle's. Curling his legs, he sprang to the attack like a panther loosed from a cage.

"One more step," Maggie warned, whipping up the .22, "and the White Wolf will have to sire a new cub."

He pulled up short. In the stark light of the overhead bulb, his scar stood out like a river of pain across his cheek.

"So, Dr. St. Clare," he said at last. "It appears we've reached what the military would call a countervailing force of arms."

Maggie arched a brow. "It doesn't strike me as particularly countervailing. I'm the only one with a weapon here. Unless you have something hidden that my search failed to turn up…and I conducted a *very* thorough search."

Thorough enough to discover that Nikolas Cherkoff's face wasn't the only portion of his anatomy that bore the scars of combat. Maggie hadn't actually seen phosphorus-grenade wounds before, but Jaguar had described them in enough detail for her to guess what had caused the horrible, puckered burns on the major's stomach. And she didn't think he'd taken that bullet through the shoulder in a hunting accident.

He jerked his chin toward her left hand. "Do you really think a weapon of that small caliber can stop a man of my size and weight before he does serious damage?"

"Well, yes…when it's loaded with long-rifle hollow-point stingers, which, as I'm sure you're aware, do as much tissue damage as a .38 special."

His black eyes narrowed dangerously. "Do you care to tell me what a UN geologist is doing with such a weapon?"

"I might, if you tell me what you're doing in said geologist's room."

His jaw worked at her swift, uncompromising response. "I came to speak with you."

"Really? And you attack everyone you wish to speak with?"

"Don't be foolish. Naturally, I was alarmed to find you gone. So when a figure dressed all in black...and of considerably different proportions than the one I expected... stepped into the room, I reacted accordingly."

Maggie had to admit her knit slacks and turtleneck were a bit more slenderizing than the baggy tan pants and thick wool shirt, but she wasn't ready to buy his story of mistaken identity. She kept the .22 level.

"What did you wish to speak to me about, Major?"

He didn't respond for several seconds. "Your team goes from Balminsk to Karistan, does it not?" he said at last.

"It does."

"I came to warn you. You travel into harm's way."

Maggie regarded him steadily. "Why?"

"Why what?"

"Why do you warn me? What's in this for you?"

At her soft question, he went still. Like an animal retreating behind a protective screen, he seemed to withdraw inside himself, to a place she couldn't follow and wasn't sure she wanted to even if she could. Black shutters dropped over his eyes, leaving behind an emptiness that made Maggie shiver.

As the seconds ticked by, the deep, gut-level instincts that the other OMEGA agents joked about and Adam Ridgeway swore added to the silver strands at his temples, stirred in Maggie. She chewed on a corner of her lower lip for a few endless moments, then rose.

Lifting the hem of her turtleneck, she slid the .22 into the specially designed and shielded holster at her waist.

"Tell me," she said quietly, walking toward him.

The scar twitched.

She laid a hand on an arm composed entirely of taut sinew and rock-hard muscle. "Tell me why you came to warn me."

With infinite, agonizing slowness, Cherkoff looked down at her hand. When he raised his head, his eyes were as flat and as desolate as before, but focused on her face.

"Balminsk is a series of catastrophes waiting to happen. If not this week, then the next."

"And?"

He spoke slowly, his voice harsh with effort. "And I've seen enough of war to know that this time, when our world explodes with guns and bullets, the wounds could be fatal. To us. To Karistan. To any caught between us."

"Cowboy, this is Chameleon. Do you read me?"

Nate hunkered down on both heels and pressed the transmit button.

"I read you, Chameleon, but talk fast. I've got about a minute, max, before someone notices Red and I have taken a slight detour and comes looking for us."

Maggie's voice filtered through the darkness surrounding Nate. "I'm in Balminsk's capitol. I'm convinced they don't have the decoder here. But I'm also convinced that all hell's about to break loose."

"What kind of hell?"

"A raid on Karistan is imminent, but I can't confirm when or where. My source is convinced that it will reopen hostilities and escalate into something really nasty, really fast."

"Is your source reliable?"

"I think so. My instincts say so."

"That's good enough for me," Nate muttered.

"Any progress in finding the decoder on your end?"

Nate's jaw clenched. "No."

A little silence descended, and then the sensitive transmitter picked up Maggie's soft caution.

"Things in this corner of the world are turning out to

be a lot more desperate than any of the intelligence analysts realized. Be careful, Cowboy.''

"I know. I've got my boots on."

"What?"

Nate allowed himself a small smile. "When the corral's this full of horse manure, Wily Willie always advised pulling on a good pair of boots before going in to shovel it out. I'm wearing my Naconas. Make sure you keep those clunkers of yours on."

He could hear an answering smile seep into Maggie's voice. "I will. I promise."

"And keep me posted, Chameleon."

"Will do." She paused, then added in a little rush, "Look, I think I might be able hold them off at this end for a few days. Two, maybe three, at the most. Will that help?"

"It wouldn't hurt," he returned. Two, possibly three, more days to work his target. To break the shell around her. To learn the desperate secret she hid behind that proud, self-contained exterior. It wouldn't take him that long, he vowed to himself. And to Alex.

"What have you got in mind?" he asked Maggie.

"The team is scheduled to go down into the first silo tomorrow. Uh…don't be alarmed if you hear reports of a low-grade nuclear fuel spill."

The hairs on Nate's neck stood on end. "Good Lord, woman!" he shot back. "That's not something you want to fool around with!"

"Oh, for Pete's sake. I'm not going to actually *do* anything. But maybe I can make some people think I did."

"Chameleon!" Nate caught his near shout and forced himself to lower his voice. "Listen to me! Don't mess around down in that silo. Those missiles are old and unstable. You don't know what you're dealing with there."

"I may not, but one of the world's foremost nuclear physicists is leading this team, remember? I'm fairly sure I can convince him to cooperate."

"Why the hell would he cooperate in something like this?"

"It has to do with endocrine systems, but I don't have time to go into that right now. Just trust me, this man knows what he's doing."

Nate almost missed her last, faint transmission.

"I hope."

When Maggie signed off, Nate remained in a low crouch, staring at the illuminated face of his watch.

She wouldn't, he told himself. Surely to God, she wouldn't. With a sinking feeling, he acknowledged that she would.

Holy hell! Maggie intended to fake a nuclear fuel spill! Nate shook his head. He'd just as soon not be around when she tried to explain this one to Adam Ridgeway.

Contrary to the trigger-happy Hollywood stereotype, OMEGA agents were highly skilled professionals. They employed use of deadly force only as a last, desperate resort. Most had used it at one time or another, but no one ever spoke of it outside the required debrief with the director. Eventually a sanitized version of the event would circulate so that other agents could learn from it and, hopefully, avoid a similar lethal position.

Within that general framework, OMEGA's director gave his operatives complete discretion in the field to act as the situation warranted. Still, Nate suspected Maggie might have to do some pretty fast talking to convince Ridgeway the situation warranted what she had in mind.

Whatever the hell it was she had in mind!

Nate's stomach clenched as he considered the awesome

possibilities. He rose, feeling as twisted and taut as newly strung barbed wire. Maggie's transmission had added a gut-wrenching sense of urgency to the edgy tension already generated by the hours Nate had just shared with Alex on the shallow ledge.

Instead of easing after he'd settled back against the wall and put some space between himself and his target, his desire had sharpened with every glance of her black-fringed eyes, deepened with every movement of her bare flesh under her coat. By the time the storm's violence had subsided enough to allow safe travel, Nate's physical and mental frustration had left him feeling as surly as a kicked mongrel, and twice as ugly.

The long ride hadn't improved his mood. An hour after they rejoined Dimitri and the others, a silent signal had pulsed against the back of Nate's wrist. His impatience had mounted as he waited for an opportunity to shake his companions and answer the signal. He knew he had to do it on the trail, if possible. Once he returned to camp, it would be even harder to slip away from Ivana and Anya, not to mention Katerina.

The Karistani campfires were distant pinpoints of light against the velvet blackness before he managed a few moments alone. Dimitri had halted beside a blackened, smoldering tree split lengthwise by lightning. When Alex and the others clustered around to examine the storm's damage, Nate had used the cover of the colt's restless prancing at the end of his tether to slip away.

He'd known he had only a few moments, and he'd used them. Now he had to deal with what he'd learned from Maggie. As Nate moved toward Red, standing patiently nearby, tension gnawed at him.

Where the hell was that decoder? How would it come into play if Balminsk launched an attack? And what was he going to do with, or to, Alexandra if Maggie couldn't hold off the raiders?

Despite the cool night air, sweat dampened his palms. How could he protect Alex? Especially when the blasted woman didn't want protection. She took her responsibilities as *ataman* of this tattered host so fiercely, so personally, that Nate didn't doubt she'd be in the middle of the action. His gut twisted at the thought.

Reins in hand, he stopped and stared into the distance. The star-studded Karistani night took on a gray, hazy cast. The open steppes narrowed, closed, until they resembled a fog-shrouded street. The vast quiet seemed to carry a distant, ghostly echo of automatic rifle fire. The sound of panting desperation. A low grunt. The gush of warm, red blood...

The soft plop of hooves wrenched Nate from his private hell.

Instantly he registered the direction, the gait and the size of the horse that made the sound. The tension in him shifted focus, from a woman who'd been part of his past to a woman he damned well was going to make sure had a future.

The metallic click of a rifle bolt being drawn back sounded just before Alex's voice drifted out of the night.

"I hope that's you, Sloan. If it is, you'd better let me know in the next two seconds."

"It's me," he replied, in a low, dangerous snarl, "and the name's Nate."

She didn't respond for a moment. When she did, her tone was a good ten degrees cooler than it had been.

"Before you take another step, I suggest you tell me just why you separated from the rest of us...and why you suddenly seem to have a problem with what I call you."

Nate wasn't in the mood for threats. He took Red's

reins, shoved a boot into the stirrup and swung into the saddle. Pulling the stallion's head around, he kneed him toward the waiting woman. Her face was a pale blur when he answered.

"It's like this, *Alexandra.* If you Karistani women insist on sneakin' up on a man while he's tryin' to commune with nature, I figure you ought to at least call him by his given name."

Her chin lifted at his drawling sarcasm. "All right, *Nate.* I'll use your given name. And you won't disappear again. For any reason."

She might've thought she was calling his bluff, but he smiled in savage satisfaction at her response.

"You know, Alex, Wily Willie always warned me to chew on my thoughts a bit before I spit them out. You don't want me to disappear on you again? For any reason? Fine by me. From here on out, sweetheart, you're going to think you've sprouted a second shadow. You'd better look over your shoulder before you…commune with nature, or with anyone else."

Nate smiled grimly when he heard a familiar sound. The short whip cracked twice more against her boot top before she replied in a low, curt voice.

"You know that's not what I meant."

"Well, *you* may not have meant it, Alexandra, but *I* sure did."

It didn't take Alex long to discover Sloan did mean it.

Without a word being spoken between them, he and Dimitri somehow exchanged places. The tired, stoop-shouldered lieutenant fell back, and Nate took his position at Alex's side as though he belonged there.

The small band rode into camp an hour later. The temperature had dropped, and the wind knifed through their still-damp garments with a bone-chilling ease. Her hands numb, Alex could barely grip the reins when she at last slid out of the saddle.

A small crowd gathered to meet them and hear what news, if any, they brought. While the men took charge of the horses and the women pressed mugs of hot tea into their hands, Katerina drifted to Nate's side to welcome him back personally.

"You...you wear the wet!" she exclaimed, plucking at his jacket sleeve. She glanced around at the rest of the small party. "All of you."

Anya, her pale hair dangling down her back in a fat braid, clucked and murmured something in her soft voice.

"Come," Katerina urged, tugging on Nate's arm. "Anya says the water is yet hot in the steaming tent. She left the fires...how is it? Stroked?"

"Stoked," Alex supplied between sips of hot, steaming tea.

The thought of Nate being hustled to the small tent that served as the camp's communal steam bath almost made her forget the shivers racking her body. Like most of their European counterparts, the Karistanis had few inhibitions about shedding their clothes for a good, invigorating soak. Alex herself had long ago learned to balance her more conservative upbringing in the States with the earthier and far more practical Karistani traditions. But she knew that few Americans took to communal bathing. Folding her hands around the mug, she waited to watch Sloan—Nate— squirm.

If the thought of stripping down in front of strangers disconcerted him, he didn't show it.

"Thanks, Katerina," he responded with his lazy grin. "We could use some thawing-out. But the steaming tent won't hold us all. Let Dimitri and the others go first. I'll take the next shift...with Alexandra.''

Katerina sent Alex a quick, frowning glance over the heads of the others.

"It is not...not meet for you to bathe with an unmarried woman," she said primly to Nate.

Ha! Alex thought. If he'd suggested Katerina go into the steam tent, she would've joined him quickly enough.

The cattiness of her reaction surprised Alex, and flooded her with guilt. Deciding she'd had enough for one day, Alex passed Anya her mug.

"I'll leave the second shift to you," she conceded to Nate, not very graciously.

"God keep you until the dawn, Alexandra Danilova."

"And you...Nate Sloan."

Alex rose with the sun the next morning and walked out into the brisk air. The wind had taken on a keenness that brought a sting to her cheeks and made her grateful for the warmth of her high-collared, long-sleeved shirt in soft cream wool, which she wore belted at the waist. Its thick cashmerelike fabric defied the wind, as did the folds of her loose, baggy trousers. Fumbling in her pocket for a box of matches to light the charcoal in the samovar, she saw with some surprise that the brass urn was already steaming.

"Will you take tea, *ataman?*"

Turning, she found Dimitri waiting in a patch of sunlight beside the tent. Gratefully Alex reached for the tin mug he offered.

"Thank you. And thank you, as well, for lighting the samovar."

"It was not I," he replied. "The *Amerikanski*, he did so."

Alex folded her hands around the steaming mug, her spine tingling in awareness. Nate had been up before dawn? To light the samovar? Involuntarily she glanced over her shoulder, half expecting, half wanting, to see him behind her.

Dimitri picked up his own mug, then gave a mutter of disgust as tea sloshed over the sides. Seeing how his stiff hands shook, Alex felt a wave of compassion for this loyal and well-worn lieutenant.

"Why are you awake so early?" she asked. "Why don't you wait until the sun takes the chill from the winds to leave your tent?"

"Until the sun takes the stiffness from my bones, you mean?" His pale, rheumy eyes reflected a wry resignation. "I fear even the summer sun can no longer ease the ache in these bones."

Alex felt a crushing weight on her heart. "Dimitri," she said slowly, painfully, "perhaps you should go to the low-lands for the winter. You and the others who wish it. This...this could be a harsh time for Karistan."

"No, my *ataman*. I was born on the steppes. I will die on the steppes." His leathered face creased in a smile. "But not today. Nor, perhaps, tomorrow. Drink your tea, and I will tell you what Gregor learned from listening to his wireless in the small hours of the night."

As the lieutenant related an overheard conversation be-tween two shortwave-radio operators in Balminsk, a band seemed to tighten around Alex's chest.

"And when is this raid to take place?" she asked, her eyes on the distant horizon.

"Gregor could not hear," Dimitri replied with a shrug. "Or the speakers did not say. All that came through was that Karistani beef must provide filling for *peroshki*, or many in Balminsk will die this winter."

"I suppose they care not how many Karistani will die if they take the cattle!"

"It has always been so."

Alex swallowed her bitterness. "Yes, it has. Although it will leave the camp thin, we must double the scouts along the eastern border. Make sure they have plenty of flares to give us warning. Send Mikhail and one other to move the cattle in from the north grazing range. I'll bring in those from the south."

Dimitri nodded. "It is done."

He threw the rest of his tea on the ground, then half turned to leave. Swinging back, he faced her, an unreadable expression on his lined countenance.

"What?" Alex asked. "What troubles you?"

"If the raiders come and I'm not with you," he said slowly, "keep the *Amerikanski* close by you. To guard your back."

Alex stared at him in surprise. "Why should you think he cares about my back?"

The somber light in his eyes gave way to a watery smile. "Ah, 'Zandra. This one cares about most parts of you, would you but open your eyes and see it. You should take him to your bed and be done with it."

Her face warming, Alex lifted her chin. "Don't confuse me with Katerina or Ivana. I'm not in competition for this man's…services."

"Nevertheless, sooner or later he will offer them to you. Or force them on you, if he's half the stallion I think he is."

His pale eyes fastened on something just over Alex's left shoulder, and he gave a rumble of low laughter.

"From the looks of him this morning, I would say it may be sooner rather than later."

He strolled away, leaving Alex to face Sloan.

Gripping her tin mug in both hands, she swung around. As she watched him stride toward her, she realized with a sinking sensation that she wasn't quite sure how to handle this man. The balance between them had shifted subtly in the past twenty-four hours. Alex felt less sure about him, less in control.

She didn't understand why. Unless it was the determined glint in his eyes. Or the set of his broad shoulders beneath the turned-up collar of his jacket. Or the way his gaze made a slow, deliberate journey from the tip of her upthrust chin, down over each of the buttons on her shirt, to the toes of her boots, then back up again. By the time his eyes met hers once more, she felt as though she'd been undressed in public...and put together again with everything inside out.

"Mornin', Alexandra."

"Good morning, Sl—Nate."

"I like your hair like that." A smile webbed the weathered skin at the corners of his eyes. "Especially with that thingamabob in it."

Alex fingered the French braid that hung over one shoulder, its end tied with a tasseled bit of yarn and horsehair. The compliment disconcerted her, threw her even more off stride.

"Thank you," she replied hesitantly.

"You ready to ride?"

She tipped him a cool look. "Ride where?"

"I talked to Dimitri earlier. You need to bring your cattle in."

"That so?"

His smile deepening, he reached for a mug and twisted the spigot on the samovar.

"That's so."

It was only after his soft response that Alex realized

she'd picked up one of his favorite colloquialisms. Good Lord, as if her jumble of Karistani, North Philly establishment and Manhattan garment-district phrasing weren't confusing enough.

Disdaining sugar, he sipped at the bitter green tea. "How many head do we have to bring in?"

Alex hesitated. She didn't particularly care for this air of authority he'd assumed, but it would be foolish to spurn his help. Any help. With the feeling that she was crossing some invisible line, she shrugged.

"A hundred or so from the north grazing. Mikhail will bring those to the ravine. There are another thirty, perhaps forty, south of here."

"We're going after them?"

She forced a reluctant response. "I guess we are."

He set aside his mug and stepped closer to curl a finger under her chin. Tilting her face to his, he smiled down at her.

"That wasn't so bad, was it?"

When she didn't answer, he brushed his thumb along the line of her jaw. "Listen to me, Alex. It's not a sign of weakness to ask for help. You don't have to ride this trail all alone."

"No, it appears she does not."

Katerina's voice cut through the stillness between them like a knife.

Alex jerked her chin out of Nate's hold as her cousin let the tent flap fall behind her and sauntered out. Tossing her cloud of dark hair over one shoulder, she glared at them both.

Apparently the peace between her and her cousin was as fragile as the one between Karistan and Balminsk, Alex thought with an inner sigh. Anxious to avoid open hostilities with the younger woman, she suggested to Nate that they saddle up.

Chapter 11

Within two hours, Alex and Nate had driven the cattle into the ravine where their small band merged with the herd Mikhail and his men had brought down from the north. Leaving the beefy, red-faced Karistani with the black Denver Broncos ball cap on his head in charge, Alex insisted on returning to camp immediately.

They were met by Katerina and Petr Borodín, who was practically hopping up and down in excitement.

"You will not believe it, *ataman!*" he exclaimed in Karistani as they dismounted. "Such news Gregor has just heard over his wireless!"

Alex's heart jumped into her throat. She thrust her reins into Katerina's hands and rushed over to the thin, balding warrior.

"What news, Petr? Tell me! What has happened? We saw no flares. We heard no shots."

"There's been some sort of accident in Balminsk. No

one knows exactly what. The radio reports all differ. The head of the team says it is cause for concern.''

''What team?'' she asked sharply.

Petr waved his one arm, causing the medals on his chest to clink in a chorus of excitement. ''The team that checks the missiles. From the United Nations.''

''They're there, then,'' Alex murmured, half under her breath.

Petr cackled gleefully. ''Yes, they are there, and there they will stay. This team leader has said that Balminsk's borders must be closed, and has called in UN helicopters to patrol them.''

''What!''

''No one may travel in or out of Balminsk, until some person who checks the soils...some geo...geo...''

''Geologist?''

''Yes, until this geologist says there is no contamination.''

''Oh, my God.''

Her mind whirling, Alex tried to grasp the ramifications to Karistan of this bizarre situation. If what Gregor had heard was true, no raiders would ride across the borders from Balminsk, at least not for some days. But neither would anyone else!

The one person she'd been waiting for, the one whose advice she'd been counting on, was stranded on the other side of the border.

''You want to let me know what's going on here?''

The steel underlying Nate's drawl swung Alex around. ''There are reports of an accident in Balminsk.''

His eyes lanced into her, hard and laser-sharp. ''What kind of an accident?''

"No one quite knows for sure. The reports are confused. Something about soil contamination."

"Anyone hurt?"

Alex relayed the question to Petr, who shook his head.

"Not according to reports so far. But supposedly they've closed the borders until a geologist with the UN team verifies conditions. No one may go into or out of Balminsk for several days, at least."

"Holy hell!" Nate raked a hand through his short, sun-streaked hair. "I hope she's got her boots on," he muttered under his breath.

Katerina sauntered forward, her dark eyes gleaming. "So, cousin, this is good, no? We have the...the reprieve."

"Perhaps."

"Pah! Those to the east have worries of their own for a while. I? I say we should take our ease for what hours we may."

"Well..."

"As the women say, my cousin, life is short, and only a fool would scrub dirty linens when she may sip the vodka and dance the dance."

Strolling forward, Katerina hooked a hand through Nate's arm and tilted her head to smile provocatively up at him. "Come, I will show you the work of my aunt, Feodora. She paints the...the...*pysanky*."

"The Easter eggs," Alex translated, fighting a sudden and violent surge of jealousy at the thought of Katerina sipping and dancing with Nate.

"Yes, the Easter eggs," her cousin cooed. "They are most beautiful."

Lifting her chin, Alex gave Nate a cool look. "You should go with Katerina. My aunt is very talented. One of her pieces is on permanent display at the Saint Petersburg Academy of Arts.''

Nate patted the younger woman's hand. ''Well, I'd like to see those eggs, you understand. But later. Right now, I'd better stick with Alexandra and Petr. We need to find out a little more about what's happened in Balminsk.''

Katerina pursed her lips, clearly not pleased with his excuse. With a petulant shrug, she flipped her dark hair over one shoulder.

''Stay with them, then. Perhaps later we will play a bit, no?''

''Perhaps,'' he answered with one of his slow grins, which instantly restored Katerina's good humor and set Alex's back teeth on edge.

''Come, Petr,'' she snapped. ''Let us go see what additional news Gregor may have gleaned.''

Alex turned and headed for the camp. With the sun almost overhead, she didn't cast much of a shadow on the dusty earth. But Sloan's was longer, more solid. It merged with hers as they strode toward the tent that served as the Karistanis' administrative center.

For the rest of the day, Gregor stayed perched on his shaky camp stool in front of his ancient radio. Static crackled over the receiver as he picked up various reports. The residents of the camp drifted in and out of the tent to hear the news, shaking their heads at each confused report.

No Karistani would wish a disaster such as Chernobyl on even their most hated enemy—and it was soon obvious that the accident in Balminsk was not of that magnitude or seriousness. It kept the White Wolf trapped within his own lair, however, and that filled the Karistanis with a savage glee.

Long into the night, groups gathered to discuss events. The tensions that had racked the camp for so long eased perceptibly. Having lived on the knife edge of danger and war long, the host savored every moment of their reprieve. It was a short one, they acknowledged, but sufficient to justify bringing out the vodka bottles and indulging themselves a bit.

By the next morning, an almost festive air permeated the camp, one reminiscent of the old days. One Alex hadn't seen since her return.

The Karistani were a people who loved music, dance and drink, not necessarily in that order. In the summers of Alex's youth, they had needed little excuse to gather around the campfires at night and listen to the balalaika or sing the lusty ballads that told of their past—of great battles and warrior princes. Of mythical animals and sleighs flying across snow-blanketed steppes.

On holy days or in celebration of some triumph, the women had cooked great platters of sugared beets and spicy pastries. Whole sides of beef had turned on spits, and astonishing quantities of vodka had disappeared in a single night. Karistani feasts rivaled those rumored to have been given by the Cossacks of old, although Alex had never seen among her mother's people quite the level of orgiastic activity that reputedly had taken place in previous centuries.

As she and Nate walked through the bright morning sunlight, blessed by a rare lack of wind, she saw signs of the feverish activity that preceded a night of revelry.

Alex herself wasn't immune to the general air of excitement. For reasons she didn't really want to consider, she'd donned her red wool tunic with the gold frogging, freshly cleaned after its dousing in the storm two nights ago. Her hair gleamed from an herbal shampoo and vigorous brushing, and she'd dug out the supply of cosmetics she usually didn't bother with here on the steppes. A touch of mascara, a little lipstick, and she felt like a different woman altogether.

One Sloan approved of, if the glint in his eyes when he met her outside the tent was any measure. Ignoring him and the flutter the sight of his tall, lean body in its usual jeans and soft cotton shirt caused, Alex strode through the camp.

Anya stood at a sturdy wood worktable, her sleeves rolled up and her arms floured to her elbows, slamming dough onto the surface with the cheerful enthusiasm of a kerchiefed sumo wrestler. Her pretty face lighted up as she caught sight of Nate, and she called a greeting that Alex refused to translate verbatim. It never failed to astound her that Anya—pale, delicate Anya—should have such an earthy appreciation of the male physique.

Ivana, honey pot in hand, came out of the women's tent as they approached. Alex translated the widow's laughing invitation for Nate and Ole Red to join her on an expedition in search of honeycombs, and Nate's good-natured declination.

Secretly pleased, but curious about his refusal, Alex tipped her head back to look up at him. "Why don't you go with her? I have things I must do. I don't need you on my heels every minute."

Sloan hooked his thumbs in his belt, smiling down at her. "You know, Alexandra, Wily Willie used to warn me to be careful what I wished for, because I just might get it. You wanted me to stick close? I'm stickin' close."

Alex wasn't sure whether it was the smile or the soft

promise that sent the ripple of sensation down her spine. To cover her sudden pleasure, she shrugged.

"I'm beginning to think your Willie has Karistani blood in his veins. He has as many sayings as the women of this host. One of which," Alex warned, "has to do with skinning and tanning the hide of a bothersome male. At least if one makes a rug out of him, he can be put to some use."

Laughter glinted in his hazel eyes. "Ah, sweetheart, when this is all over, I'll have to show you just how many uses a bothersome male can be put to."

The ripple of sensation became a rush of pleasure. He'd called her "sweetheart" several times before. At least once in anger. Several times in mockery. But this was the first time the term had rolled off his lips with a low, caressing intimacy that sent liquid heat spilling through Alex's veins. The sensation disconcerted her so much that it took a few moments for the rest of his words to penetrate.

"When what is all over?" she asked slowly.

The laughter faded from his eyes. "You tell me, Alex. What's going on here? What have you got planned?"

They stood toe-to-toe in the dusty square. The camp bustled with activity all around them, but neither of them paid any attention. The sun heated the air, but neither of them felt it.

"Tell me," he urged.

Alex wanted to. She might have, if one of the women hadn't called to Petr at that moment, asking him if he thought it safe for her to go collect wild onions for the beefsteaks without escort. The question underscored the impermanence of these few hours of reprieve, and brought the realities of Alex's responsibilities crashing down on her.

"I...I can't."

She turned to walk away, only to be spun back around. "Why not?"

His insistence rubbed against the grain of Alex's own strong will.

"Look, this isn't any of your business. Karistan isn't any of your business."

"Bull."

She stiffened and shot him an angry look. "It's not bull. I'm the one responsible for seeing these people don't starve this winter. I'm the one who has to keep the White Wolf away from our herds."

"There's help available. The president..."

"Right. The president. He's so caught up with the troubles in the Middle East and Central America and his own reelection difficulties that he doesn't have time for a tiny corner of the world like Karistan."

"He sent me, didn't he?"

"Yes, and Three Bars Red." Her lip curled. "As much as we appreciate the offer of your services, Karistan's problems need a more immediate fix."

"Then why the hell didn't you take the aid package that was offered?"

"You know about that, do you? Then you ought to know what this so-called package included. No? Let me tell you."

Alex shoved a hand through her hair, feeling the tensions and worries that had built up inside her bubble over.

"Some fourth-level State Department weenie came waltzing in here with promises of *future* aid...*if* I agreed to open, unannounced inspections of Karistan by any and every federal agency with nothing better to do. *If* I converted our economy and our currency to one that would 'compete' on the European market. *If* I agree to an agricultural program that included planting rice.''

Sloan's sun-bleached brows rose in disbelief. ''Rice?''

''Rice! On the steppes! Even if my ancestors hadn't turned over in their graves at the thought of our men riding tractors instead of horses, these lands are too high, too arid, for rice, for God's sake.''

''Okay, so some bureaucrat didn't do his homework before he put together a package for Karistan…''

The blood of her mother's people rose in Alex, hot and fierce. ''Let's get this straight. No one's going to *put together* anything for Karistan, except me. I didn't ask for this responsibility, but it's mine.''

He took her arm in a hard grip. ''Listen to me, Alex. You don't have to do this alone.''

She flicked an icy glance at the hand folded around the red of her sleeve, then up at his face. ''Aren't you forgetting the ground rules, Sloan? You won't touch me without my permission, remember? Unless you want to feel the bite of the *nagaika*.''

His fingers dug into her flesh for an instant, then uncurled, one by one. Eyes the color of agates raked her face.

''You better keep that little horsetail flyswatter close to hand, Alexandra. Because the time's coming when I'm going to touch a whole lot more of you than you've ever had touched before.''

He turned and stalked away, leaving Alex stunned by the savagery she'd seen in his eyes. And swamped with heat. And suddenly, inexplicably frightened. She wrapped her arms around herself, trying to understand the feeling that gripped her.

She could remember feeling like this only once before. One long-ago summer, when the half-broken pony she was riding had thrown her. She'd been far out on the steppes, and had walked home through gathering dusk with the echo of distant, eerie howls behind her.

With a wrenching sensation in the pit of her stomach, Alex now realized that Nate Sloan loomed as a far more powerful threat to her than either the gray wolves of the steppes or the White Wolf of Balminsk. Not because she feared him or the look in his eyes. But because her blood pumped with a hot, equally savage need to know what would happen if...when...he touched her as he'd promised.

Swallowing, she watched him brush by Katerina with a nod and a curt word. Her cousin's brows rose in astonishment as she, too, turned to stare after him.

No wonder Katerina was surprised. The Sloan who strode through the camp was a different person than either she or Alex had thought him.

This wasn't the dusty outsider who'd laughed when she threatened to teach him to dance, Cossack-style.

Nor the man who'd warmed her frozen toes with his hands, and her heart with his tales of his improbable youth.

This was a stranger. A hard, unsmiling stranger who radiated anger and authority in every line of his long, lean body. One who challenged her as a woman as much as he now seemed to challenge her authority.

Alex gave a silent groan as a scowling Katerina made her way across the square. Still shaken by the confrontation with Sloan, she was in no mood for more of her cousin's dark looks.

"So, cousin. The *Amerikanski* stomps through the camp like a bear with one foot in the trap, and you, you pucker your lips like one who has eaten the persimmon. You fight with him, no?''

Alex ground her teeth. ''Can't a person have a single conversation or thought in this camp without everyone watching and commenting on it?''

''No, one cannot,'' Katerina retorted. ''You know that! Nor can one spend every waking moment with a man and not raise comment. Why has he stuck to you like flies to the dungpile these last few days?''

Alex twisted her lips at the imagery.

Katerina mistook the reason behind that small, tight smile. Planting her hands on her hips, she glared at Alex.

''So, it appears you change your mind about him, no? Is that why you dress yourself in your prettiest tunic? Is that why you wear the lipstick? Do you now think to take him to stud yourself?''

''Don't be crude, Katerina.''

''I, crude? I'm not the one who proposed such a plan. You *said* you didn't want him, cousin. You *said* one of us was to have him.''

Alex's temper flared. ''You may have him, Katerina, I told you that! If you're woman enough to hold him.''

Katerina stepped back, her eyes widening at the sharp retort.

Alex wasn't about to stay for the next round in this escalating war between them. She'd had enough of Katerina. Enough of Nate Sloan. Enough of this whole damned cluster of goathide tents and curious aunts and cousins and aged, bent warriors.

''Tell Dimitri I'll be at the ice cave. And you, my cousin, may go to—go to join the rest who cook pastries and pour vodka!''

Whirling, Alex strode to the north pasture. In three

minutes she had a snaffle bit and saddle on her gray. In five, she was heading for the retreat that had been her special place since childhood.

With the feel of the gelding's pounding hooves vibrating through her body and the sun beating down on her shoulders, Alex rode across the plains.

For an hour or so, she would leave the camp behind. She would leave her responsibilities and her worries and her cousin's animosity. She would pretend, if only for an hour or so, that she was once again the thin, long-legged teenager who had galloped across the steppes as though she owned them.

When she reached a line of low, serrated hills, Alex guided the gelding toward a rocky incline. Halfway up, she found the narrow, almost indiscernible path between tumbled, sharp-sided boulders. After a few moments, Alex reined the gray in on a flat, circular plateau surrounded by boulders and dismounted.

"Well done, my friend."

She gave the gray's dusty neck a pat, then slid her rifle from its case and pulled the reins over the animal's head to let them drag the ground. Trained by Petr himself, the gelding would not move unless or until called by its rider.

For a moment, Alex paused to look out over the rim of tumbled rocks. High, grassy seas stretched to the distant horizon. Gray-green melted into blue where earth and sky met. From this elevation, she could see the jagged scars in the surface, the sharp ravines and deep gorges carved by centuries of rains and swollen spring rivers.

She could see, as well, a distant horseman patrolling a small, barbed wire compound. Inside that wire, beneath a grassy, overgrown mound, was a cylinder of steel and death.

The missile site looked so innocent from this distance and this height. A slight bulge in the earth. A patch of shorter grass in a sea of waving stalks. Miles from the deserted launch facility that straddled the border between Karistan and Balminsk.

From her research, Alex knew that the U.S. missile sites scattered across Montana and Utah and Wyoming were just as isolated, just as remote. Just as innocuous-looking. Linked by underground umbilical cords to launch facilities hundreds of miles away, the weapons themselves were protected by an array of sophisticated intrusion-detection systems.

In more peaceful times, cattle had grazed near the Karistani site and scratched their backs on those twists of barbed wire. Soldiers in Soviet uniforms had come to inspect the warheads and the intrusion-detection systems. Now the soldiers were gone, and only a lone Karistani rider patrolled the site. Watching. Waiting. As they all waited.

Sighing, Alex turned toward a crack in the stone wall behind her. Angling sideways, she edged through the opening and left the twentieth century behind.

She stood in a high-ceilinged cavern lighted by narrow fissures in the cliff overhead. The air was cool, the temperature constant. It was an ice cave, her grandfather had told her when he first brought her here, so many years ago. It had been cut into the rock by long-ago glaciers, and had been used by hunters and travelers down through the ages.

As her eyes grew accustomed to the gloom, Alex sought the faint, fading splotches of color on a far wall. Propping her rifle against the stone, she went over to examine the paintings. She had too much respect to touch them. She wouldn't even breathe on them. A team of paleontologists from Moscow had examined them some years ago, promising funds to study and protect them. But these pictographs, like so much else, had fallen victim to the disintegration of the Soviet state.

One of Alex's goals, when—and if—she secured Karistan's future, was to protect this part of its past.

Her fingers itched for her sketch pad as she studied the outline of a shaggy-humped ox, an ancestor of the yak that had migrated centuries ago to Tibet and Central Asia. She drank in the graceful lines of a tusked white tiger, similar to those that had inhabited these parts long before encroaching civilization drove them east to Siberia. And the artist in her marveled at the skill of the long-ago painter, who'd captured in just a few strokes the determination of the naked, heavily muscled hunters moving in for the kill.

Alex walked farther into the cavern, to where the chamber divided into smaller, darker tunnels. There were more paintings in these spokes, she knew, and a few piles of bones.

The hunters had wintered here, according to the paleontologists. They'd eaten around fires in the main cavern, stored their supplies of meat and roots in the tunnels, wrapped their dead in hides and left them in the small, dark fissures because the ground was too frozen for burial. If they'd believed in burial.

Ducking her head, she entered one of the narrow tunnels. Enough light came from the main chamber behind her to show her the way, although she'd been here often enough to know it even in the dark. She was halfway to her special place when a faint rattle made her pause.

She glanced over her shoulder, listening intently. Was someone or something in the main cavern? It couldn't be Dimitri, or anyone else from camp. They would call out to her, signal their presence.

An animal? A bear, or one of the silver foxes that made their lairs in the stony precipices?

No, her horse would have whinnied, given notice of a predator's approach.

A rodent of some kind, a cave dweller whose nest she had unwittingly disturbed in passing?

Another chink of stone against stone told her that whatever came behind her was too large to be rodent.

Instinctively Alex dropped to a crouch and balanced on the balls of her feet. Her arms outstretched, fingertips pressing against cool stone, she peered through the dimness.

Only shadows and stillness stretched behind her.

Her heart began a slow, painful hammering. Her eyes strained.

One of the shadows moved. Came closer. Took on the vague outline of a man.

Alex didn't waste time cursing her stupidity in leaving her rifle in the cavern. Her grandfather had taught her not to spend energy on that which she could not change. Instead, she must concentrate on that which she could.

All right, she told herself. All right. Someone was between her and the Enfield. Someone who had seen the gelding outside. Someone who now stalked her with silent, deliberate stealth.

Alex took a swift inventory of her weapons. She had the bone-handled knife in her boot. And the short braided whip looped around her wrist. And the fissures along the tunnel to conceal herself in.

The dim shadow, hardly more than a notion of movement along the dark wall, drifted toward her.

Her breath suspended, Alex eased upright and flattened her back against the stone. Moving with infinite caution, she inched her shoulders along the wall until the left one dipped into a crevice.

When her left side fit into the opening, Alex wanted to sob with relief. Instead, she swallowed the fear that clogged her throat and carefully moved her body into darkness. She didn't let herself think what might be behind her. If there were bones, they could do her no harm. If there were pictographs painted on the slick, cold stone, she'd explore them some other time. Assuming she lived to explore another time.

She didn't have any illusions about what could happen to her if the man coming toward her had, somehow, slipped across the border from Balminsk.

For many years, just the threat of her grandfather's retribution had laid a mantle of protection over the women of the host. Justice was swift and sure to any who violated a Karistani woman. But the wars, the killings, the mutilations—by both sides—had stripped away the thin veneer of civilization of the people of this area.

They were descended from the Cossacks. Some from the Tartars, who took few prisoners and made those they did take beg for death. That so few of the Karistani men survived today was evidence of the savagery and the hate the wars with Balminsk had generated.

The shadow merged with the darkness of the tunnel. Alex couldn't see anything now. Nor could she hear anything. Except silence and the pounding of her own heart.

She sensed the intruder's presence before she saw him.

Her fingers gripped the knife's bone handle. She held it

as her grandfather had taught her, with the blade low and pointed upward to slash at an unprotected belly.

A low growl drifted out of the darkness.

"I'm going to get stuck if I go much farther into this tunnel. You'd better come out, Alex."

Relief crashed over her in waves. Followed immediately by a wave of fury.

"You fool!" She slid sideways through the narrow aperture. "You idiot! Why didn't you call out? Let me know who you were? I was about to gut you!"

"You were about to try," he said, with a smile in his voice that sent Alex's anger spiraling.

"You think this is funny? You think it's something to laugh about?"

"No, sweetheart, I don't. I was just remembering the first time we met. Best I recall, you used about the same terms of endearment."

"Don't *sweetheart* me, you damned cowboy. I ought to…"

"I know, I know." He reached out and gripped her wrist, twisting it and the knife downward. "You ought to gut me and tan my hide. Or boil me in fish oil. Or feed me to the prairie dogs. You Karistani women are sure a bloodthirsty lot."

"Sloan…"

"Nate," he reminded her, using the hold to tug her closer.

"Let go of me."

"I'm just keeping that rib-tickler out of our way while we settle some things between us."

"There's nothing to settle."

With a smooth twist of his arm, he had Alex's wrist tucked behind her and her body up against his.

"Yes, Alexandra Danilova, there is."

"Sloan…"

The arm banding her to him tightened. "Nate."

"Let me go."

Even in the dim shadows, she could see the glint in his eyes. "Did anyone ever tell you that you're one stubborn female?"

"Yes, as a matter of fact. My grandfather, twice a day, every day I spent with him. Now let me go."

"I don't think so."

The soft implacability in his voice sent a shiver dancing along Alex's nerves.

"Aren't you forgetting the *nagaika?*"

His breath fanned her lips. "I guess I'll just have to take my licks."

"Sloan… Nate…"

His lips brushed hers. "It's too late, Alexandra. Way too late. For both of us."

Chapter 12

Ever afterward, when she thought about that moment of contact in the dark, narrow tunnel, Alex would know it was Sloan's combination of gentleness and strength that shattered the last of the barriers she'd erected around herself.

He was a man who knew his strength, and wasn't afraid to show gentleness. His mouth moved over hers with warm insistence. Tasting. Exploring. Giving a pleasure that stirred a response deep within her.

At first, Alex refused to acknowledge it. She held herself stiff and unmoving, not fighting, not cooperating.

At first, he didn't seem to mind her lack of participation. He drew what he needed from her lips, like a thirsty man taking a long-awaited drink.

All too soon, the situation satisfied neither one of them. Alex made a little movement against him, as if to pull away, and discovered that his hand had already loosened its grip on her wrist. She'd been held, not by his strength, but by his gentleness.

Though she knew she was free, she didn't move. She should, she told herself. She should push away from the seductive nearness of this man. She should go outside, back to the camp. Back to her responsibilities.

At the thought, something deep within her rebelled. For weeks now, she'd carried this burden that had been thrust on her. For weeks, she'd sublimated her own life, her own desires, for those of the others. A sudden, totally selfish need rose in her. She wanted a few more minutes with Nate. She wanted to lean into his power. She wanted his arms around her. His mouth on hers.

Oh, God, she wanted him.

With the admission came a molten spear of heat. She was woman enough to recognize the heat for what it was. And honest enough to acknowledge what she intended to do about it.

Reaching up on tiptoe, she wrapped her arms around Nate's neck and brought his head to hers.

This was right.

The moment she tasted the hard, driving hunger in his kiss and felt her own rise to meet it, she knew this was right.

Here in the darkness, in the cold splendor of the caves where her ancestors had found shelter and perhaps survival, the primitive urge that surged through her was right. And natural. And shattering in its intensity.

He was made for this. She was. Their bodies fit together at knee and thigh and hip. She had to stretch a bit, he had to bend a little, but they managed to make contact everywhere that mattered. Her blood firing, she arched into him. His mouth ravaged hers. Her hips ground against his.

She wasn't sure whether it was minutes or hours later

that he speared both hands through her hair, holding her head still as he dragged his own back. She waited unmoving, her breath as ragged as his.

Calling on every ounce of discipline he possessed, Nate willed himself to control. This was crazy. Insane. He hadn't intended for this to happen when he followed Alex across the plains, spurred by the twin needs to protect this stubborn woman and to know where she was going. He hadn't intended to let his desire to hold her, to drink in her taste and texture, get out of hand like this.

But even as he fought his own pumping desire, he felt hers in the ragged, panting breath that washed against his throat and the hard nipples that pushed through the red wool of her blouse.

Any hope of control shattered when she arched her lower body into his with an intimacy that sent a white-hot heat through his groin.

"I want you, Nate," she whispered. "Just for a little while, I—need you to hold me."

She did. More than she realized. Even more than he himself had realized until this instant. Nate heard the vulnerability in her voice, the aching loneliness.

With stunning intensity, a dozen different forces collided within him. The driving male urge to mate that had him hard and rampant. The masculine impulse to claim the woman who'd haunted his nights and filled his days. The purely personal and far more urgent desire to lose himself inside this shimmering, complex, compelling creature that was Alex. The simple need to give her pleasure.

He'd hold this woman…for a whole lot longer than the little while she'd asked for.

"I want you, too, Alexandra. I have since the first moment I met you. But not like this. Not in the darkness and the shadows."

She made a murmur of protest.

"I want to see your eyes dilated with pleasure and your mouth swollen from my kisses. I want to see your forehead."

"What?"

"Just come with me."

He wouldn't, couldn't, take the time to tell her now that his entire being was concentrated on erasing every damn worry line from her face and replacing them with a flush of pleasure.

When they slipped through the opening in the cliff face, the bright, dazzling sunlight blinded them. Alex stumbled and would have fallen if Nate hadn't caught her with an arm around her waist and swung her back against the cliff face. Pinning her body to the stone with his, he took up where they'd left off in the dark cave.

Nate couldn't have said how long it was before hard, hungry kisses and the friction of their clothed bodies against each other weren't enough...for either of them.

Her mouth locked with his, Alex slid her hands inside his jacket and peeled it over his shoulders. While her tongue played with his and he drank in her soft little sounds of pleasure, her fingers groped at the buttons on his cotton shirt.

With one arm still wrapped around her waist to cushion her from the rock wall, Nate tugged at the high collar of her red top. Frustrated at the small patch of soft skin her collar gave him access to, he put just enough distance between them to fumble with the buttons on the tunic.

Alex leaned against the wall, her mouth satisfactorily swollen and her forehead free of all lines, while Nate worked the gold frog fastenings that marched with military precision down the front of her blouse. He soon found himself cursing under his breath at the elaborate fastenings. They looked impressive, but they were hell for a man with hands the size of his to get undone. Impatient, he worked the last one free and shoved the soft red wool down to her elbows. When he saw the bra that cupped her breasts, Nate didn't know whether to grin or to groan.

He'd held that bit of lace in his hands the night Red raided Ivana's honey pot, and spent more than one sweat-drenched hour wondering how it would look on Alex's body. None of his imaginings had ever come close to reality, he discovered as he stripped away the rest of her clothes.

She was glorious. As slender and smooth as a willow sapling. Long-legged as a newborn colt, but far more graceful. Her skin gleamed with ivory tints and satin shadows in the sunlight. Dusky nipples crowned her small, high breasts, and the triangle at the juncture of her thighs was as dark and as silky as her mane of tumbling sable hair. But if Nate had been allowed only one memory to take away with him of that moment, one vivid impression, it would have been her eyes. Golden and glorious, they held no hint of fear, no shadow of worry. Only a smiling invitation that made him ache with wanting her.

"I want to see you, too," she murmured, sliding her hands inside his shirt. "All of you."

By the time Alex had managed—with Nate's ready assistance—to rid him of his clothing, she was liquid with need.

He was magnificent. Lean, finely honed by exercise or work, each muscle well-defined under supple skin lightly furred with soft golden hair. His body showed evidence of the hard youth he'd told her of that day when the storm cocooned them on the shallow ledge. There were long white scars that traced back to his rodeo days, she suspected. Hard ridges of flesh. And a small round patch of puckered skin on the right side of his chest.

Alex had spent enough summers on the steppes to recognize a bullet wound when she saw one.

"When did you get this?" she asked, her voice husky.

"A long time ago."

Her fingers traced the scarred flesh. "How?"

His hand closed over hers, trapping it against his skin. "It doesn't matter. It's part of my past. At this particular moment, I'm more concerned about the present."

Alex felt a rush of dissatisfaction that Nate would shut any part of himself off from her. The feeling was irrational, she knew. At this point in time, she probably had many more secrets tucked away inside her than he did.

With a sudden, fierce resolve, she shoved aside the past and refused to think about the future. He was right. For this slice of time, at least, there was only here. And now. And Nate.

She slid her hand free of his loose hold and let it travel slowly down his chest. Across his smooth-planed middle. Over his flat belly. With the tip of one nail, she traced the length of his hard, rampant arousal.

Her eyes limpid, she smiled up at him. "I don't think you have to be too concerned about the present."

He half laughed, half groaned.

Alex closed her fingers around his rigid shaft, then blinked in surprise when he pulled away.

"Wait," he ordered softly. "Wait a moment."

He turned and hunkered down to dig through their pile of discarded clothing. While Alex admired the smooth line of his tanned back and his tight white buns, he emptied the pockets of his jeans. He tossed an old pocketknife, what looked like a half-empty package of chewing gum and a handful of coins on top of her crumpled tunic before he found what he wanted.

Straightening, he walked back to her side.

Alex fought a feeling of feminine pique as she stared at the foil packet. She should've known someone with Nate's laughing eyes and rugged handsomeness would be prepared for just these circumstances.

"Do you always carry an emergency supply?" she asked, a hint of coolness in her voice.

He propped an arm against the cliff and used his free hand to tip her head back.

"Always, sweetheart. Wily Willie taught me that a man isn't a man if he doesn't protect his spread, his horse, and his woman."

"I can imagine which one came first with Willie," she retorted, refusing to acknowledge the shiver that darted down her spine at his use of the possessive.

"I never had the nerve to ask," he responded with a grin. "But I can tell you which comes first with me. You, Alexandra Danilova Jordan. You, my wild, beautiful woman of the steppes."

When he bent to nuzzle her neck, Alex arched against him. His teeth and his tongue worked her flesh, causing explosions of heat in parts of her body well below her neckline. The unyielding stone wall held her immobile, unable to withdraw any part of herself from him even if she'd wanted to.

And she didn't.

Sweet heaven above, she didn't.

When his hand shaped her breast and tipped it up for a small, biting kiss, she gasped and lifted herself higher. When he suckled the aching nipple, streaks of fire shot straight from her breast to her loins. When one of his hair-roughened thighs parted hers, and a hand slid down her belly to delve into the moist warmth at her center, Alex buried her face in his neck to muffle her moan.

Sometime later, he rasped softly in her ear, "Look at me, Alexandra."

She shook her head, keeping her face against his neck. She didn't want to see, to think, to do anything but feel the exquisite sensations his hands and his mouth were bringing her. And return them in some way.

"Alex, I want to see your eyes."

"I...I thought it was my forehead," she gasped, wriggling desperately as his thumb pressed the nub of flesh between her thighs.

"Whatever," he growled.

She brought her head back, her eyes narrowed against the sun and her own spiraling pleasure. Wanting, needing, to give in return, she matched him stroke for stroke, kiss for kiss.

When she felt as though she were about to drown in the waves of sensation that washed over her, he stepped back to tear open the packet and sheathe himself.

Then his strong, square hands circled her waist.

Holding her back away from the rough cliffside, he lifted her, and brought her down onto him. Alex gave a ragged groan as his rigid shaft entered her slick channel. Her muscles tightened involuntarily, then loosened to accept him.

Fierce masculine satisfaction flared in his eyes for a moment, before giving way to an emotion Alex might have tried to identify if she hadn't been caught up in a whirling, spinning vortex of pure sensation. Using his muscled thigh, his straining member, his hands and his mouth, Nate stoked the fires within her, fanning the leaping flames, until at last she exploded into shards of white light and blazing red heat.

When the spasms that held her rigid subsided, Alex slumped against his chest. Which was when she first realized he hadn't climaxed. Or, if he had, he didn't give any evidence of it that she could tell.

"Oh, Nate," she murmured breathlessly. "I'm sorry. I can't... I've never..."

She swallowed, and tried unsuccessfully to force her limp muscles to move. "Just give me a little while."

He managed a grin and eased himself out of her. "Isn't that usually the man's line?"

"Yes, well..."

Alex wet her lips, not wanting to confess that she'd never before exploded into so many pieces, and wasn't sure exactly how to put herself back together.

"It's okay, sweetheart," he assured her, brushing a strand of limp hair from her forehead. "I'll live."

At his words, Alex felt a mix of guilt and satisfaction and responsibility. She wasn't the kind of woman to take and not give.

"I want you to do more than just live, Nate. You just made me feel as though I was..."

His eyes glinted. "Yeah?"

"Flying across the steppes on a wild pony," she told him with a wry smile. "I want you to fly, too."

"Well, I wouldn't mind a little flying, you understand, but I'm afraid my emergency supply won't make it through another ride across the steppes."

She gave the supply in question a quick inspection, then sent him a look of inquiry.

"I don't want to risk tearing it, Alex. I won't add to your worries."

She tilted her head, unused to having decisions taken out of her hands so summarily. After a moment, she put her palms on his chest and pushed him away.

"Fine. We won't risk it. You just sit on that boulder over there, and I'll show you how the women of Karistan solve a problem like this."

"Alex…"

"We have a saying," she told him, shoving him toward the low, benchlike rock. "One passed from mother to daughter for centuries."

"I'm not sure I want to hear this."

Hands on his shoulders, she pressed him down.

"A man may be more difficult to trap than a wild goat," Alex purred, "but he's far easier to milk."

Later, much later, when they had trapped and milked and flown across the steppes to everyone's mutual satisfaction, Nate dragged on his jeans. In no hurry to see Alex's long, slender legs covered up, he dug only her panties and his jacket out of the pile of scattered clothing.

After wrapping the warm felt-lined denim around her shoulders, he settled down with his back against the cliff and took her on his lap. Resting his chin on the top of Alex's head, Nate stared out at the vast, endless vista.

For a while, the only sounds that disturbed the stillness were the occasional shuffle of the horses as they shifted in and out of their sleepy dozes and the distant call of a hawk circling far out over the plains. The sun hovered just above the line of boulders at the edge of the rocky plateau and bathed the grass below in a golden hue.

Alex pulled the front edges of the jacket closer. The thin felt lining carried traces of Nate's scent, warm and masculine and comforting. As comforting as the feel of his rock-solid chest behind her and the arms wrapped loosely around her waist.

She shifted on his lap and felt a stone dig into one bare heel. Wincing, she rubbed her foot along the rocky ground to dislodge the sharp pebble, then glanced around the bare, rocky plateau. The place probably wouldn't rate on anyone's list of the top ten most romantic rendezvous. No soft bed with silken sheets. No dreamy music or chilled champagne. Not even one of the thick, cushioning wolf pelts the Karistani women had been known to tuck under their saddles when they rode off to bring food and other comforts to their men riding herd at some distant grazing site. But at that moment, Alex felt more bonelessly, wonderfully comfortable than she'd ever felt in her life. She wouldn't have traded Nate's lap and the open, sunswept plateau for all the silk sheets and wolf pelts in the world.

"Just imagine how many people never see anything like that," he murmured above her.

She lifted her head from its tucked position under his chin and looked up to see his eyes drinking in the vast, empty distance.

"It calls to you, doesn't it?" she asked with a hint of envy.

He glanced down at her. "It doesn't call to you?"

Alex turned her face to the open vista, frowning. "It used to. Sometimes, at night, I think it still does. But..." She gave a little shrug. "But then I decide it's just the wind."

He tightened his arms, drawing her closer into his warmth. "You were born here, weren't you?"

"Yes."

"And?" he prompted.

"And I grew up as sort of an international nomad," she answered lightly. "I spent the summers in Karistan. In the winters, I attended school in North Philadelphia."

"And now that you're all grown up? Very nicely grown up, I might add. How do you live now, Alex?"

"Until a few weeks ago, I commuted between Philly

and Manhattan. With occasional trips to London and regular treks to Paris for the spring and fall shows thrown
in.''

''Not to Karistan?''

She stared out over the empty steppes. ''No, not to
Karistan. I hadn't been back here for almost ten years
when my grandfather died.''

He shifted, bringing her around in the circle of his arms
to look down into her face.

''Why?''

''What is this?'' Alex returned. ''Are we playing twenty
questions? We don't have time for games, Nate. I need to
get back.''

She curled a leg under her, intending to push herself off
his lap. His arms held her in place.

''Tell me, Alex. Tell me who you are. I want to know.''

She turned the tables on him. ''Why?''

''A man wants to know all he can about the woman
he's going to be riding across the steppes with.''

Alex caught her breath at the steely promise in his
voice.

''Tell me,'' he urged. ''Tell me who you are.''

Alex hesitated, then slowly, painfully articulated aloud
for the first time in her life the doubts she'd carried for so
long.

''I don't know who I am, Nate. I guess I've never really
known. I've always been torn by divided loyalties.''

''Yet when the chips were down, you came back to
Karistan.''

''I came back because I had to. I stay because…''

''Why, Alex?''

''Because Karistan's like me, caught between two
worlds. Only its worlds aren't East and West. They're the
past and the present.''

She stared up at him, seeing the keen intelligence in his eyes. And something else, something that pulled at the tight knot of worries she'd been holding inside her for so long.

His thumb brushed the spot just above her eyebrows. "And that's what's causing this crease? The idea of leading Karistan out of the past and into the future?"

The knot loosened, and the worries came tumbling out.

"I know I may not be the best person to do it. I've made some mistakes. Well, a lot of mistakes. Maybe I should have accepted the aid package. Maybe I should have agreed to the conditions that State Department weenie laid out. I've lain awake nights, worrying about that decision."

"Alex..."

She twisted out of his arms to kneel beside him. "But I couldn't do it, Nate. I couldn't give away the very independence my grandfather fought for. I couldn't just hand over the trust he passed to me."

She broke off, biting down on her lower lip.

Nate didn't move, didn't encourage her or discourage her by so much as a blink. With a gut-twisting need that had nothing to do with his mission to Karistan, he wanted Alex to trust him. Not because he'd convinced her to. Because she wanted to.

She chewed on her lip for long, endless seconds, then pushed herself to her feet.

"Wait here," she told him. "I...I want to show you something."

Alex scrambled up. Pausing only to pull on her pants and boots, she slipped through the narrow entrance in the cliff wall.

Chapter 13

Nate got to his feet slowly. As he watched Alex disappear through the dark entrance to the cavern, he tried to decide what to call the feeling that coiled through him.

Not lust. He knew all the symptoms of lust, and this wasn't it.

Not desire. Holding Alex wrapped in his arms and hearing her open up had taken him far beyond desire.

What he felt was deeper, fiercer, more gut-wrenchingly painful.

He turned to stare out over the steppes, thinking about what she'd knowingly and unknowingly revealed in the past few minutes. He suspected that Alex herself didn't realize how deep the conflict in her went.

Nate himself had never known a home, as most people knew it. He'd never wanted or needed one. Rattling around with Willie in their old pickup had filled all his needs. Even after the authorities caught up with them and forced Willie to leave Nate with family friends during the school year, he'd snuck away whenever possible to hitchhike to whatever dusty, noise-filled town was hosting the next rodeo.

He'd never put down roots, and he'd never felt himself pulled in different directions by those deep, entangling vines. Alex had roots in two different worlds, but nothing to anchor them to.

Everything in Nate ached to give her that anchor. She was so strong, so fiercely independent, and so achingly lost in that never-never land of hers. With every fiber of his being, Nate wanted to give her world a solid plane. Instead, he knew, he was about to tear it apart.

His savage oath startled the horses out of their sleepy dozes. Ole Red tossed his head, chuffing through hairy lips as he came more fully awake and threw Nate an inquiring look.

"Hang loose, fella. We'll be heading back to camp soon."

The words left a bitter taste in Nate's mouth, and he turned once more to stare out at the empty vastness of the steppes.

A rattle of stone at the cave's entrance announced Alex's return a little while later. He swung around as she emerged into the waning sunlight and hurried toward him, his heart constricting at the sight of her.

Her hair tumbled over her shoulders in a dark, tangled mass, and the lipstick she'd worn earlier had long since disappeared. She looked like a refugee from a homeless shelter in those baggy pants and his oversize jacket. But as he watched her come toward him, bathed by the glow of the setting sun, Nate could finally give a name to the feeling knifing through him.

He loved her, or thought he did. The emotion wasn't one he had a whole lot of practice or familiarity with.

The thought of what he was about to do to that love curled his hands into fists. When she stopped beside him, he didn't have to glance down to know that one of the items she held in her hands was a small black box.

"My grandfather passed these to me when he died," she told him breathlessly.

A small metallic chink drew Nate's reluctant gaze to the tarnished silver snaffle bit she held up. The D-rings to which reins would have been attached were carved in an intricate design, as ornate as any museum piece.

"This was used by a long-ago *ataman* of our host," Alex said, her voice low and vibrating with pride. "He led five hundred men against the Poles at Pskov, in 1581, when the steppes were still known as the Wild Country. The czar himself presented this bridle bit in recognition of that victory."

Her mouth twisted. "The same czar tried to reclaim it not two months later, when he decided the Cossacks had grown too powerful. The plains were awash with blood for years, but the Cossacks held the Wild Country. They chose to die before they would give up their freedoms. No Cossack was ever a serf. Not under the czars."

Her hands closed over the tarnished silver bit. Nate saw the fierce emotion in her eyes, and for the first time understood the power of the forces that pulled at her.

"Scholars say true Cossackdom died after World War I, when long-range artillery made horsemen armed with rifles obsolete. The Cossack regiments were absorbed into the Soviet armies, and the red bear spread its shadow over the steppes. The hosts disintegrated, and people fled to America, or to Europe, or China. Except for a few stubborn, scattered bands."

She drew in a ragged breath. "My grandfather's father led one of those bands, and then my grandfather. Rather than see his people exterminated during Stalin's reign of terror, he accepted Moscow's authority. But he never gave up fighting for them, never stopped working for Karistan's freedom. Our men died, one by one, in the last battles with the Soviet bear, and with the wolves of Balminsk, who wanted to take the few resources left to us.''

Nate caught the shift in pronouns that Alex seemed unaware of. In her short, impassioned speech, she'd shifted from *his* people to *our* men. From *them* to *us*. The roots that pulled at Alex went deeper than she realized.

''When the Soviets planted their missiles on our soil, they didn't care that they made Karistan a target for the West's retaliation. But in the end, those missiles will give us the means to keep the freedom we won back.''

Lifting her other hand, she uncurled her fingers. ''This has more power for Karistan than the Soviets or the West ever intended it to have.''

Nate didn't look down, didn't look anywhere but into Alex's eyes. ''What do you intend to do with it?''

A flicker of surprise crossed her face. ''Don't you want to know what it is?''

''I know what it is, Alex.''

She stared at him, her brows drawing together in confusion. ''How do you know? How could you?''

As with most moments of intense drama, this one was broken by the most mundane event.

A deep, whoofing snuffle made both Alex and Nate glance around. Red had ambled across the rocky plateau and was now investigating the articles of clothing still scattered on the ground.

''Get out of there.''

The stallion's ears twitched, but he ignored Nate's growled command. One big hoof plopped down on the braided *nagaika*. Nosing Alex's bra aside with his nose, he lipped at the red wool tunic.

"Red! Dammit, get out of there! Oh, hell, he's after the package of chewing gum!"

Still confused, still not quite understanding the inexplicable tension in the man who had only moments before cradled her in his warmth, Alex watched Nate stride across the plateau.

"Come on, Red, spit out the paper! I don't want to have to shove a fist down your windpipe to dislodge it if it gets stuck."

As Nate tried to convince Red to relinquish his prize, the sun sank a little lower behind the rim of boulders. A chill prickled along Alex's arms that wasn't due entirely to the rapidly cooling air. Feeling a need to clothe herself, she tucked the silver bit and the black box in her pants pocket, then shed Nate's jacket to pull on her red top.

Kneeling, she reached for the short braided whip no steppe horseman ever rode without. Her fingers brushed over the handful of loose coins and the old pocketknife that Nate had dug out of his jeans earlier. When she touched the bone handle of the knife, she gave a start of surprise.

The first thing Nate noticed when he finally convinced Red to give up the wadded paper and gum and swung around were the tight, grooved lines bracketing Alex's mouth.

The second was the pocketknife resting on her upturned palm. Although he couldn't see any movement, Nate knew the knife was vibrating against her palm.

"If I thought you were the kind of man to go in for kinky sex toys, I'd say this is another one of your emergency supplies." Her lips twisted in a bitter travesty of a smile. "But then, I don't really know *what* kind of man you are, do I, Sloan?"

"Alex…"

"This is some kind of a device, isn't it? An electronic homing device of some kind?"

"Close enough."

"What set it off?"

He met her look. "The decoder."

"You bastard."

The way she said it sliced through Nate like a blade. Without heat. Without anger. Without any emotion at all. Except a cold, flat contempt.

"That's what you came to Karistan for, isn't it? The decoding device?"

He hooked his thumbs in his belt. "Yes."

"That's it?" she asked after a long, deadly moment. "Just 'yes'? No excuses? No explanations? No embarrassment over the fact that you just used me in the most contemptible way a man can use a woman to get his hands on what he wants."

"No, Alex. No excuses. No explanations. And I didn't *use* you. We used each other, in the most elemental, most fundamental way a man and woman can. What we had… What we have is right, Alex."

Her lip curled. "Oh, it was right. It was certainly right. You're good, Sloan, I'll give you that. If there's a scale for measuring performance at stud, I'd give you top marks. I suspect not even Three Bars Red is in your class. But I hope you don't think that one—admittedly spectacular— performance is enough to convince me to give you this little black box."

They both knew it wasn't a matter of giving, that he could take it from her any time he wanted. They also knew he wouldn't use force against her. Not yet, anyway, Nate amended silently.

"I'm going to mount and ride out of here," Alex told him, spacing her words carefully. "I'm going to ride back to camp. You and that damned horse of yours will be out of Karistan by dawn, or I'll shoot you on sight."

"Then you'd better keep your Enfield loaded, sweetheart. I'll be right behind you. Like a second shadow, remember?"

"Sloan…"

"Think about what happened here during the ride back to camp, Alex. It had nothing to do with that decoder. When you work your way past your anger, you'll admit that. You're too honest not to. Think about this, too."

There wasn't anything gentle about his kiss this time. It was hard and raw and possessive. And when Alex wrenched herself out of his arms and stalked to her gelding, Nate could only hope that the glitter in her eyes was fury, and not hatred.

He stood beside Red while Alex worked her way down the steep incline. His every muscle was tense with the strain of wanting to go after her. But he knew she needed time. Time to work through her anger and her hurt. Time to get past this damned business of the decoder.

But not too much time, Nate vowed grimly.

He was halfway back to camp when the chronometer pulsed against his wrist with a silent signal. Nate glanced at the code and reined Red in.

"Cowboy here. Go ahead, Chameleon."

Maggie's voice cut through the shadowy dusk, tense and urgent. "I think you ought to know the horse poop just got deeper at this end. In fact, it's over my boot tops at this moment. Hang on. I'm going to code Doc in. He needs to hear this, too.''

The few seconds it took for her to call up OMEGA Control spun into several lifetimes for Nate. His eyes narrowed, he searched the shadows ahead for a sign of Alex.

"This is Doc. Thunder's here, too, listening in. Go ahead, Chameleon.''

The sensitive transmitter picked up Maggie's small, breathy sigh. Nate couldn't tell whether it was one of dismay or relief at the news that Adam Ridgeway, code name Thunder, was present in the Control Center. Nate suspected Maggie was already dreading the debrief she'd have with the director when this mission was over, but there wasn't anyone either one of them would rather have on hand when the horse manure was about to hit the fan. Which it apparently was.

"Okay, team, here's the situation,'' Maggie reported. "Cherkoff, Sr., dug up a team of Ukrainian scientists with some radiation-measuring equipment of their own. He had them flown in this afternoon. When their equipment showed no evidence of soil contamination, he insisted on watching while we remeasured with ours. He wasn't too happy when he discovered we'd exaggerated the readings a bit.''

"Fabricated them, you mean,'' Thunder put in coldly.

"Whatever. In any event, Richard—Dr. Worthington— was forced to rescind the order closing the borders.''

"Hell!''

"I'm sorry, Cowboy.'' Maggie paused, then plunged ahead. "There's more. Since the soil samples showed clear, the White Wolf also insisted that the silos be inspected. Richard and I were the first ones to go down. Turns out we were the only ones. We're, uh, still here.''

"Are you all right?'' Adam's sharp question leaped through the air.

Nate glanced down at the chronometer in surprise. As one of OMEGA's old-timers, he'd worked for Adam Ridgeway for a goodly number of years. He knew that the safety of field operatives overrode any mission requirement as far as the director was concerned. But Nate had never heard that level of intensity in Ridgeway's voice before. He wondered if Maggie had caught it, as well.

Evidently not.

"We're fine," she assured Adam blithely. "We're just sort of…trapped here. Richard's working on the silo hatch mechanism right now. He thinks it's been tampered with."

"Cherkoff," Nate growled.

"Exactly." Her voice sharpened, took on a new urgency. "Look, Cowboy, I don't know how long it will take us to get out of here. In the meantime, I can't control what's going on topside. But I do know the Wolf's fangs were bared last time I saw him. He's out for blood. Any blood. If not that of the capitalist scum he hates so much, then that of the Karistanis, whom he hates even more."

"Guess it's time we pull his fangs," Doc interjected. "Your play was more effective than you realized, Chameleon. It bought enough time for me to deploy a squadron of gunships from Germany to a forward base in Eastern Europe. They can be in orbit over Karistan in…one hour and fourteen minutes. Less, if the head winds drop below twenty knots."

The tension at the base of Nate's neck eased considerably. "Well, now, with that kind of firepower, this might just turn out to be an interestin' night. Sorry you're going to be stuck down in that hole and miss it, Chameleon."

"Try not to start the party without me, Cowboy. I'll get out of here yet. Hey, I'm sitting on a couple of megatons of explosives, aren't I?"

Three startled males responded to that one simultaneously. Nate and David conceded the airwaves to Adam, who gave Maggie several explicit instructions, only one of which had to do with sitting on her hands until they got an extraction team to pull her and Worthington out of that damned hole.

Nate signed off a few seconds later, his eyes thoughtful. With a squadron of AC-130 Spectre gunships backing him up, he could hold off anything the White Wolf threw at Karistan, with plenty of firepower left over.

What he wouldn't be able to hold off was Alex's fury when he told her that the United States, in the person of Nate Sloan, was preempting every one of her options when it came to deciding Karistan's future.

There was no way he could leave that decoder in her hands, not with tensions about to escalate from here to Sunday. Nor could he stand by while Alex put herself in harm's way. She was good, too damn good, with that Enfield and that knife of hers, but she didn't have Nate's combat skills or even Maggie Sinclair's training. Somehow, he had to convince her to trust him enough to see them through the battle that was about to erupt.

Wishing Maggie was here to assist in what he feared would be a dangerous situation, Nate smiled grimly at the thought of her and Alex together. Talk about a combination of brains, beauty, and sheer determination.

When this was all over, Nate promised himself silently as he kneed Red into a gallop, he was going to enjoy watching those two meet.

When this was all over, Maggie promised herself a half hour later, she was never, *never,* going down into anything round and dark and sixty feet deep again.

Flattening her palms against the concrete wall behind her, she stayed as far back as possible from the edge of the narrow catwalk that circled the inside of the silo like a dog collar. Craning her neck, she peered up through the eerie greenish gloom.

Richard had managed to activate one of the auxiliary lights in the silo. It had just enough wattage to illuminate the huge, round, white-painted missile a few feet from Maggie's nose and to show the vague shadow of Richard's boots above her.

The boots were perched on the top rung of the ladder that climbed the height of the silo. An occasional grunt told Maggie the young scientist was still wrestling with the manual levers that were supposed to open the overhead hatch when the pneudraulic systems failed.

"Any luck?" she called into the echoing murkiness. The boots swiveled on the ladder as he bent to peer down at her.

"The hatch cover won't budge."

"Richard, be careful. Don't twist like that. You might— Oh, my God!"

Horrified, Maggie saw one of his boots slip off the rung completely. He jerked upright to clutch at the ladder, causing the other foot to lose its hold, as well. While his hands scrambled for a grip on the slippery metal, his shins whacked against the lower rungs.

Instinctively Maggie grabbed for the rung nearest to her. There were only three feet of space between the concrete wall and the gleaming surface of the missile. If she hung on to the ladder with one hand and braced the other against the missile, she might be able to break Richard's fall with her body.

"I'm...I'm okay," he called out a moment later. "I'm coming down."

Swallowing heavily, Maggie reclaimed her spot on the catwalk. Richard had told her that the narrow steel platform encircling the silo could be raised and lowered to allow maintenance on the missile. At this moment, however, it hovered some forty feet above ground zero, as he had ghoulishly termed it.

She edged sideways to make room for Richard on the metal platform. His face, tinted chartreuse by the light, scrunched up in frustration.

"I simply don't understand why the hatch won't open. The manual systems are completely independent of the pneudraulic lifts."

He slumped back against the concrete wall, making Maggie quiver with the need to grab at him. Those big feet of his could slide off the narrow catwalk just as easily as the ladder.

"Can't you think of something to make it work?" she snapped, her eye on the minuscule distance between his feet and oblivion.

"Why don't *you* think of something?" he shot back. "You got us into this. God, I can't believe I let you talk me into faking a nuclear fuel spill!"

Maggie arched a brow. "As I recall, you didn't need much talking."

"I must have been out of my mind!" He speared a hand through his hair. "That's what happens when the endocrine system fluctuates. The overproduction of bodily fluids, particularly the hormonal serums, can upset the chemical bal—"

"Look, could we finish this discussion some other time? We've got other things to worry about right now besides your hormonal serums."

He leaned his head back against the wall for a moment, expelling a long, slow breath. When he faced Maggie again, his green face was softened by a look of apology.

"I'm sorry, Megan. I shouldn't blame my lapse in judgment on you. I'm not usually swayed by illogic, nor do I normally indulge in irresponsible acts. But you're...well, you must know you're impossible for any man to resist. And when you mentioned this ruse might delay an attack on Karistan, I felt obligated to help."

Maggie wasn't sure whether to be offended, flattered, or amused. Deciding on the latter, she gave him a small grin.

"Maybe you won't think it was so irresponsible or illogical when I tell you that our little ruse worked. We bought enough time for a squadron of Spectre gunships to deploy from Germany."

His face settled into a thoughtful frown.

"I thought I heard you talking while I was up on the ladder," he said slowly. "To receive that kind of information, I must assume you have some kind of a satellite transceiver on your person. A small, but powerful one. With at least twenty gigahertz of power to penetrate this level of concrete density."

"Something like that."

"Then I may also assume you're not a geologist?"

"Not even a rock collector," she admitted.

"Who are you?"

"I can't tell you that. But I can tell you that there's a team on the way to Balminsk to get us out of here." Her grin faded as the realities of a possible hostile extraction filtered through her mind. "I don't suppose you know how to use a .22?"

She reached under her shirt and slipped her Smith and Wesson out of the holster nestled at her waist.

"I know how to use a .22, a .38, a .45, and any caliber rifle you care to name," Richard replied quietly.

At her quick, startled look, he lifted one shoulder. "I'm no stranger to violence. I shot a man when I was six years old. In the kneecap. By luck, more than by aim, but it disabled him enough for me to get away. I made sure luck wouldn't be a factor in my aim after that."

Maggie stared up into his green-tinted face. Richard might have lost the tip of his pinkie when he was kidnapped as a child, but he'd gained a confidence few people would exhibit with the threat of violence staring them in the face. Without a word, she passed him the .22. He checked the magazine with careful expertise, then tucked it into his jacket pocket.

Maggie assembled the arsenal of other weapons supplied by OMEGA, then propped her shoulders against the wall beside Richard. She glanced up at the shrouded tip of the missile, shivering a bit as she thought of the warhead encased in the cone.

"Isn't it ironic that we've got all that explosive power within a few feet of us and we can't use it to blow that hatch?"

Richard followed her line of sight, then looked up at the circular steel silo cover. "I suppose we could," he said slowly. "Blow it, I mean."

"*What?* No, I don't think that's a good idea. Really, Richard, I was just making small talk. You know, the idle chitchat everyone indulges in when they're stuck in a nuclear missile silo."

He pushed his shoulders off the wall and leaned over to peer down into the murky depths. "It could be done," he murmured.

Maggie grabbed his arm and hauled him back. "Richard, listen to me! This is *not* a good idea!"

"Just how much do you know about physics, Megan?"

"I remember exactly two things from high school! One, for every action there's an equal and opposite reaction. Two…" She waved a hand wildly. "I forget the second. Richard, I swear, if you go *near* that warhead I'll…I'll…"

"I have no intention of touching the warhead." He wrapped his hands around her upper arms. "I'm talking about imploding the pneudraulic systems. They're simply mechanisms, really. Quite similar in concept to hydraulics."

"Oh, that helps."

He grinned, his white teeth startling in his green-tinted face. "When gas pressure trapped in the pneudraulic cylinder expands, it forces up the lift, which in turn raises the hatch. The more gas, the greater the force when it expands."

She eyed him suspiciously. "So?"

"So this missile has three stages. Three separate rockets, to launch the warhead into an orbital trajectory."

"So?"

"So each of those stages has a separate motor."

"So *what,* Richard?"

"So the motors require periodic inspection and maintenance. Which is done through their separate hatches. Which lift via pneudraulic canisters. Four per hatch."

He gave her a little shake.

"Don't you get it? The second-stage motor is only about four feet below where we're standing. If you hang on to me while I reach over the edge of the catwalk, I can open the hatch and extract the gas canisters. I'll then insert them into the lifts for the overhead hatch cover. With that extra firepower, we can blow the lid right off this silo."

The absolute certainty in his dark eyes almost convinced

Maggie. She glanced sideways at the white shell of the missile and repressed a shudder.

"Are you sure there won't be any, uh, secondary explosions when the lid goes?"

"Positive. That sucker will shoot straight up in the air. The energy from the canisters will expel upward with it. Trust me."

Maggie groaned. "Oh, Richard! Don't you know those are the last two words a woman wants to hear when a man's trying to talk her into something she knows she shouldn't be doing in the first place!"

Chapter 14

Nate kept Red to a hard, pounding gallop. He was still some miles from the Karistani camp when he caught sight of a dim figure ahead. His jaw hardening, he urged the stallion to even greater speed.

At the sound of drumming hoofbeats behind her, Alex twisted to look over her shoulder. She couldn't fail to identify Red's distinctive silhouette, even in the gathering dusk. Realizing that there was no way her gray could outrun the faster, stronger quarter horse, she pulled her mount around.

Nate was out of the saddle in a swift, surefooted leap, and he grabbed her reins, almost jerking them out of her hands. The startled gelding tried to dance away.

"Let go of my mount!"

"No way, lady. We need to talk."

Her mount skittered sideways, its hooves raising a small cloud of dust.

"We've talked all we're going to! Let go of the reins."

Her angry shout added to the gray's nervousness. Jerking its head back, it reared up against Nate's hold. As Alex fought for balance, her arm swung in a wild arc, the braided whip slicing through the air.

When the *nagaika* descended, Nate raised a forearm. The tail hissed viciously as it whipped around his jacket sleeve. With a twist of his wrist, he caught the stock in his fist and gave it a hard yank.

Tethered by the loop around her wrist, Alex tumbled out of her saddle. With a startled cry, she landed in Nate's arms.

He held her easily, despite her furious struggling, and drew her up on her toes. "Listen to me, Alex. It turns out there wasn't any spill in Balminsk. The borders are open again."

She stopped jerking against his hold. "What? When?"

"An hour ago, maybe less."

She stared up at him, the planes of her face stark in the rising moonlight. Her breath puffed on the cool air in little pants as she fought to take in the implications of his news.

Nate's fingers dug into her arms, unconsciously communicating his own tension. "That means the situation here could get real nasty, real quick."

"Is that why you came after me? To warn me?"

"That's one of the reasons."

"Or because you wanted to secure the decoder?"

"That, too," he told her with brutal honesty. "It's not something you need to be worrying about in the middle of a firefight. Left unsecured, something like that could make matters escalate out of control."

She went utterly still. Shock widened her eyes to huge golden pools. "Escalate? My God, do you think I would allow that to happen? That I would try to…to actually arm the warheads? Even to save Karistan?"

"Of course not, you little idiot. But hasn't it occurred to you that the White Wolf might be after something other than cattle? That he might just want to get his hands on that bit of electronic gadgetry? You may not be planning to hold the world as a nuclear hostage, but he would."

"He couldn't."

The absolute certainty in her voice made Nate's eyes narrow. "Why not?"

She wrenched out of his hold. "Because the device is useless. I disabled it weeks ago."

"Come on, Alex! We're not talking about a TV remote control here. You don't just unscrew it and take out the batteries."

In answer, she dug into her pants pocket, pulled out the small black box and heaved it at him.

"Jesus!"

Nate jumped to catch the device, fumbling it several times, like a football player bobbling a poorly thrown pass. Although his rational mind told him there was no possibility of any disaster occurring if he dropped the thing, his subconscious wasn't taking any chances.

Alex watched his performance with a tight, derisive smile. "For your information, it *is* very similar to a TV remote control. I contacted an acquaintance—actually, the son of an acquaintance—and he told me how to open the casing and remove the transistors."

"I don't believe this! You've been talking about nuclear devices with the son of an acquaintance!"

"Richard's a brilliant young physicist and engineer."

"Richard?" Nate froze, the decoder clutched in both hands.

"Dr. Richard Worthington."

"How do you know him?" He rapped the words, his mind racing with all kinds of wild possibilities.

"Not that it's any of your business, but his mother bought some of my early designs when I was just launching my own line. She invited me to their home—more of a fortress, really—and Richard had dinner with us. When I came back to Karistan, I called him for advice. He arranged to be part of the UN team so he could assess the situation and give me some suggestions regarding the nuclear reduction treaty."

"Why in hell would you trust him, when you don't trust the representatives of the State Department?"

"Maybe because he has some ideas for Karistan's future that don't include growing rice!"

"Christ!" Nate muttered, hefting the black box in his hand. "I can't believe it. You've been bluffing all along. Remind me to stake you in poker against Willie one of these days. You'd clean him out."

She sent him a look of mingled resentment and wariness. "I only need a few more days. Just until Richard gets here."

It was as close as someone with her proud background would come to begging, Nate realized. She still simmered with anger over his deception, still eyed him with wariness and resentment, yet she would put aside her personal feelings in the face of the responsibilities she carried. The tightness around Nate's chest ratcheted up another notch.

Slowly, he held out his hand. As she reached for the small device, his fingers wrapped around hers.

"Even if I wanted to give you those few days, Alex, I can't. I'm not the only one who's called your bluff. The White Wolf has, too. If the reports I got tonight are accurate, you've just run out of time."

Her face paled, and Nate lifted their intertwined hands until hers rested on his breastbone.

"You're not alone in this. Not by a long shot. There's

backup firepower on the way. And until it arrives, I'm going to take a real active role in the camp's defense." His hand tightened around hers. "I want your word you'll do exactly as I say, at least until help arrives."

"I can't just turn over leadership of the host to you! Not now, not when…"

"I'm not asking you to abrogate your responsibilities. I know you wouldn't, in any case. But I've got more experience in what's coming down. Let me do this. Let me help you, Alex."

She tugged at her hand. "Why? Why should you do this? You accomplished your mission. You got what you came for. Why don't you get out of here while you can?"

"Oh, no, Alex. I'm not leaving. And I haven't got everything I came for. Not by a long shot."

He stood a heartbeat away, his face tipped with shadows and his long body radiating a tension that matched hers.

"I didn't realize when I rode onto the steppes that I was looking for you, Alexandra Danilova. I sure as hell didn't know I'd find you. But I was, and I did. And now that I have, I'm not about to lose you."

They rode back to camp at a fast, ground-eating gallop.

Her mind whirling, Alex tried to absorb everything she'd learned, everything she'd felt, in the past few hours. The thought of Americans coming to Karistan's aid sent a rush of relief through her, tinged with the faintest touch of bitterness. Relief that her ragged band of warriors would have assistance in whatever occurred tonight. Bitterness that, once the crisis was over, the gunships would return to their base and Karistan would again face an uncertain future.

Alex didn't pretend to be any kind of an expert in world affairs, but she knew that this tiny country couldn't claim a superpower's attention for very long. There were too many crises all over the world, too many trouble spots erupting into war. U.S. forces were spread thin as it was. She couldn't expect them to stay in Karistan, not without an inducement.

The only inducement for keeping the West's attention on Karistan, the only bargaining chip she'd had, was those missiles and the wild card of the decoder. She'd played that wildcard as long as she could, knowing someone might call her bluff at any moment.

Someone had.

She slanted a quick glance at the man beside her. His face was taut with concentration, his eyes were narrowed on the dark plains ahead. He absorbed the impact of Red's pounding stride with an unconscious coordination.

Alex tried to whip up some of the anger and resentment she'd felt when she left the plateau outside the cave. The sense of betrayal. The conviction that Nate had used her to get to the decoder.

She made a moue of disgust at her own choice of terms. Nate was right. He hadn't used her, any more than she had used him. They'd come together in a shattering explosion of need that had nothing to do with his mission to Karistan and everything to do with the attraction that arced between them. Had arced since the first moment they'd faced each other at either end of her rifle.

Alex had told herself she wanted to draw from his strength, if only for a few hours. Take comfort in his gentleness, if only for an afternoon. But now, with the world about to explode around them, she could admit that a few hours hadn't been enough. Not anywhere near enough.

He'd promised that they'd finish what was between them when this was all over. Alex tucked that promise away in a corner of her heart, knowing that it would give her something to hold on to in the desperate hours ahead.

When they rode into camp, the horses lathered and blowing, she felt a sharp sense of disorientation. The muffled laughter and sounds of singing took her by surprise. It took her a moment to remember that when she left, Anya had been happily rolling out pastries and Ivana had gone to collect honeycombs. So much had happened in the past few hours that the bright, sunny morning filled with the promise of a reprieve seemed a lifetime ago.

"So, cousin," Katerina called out, coming forward. "It is time you returned."

Her dark eyes shifted to Nate and seemed to go flat and hard for a moment. Alex dragged the reins over the gray's head, preparing to inform her cousin this was not the time for jealousies between them, but then the younger woman gave a small, defeated sigh.

"We have meat roasting, and fresh bread," she said, her shoulders sagging. "Come, you must be hungry."

"There's no time to eat," Alex responded. "We have news from the east, and it's not good. Tell Dimitri I must speak with him, if you would, and spread word for the men to gather their weapons. I'll meet with everyone in the square in ten minutes."

She turned to pass the reins to one of the men who'd appeared at her side. For an instant, the enormity of what was about to happen washed over her. Her hand trembled, the leather leads shook.

A strong, steady hand took the reins from her grasp. Giving both Red and the gray into the care of the waiting man, Nate stood before her.

"Remember, you're not alone in this."

She flashed him a quick, uncertain look.

"You'll never be alone again, Alex," he told her quietly, then took her arm and turned her toward the camp. "Let's go talk to Dimitri."

The gray-bearded lieutenant listened without comment as Alex quickly outlined the situation.

"So," she finished, "if the White Wolf leads a force of any size into Karistan, these Spectre gunships with their infrared scopes will detect them and give us warning. If only small bands come, from different directions, as they have done in the past, they'll be more difficult to detect. Then we must rely, as we have before, on our sentries to signal the alert and our men to hold the camp until Nate calls in the air cover."

"We can hold them off until the gunship arrives, *ataman*." Although Dimitri spoke to Alex, his eyes were on the man standing at her shoulder.

With a wry smile, Alex translated his words for Nate. Since the moment the aged lieutenant had joined them, she'd felt the subtle shift of power from her to Nate. Not so much a lessening of her authority as a recognition that another shared it. Dimitri knew these gunships would come because of the man beside her. He understood that the *Amerikanski* could control and direct their firepower. Whether she wanted to or not, she now shared the burden that had been given her.

As the two men bent over the sketches Alex had drawn of the camp's defenses, Katerina stepped out of the shadows.

"What if we do not fight with the men of Balminsk?"

"What are you saying?" Alex asked sharply.

"What if we give them that which they seek? What if we end this ceaseless feud?"

"You would have me just hand over our cattle? Our grazing lands?"

"We…the women…we don't wish to see more bloodshed. We want none of this, 'Zandra."

"It's only this night, Katerina. Just this night. You'll be safe. You'll go to the ice caves, with the other women, until it's over."

She shook her head. "It is already over. We don't wish to live like this anymore. We take the children and we leave in the morning for the lowlands."

Alex felt Nate's presence behind her.

"Do we have a problem?"

Slowly, her heart aching, Alex translated for him.

For Alex, the few hours were a blur of tension and terror, relief and regret.

Nate organized the men. Petr Borodín, who had won renown and a chestful of medals for his activities as a saboteur during World War II, took fiendish delight in helping Nate plant what he called perimeter defenses.

Dimitri sent men with flares and weapons to guard the cattle, while others saddled the horses and tied their reins in strings of six, as had the Cossacks of old, to make it easier to lead them through battle if necessary.

Mikhail and a heavily armed squad shepherded the women and children to the protection of the ice cave…all except Katerina, who refused to leave. She would stay, she insisted, because she was of Karistan. For this night, at least.

Alex herself oversaw the distribution of the pitiful supply of arms and ammunition. A few grenade launchers her grandfather had bartered with the Chinese for. A Pakistani shoulder-held rocket launcher, still in its protective Cosmoline coating. The miscellaneous collection of rifles.

She told herself that the gunships hovering somewhere

far overhead would make the difference. That their firepower was swifter, surer, more devastating. The thought gave her little comfort.

When the first, distant *whump-whump-whump* came out of the sky, Alex thought the attack had come. Desperate determination and an icy calm overlaid the churning fear in her stomach. Following Nate's terse order, she took a defensive position on a low, rolling hill at the rear of the camp, just above the stream. Katerina crouched beside her, unspeaking, a pistol in her hand and a flat, unreadable expression on her face.

A dark-painted helicopter skimmed out of the darkness from the east. Its searchlights swept the camp like flashlights swung from a giant hand. They illuminated a lone figure standing in the middle of the square. His rifle to his shoulder, old Gregor squinted along the barrel at the hovering aircraft.

''No!'' Nate raced out of the darkness, into the undulating circle of light. ''No! It has UN markings!''

Although Gregor didn't understand the words, Nate's urgency communicated itself, and he lowered the rifle. They stood together while the hovering helicopter settled in the dusty square.

When Richard clambered out, his eyes wide and his body jackknifed to avoid the whirling rotor blades, Alex recognized him at once. But she didn't recognize the long-legged brunette who jumped out behind him and was promptly swept against Nate's side in a bone-crushing squeeze. The woman whipped off her glasses and waved them in the air as she and Nate ducked away from the rotor blades, talking urgently.

As she strode across the square, Alex caught snatches of the woman's comments. ''Blew the hatch…small explosion, nothing to worry about… Right behind us, about fifty strong. Heading right for the camp… This is no cattle raid, Cowboy. I'm going back up in the helo. Richard and I devised a few small surprises that might delay them a little.''

Nate whirled at Alex's approach. ''There's no time for long introductions, sweetheart. Things are moving too fast. But you know Worthington.''

Alex sent the young scientist a quick smile. ''Hello, Richard.''

''Hello, Sandra. Sorry it took me so long to get here. We had…uh, an unexpected delay.''

The tall, confident brunette in lumberjack's clothing stepped forward. ''I'm Nate's partner. I've been hoping to meet you.'' Her generous mouth quirked. ''You wouldn't know it to look at me right now, but I'm a great admirer of your work. Look, I've got to get back in the air, but maybe when this is all over, we can talk.''

As drawn by the woman's vitality and confidence as she was unsettled by the easy camaraderie between her and Nate, Alex nodded. ''When this is all over, we'll definitely talk.''

The brunette flashed Nate a cheeky grin and a thumbs-up, then headed for the helicopter. ''Come on, Richard. Let's get this hummer up and see if those little canisters work as well from the air as they did from the bottom of a silo.''

The helo lifted off in a wash of swirling air and whining engines. Her stomach twisting, Alex turned to Nate.

''Tell me what we face.''

In brief, succinct phrases, Nate related the bald facts. Small, separate groups had slipped out of Balminsk, avoiding surveillance. They'd converged some twenty miles from the camp. Were heading this way. The gunships were in the air, closing fast.

"It's going to be tight, but we should be able to keep the attackers occupied until the real firepower arrives."

"Nate—"

Whatever she would have said was lost in the sudden, distant boom of an explosion.

Nate whipped around, his eyes searching the impenetrable darkness. When he turned back, his eyes held a wry smile.

"That was one of Petr's booby traps. A satchel charge. It'll cause more confusion than damage, but at this point, confusion will work for us as well as anything. Get Katerina, Alex, and take cover. This could be an interestin' half hour."

Ever afterward, Alex would remember the events of the next few moments as a blur of confusion, shouts, and sudden, gripping fear.

She was halfway across the square when another explosion sounded, then another. She whirled, watching Nate freeze beside Dimitri as they strained to peer through the darkness beyond the barricades. And Petr, his bald head shining in the moonlight as he held a rifle tucked in his armpit.

Oh, God, she would remember thinking. Has it come down to this? Have all her grandfather's hopes for Karistan, all her own plans, come down to this last, desperate hour?

Another explosion. And then the sound of drumming hooves.

Alex raced across the square to Katerina, her stomach twisting at the blank emptiness on the girl's face as she calmly, mechanically, loaded a magazine clip into an automatic rifle. No fear. No terror. She'd done this before.

Many times. She was so young, yet she'd seen so much death. And was about to see more.

As she closed the distance to her cousin, Alex thought of her father. Of the way Daniel Jordan had stood by his principles in the face of the hawk-eyed chieftain's vitriolic scorn. He'd insisted guns weren't the answer for Karistan, but he'd had no other.

Once again, the forces that had pulled at Alex for so many years ripped at her soul. Who was right? *What* was right?

Pulling Katerina behind the shelter of an overturned van, Alex slid a hand in her pocket and gripped the silver bridle bit in a tight, hard fist. Her knuckles nudged the small black box.

When Katerina turned her head and met her cousin's eyes, Alex's disparate worlds seemed to rush toward each other like two comets hurtling through the heavens.

When Nate shouted a warning and Alex slewed around to see him standing tall and commanding, in charge of a battle he had no stake in, no responsibility for, her separate worlds collided.

And when a lone rider hurtled out of the darkness and soared over the barricades a few heart-stopping moments later, she knew what she had to do.

"Hold your fire!"

Her command rang through the camp, echoing Nate's.

For a few moments, no one moved. They were all caught up in the drama of watching the rider yank his mount's head around and bring it to a dancing, skidding, shuddering stop.

When the uniformed man dismounted, the scar on his face stood out in the moonlight, as did the cold expression on his face. He searched the shadows, then fastened his gaze on Nate.

"I am Cherkoff. I have ordered the men of Balminsk to hold outside the mine field you have planted while I come to speak with you."

Nate walked out into the center of the square. Slowly, deliberately, he measured the stiff figure.

"No," Nate replied, "you come to speak with the *ataman*."

Alex heard the soft response as she came up behind Nate, Katerina at her side. The splinter of private joy his words gave her helped shatter the tight knot of pain at what she was about to do.

"The *ataman* is here," she replied.

Cherkoff turned to face her, his dark eyes piercing, his shoulders rigid in his brown uniform with red tabs at the shoulder denoting his rank.

"You have something my father wishes to possess."

"No, I have not."

A muscle twitched at the side of his jaw. "You don't understand the depths of my father's hatred."

Alex swallowed. She understood it. Her grandfather had passed her the same hatred.

"Why have you come?" she asked him. "And wearing that uniform?"

"I wear it," the major said slowly, as though each word were dragged from his heart, "because it is a symbol of what was before."

His hand lifted to the leather strap that crossed one shoulder, holding his service holster and pistol. His fingers brushed a gleaming buckle.

As Alex watched, her breath suspended, he lifted the strap's end, undid the buckle and removed the holster. Opening his fist, he let the weapon fall to the ground.

"It's time to put this past behind us. I would speak with

you about the future, and about this device you hold that
so incites my father's fury.''

Katerina stepped forward. ''I have the device which you
seek. You will speak with me.''

Chapter 15

"All right, let's get down to some serious negotiations here."

Maggie pushed the black glasses up the bridge of her nose and shrugged off the weariness of a long night and frantic morning. Folding her arms on the scarred surface of the table, she waited while the two officials who'd been standing by in Germany ever since the crisis over the decoder first surfaced took their seats. They'd arrived just moments ago, aboard the transport that would take Maggie and Nate back to the States. Before that plane lifted off, the parties gathered in the dim, shadowy tent needed to reach agreement.

The State Department representative, a big, burly man in a crumpled navy suit and white shirt, looked Maggie up and down.

"Just who are you?" he asked coolly. "And what authority do you have to participate in these negotiations?"

"She's Dr. Megan St. Clare," Alex supplied from her

seat next to Maggie's, her tone several degrees colder than
the official's. "She's here at my request, and that of my
cousin, Katerina Terenshkova. As is our technical advisor,
Dr. Richard Worthington."

A thin, well-dressed woman in her mid-forties seated
beside the State Department official peered across the table. "Richard Worthington? From MIT?"

"Well, I, uh, consult with several institutes."

The woman, a midlevel bureaucrat with the Nuclear
Regulatory Agency, frowned. "This is highly irregular,
you know. Negotiations like this are quite sensitive. We
don't generally allow outsiders to participate."

"You are in Karistan," Alex reminded her with a lift
of one brow. "You're the outsider here. My cousin and I
will decide who does and does not participate."

The woman blinked, then sat back. "Yes. Of course."

The burly State Department rep, who looked as though
he'd be more at home roaming the back streets of D.C.
than the corridors of the granite federal building in Foggy
Bottom, frowned.

"Before we begin, I understand you have a certain device which we'll take possession of."

Alex turned to Katerina, who dug into the pockets of
her skirts. She pulled out the decoder and dropped it on
the table with a loud clatter.

The officials winced.

"Here, take it," Maggie urged, pushing the thing across
the table with a cautious finger. Since her hours in that
dark silo with Richard, she didn't want anything associated
with nuclear matters within her sight. Ever again.

She picked up the papers torn from Alex's sketch pad,
which were now filled with the figures they'd hurriedly
put together in the small hours of the night.

"All right, here's the bottom line. We estimate that the

total cost to dismantle all nuclear weapons in Balminsk and Karistan at approximately three billion dollars."

"What?"

"That includes a system to verify the warheads' destruction, and compensation for the enriched uranium that will be extracted."

"Now see here, Dr. St. Clare..."

"It also includes approximately ten million dollars," Maggie interjected ruthlessly, "to establish a science and technology center here. The center will bring in outside expertise—researchers, technicians, and their support staffs."

"Perhaps a hundred men or more," Katerina murmured, her eyes gleaming. "My aunts will be most pleased."

A wave of red crept up the State Department rep's bulllike neck. "This is absurd."

Richard cleared his throat. "Uh, no, actually, it's not. This is exactly half what the United States offered the Ukraine less than a year ago as inducement to sign the Strategic Arms Reduction Treaty. The Ukraine had fewer missiles, as I'm sure you're aware, giving the Karistanis the advantage of 6.4 times the throw weight."

The woman across from Maggie jerked her head up. "Dr. Worthington! We don't negotiate treaties dollar for dollar based on throw weight. It's highly irregular!"

"There is more," Katerina added. "The major, he has the thoughts about con...con..."

"Conventional arms," Nikolas supplied, coming forward out of the shadows at the back of the tent to stand behind Katerina's chair.

She sent him a slow, provocative smile over one shoulder. *"Da!* Nikolas will talk with you about such conventional arms, so we may protect our borders when the missiles are gone."

"Now wait just a minute…"

The blustering official faltered as Nikolas Cherkoff placed his hands on Katerina's shoulders and leaned into the light. His scar livid against his cheek, he bared his teeth in a smile.

"No. No more waiting. We have waited long enough for peace in this land. We will proceed."

Several hours later, Maggie stepped out of the black tent and wiped an arm across her forehead. "Whew! That was almost as nerve-racking as being trapped in a hole with Richard."

"I can imagine," Alex replied, her eyes on the two stiff-backed bureaucrats who were stalking toward the aircraft that squatted like a camouflaged quail on a flat stretch of plain just outside camp.

A ripple of sound inside the tent caught Maggie's attention. The young scientist gave an indignant sputter, Katerina a teasing laugh. For a crazy moment last night, when she first saw Richard approached by a young woman with a cloud of dark, curling hair, a sultry smile and a chest that drew his eyes like a magnet, Maggie thought—hoped!—that Katerina might go to work on Richard's endocrine system. But either the physicist's hormonal serums went out of whack only with older women, or Katerina wasn't interested in awkward young scientists. After a brief greeting to Richard, she'd never taken her eyes, or her hands, off Nikolas Cherkoff, and the young scientist had stuck to Maggie like gum on the bottom of a shoe.

Maggie sighed, deciding she'd just have to take Richard in hand when they got back to the States and introduce him to more older women.

Why did her life seem to grow more complicated after each mission? If she wasn't collecting German shepherd-size blue-and-orange-striped iguanas, she was taking charge of organizing a brilliant physicist's love life.

Hearing Cherkoff's quiet voice, Maggie turned to Alex. "Do you think your cousin and the major will keep the peace between Balminsk and Karistan?"

"They will, if Katerina has anything to say about it, and my cousin is a most...persuasive woman." She paused, and gave Maggie a tired smile. "I don't know how to thank you for your help last night. And this morning. I thought I drove a pretty hard bargain with my suppliers when I negotiated for materials, but you made me realize I'm still in the minor leagues." Her smile became a little forced. "Nate told me you were good. One of the best, he said, although he failed to specify at what."

Maggie caught the faint, almost imperceptible hint of acid in her voice, and decided to ignore it. Until Nate and Alex worked out whatever had driven him away this morning, she wasn't going to get in the middle.

"No thanks are necessary," she said with a grin. "Unless..."

"Yes?"

"Unless you might have a dress or two in your tent that would fit me. One of your own designs, maybe, that I could purchase at a reasonable price."

Alex gave her a quick once-over. They were about the same height, although Maggie carried a few more inches on her curving frame than Alex did.

"I think I might just have something."

"You wonderful person!"

"In cashmere."

Maggie groaned with pleasure.

Alex's eyes sparkled in response. "Dyed a shade of burnt orange that will pick up the glossy highlights in your hair and always remind you of the steppes at sunset."

Maggie tugged off her glasses and tucked them into the pocket of her plaid shirt, staring at this Alex. No wonder Cowboy had disappeared to lick his wounds this morning. If he was hit as hard as Maggie suspected he was, it was going to tear him in two to leave this vibrant, glowing woman behind.

"Thanks, Alexandra. I'll admit I wasn't looking forward to flying back to the States and facing my boss for a mission debrief wearing this outfit. It's going to be tough enough without feeling like I just crawled out of…of a silo."

At the mention of flying, the smile faded from Alex's eyes. She lifted a hand and toyed absently with one of the small tassels decorating the yoke of her swirling fitted greatcoat.

"You're leaving this morning?"

"In a couple of hours. Richard wants time to inspect the missiles on Karistan's soil before we leave."

"Is Nate going with you?"

Maggie gave her a level look. "Yes. And Three Bars Red, evidently. Nate asked me to have the pilot rig a stall for him. He said that you weren't satisfied with the stud's, er…performance."

Maggie had to bite her lip to hold back a grin. The memory of Nate's choked voice when he'd told her just which stud Alexandra had decided to accept on behalf of Karistan was one she'd always treasure.

"It's not his performance that's the problem," Alex replied in a tight, small voice, then gave herself a little shake.

"Red's already covered half the mares in Karistan," she continued. "We just can't seem to keep him in the pastures and out of the tents. Not if he gets a whiff of anything sweet. He destroyed my aunt Feodora's latest *pysanky*—Easter egg—when he..."

Alex broke off at the sound of muffled thunder from outside the camp. Frowning, she glanced over her shoulder. The thunder rolled closer, then separated into the pounding tattoo of hooves drumming against the earth.

It happened so quickly, Alex had no time to react. One moment she was standing in the open square beside Maggie, staring at the barricades still ringing the camp. The next, Red came soaring over the low wall, ears flat, nose stretched out, legs tucked. He landed with a fluid grace and flowed into a smooth gallop.

Nate was bent low over the stallion's neck, his eyes on Alex, one hand gripping the reins.

In the same instant Alex realized what he intended, she knew she couldn't stop him. Instinctively, she stumbled backward, without any real hope of getting away.

Nate leaned lower, his arm outstretched. It wrapped around Alex's waist with the force of a freight train and swept her up as Red thundered by. Her thick coat padded most of the impact, but her bottom thumped against a hard leg, then a hip, before he dragged her across his thighs.

She grabbed at his jacket and wiggled frantically to find purchase.

"Are you crazy?" she shouted, gasping for breath. "What is this?"

"Just a little circus trick I picked up from Peter the Great. Hang on, sweetheart."

Alex did, with both hands, as Red slewed to one side and then the other, weaving through the tents with the agility of a world-class cutting horse. He cleared the barricade at the opposite end of the camp with the same flying ease.

Her hair whipping her eyes, Alex caught a glimpse of

Petr's startled face behind them. And Dimitri's grinning one. She heard a distant shout, a surprised oath, and then nothing but the sound of Red's steady gait and the wind rushing in her ears.

Nate didn't slow, didn't stop to let her find a more secure seat. Holding her against his chest with one iron-hard arm, he took Red across the steppes.

When at last he drew rein beside a low outcropping of rock, Alex had regained some of her breath and most of her equilibrium. Still, she was forced to cling to him with both hands as he kicked a boot out of the stirrup, swung his leg over the saddle horn and slid off Red with her still banded to his body.

She shoved at his shoulders with both hands, leaning back to look up at his face.

"Were you just trying to impress me with a last demonstration of your horsemanship?" she panted. "Or is there a point to this little circus trick?"

"Oh, there's a point. Which we'll get to in a few moments. After we straighten out a couple of things between us."

Alex wasn't sure she cared for the hint of steel under his easy tone. It was as hard and unyielding as the arms that held her.

"First," he said, "you want to tell me just what Katerina was doing with that decoder? I just about blew it when she pulled it out last night."

"I gave it to her."

His eyes narrowed. "Why, Alex?"

"I closed my ears to what the women were trying to tell me," Alex admitted, still breathless and shaky. "When I saw you caught in the middle of the feud that my grandfather had helped perpetuate for so long, I realized I was trying to hold Karistan to his vision, instead of shaping it to theirs.''

''I'd say you did some pretty fair shaping this afternoon. I just talked to two very uptight bureaucrats at the plane.''

She managed a smile. ''With Maggie's help. I still can't quite believe I haggled over nuclear warheads like a horse trader bringing a new string to the bazaar.''

The knowledge that she'd just bought Karistan a future went a long way toward easing the ache in Alex's heart. Not all the way, but a long way.

''What's the second thing?'' she asked, staring up at Nate's lean, sun-weathered face. Alex knew that the little pattern of white lines at the sides of his eyes would stay in her memory forever. And the gold-tipped sweep of the lashes that screened those gray-brown eyes. And the small half smile that lifted one corner of his lips. ''What else do we have to get straight between us?''

''I love you, Alex. With a love that doesn't know any borders, or states, or cultures. I want to bind your life to mine, but not your soul. That has to stay free. That's what makes you unique. And wild and proud and too damn stubborn for your own good. It's also what makes you the woman I can't live without. I figure I've got about two hours until I have to go back to the States to wrap up some loose ends, but then I'll be back. And when I come back, I'm staying. We're going to do some serious flyin' across the steppes, my darlin'. For the rest of our lives.''

She didn't move, didn't speak, for long, endless moments. ''You'd live here, with me?''

''I'd live in the back of a pickup with you, Alexandra Danilova. Or in North Philly, or Wolf Creek, or Parsnippety, New Jersey. I never needed an anchor in this world until I met you. Now you are my anchor.''

Alex felt her separate halves shimmer, then splinter into

a hundred smaller and smaller pieces, until the different worlds that had pulled at her for so long disappeared in a shower of dust. With a feeling of coming home, she slid her arms around Nate's neck.

"The decoder wasn't all I gave Katerina," she whispered. "I also passed her the silver bridle bit, the one the czar presented to my ancestor. The one my grandfather gave to me."

It was Nate's turn to go still. He stared down at her, his skin drawing tight across his cheeks as he waited for her to continue. This had to come from her, he knew. As much as he wanted to pull it out, or force it out, or kiss her until she breathed it out between gasps of raw passion, he knew it could only come from her.

"Katerina's stronger than she thought she was," Alex said softly. "She has the strength of the steppes in her, and the wisdom of our people's women. She's of my grandfather's blood. She should be *ataman* of this host."

"And you, Alex? What do you want to be?"

Her eyelids fluttered for a moment. Nate could count each black, sooty lash, see each small blue vein. Then the lids lifted, and her glorious, golden eyes called him home.

"I want to be your anchor, Nate."

Alex thought he'd kiss her then. Her heart thudded painfully against her breastbone with anticipation. Her breath seemed to slow, until she forgot to draw in any at all.

Instead, his lips curved in one of those lazy, crooked grins that set her pulse tripping and sent a liquid heat to her belly.

"Which brings us to the point of my little circus act, as you called it."

Tugging her arms from around his neck, he set her to one side. Dazed, Alex watched as he untied a rolled bundle from behind the saddle. He walked a few steps into the high grass, then knelt on one knee.

Alex raised a hand to shove her hair back. "What are you doing?"

Even as she asked the question, she knew the answer. Desire, hot and sweet and instantaneous, flooded through her.

"I'm making us a bed," he replied, confirming her hopes.

She swept the open, windswept plain and endless blue sky with a quick glance. "Here?"

"Here. Katerina told me that when a woman of the steppes chooses a man to take to her bed, she'd best be sure the bed is movable, because it's a sure bet the man will be. I figured it works both ways."

"Kat—Katerina told you that?"

The leather laces gave, and a thick, shaggy wolf pelt gleaming with silvery lights rolled out onto the thick grass.

"Uh-huh. Right after she reminded me that the Cossacks of old didn't take a whole lot of time for courting. They just swooped down and carried their brides off."

Tucking the knife back in his pocket, he spread one of the feather-soft mohair blankets that kept the Karistanis warm, even in the bitterest of winters, on top of the wolf pelt. That done, he squatted on one heel and grinned up at her.

"Come here, Alex. Come, shed your clothes and your worries and your inhibitions, and fly across the steppes with me."

She took a half step, then hesitated.

"Still have some doubts?" he asked with a little twist of pain at the crease that etched a line between her eyes. "Some worries?"

"One," she murmured, taking a slow step toward him.

"Tell me. Share it with me."

Her fingers touched his, then slid across his palm and folded around it.

"I'm just hoping you don't have any chewing gum in your pockets. I don't want Red nosing under the blanket at…an inopportune moment, to get at it."

Laughing, Nate tumbled her to the blanket.

If Alex had thought this joining of their bodies and their hearts would be a gentle one now that they'd torn down the barriers between them, she soon realized her mistake.

It started easily enough. His hands worked the buttons on her coat with lazy thoroughness, while his mouth played with her, touching, tasting, rediscovering. Her fingers worked their way inside his jacket, planing across the wide spread of his chest. With each outer layer shed, however, their legs tangled more intimately. With each touch, their bodies caused more friction.

By the time Nate tore the last button loose on her tunic and yanked it open, his breath was a river of heat against her skin.

By the time Alex fumbled open the snap on his jeans and pushed them down over his lean hips, her fingers trembled with the need to feel the warmth of his flesh.

Nate crushed her into the mohair, his body hard and urgent against hers. Alex opened for him her arms, her mouth, her legs.

They twisted together, straining against each other, aching with want and with need. Nate buried both hands in her hair, anchoring her head while his mouth slanted across hers.

Alex arched under him, grinding her pelvis into his until at last frustration and need made her twist her hips and thrust him off.

Panting, she propped herself up on one elbow. "The

women of Karistan have a saying about a situation like this.''

''Oh, no, Alex…'' he groaned, flopping back on the blanket. ''Not another one. Not now.''

''Oh, yes, another one.'' She slid a leg across his belly, then pushed herself up. Planting both palms against his chest, she straddled his flanks.

''Once a woman decides where it is she goes, she must simply mount and follow the sun across the steppes until she gets there.''

Steadying herself against his chest, Alex lifted her hips and mounted.

Later, much later, when Alex had followed the sun until it exploded in a million shards of light and Nate had flown across the steppes twice, they lay wrapped in a cocoon of mohair and body heat, cooling sweat and warming sun.

Pressed against the shaggy pelt by Nate's inert body, Alex slid one foot along the blanket to ease the ache in one hip joint from her splayed position. Her toes slipped off the edge of the blanket and into the rough grass. She smiled, remembering another rocky bower under another open sky.

''Nate?'' she murmured against his ear.

''Mmm?''

''I love you. I'll live with you in the back of that pickup, if you want, or in Parsnippety or Wolf Creek or wherever. But do you suppose we might invest in a bed, or at least a real mattress? And make love on something other than the hard ground once in a while?''

He lifted his head, and Alex's heart contracted at the wicked gleam in his eyes.

''If we're going to do as much flying across the steppes

as I think we are, sweetheart, we'll invest in a whole houseful of beds. One for each room.''

He brushed a kiss across the tip of her nose. ''One for the attic.''

Another kiss feathered along her cheek. ''One for the back porch.''

Alex gasped as he withdrew a bit and bent to reach her lips. ''One for the...''

''Never mind,'' she breathed, arching her hips to draw him back into her depths. ''This wolf pelt seems to be working just fine.''

Chapter 16

The hazy September sun added a golden glow to the smog hovering above Washington's noontime streets. In offices on both sides of the Potomac, senior-level officials and lobbyists just back from their power lunches shed their tailored jackets and settled down to return their stacks of phone messages before starting their afternoon round of meetings. It was a well-established routine, one respected and adhered to by most denizens of the capital.

In one particular office on a quiet side street just off Massachusetts Avenue, however, the routine had been disrupted. OMEGA's director had called an immediate meeting with two of his operatives.

While she waited for Adam Ridgeway to finish with a phone call, Maggie perched on a corner of his receptionist's desk, swinging a foot encased in one of Alexandra Jordan's supple, cream-colored calf-high boots. The boot, with its decorated tassels edging the top, just skimmed the hem of her flowing umber skirt. A matching tunic in the same burnt orange draped her from shoulder to hip, and was banded at the wrist and neck with wide strips of corded piping in cream and gold. Maggie rubbed her hands up and down her arms, luxuriating in the sinful feel of the finest, softest cashmere against her skin.

She'd used the transport's tiny bathroom to wash both her eyebrows and her hair in a shallow stainless-steel sink. The shoulder-length brown mass now hung shiny and clean in its usual smooth sweep, and her brows were restored to their natural lines.

But Adam's receptionist, Elizabeth Wells, nibbled on her lower lip delicately as she stared at the kidney-shaped blemish on Maggie's jaw.

"Are you sure it will fade, dear?"

"The guys in Field Dress say it will," Maggie replied, a little doubtfully. Her faith in the wizards of the wardrobe was severely shaken. The formula that was supposed to dissolve the ink they'd injected under her skin had only dimmed it to a purplish hue.

Forgetting the blemish in view of more pressing concerns, she swung her foot. "Are you sure Adam said he wanted to see us as soon as we arrived at the headquarters? Usually he talks to us after the debrief."

Kind, matronly Elizabeth sent her a sympathetic look. "He took a call from the president just moments before you and Nate landed. The notes he gave me to transcribe from that conversation include some rather inflammatory remarks from the director of the Nuclear Regulatory Agency. And a highly agitated senior official from the State Department is on the line right now."

"Oh."

Sprawled with his customary loose-limbed ease in an antique chair set beside Elizabeth's desk, Nate grinned.

"Maggie, sweetheart, this next half hour might be one

of those scenes Willie says looks a whole lot better when you're peering at it through the rearview mirror instead of the windshield.''

Maggie laughed and tucked the sweep of her hair behind one ear. "I just hope it's only a half hour. Neither one of us has slept in the last thirty-six. What's more, we just shared a twenty-four-hour plane ride with a horse. I need a bath and some sleep, preferably at the same time.''

When Elizabeth's intercom buzzed a moment later, she lifted the receiver, listened a moment, then nodded.

"Go on in, dear. You too, Nate.''

Maggie edged off the desk and smoothed her hands over her hips. The soft cashmere settled around her in elegant, body-hugging lines. She might not have had recourse to her perfumed body lotion to counter the effects of Red's companionship, but at least she looked better than she smelled. A *lot* better.

When Maggie walked into the director's office a few steps ahead of Nate, Adam felt his shoulders stiffen under the wool of his tailored navy wool blazer. With considerable effort, he refrained from reaching up to tug at the Windsor knot in his crimson-and-gray-striped Harvard tie. He stood quietly behind his desk, absorbing Maggie's vivid impact.

Sunlight streaming through the tall windows behind him highlighted the golden glints in her chestnut hair and picked up the sparkle in her wide brown eyes. It also illuminated every one of the soft peaks and valleys of her body, displayed with stunning, sensual detail in a sweater dress that caused Adam's fingers to curl around the edge of his mahogany desk.

He returned the two agents' greetings calmly enough, and waited until they were seated in the wingback chairs in front of his desk before taking his seat.

"I realize that it's somewhat unusual to call you in before the debrief in the control center," he began. "But there are certain matters that need clarification immediately."

Opening a manila folder centered on his desk, he pulled out a hand-scribbled note. "Before the president calls the rather substantial campaign contributor who offered Three Bars Red to Karistan in the first place, he'd like to know why Alexandra Jordan turned the stud down. Was his performance unsatisfactory?"

Maggie folded her hands in her lap and waited gleefully for Nate's response. She hadn't had the nerve to mention "performance" matters in front of Cowboy during the trip back, not with Alexandra Jordan curled in his lap for most of the way.

Nate gave Adam one of his easy grins and sidestepped the issue.

"Let's just say Karistan has more pressing matters to attend to right now than horse-breeding."

"So I understand," Adam responded, turning to Maggie. "One of which is establishing a science and technology institute at the cost of…"

Maggie swallowed a groan as he extracted a sheet filled with rows of neatly typed figures.

"…of eight million dollars. A price, I'm informed, that was negotiated by a certain Dr. St. Clare."

She gave a small shrug. "Well, we were asking for ten million."

"I suppose you have a good reason for entering into negotiations on behalf of a foreign government…against your own."

Maggie hesitated, then leaned forward, trying to articulate the feeling that had crept over her with chilling intensity during her hours in that silo.

"If a future graduate of that institute finds a way to make nuclear power obsolete, the world will be a safer place for everyone. Eight million dollars will be a small price to pay. That stuff's scary, Adam. Especially when you're locked down in a hole with it."

"I see. Perhaps that explains why you decided to blow the silo hatch, causing a wave of unsubstantiated reports of a nuclear explosion to ripple across the globe?"

Maggie sat back, nodding. "Yes, that explains it. That and the fact that Cowboy needed me."

"Our forces were pretty thin in Karistan, Adam. We were real relieved when Maggie and Richard Worthington showed up."

Instead of placating OMEGA's director, Nate's quiet contribution caused an unexpected reaction. Maggie held her breath as Adam's blue eyes frosted over until they were positively glacial.

"Yes, let's discuss Dr. Richard Worthington."

He slid the typed list inside the folder and pulled out a faxed copy of a memo. "This is an interagency request for the permanent assignment of a geologist to Dr. Worthington's team. At his own insistence, he's been assigned as the chief inspector for the START treaty provisions. He will be traveling extensively all over the world for the next few years, inspecting silos."

Maggie shuddered at the thought of Richard—sweet, clumsy Richard—climbing down into an endless series of silos.

"This request has the highest national priority," Adam added. "Since the geologist in question is one Megan St. Clare, the president has asked me to favorably consider it."

"I was expecting this," Maggie muttered.

"You were?"

"Yes. It has something to do with endo—" She glanced at Adam's rigid face and waved a hand. "Never mind."

"I need an answer for the president," he reminded her.

"Look, Adam, when you turn this request down would you include a suggested alternate name? I know a geologist who's worked with my father. She's superbly qualified. A widow with no children, so she'll be able to travel. And she's just a couple years older than I am," Maggie finished, with a private, satisfied grin.

"You're assuming I'm going to turn down a personal request from the president?"

Maggie met Adam's eyes across the acre of polished mahogany that served as his desk. What she saw in them caused a tight curl of pleasure.

"No," she replied softly, the smile in her eyes for Adam alone. "I'm not assuming that you'll turn it down. I know you will."

Nate glanced from one to the other. Then his lazy drawl broke the silence. "If that's all, Adam, I need to go upstairs and get with Doc before the debrief. He's got some questions for me."

Adam stood and tucked the ends of his tie inside his blazer. "That's all I needed you for, but you don't have to rush your session with Doc. He's planning to stand by after the debrief for an extended session with you and Maggie."

Nate shook his head as he pushed himself to his feet. "Can't do it. I've got to make this debrief as quick as possible. I'm on borrowed time here, folks."

He hooked his thumbs in his belt, grinning. "Alexandra's picking Willie up at the airport in two hours, and then they're going to put their heads together. About wedding clothes. Unless I want to find myself walking down the aisle in Willie's unique concept of formal wear, all decorated with Alex's thingamabobs, I'd better go protect my interests.''

''Since I'm going to be giving you away, ask her to design something for me,'' Maggie begged.

Nate's blond brows lifted. ''*You're* giving *me* away?''

''I am. Alex says it's a custom among the Karistanis. The women of her host have a saying, something about only a woman being able to make sure the man is where he is supposed to be when.''

''I might have known,'' Nate groaned.

''Oh, by the way,'' she added, sailing toward the door, ''one of my responsibilities in this role is to call out a list of your positive and negative character traits, so the bride can decide whether she'll accept you or not. I've already made up the lists, Nate. One of them is *really* long.''

She almost made it out the door on the wake of Nate's laughter.

''Just a moment, Maggie. I'm not quite finished with you.'' Adam nodded to Nate as he walked around the corner of the desk. ''We'll join you upstairs for the debrief in a few moments.''

Nate gave her an encouraging wink and left.

Maggie ascribed the sudden weakening in her knees to the fact that she'd been without sleep for the last thirty-six hours. It had nothing to do with her body's reaction to the controlled grace of Adam's movements or the over-whelming impact of his nearness. Or to the way his eyes seemed to survey every square centimeter of her face before he spoke in that cool Boston Brahmin voice of his.

''You will never…*never*…again attempt to blow any-thing up when you're locked inside it. Do I make myself clear, Chameleon?''

Since he was standing two heartbeats away and Maggie drew in the spicy lemon-lime scent of his aftershave with every breath, it would've been hard for him to be any clearer.

Still, she wasn't about to let Adam know quite the impact he was having on her hormonal serums. Keeping her voice cool and her eyes steady, she returned a small smile.

"Loud and clear, Chief."

For a moment, she thought he was actually going to admit that he was furious.

Fascinated, Maggie watched a tiny muscle at the side of his jaw twitch. To her profound disappointment, the twitch subsided.

"Good," he said quietly.

Well, maybe next time, she thought.

Summoning up a cheeky grin, she tipped him her version of a military salute, the one that always brought a pained look to his aristocratic features.

"By the way," she tossed over her shoulder as she headed for the door, "remind me to tell you about the interesting uses the women of Karistan have for yak oil sometime."

*   *   *   *   *

PERFECT DOUBLE

Merline Lovelace

THE ULTIMATE COLLECTION

First Published 1996
Second Australian Paperback Edition 2005
ISBN 0 733 55761 9

Published by
Harlequin Mills & Boon
3 Gibbes Street
CHATSWOOD NSW 2067
AUSTRALIA

HARLEQUIN MILLS & BOON and the Rose Device are trademarks used
under license and registered in Australia, New Zealand, Philippines, United
States Patent & Trademark Office and in other countries.

Printed and bound in Australia by
McPherson's Printing Group

Prologue

She had to die.

That was the best solution.

The only solution.

He stood at the window and stared, unseeing, at the winter-grayed streets. The thought of killing her, of snuffing out her vibrant essence, twisted his gut. But there wasn't any other way. She didn't know she held a tiny scrap of information that could bring him and his world tumbling down. She had no idea she possessed the power to destroy him.

She had to die before she discovered she held that power.

And a part of him would die with her.

Chapter 1

Softly falling snow blanketed Washington, D.C., adding a touch of lacy white trim to the elegant town houses lining a quiet side street just off Massachusetts Avenue. The few residents of the capital who weren't glued to their TV sets this Superbowl Sunday scurried by, chins down and collars turned up against the cold. Intent on getting out of the elements, they didn't give the town house set midway down the block a second glance. If they had, they might have noticed the discreet bronze plaque set beside the entrance that identified the offices of the president's special envoy.

Most Washington insiders believed the special envoy's position had been created several administrations ago to give a wealthy campaign contributor a fancy title and an important-sounding but meaningless title. Only a handful of the most senior cabinet officials knew that the special envoy secretly served in another, far more vital capacity.

From a specially shielded high-tech control center on the third floor of the town house, he directed a covert agency.

An agency whose initials comprised the last letter of the Greek alphabet, OMEGA. An agency that, as its name implied, sprang into action as a last resort when other, more established organizations, such as the CIA, the State Department or the military, couldn't respond.

Less than an hour ago, a call from the president had activated an OMEGA response. From various corners of the capital, a small cadre of dedicated professionals battled the snow-clogged streets to converge on the scene.

Maggie Sinclair unwrapped the wool scarf muffling her mouth and nose and stomped her calf-high boots to remove the last of the clinging snow. Stuffing the scarf in her pocket, she hurried through the tunnel that led to OMEGA's secret underground entrance. At the end of the passageway, she pressed a hand to a hidden sensor and waited impatiently for the computers to verify her palmprint. Seconds later, the titanium-shielded door hummed open. She took the stairs to the second floor and scanned the monitors set into the wall. Satisfied that only the special envoy's receptionist occupied the spacious outer area, she activated the sensors.

Gray-haired, grandmotherly Elizabeth Wells glanced up in surprise. "My goodness, Chameleon, you got here fast."

"I took the subway. I wasn't about to try driving through this mess." Shrugging out of her down jacket, Maggie hooked it on a bentwood coat tree. "Besides, I wanted to leave my car for Red. Just in case."

Elizabeth's kind face folded into sympathetic lines. "What a shame you were called in right in the middle of your father's visit. He doesn't get back to the States all that often, does he?"

"No, he doesn't."

Actually, Red Sinclair was lucky if he managed a quick

trip stateside once a year. As superintendent of an oil-field
exploration rig, the crusty widower traveled continually
from one overseas job to the next. He might be drilling in
Malaysia one week, Saudi Arabia the next.

"And when he does come home," Maggie added with a
grin, "he usually times his visits to coincide with the Superbowl. I left him and Terence ensconced in front of the
TV, alternately cheering the Cowboys and cursing the Redskins."

"You left the poor man with Terence?" A ripple of dis-
taste crossed Elizabeth's face. Like most of the OMEGA
team, she actively disliked the bug-eyed blue-and-orange-
striped iguana a certain Central American colonel had given
Maggie. The one time the receptionist had been pressed into
lizard-sitting, the German shepherd-size creature had devoured her prized water lilies.

"Honestly, dear, I don't understand how you can keep
that…that creature as a house pet. I find him utterly repulsive."

"Dad does, too," Maggie replied, laughing. "Unfortunately, the reverse doesn't hold true. Terence hates this cold
weather. He's been trying to climb into Red's lap to share
his warmth, not to mention his beer, all afternoon long. I
left them just before halftime, tussling for possession of a
bottle of Coors."

"Perhaps I should give your father a call," Elizabeth
mused. "If you're going out of town, he might like to get
away from that disgusting reptile for a while. Maybe have
dinner with me."

Maggie's brows rose. "*Am* I going out of town?"

Elizabeth gave a little cluck of disgust at her uncharacteristic slip. Having served as personal assistant to
OMEGA's director since the agency was founded, she knew
when and how to keep secrets. She also knew how to use

the Sig Sauer 9 mm pistol she kept in her upper-right-hand desk drawer. She'd fired the weapon only once in the line of duty, to deadly effect.

Maggie grinned to herself. This kind, lethal woman had a background and a personality as intriguing as her father's.

"I wish you would give Dad a call, Elizabeth. I'm sure he'd enjoy having dinner with someone who doesn't prefer bugs as an appetizer."

The receptionist grimaced and reached for the intercom phone. "I will, I promise. Right now, though, I'd better tell the chief you're here. He's waiting for you."

While Elizabeth announced her arrival, Maggie raked a hand through her snow-dampened, shoulder-length brown hair. A quick tug settled her faded maroon-and-gold Washington Redskins sweatshirt around her jeans-clad hips. This wasn't quite her standard professional attire, but the coded message summoning her to headquarters had signaled a matter of national importance, and she hadn't taken the time to change. Oh, well, OMEGA's director had seen her in worse rigs than this. Much worse.

Now all brisk efficiency, Elizabeth nodded. "Go on in, dear."

As Maggie walked down the short corridor leading to the director's private office, a flicker of anticipation skipped through her, like a tiny electrical impulse darting across a circuit board. She tried to tell herself that her suddenly erratic pulse was due to her imminent mission, whatever it might be. Herself wasn't buying it. She knew darn well what was causing the shimmer of excitement in her blood.

He was waiting a few steps away.

Maggie paused outside the door to draw in a deep, steadying breath. The extra supply of air didn't do her any good. As soon as she walked into his office and caught her first glimpse of the tall, dark-haired man standing at the window, her lungs forgot to function.

After almost three years, Maggie thought wryly, she ought to be used to Adam Ridgeway's effect on her respiratory system. The sad fact was that each contact with this cool, authoritative, often irritating man left her more breathless than the last.

He turned and gave her one of his rare smiles. ''Hello, Maggie. Sorry I had to drag you away from the game.''

She forced the air trapped in her chest cavity to circulate. Okay, the man looked like an ad for *GQ* in knife-pleated tan wool slacks, a white oxford shirt and a V-necked cashmere sweater in a deep indigo blue that matched his eyes. And, yes, the light from his desk lamp picked up a few delicious traces of silver in his black hair, traces he claimed she herself had put there.

But he was her boss, for heaven's sake, and she was too mature, too professional, to allow her growing fascination with Adam Ridgeway to complicate her relationship with the director of OMEGA. Unfortunately.

''Hi, Adam,'' she replied, moving to her favorite perch on one corner of his massive mahogany conference table. ''I don't mind the weather, but if the Skins lose this game because I'm not there to cheer them on, Red's going to gloat for the rest of his visit. He still can't believe I've transferred my allegiance from the Cowboys.''

''That is a pretty radical switch for an Oklahoman,'' the Boston-bred Adam concurred gravely.

''No kidding! A lot of folks back home think it ranks right up there with abandoning your firstborn or setting fire to the flag.''

Actually, Maggie's move to Washington three years ago had resulted in far more than a shift in allegiance in football teams. Until that time, she'd chaired the foreign language department at a small Midwestern college. An easy mastery of her work and a broken engagement had led to a growing restlessness. So when she received a late-night call from the strange little man Red Sinclair had once helped smuggle out of a war-torn oil sheikhdom, she'd been intrigued. That call had resulted in a secret trip to D.C. and, ultimately, her recruitment as an operative.

From the day she joined OMEGA, Maggie had never considered going back to sleepy little Yarnell College. What woman could be content teaching languages after leading a strike team into the jungles of Central America to take down a drug lord? Or after being trapped in a Soviet nuclear-missile silo with a brilliant, if incredibly clumsy, scientist? Or dangling hundreds of feet above the dark, crashing Mediterranean to extract a wounded agent from the subterranean lair of a megalomaniacal film star? Not this woman, at any rate.

Although…

If pressed, Maggie would have admitted that the life of a secret agent had its drawbacks. Like the fact that most of the men she associated with in her line of work were either drug dealers or thieves or general all-around sleazebags.

Oh, there were a few interesting prospects. A certain drop-dead-gorgeous Latin American colonel still called her whenever he was in D.C. And one or two operatives from other agencies she'd worked with had thrown out hints about wanting to know the woman behind the code name Chameleon. But none of these men possessed quite the right combination of qualities Maggie was looking for in a potential mate. Like a keen, incisive mind. A sense of adventure. A hint of danger in his smile. A great bod wasn't one of her absolute requirements, but it certainly wouldn't hurt.

So far Maggie had only met one man who came close to measuring up in all categories, and he was standing a few feet away from her right now. The problem was, whenever they came face-to-face, it was generally just before he sent her off to some far corner of the world.

As he was about to do now, apparently.

"So what's up, Adam?" she asked. "Why are we here?"

"I'm here because I got a call from the president an hour ago," he said slowly, his eyes on her face.

"And?" Maggie prompted.

The tingling tension that always gripped her at the start of a mission added to the fluttering in her veins that Adam's presence generated. Anticipation coursed through her, and her fingers gripped the smooth wood as she focused her full attention on his next words.

"And you're here because you're going to impersonate the vice president for the next two weeks."

Maggie's jaw dropped. "The vice president? Of the United States?"

"Of the United States."

"Taylor Grant?"

"Taylor Grant."

Maggie's astonishment exploded into shimmering, leaping excitement. In her varied career with OMEGA, she'd passed herself off as everything from a nun to a call girl. But this would be the first time she'd gone undercover in the topmost echelons of the executive branch.

"Now *this* is my kind of assignment! The vice president of the United States!" She shoved a hand through the thick sweep of her brown hair. "What's the story, Adam?"

"For the last three months, the vice president has been working secretly on an international accord in response to terrorism. According to the president, the parties involved are close, very close, to hammering out the final details of an agreement. One that will send shock waves through the terrorist community. When this treaty is approved, all signatories will respond as one to any hostile act.''

''It's about time!''

In the past few years, Maggie had seen firsthand the results of differing government approaches to terrorism. Depending on the personality of the people in high office, the response could be swift or maddeningly slow, strong or fatally indecisive.

''The key players involved in crafting the treaty are gathering at Camp David to hammer out the final details,'' Adam continued. ''No one—I repeat, no one—outside of the president, the VP herself and a few trusted advisors know about this meeting.''

Maggie eyed him shrewdly. ''So I'm to deflect the world's attention while this secret meeting takes place?''

''Exactly.''

She chewed on her lower lip for a moment. ''Why me?''

''Why not?'' he countered, watching her face.

''Mrs. Grant has at least half a dozen women assigned to her Secret Service detail,'' Maggie said bluntly. ''They know her personal habits and routine intimately. They wouldn't need the coaching I will to double for her.''

''True, but none of them matches her height and general physical characteristics as well as you do.''

Maggie composed a swift mental image of the attractive young widow. Tall. Auburn-haired. Slightly more slender than Maggie herself. A full mouth that quirked in a distinctive way when she was amused, which was often. Stunning violet eyes that sparkled with a lively intelligence.

Far more important than any physical characteristics, however, were the vice president's personality traits. Taylor Grant was totally self-assured. Gracious, yet tenacious as a pit bull when it came to the political issues she championed. And she carried herself with an easy confidence that Maggie knew she projected, as well. With a flash of insight, she sensed that was the key to this assignment.

She'd earned her code name, Chameleon, because of her ability to dramatically alter her physical appearance when going undercover. But she'd survived in the field because she knew that a successful impersonation came from within, not from without. The trick was to believe you were the person you pretended to be—if you did, you could convince others. This mission would take intense concentration and all of Maggie's skills, but she could do it. She would do it.

"Imagine," she murmured, her brown eyes gleaming. "I'll be presiding over joint sessions of Congress. Just think of the bills I can push through in the next couple of weeks. The bloated bureaucratic budgets I can slash."

"I'm afraid you won't have much opportunity to exercise your political clout," Adam said dryly. "To cover her absence, the vice president has announced that she's taking a long-overdue two-week vacation to her home in the California Sierras."

With real regret, Maggie abandoned her plans to ruthlessly streamline the entire federal government.

"Okay, what's the catch?"

One of Adam's dark brows rose.

"A two-week vacation in the High Sierras is too easy. I've got this tingly little feeling there's more to this role than what you've told me so far."

The ghost of a smile curved Adam's lips. "Your tingles are on target."

"They usually are," she said with a trace of smugness.

His smile faded as he studied her face. "Early this morning, Taylor Grant received a death threat. Your mission while you're undercover will be to discover the source of this threat."

The fact that Mrs. Grant had received a death threat

Merline Lovelace							15

didn't particularly surprise Maggie. A Secret Service contact she'd once worked with had mentioned that the White
House switchboard screened upward of fifty thousand calls
a day. A battery of skilled operators separated disgruntled
voters from dangerous malcontents and forwarded the ''sin-
isters'' for investigation. Maggie had been amazed at both
the number and the content of the wacko calls that came
over the switchboard. One, she'd been told, had ended with
a long-drawn-out shriek and the sound of the caller blowing
out his brains.

But in addition to outright kooks and psychotics who
might target Taylor Grant, Maggie could name at least half
dozen ultraright-wing groups the vice president had out-
raged. An intelligent, outspoken woman with strong liberal
leanings, she'd been chosen as the president's running mate
to balance his more conservative platform and to guarantee
California's huge block of electoral votes. No, Maggie
wasn't surprised Mrs. Grant had received a death threat.

Still, the Secret Service was charged with investigating
such threats. Once again, Maggie puzzled over the reason
for her involvement in this mission. She knew Adam too
well to suppose that he'd called her in just because she
resembled Taylor Grant in general size and shape.

''So what was different about this threat, that it activated
an OMEGA response?'' she asked.

''The call came in over the VP's personal line. Whoever
made it knew how to bypass the filters that protect her from
such calls, and how to electronically synthesize his voice.''

''His voice? If it was electronically disguised, how do
we know the caller was a he?''

Adam regarded her steadily across the half acre of polished mahogany that constituted his desk. ''Because the nature of the call suggests it was made by someone who

knows Mrs. Grant well. *Very* well. Well enough to mention her husky little gasp at moments of extreme passion.''

''Extreme passion?'' Maggie's jaw sagged once more. ''Good grief, are you saying the vice president of the United States is being threatened by...by a former lover?''

''So it appears.''

While Maggie struggled to absorb this astounding information, Adam rose, a sheet of notepaper in his hand.

''This is a list the VP supplied of the men she's known intimately.''

Eyes wide, Maggie glanced down at the list he handed her. To her surprise, she saw that it was very short. *Amazingly* short, for a charismatic, dynamic woman who'd been a widow for over ten years. A woman who kept the press and the public titillated with a string of very handsome and very eligible escorts.

There were only four names on the list:

Harold Grant, the vice president's husband. The California sculptor had died from a rare form of bone cancer more than a decade ago.

Peter Donovan. Maggie couldn't place him, but the notation beside the name indicated that he had managed the VP's first campaign for governor.

Stoney Armstrong. That name she recognized immediately! The handsome, square-jawed movie star had escorted then-Governor Grant one whole, tempestuous spring. Their pictures had been splashed across every tabloid and every glossy magazine on several continents.

And...

Maggie's eyes widened. ''James Elliot?'' she gasped. ''The secretary of the treasury?''

Adam nodded. ''Elliot met Mrs. Grant after the president named him to head Treasury. Their liaison was reportedly short, but passionate.''

"So that's why OMEGA's running this show instead of the Secret Service!" Maggie exclaimed.

In addition to his responsibilities for the fiscal policies of the United States, the secretary of the treasury also directed the Secret Service. The idea that the supervisor of the very agency charged with protecting the vice president was one of three men suspected of threatening to kill her boggled Maggie's mind.

"Elliot himself suggested OMEGA take the lead in this case," Adam said slowly. "He recognized that his liaison with Mrs. Grant, as brief as it was, compromised him in this case."

"No kidding!"

Her forehead wrinkling, Maggie studied the short list once again. Four names, three suspects—one of whom was a close personal friend of the president, and a member of his cabinet. Whew!

"There's another name that should be included on the list," Adam added in a neutral tone.

"Really?" she murmured, still absorbing the implications of James Elliot's involvement. "Whose?"

"Mine."

With infinite care, Maggie raised her eyes from the paper in her hand. As she searched Adam's face, a wave of conflicting emotions crashed through her.

Instinctive denial.

Instant awareness of the staggering impact this had on her mission.

And jealousy. Sheer, unadulterated jealousy. The old-fashioned green-eyed kind that was embarrassing to own up to but impossible to deny.

Taylor Grant was just the kind of woman who would attract Adam, Maggie admitted with painful honesty.

Polished. Sophisticated. At ease with politicians and

princes. She moved in the same circles Adam did. Circles that Maggie, content with herself and her world, had never aspired to…until recently.

Summoning every ounce of professionalism she possessed, she sent him a cool look. "Well, that certainly puts a new twist on this mission. Suppose you tell me why the vice president didn't include your name on her list."

A glimmer of emotion flickered through his eyes at her tart rejoinder. It might have been amusement or irritation, but it disappeared so quickly, Maggie couldn't tell. With Adam, she rarely could.

"Because I'm her future, not her past, lover," he replied evenly.

For the space of several heartbeats, silence blanketed the spacious office. Maggie fabricated and rejected a dozen possible interpretations of his statement. Only one of them made any sense, and she wouldn't let herself believe that one.

"Come again?" she asked.

Navy cashmere contoured Adam's well-defined shoulders as he crossed his arms. "Until this point, I've enjoyed only a casual friendship with Taylor Grant."

Maggie fought down a ridiculous rush of relief.

"That friendship is about to deepen."

"It is?"

"It is."

She cleared her throat. "Just how deep do you intend to take it?"

"As deep as necessary."

She refused to acknowledge the slow curl of heat his words generated. "I think you'd better give me something more specific."

"For the duration of the time you're undercover, I'll be your sole contact. We'll be together night and day for the next two weeks. As far as the rest of the world is concerned, we're in love. Or at least in lust.''

Right. As far as the rest of the world was concerned. Maggie bit down on the inside of her lower lip and forced herself to concentrate as Adam continued.

''We'll debut this new relationship at the VP's last official Washington function before she leaves for California.''

''Which is?''

''A special benefit performance at the Kennedy Center tomorrow night.''

''Tomorrow night?''

Maggie jumped off the corner of the conference table, her mind racing. She had less than twenty-four hours to transform herself into the person of the vice president of the United States. And into Adam Ridgeway's latest companion/lover.

At that moment, she wasn't sure which role daunted her—or thrilled her—more.

Chapter 2

The next hours were the most intense Maggie had ever spent preparing for a mission.

A quick call to her father glossed over the reason for extended absence. Although she'd never told Red Sinclair about her work for OMEGA, he knew his daughter too well to believe that her civilian cover as an adjunct professor at D.C.'s Georgetown University occupied all her time.

Grumbling something about making clear to a certain reptile who was in charge during Maggie's absence, Red hung up and went back to the Superbowl.

After that, the OMEGA team moved at the speed of light.

Jake MacKenzie, code name Jaguar, arrived to act as headquarters controller for this operation. Since his marriage last year to a woman he'd rescued from a band of Central American rebels, Jake hadn't spent much time in the field, but he was one of OMEGA's most experienced agents. There wasn't anyone Maggie trusted more to orchestrate the behind-the-scenes support for this mission than the steely-eyed Jaguar.

With Jake beside her, she listened to the chilling tape of the early-morning phone call.

"You were so good," the eerie, electronic voice whispered, *"so beautiful. I can still hear your soft, sweet moan, that little sound you make when…"*

Disgust twisted Maggie's mouth. That someone could speak of love in one breath, and death the next, sickened her.

"I must kill you. I don't want to, but I must. Try to understand.…"

The call ended with a click, and Taylor Grant's swift, indrawn gasp.

"All right," Jake said, his mouth grim. "Let's go over these dossiers on the three suspects one more time. Intel is champing at the bit to start your political indoctrination."

The dossiers didn't give her any more insight into which of the three prominent men might want to assassinate the vice president, but Maggie studied their backgrounds in minute detail. Then she spent hours in briefings on the political personalities and issues the vice president dealt with daily.

Finally she closeted herself in a small room to study videotapes of Taylor Grant's speech patterns and gestures. Given her background in linguistics, Maggie soon had the vice president's voice down pat. Copying her gestures and facial expressions took a bit more work, but after hours in front of the mirror and a video camera, Maggie passed even Jake's and Adam's critical review.

At that point, the wizards of the wardrobe, as she termed OMEGA's field dress unit, whipped into action. A gel-like adhesive "bone" shaped her chin and nose to match Mrs. Grant's profile. A quick dye job and an expert cut resulted

in the well-known stylish auburn shag. Tinted contacts duplicated the vice president's distinctive violet eyes.

Reducing Maggie's more generous figure to the vice
president's exact proportions, however, required a bit more
ingenuity. After taking some rather intimate measurements
and stewing over the matter for a while, the pudgy, frizzy-
haired genius who headed Field Dress produced a nineties
version of a corset that also, he proclaimed proudly, doubled as protective body armor. The thin Kevlar wraparound
vest flattened Maggie's bust and trimmed several inches off
her waist. The vice president's well-known preference for
pleated pants and long tunic-style jackets would disguise
her slightly fuller hips.

"Suck it in, Chameleon," the chief wizard ordered
sternly, yanking on the adjustable straps at the waist of the
bodysuit-corset.

Maggie clutched at the edge of a table. "Hey! Go easy
there," she said over one shoulder. "I've got to be able to
breathe for the next few weeks, you know."

"Don't panic," he replied, grunting a little with effort.
"This baby should fit more easily in a day or so."

"It should?" she gasped. "Why?"

He backed away, surveying his handiwork. "A couple of
days on the VP's diet will shave a few pounds off you."

Maggie straightened and took a few shallow, experimental breaths. "The vice president is on a diet?"

"Uh-oh. You didn't know?"

"Intelligence is going to cover her personal habits as
soon as we're through here. What kind of a diet?"

"You'd better let intel brief you," the chief replied eva-
sively. Not meeting her eyes, he held out a cobalt blue St.
John knit tunic with a double row of gold buttons.

Maggie poked her head through the square-cut neck of
the tunic and eyed the pudgy chief suspiciously.

relay the necessary information to OMEGA headquarters via his own, more powerful device.''

''Which is why we won't be more than a few miles apart during this entire operation,'' Adam said, coming to stand beside her. He took the ring from her unresisting fingers to examine it himself.

Maggie frowned, not entirely sure she liked this turn of events. She was used to operating independently in the field. Very independently. The idea of passing all her communications through Adam was a little unsettling.

She slanted him a quick speculative look as he hefted the gold band in his palm. She'd worked for and with Adam Ridgeway for three years now. In the process, she'd learned to respect his sharp, incisive knowledge of field operations. Like the other OMEGA operatives, she trusted him with her life every time he sent her into the field.

Still, for all her personal and very private admiration of Adam, Maggie had to admit they sometimes clashed professionally. They'd had more than a few disagreements in the past over her occasionally unorthodox methods in the field. In fact, the only times any of the OMEGA agents had ever seen Adam come close to losing his legendary cool were during Maggie's mission debriefs.

Well, the next few weeks would no doubt provide a severe test of his restraint, she thought. She was the field operative on this mission, and she fully intended to follow her instincts, just as she always had. Her generous mouth curved in a private smile. She'd always hoped to be on the scene when the iron-spined Adam Ridgeway's control finally slipped its leash.

Maybe, just maybe, she would be.

He caught her sideways glance. ''Let's see how well this works,'' he said, holding out his hand.

A funny little quiver darted through her stomach as she

placed her left hand in Adam's right. His palm felt warm and smooth beneath her fingertips, like supple, well-tanned leather. Nibbling on her lower lip, she watched him slide the gold band over the knuckle of her ring finger. When it slipped into place, his hand closed over hers.

Startled by both the tensile strength of his hold and the intimacy of the gesture, Maggie glanced up at the face so close to her own. His blue eyes locked with hers.

A voice at her shoulder jerked her attention back to the hovering technicians. "How does it feel?"

Her hand slipped from Adam's hold. "Fine."

Actually, the heavy circle felt odd. Unfamiliar. Maggie rarely wore jewelry, and when she did, it was more the funky, fun kind. This solid ounce of precious metal weighting her hand was a new experience for her. Using her thumb, she twisted the ring around her finger. It fit perfectly. Not too tight, not too loose. Yet when she tried to remove it, the thing balked at her knuckle.

"The inside of the band is curved to slide on easily, but that sucker won't ever come off," the team chief told her with a smug grin.

Her newly dyed dark red brows snapped together. "What?"

"Not without a special lubricant."

"Wait a minute. This special lubricant isn't another one of your no-fail formulas, is it? Like the solvent that was supposed to instantly remove the tattoo you put on my chin? It took three months for the thing to fade completely."

The technician waved a hand to dismiss that minor inconvenience. "The lubricant will work, I'm sure."

"You're *sure?* You mean you haven't tested it yet?"

"As a matter of fact, we haven't quite developed it yet. But we will by the time this mission is over. Besides, the chief suggested we size the ring like that."

"Oh, he did?" She turned to the man at her side, her brows arching.

"So you won't have to worry about losing it," Adam said easily. "And I don't have to worry about losing you."

After another round with intelligence and a final mission prebrief with Jake and Adam, Maggie pulled on the cobalt blue pea jacket that matched her designer knit outfit and slid into the back seat of a limo. A slow, simmering excitement percolated through her veins during the ride to the target point. She locked her gloved hands in her lap to keep from beating a nervous tattoo on the leather armrest and stared out at a capital still blanketed by a layer of white, now more slush than snow.

They'd decided to make the switch at the vice president's official residence. The old executive office building, where the VP's office and staff were located, swarmed with people all day and far into the night. By contrast, the pillared, three-story residence tucked away on the wooded grounds of the naval observatory in northwest Washington had limited access and much less traffic.

Outside of OMEGA, only three people knew exactly when and how the switch would take place. The vice president, of course. Lillian Roth, Mrs. Grant's personal assistant and dresser. And the SAIC—the special agent in charge of her personal security detail—William "Buck" Evans.

Maggie, Adam and Jake had debated strenuously whether or not to read Buck Evans into the script. With the treasury secretary himself under suspicion, they hesitated to include anyone in his chain of command in this deep-cover operation. But Mrs. Grant had insisted, and the president himself had concurred.

Evans had been assigned to the vice president's detail since the early days of the campaign. At one whistle-stop, he'd thrown himself in front of a two-hundred-and-fifty-pound crazy who objected to her stand in favor of government subsidies for AIDS research and treatment. In the ensuing brawl, the protester had chewed off the tip of Buck's ear. The agent had declined cosmetic surgery, claiming that the mangled ear added to his character. From that day on, he'd been permanently assigned to Taylor Grant's detail, and she trusted him with her life.

Besides, the vice president had said tartly, without Buck's assistance, it would be impossible to pull off this masquerade. As SAIC, he screened the agents assigned to her protective detail, approved all security procedures and set the duty schedules. He could ensure that the people accompanying the VP on her long-planned vacation were the ones least familiar with the twists and turns of her personality. He would also provide the real Mrs. Grant with protection during her secret treaty negotiations at Camp David.

So when Maggie's limo drove around to the back of the turreted turn-of-the-century mansion that served as the vice president's official residence, it was Buck Evans who stepped out of the shadows and yanked open the rear door. Digging a hand into her arm, he half helped, half hauled her out of the back seat.

"I've diverted the surveillance cameras. Let's get you upstairs, fast."

He hustled her through a side door, past a darkened room and up a set of narrow stairs. After scanning the wide hallway that ran the length of the second floor, he tugged her after him, toward a door set halfway down the hall.

"Go on inside. I'll reset the cameras, then come back for Mrs. Grant when she calls."

Maggie had barely stepped into a small foyer before the door shut behind her. She stood still for a moment, trying to slow her pounding heart. From her breathless state, she guessed that the total elapsed time from the moment Buck Evans pulled open the limo's door until he shut this one behind her had been less than a minute.

"Harrumph!"

At the sudden sound, Maggie spun to the left and dropped into an instinctive crouch. Her hand reached for her weapon before she remembered she wasn't armed.

"So you're the one!"

A diminutive figure in a severely cut navy blue suit, thick-soled lace-up shoes, and an unruly mass of steel gray curls stood framed in a set of glass-paned French doors. She held herself ramrod straight, her chin tilted at a belligerent angle and her mouth thinned to a tight line as she surveyed the newcomer from the tip of her auburn head to the toes of her black leather boots.

Maggie straightened slowly. From her intelligence briefings, she recognized the other woman instantly. Lillian Roth, the vice president's personal confidante and assistant for almost twenty years. The sixty-three-year-old woman had appeared rather formidable in the few photographs intel had dug up of her. Maggie now discovered that the photos hadn't really captured the full force of Lillian's character. In person, she radiated all the warmth and charm of a Marine Corps drill sergeant on a bad hair day.

"Well, I must say you've achieved a startling resemblance," the dresser said with a small sniff. "But it takes more than mere physical presence to emulate someone of Mrs. Grant's stature."

"I agree completely."

Maggie's cool reply duplicated exactly the vice president's voice and intonation. Lillian's gray brows rose, but she obviously couldn't bring herself to unbend enough to praise what Maggie considered a rather impressive performance.

"I'll take your coat. The vice president is waiting for you in her sitting room."

Having memorized the floor plans of the residence, Maggie walked confidently through the double doors into a tall-ceilinged, airy room. She paused just past the threshold, visually cataloging the fixtures and furniture in her mind. Although an attack on the VP was unlikely in this secure environment, Maggie wasn't about to take any chances. She'd spend only one night here, but she wanted to be able to find her way around these rooms in total darkness if she had to.

The furnishings in the spacious sitting room were a tribute to Taylor Grant's exquisite taste and vibrant personality. A framed print of Monet's famous water lilies of Giverny hung in a lighted alcove between tall curtained windows. Accent pieces scattered throughout the room took their cue from this masterpiece of swirling blues and greens and purples. A magnificent green jade Chinese temple dog, one paw resting imperiously on a round ball, dominated the huge coffee table set between two facing sofas, which were covered in a shimmering blue-and-purple plaid. A collection of crystal candlesticks in varying shapes and sizes decorated the white-painted wood mantel, reflecting the light from the fire in a rainbow of glowing colors.

But it was the woman standing beside the fireplace who drew Maggie's attention. For an eerie moment, she felt as though she were looking at her own reflection through a large invisible mirror.

The vice president wore royal blue pleated slacks and tunic exactly like the one Field Dress had procured for Maggie. Overhead spots highlighted the subtle gold tints in her wine-colored hair, which was styled in the simple, elegant shag the OMEGA agent now sported. Her eyes, deepened to a dusky violet by the bold color of her outfit, stared at Maggie with the same unwavering scrutiny.

For a long moment, neither woman spoke. Then Mrs. Grant's full mouth twisted.

"It's kind of a shock, isn't it? Every woman wants to think she's unique. Special in her own way. Yet here we are, two identical clones."

"Not quite identical," Maggie replied, smiling. "Underneath this very flattering outfit, I'm trussed up like a Christmas turkey."

The vice president's lips quirked in response. Without thinking, Maggie duplicated the small smile.

Mrs. Grant's eyes widened. "Good grief, you *are* real, aren't you?"

"Yes, ma'am."

"Adam said you were good," the vice president murmured, "but I see now that was somewhat of an understatement."

Adam, Maggie noted. Not the special envoy. Not even Adam Ridgeway. Just that casual, familiar *Adam*. A little too familiar, in her opinion.

Taylor Grant gestured toward one of the sofas, then took the other. "You go by the code name Chameleon, don't you?"

Maggie nodded. No one, not even the president, knew the OMEGA operatives' real names or civilian covers. That simple but rigid policy protected the president in the event anything should go wrong on a mission. It protected the agents, as well. With OMEGA maintaining absolute control over such privileged information, they didn't have to worry about the inevitable leaks that plagued the CIA or FBI.

"Well, I can certainly understand how you earned that particular designation," the vice president said. She eyed Maggie for a moment, her expression uncompromising.

"You understand that I'm not happy about this charade? At all?"

"So I was told."

"If my presence at these secret treaty negotiations wasn't so necessary, I wouldn't allow you to be used as a decoy like this. I've never backed away from a challenge...or a threat...in my life."

"I know that, Mrs. Grant."

For all her refined appearance and well-known sense of humor, this woman was as tough and as resilient as they came. She'd battled her way up through the political ranks on her own, without a prominent family name or fortune to ease her way. Obviously, she didn't like someone else taking the heat for her. Her deep brown eyes speared Maggie.

"I understand I have approximately twenty minutes to fill you in on the more intimate details of my life."

"Yes, ma'am."

The vice president's jaw tightened. "I'm not used to sharing this kind of information," she said after a moment. "With anyone. Politics doesn't encourage a person to reveal her innermost secrets."

"Whatever you tell me doesn't go beyond this room," Maggie said with quiet assurance.

She and Adam had agreed that this half hour with the vice president would be private, unrecorded. The little bug in her ring wouldn't activate until Mrs. Grant left the compound. Maggie's innate honesty compelled her to add a kicker, however.

"Unless you tell me something that will help identify the man who called you this morning."

An emotion that wasn't quite fear, but was something pretty close to it, rippled across the vice president's face as she glanced at the phone on a table beside the sofa. Maggie could only admire the vice president's courage as she mastered that brief, unguarded emotion and turned away from the telephone with a contemptuous look.

"I don't like being threatened any more than I like revealing the details of my private life."

Realizing that they weren't making much headway, Maggie sat up straight, tucked her hands into her sleeves and assumed a soulful expression.

"I once went underground in a convent. If it helps any, just think of me as a *religiosa,* a sort of female father confessor."

Some of the stiffness went out of Mrs. Grant's slender frame. "Somehow I can't see you as a nun," she drawled.

"It wasn't my favorite assignment," Maggie admitted with a grin, abandoning her postulant's pose. "Those wool habits itch like the dickens."

The vice president chuckled. "I believe you. All right, where do you want me to start?"

"Let's start with Stoney Armstrong, since I'll be meeting him in L.A. tomorrow. You dated for almost six months, didn't you, Mrs. Grant?"

"Taylor."

At Maggie's surprised glance, she smiled. "I can't bring myself to share the most intimate details of my love life with someone who addresses me as 'ma'am' or 'Mrs. Grant.' Please, just call me Taylor."

No wonder Adam had developed such a close friendship with this woman, Maggie thought. The power of her office hadn't diminished her charm or charismatic personality.

"What do you want to know about Stoney?"

"For starters, what's behind his studio image of a muscle-bound, over-sexed, gorgeous hunk of beefcake?"

"A muscle-bound, oversexed, gorgeous hunk of beefcake," Taylor responded dryly.

"So it wasn't his, ah, intellectual prowess that attracted you to him?"

Absently the vice president plucked at the fringe on one of the sofa pillows. "No, it wasn't. But at that point in my life, I didn't need the challenge of a rousing debate on domestic politics or international affairs. I needed, or thought I needed, Stoney Armstrong."

She stopped playing with the fringe and glanced across the coffee table at Maggie. Her remarkable eyes filled with the gleam of laughter that had made her the darling of the international press corps.

"Every woman should have a man like Stoney in her life at some point or another, if only to remind her that great sex is highly overrated as the foundation for a permanent relationship."

"True," Maggie replied with an answering laugh. "But it's certainly not a bad place to start."

Twenty minutes later, Lillian Roth knocked on the sitting room door, then poked her head inside. She glanced from Maggie to the vice president for a moment in startled confusion.

"Yes, Lillian?" Maggie asked, testing her skills.

The dresser's birdlike black eyes narrowed. She studied Maggie for long, silent moments, then switched her focus to Taylor. Giving a little sniff, she spoke slowly, as if not quite sure of herself.

"Buck just called on your private line. They're just starting the shift change. You have to go, Mrs. Grant."

Pleased with the fact that she'd managed to fool the dresser, at least for a few seconds, Maggie rose.

The two auburn-haired women faced each other. Mrs. Grant—Taylor—held out her hand.

"Good luck, Chameleon."

"Thanks. I'll need it! I just hope I don't do something stupid and totally ruin your image in the next couple of weeks."

"You won't. Besides, I don't worry about my image when I'm in the Sierras. That cabin is the only place in the world where I go without makeup, don't bother with my hair, and bundle up in layers of flannel and wool. You just have to make it through a couple of brief public appearances, then you're home free."

"Right." Maggie laughed. "One huge benefit at the Kennedy Center tonight, and a dinner for two hundred of your closest friends in L.A. tomorrow."

"Don't worry. Stoney will make sure all the media focuses on him tomorrow. And tonight…well, tonight you'll have Adam at your side."

There it was again, that easy, familiar *Adam*. Maggie's grin slipped a bit.

As Taylor eased into her coat, her amethyst eyes took on a distant, almost dreamy expression. "I've been wanting to invite Adam up to the cabin for some time. If it weren't for these treaty negotiations…"

"Yes?"

The cool note in Maggie's voice drew the vice president's gaze.

"Well," she finished after a moment, "let's just say that Adam's the kind of man any woman would want to have around whenever she was in the mood for a stimulating intellectual debate…or anything else."

At that moment, the foyer door opened and Buck Evans slipped inside. His rusty brown hair, worn a little long on the sides, didn't quite cover his half-chewed ear.

"You ready to go, Mrs. Grant?"

"I'm ready."

He paused with one hand on the knob and gave Maggie

a hard look. "Officially, I'm on leave while Mrs. Grant is in California."

"I know."

"I'll be with her every moment at Camp David. Have your people contact me there if you need me."

"Roger."

The Secret Service agent's eyes narrowed. "Just for the record, I think this subterfuge is ridiculous. Every man and woman on this detail has sworn to protect the vice president with their lives."

Maggie didn't answer. The decision to keep the switch secret from everyone but Buck Evans had been made by the president himself. She wasn't about to engage in a debate, public or private, about it. But she saw the total dedication in this man's fierce, protective stance toward Mrs. Grant, and understood the depth of his anger.

"Let's go, Buck," the vice president said quietly. "We've only got an hour before the others begin arriving at Camp David."

With a final nod to Maggie, she followed the agent out the door.

Lillian closed it behind them. Clearly unhappy at being left behind, she scowled at Maggie, then reluctantly assumed her duties.

"Have you had dinner?"

"No, there wasn't time."

Her small mouth pursed into a tight bud. "I'll call down to the kitchens for a tray, then run your bath."

"Fine. In the meantime, I'll look around the suite."

"Humph."

The dresser turned and marched out, her back rigid. Lillian Roth possessed not only the disposition of a drill sergeant, Maggie decided, but the carriage, as well.

* * *

A short time later, a scrubbed and powdered Maggie tightened the belt of a fluffy terry-cloth robe. Wandering into the sitting room, she sat down at a small table pulled up to an armchair. Her stomach rumbled in anticipation as she lifted a domed silver cover.

In some consternation, she stared at the four stalks of an unidentifiable yellow vegetable. They were arranged in solitary splendor on a gold-rimmed plate bearing the vice-presidential seal. Swallowing, Maggie poked at the stalks with the tip of her fork, then cut off an experimental bite.

At the taste, her face scrunched up in a disgusted grimace. Laying down the fork, she pushed the tray to one side. Maybe she could sneak a bag of peanuts or a candy bar at the Kennedy Center during intermission, she thought hopefully.

She soon discovered that the role of vice president of the United States didn't include any intermissions.

Chapter 3

"Lillian, have a heart! Not so tight!"

As Maggie's protest pierced the well-engineered quiet of his sleek black Porsche, Adam glanced down at the gold watch on his wrist. The faint pattern of her voice had grown stronger and stronger as he neared the naval observatory. Now, less than half a mile away, it came through the receiver built into his watch with startling clarity. As did Lillian Roth's tart reply.

"Suck it in. Mrs. Grant is a perfect size eight, you know."

"Well, I'm not a perfect anything. Loosen the straps a bit."

"Humph."

Adam smiled to himself as he swung the leather-wrapped steering wheel, following the curve of Massachusetts Avenue. He had to agree with Maggie on that one. She was far from perfect.

Of all the agents he directed, Maggie Sinclair, code name

Chameleon, was the most independent and the least pre-
dictable. There was no denying her fierce dedication to her
job. Yet she approached it with a breezy self-confidence
and an irrepressible sparkle in her brown eyes that had alternately fascinated and irritated Adam greatly at various
times in the past three years. What was more, she possessed
her own inimitable style of operating in the field.

His hands clenched on the steering wheel as he remembered a few of the impossible situations Chameleon had
extricated herself from. Adam knew he would never forget
the way she'd blown her way out of a Soviet nuclear-
missile silo with the aid of a terminally klutzy physicist.
He'd noticed the first streaks of gray in his hair when Maggie returned from that particular mission.

She hadn't been any more repentant over that incident
than any of the others he'd taken her to task for. Although
respectful—most of the time—Maggie Sinclair was by turns
cheeky, irrepressible and so damned irresistible, that Adam
didn't know how he'd managed to keep his hands off her
as long as he had.

If he wasn't OMEGA's director… If he didn't have to
maintain the distance, the objectivity, necessary to send her
into danger…

The thought of touching Maggie, of tasting her, of burying his hands in that sweep of glossy, shoulder-length
brown hair and kissing her laughing, generous mouth, sent
a spear of hot, heavy desire lancing through Adam.

"Lillian! For Pete's sake!"

Willing himself back under control, Adam pressed the
stem on his watch, cutting off Maggie's indignant protest.
His jaw tight, he turned off Massachusetts Avenue onto the
approach to the U.S. naval observatory.

Sited on what had once been a hilly farm well outside
the capital, the sprawling complex still functioned as an

active military installation. A battery of scientists manned the round-domed observatory, which tracked celestial movements and produced navigational aids. More experts maintained the master clock of the United States, accurate to within thirty billionths of a second.

In addition to its military mission, however, the complex also served as home to the vice president. Since 1976, the occupant of that office had also occupied the fanciful Victorian mansion built at the turn of the century for the superintendent of the observatory.

The entire facility was guarded by an elite branch of the marine guard, one of whom stepped out of a white-painted guard post at Adam's approach. The granite-jawed gunnery sergeant bent to shine a high-powered beam into the Porsche's interior.

"Evening, sir. May I help you?"

"Good evening, Gunny. I'm Adam Ridgeway. Mrs. Grant is expecting me."

He handed over the pass issued by the vice president's office. The plastic card looked ordinary enough but concealed several lines of scrambled code. After running a handheld scanner over it, the marine squinted through the window to compare Adam's face to the digitized image on the scanner's small screen. He returned the pass, then punched a button on his belt. Heavy iron gates swung open.

"Go on up, Mr. Ridgeway."

"Thanks."

As he drove the tree-lined drive, Adam searched for signs of the highly sophisticated defensive security system that supplemented the military guards. He saw none, but knew that canine patrols roamed the area and electronic eyes swept the grounds continuously, particularly along the approach to the vice president's residence. The mansion itself was wired from attic to subbasement. Even the food, purchased from a list of carefully vetted suppliers, went through chemical and infrared screening before cooking. The security surrounding the woman who stood only a heartbeat away from the Oval Office was almost as heavy as that around the president himself.

For that reason, Adam believed that whoever had called Taylor Grant in the early hours of yesterday morning wouldn't try to make good on his threat here. The attack, when it came, would occur when she was most vulnerable. At a public appearance. Or on the road. Or in that isolated cabin of hers high in the Sierras.

Whenever and wherever it came, Adam intended to be there.

Another guard stopped him at the gate in the wrought-iron fence surrounding the residence. After scrutinizing his pass once again, the marine stood back.

Adam drove up a sloping drive toward the Victorian structure, complete with wraparound verandah and a distinctive round tower. White-painted and green-shuttered, the mansion rose majestically above a rolling blanket of snow, a picture postcard of white on white.

Adam pulled up under the pillared drive-through and shifted into park, but left the motor running. Having escorted Taylor to several functions in the past, he knew the drill. A valet would park his car around back, a safe distance from the house in the unlikely event it had been tampered with and now carried explosives. He and the vice president would ride to the Kennedy Center in her armor-plated limousine, preceded and followed by Secret Service vehicles. The agent in charge would sit beside the driver in the limo and remain a only few steps away after they arrived at their destination.

Adam and Maggie wouldn't have a private moment the entire evening. Theoretically.

He pulled his overcoat from the front seat, nodded to the valet and strolled up the wide front steps. A navy steward showed him into a paneled sitting room and offered a choice of drinks while he waited.

"Hello, Adam."

He turned at the low greeting. The heat that spiraled through his stomach had nothing to do with the swallow of Scotch he'd just downed. This was a Maggie he'd never seen before.

In the past three years, she'd gone undercover in everything from a nun's habit to a slinky gold mesh halter that barely covered the tips of her breasts. That particular article of clothing had cost Adam a number of hours of lost sleep. Yet it hadn't carried half as much kick as this elegant, deceptively demure black velvet gown.

On second observation, Adam decided it wasn't the floor-length skirt, slit to the knee, that caused his knuckles to whiten around the heavy crystal tumbler of Scotch. Or the tunic studded with jet beads that shimmered seductively with her every step. Or the feathery cut of her auburn hair, framing a face that bore an uncanny resemblence to Taylor Grant's.

It was the gleam in her violet-tinted eyes. That sparkling glint of excitement, of shared adventure. And the conspiratorial grin that vanished before the cameras in the downstairs rooms could record it—but not before Adam had felt its impact in every part of his body. Carefully, very carefully, he set the tumbler down.

Stepping forward, he brushed a light kiss across her lips. "Hello, Taylor. You look ravishing tonight."

She stared up at him, startled by the intimate greeting, but then her mouth quirked upward in the vice president's distinctive smile.

"Thank you. You look rather delectable yourself."

Actually, when she recovered from the surprise of that brief kiss, Maggie had to admit that Adam looked more than delectable. He looked delicious. Good enough to eat. Which was, she realized immediately, an unfortunate metaphor. The mere thought of digesting anything, Adam included, made her stomach growl. Loudly. Embarrassingly.

He lifted a dark brow.

"It's getting late," she said, her cheeks warming. "Shall we go?"

As if on cue, the woman designated to serve as agent in charge during Buck Evans's absence stepped into the reception room. Promoted only a week ago from her position as head of the Secret Service's Chicago field office, the sandy-haired Denise Kowalski was brisk, efficient and still very new to vice president's detail. Buck Evans had vouched for her personally.

In keeping with the occasion, she wore a chic red plaid evening jacket that disguised the weapon holstered at the small of her back. Her black satin skirt was full enough to allow her complete ease of movement if she had to throw her body across the vice president's. Which, Maggie sincerely hoped, she wouldn't have to do tonight. Or any other night.

"Your car is at the front entrance, Mrs. Grant."

"Thank you, Denise. We'll be right out."

The agent nodded and went to get the rest of the team into position. The heavy oak front door swung open behind her, its leaded glass panels refracting the light of the brass lanterns mounted on either side of the porte cochere. Golden light flooded the covered drive, but beyond that, blackness beckoned. Beyond that, a possible assassin waited.

Maggie stared at the open door, pysching herself for her first public appearance as Taylor Grant. She drew in a slow breath, and suddenly the Kevlar body shield didn't seem to bite into her flesh quite as much as it had before.

Moving to her side, Adam lifted the silk-lined black angora cloak she carried over one arm. He held it out, and when she'd wrapped herself in its sybaritic warmth, he rested his hands on her shoulders for a moment.

"I'm glad you invited me to join you tonight," he murmured.

Maggie gave him her best Taylor-made smile. "Me too."

"Ready to go?"

"As ready as I'll ever be."

Maggie had been to the Kennedy Center several times before. In fact, she'd taken her father to a performance of Andrew Lloyd Webber's *Phantom of the Opera* just last week. Red Sinclair had thoroughly enjoyed both the lavish production and the spectacle of jeans-clad students and camera-snapping tourists rubbing elbows with socialites dripping mink and diamonds.

But this was the first time Maggie had driven to a private performance in an armor-plated limousine. Or stepped out of the car into a barrage of TV cameras and bright lights.

Adam turned to help her alight, shielding her with his broad back while the Secret Service agents fanned out to open a corridor through the crowd. The smile he gave her caused a ripple of murmured comment among the onlookers and a shock of sensual pleasure in Maggie. Her fingers curled in his before she reminded herself that they were playing to the audience.

The elegantly dressed crowd parted before them like the Red Sea rolling back for Moses. With Agent Kowalski a few steps ahead, Maggie and Adam made their way toward the grand foyer at the rear of the marble-walled structure.

Since tonight's concert was a special benefit to raise

funds for a flood-ravaged province in India, the guests had been invited by that country's ambassador. The Secret Service's Office of Protective Research had run all two thousand names through its computerized list of "lookouts." Reportedly, none of the persons present tonight had triggered a flag that would identify a potential threat to the vice president. Nevertheless, by the time Maggie and Adam reached the short flight of stairs leading down to the red-carpeted grand foyer, her heart was thumping painfully against her body armor.

The ambassador and his wife awaited them beneath the striking seven-foot-high bronze bust of John F. Kennedy that dominated the wide hall. Brilliant light from eighteen massive chandeliers overhead made the colorful decorations pinned to the sash across the ambassador's chest sparkle like precious gems. The same glowing light illuminated the rich green and purple jewel tones of his wife's sari.

The diplomat bowed over Maggie's hand with polished charm. "Madam Vice President. We are most honored that you join us this evening."

"It's my pleasure, Ambassador Awani, Madam Awani. Do you know my escort, Special Envoy Adam Ridgeway?"

The tips of the ambassador's luxuriant mustache lifted in a wide smile. "But of course," he replied, pumping Adam's hand. "I have played both with and against this rogue on the polo field."

"Have you?"

Maggie arched an inquiring eyebrow at Adam, not really surprised that a man who sculled the Potomac in gray Harvard sweats to keep in shape also played a little polo on the side. Maggie herself was more the tag-football-and-long-lazy-walks type.

"Did he not tell you that he scored the winning goal for my team the last time he was in Bombay?"

"No, he didn't."

"It was a lucky shot," Adam said, with a small shrug of his black-clad shoulders. "I couldn't have done it without Sulim's fantastic pass."

The ambassador preened visibly at the compliment. With the fervor of a true enthusiast, he plunged into a recap of that memorable game. To Maggie's amusement, the ensuing conversation was soon peppered with terms like *chukker* and *grass penalty*. A spirited argument broke out over a controversial call in the last challenge for the Cup of the Americas. Even the ambassador's wife joined in, denouncing the officiating in a soft, melodic voice. Polo was a passion in India, she confided to Maggie in a smiling aside. It had been played in her country for over a thousand years.

As Maggie listened to the lively exchange, a sense of unreality gripped her. She'd been so keyed up for this first appearance as vice president. So intent on maintaining the fierce concentration necessary to stay in character. So determined to dodge any protocol gaffes—not to mention any stray bullets. Yet here she was, chuckling at the increasingly improbable tales of polo games won and lost, as though she moved in these sophisticated circles every day.

She gave most of the credit for her smooth insertion into this glittering world to Adam. This was his world, she thought, slanting him a quick glance. He moved comfortably among ambassadors and artists, Greek shipping magnates and the high-priced gunmen who guarded them. With his cool air of authority and commanding blue eyes, he appeared every bit as regal as any king or prince she could imagine. Although he wore no jewelry except the small gold studs in his white dress shirt and a thin gold watch, he didn't need to advertise either his background or his breeding. It showed in his understated, casual elegance and the ease with which he kept both the ambassador and his wife entertained.

And in the ways he displayed his interest in the woman at his side.

Adam Ridgeway didn't resort to any sort of this-is-my-woman caveman tactics to advertise his budding relationship with the vice president. The signals he sent out were subtle, but unmistakable. There was that small, private smile when Maggie laughingly asked if he'd *really* fallen off his pony in full view of India's prime minister. The glance that lingered on her face a few seconds longer than necessary. The relaxed stance at her side, not quite touching her, yet close enough for her to catch the clean scent of his after-shave with every small movement.

He was playing a role, Maggie reminded herself sternly. The same role he'd been playing when he kissed her earlier. When he'd taken her hand to help her out of the limo.

But then the foyer lights flashed, and Adam's hand moved to the small of her back to guide her toward the opera house. The gesture was at once courteous and possessive. Comforting and strangely disturbing. Maggie felt it right through her layers of Kevlar and velvet. Tiny ripples of awareness undulated through her middle.

Of course, she thought ruefully, those rippling sensations might well be hunger pangs. As their party mounted the wide, red-carpeted stairs to the opera house, she gave a silent prayer that her stomach wouldn't drown out the guest artist's performance.

Once they were inside the opera house, a black-suited usher escorted them up a short ramp to the box tier. Denise Kowalski halted the party just outside the entrance to the presidential box.

"If you'll wait here, please, I'll do a final visual."

Maggie knew that the Secret Service had swept the entire

theater for hidden explosive devices earlier this afternoon.
According to Denise, they'd done another sweep just prior
to the vice president's arrival. Now the senior agent made
personal eye contact with each of the other agents stationed
around the three-tiered red-and-gold auditorium.

Watching Denise Kowalski in operation, Maggie felt a
mounting respect for her cool professionalism. She also
tried very hard to ignore the fact that President Lincoln had
been assassinated as he sat in a theater box only a few miles
from this one.

At Denise's nod, Maggie pasted a smile on her face and
stepped into the box.

Heads twisted.

Necks craned.

Murmurs snaked through the opera house.

A seat cushion thumped against a chairback as a lone
figure rose. As if in slow motion, he twisted around to face
their box.

Adam stepped to her side, and Maggie felt her nails dig
into her palms.

Then another man rose, and the woman beside him.
Within moments, the entire audience was standing. The or-
chestra broke into "Ruffles and Flourishes," then played
the Indian and American national anthems.

Unclenching her fist, Maggie placed her palm over her
heart. She wasn't surprised to feel it drumming wildly
against its velvet-covered shield. She'd had some interesting moments in her OMEGA career, but for sheer hair-
raising, knee-knocking excitement, that second or so when
she and the man in the center section had faced each other
ranked right up there with the best—or worst—of them. By
the time she sank into the plush red seat, her smile was so
stiff, it could have been cut from cardboard.

Immediately, the lights dimmed. The featured artist, a

slender, dark-haired flutist of Indian birth and growing international fame, walked out to center stage. Maggie was certain she wouldn't hear a note over the pounding in her ears, yet the haunting woodwind call gradually pierced the drumming in her ears. The music soothed. Soared. Evoked images of the flowing Ganges and the moonlit Taj Mahal. Beat by beat, her heart picked up the flute's rhythm. Her spine slowly relaxed. When the last notes of the first half of the program died away, she joined in the thunderous applause.

During the brief intermission, the ambassador relinquished his place at her side to circulate among his other guests and to allow them access to the vice president. Maggie cast a quick glance at the buffet table, loaded with platters of lobster pastries and succulent slices of smoked ham. Suppressing a sigh, she turned her back on the forbidden feast and forced herself to concentrate on the steady stream of people vying for her attention.

With Adam at her side, she got through the nerve-racking interval relatively unscathed.

She soon discovered that most of the politicians who elbowed their way into her circle were more interested in hearing themselves speak than in anything the VP might say. The only near-disaster occurred when the chairman of the senate fiduciary committee groused that the peso's steep nosedive was going to wreak havoc on international markets.

Maggie nodded in agreement.

"Given today's unrestrained markets, that's a real possibility," Adam interjected smoothly. "Of course, the president's Pan-American Monetary Stabilization Plan, which you helped draft, will help prevent future disasters like that."

Right. The president's Pan-American Monetary Stabilization Plan.

On behalf of Taylor Grant, Maggie smiled and accepted Adam's accolade. The senator immediately launched into a long and incredibly boring explanation of his own strategy to single-handedly save third-world economies. Thankfully, the grand foyer's lights dimmed before he wound down, saving Maggie from having to formulate a reply.

By this time, she was feeling the combined effects of her few sips of champagne and her taut nerves, not to mention the pressure of Lillian's determination to make her a perfect size eight.

"Do I have time to powder my nose?" she murmured to Adam.

His mouth lifted. "You have time to powder anything you want. They won't start the second half of the program until you're seated."

The belated realization that several thousand people would have to wait while she went to the bathroom effectively eliminated Maggie's need. Before she could tell Adam she'd changed her mind, however, he had steered her toward the ladies' room on the second-floor landing.

Denise Kowalski quickly grasped the situation and stepped ahead of them. Signaling to Maggie to wait, she threaded her way through the women standing patiently in line and checked out the facility.

Good grief, it hadn't occurred to Maggie that the vice president of the United States couldn't even tinkle without a security check. She was discovering that this job wasn't quite as glamorous and exciting as it appeared to the rest of the world.

Evidently no assassins lurked in the stalls. Denise returned in less than a minute to escort Maggie to the head of the line. The other women graciously yielded their places, but Maggie, now thoroughly embarrassed by the whole affair, paused with one hand on the stall door.

"This is ridiculous," she commented. "I'll bet there isn't a line like this in the men's room."

The other woman gaped at her for a moment, then broke into laughter.

"Maybe it's time the government took a look at the distribution of public toilets by gender," one of them suggested.

"Maybe it is," Maggie agreed. "I'll put it on the agenda as soon I get back from California."

To a chorus of cheers and applause, she sailed into a stall. One way or another, she'd convince Taylor Grant to follow through on her rash promise to look into public potties.

"What was that all about?" Adam asked when she and the grinning agent in charge emerged a few moments later.

Tucking her hand in his arm, Maggie smiled demurely. "It's a woman thing."

The presence of the driver and the Secret Service agent prevented Maggie discussing the evening's events with Adam during the drive back to the naval observatory. Still wired, and reluctant to see their time together end, Maggie forced herself not to fidget, but her fingers tapped an uneven beat on the leather armrest.

When Adam's hand closed over hers, she wasn't sure whether his intent was to still the nervous movement or to further their supposed relationship. Whatever the reason, she obligingly turned her palm up and entwined her fingers with his.

"Did you enjoy the concert?" he asked conversationally.

"Very much." She gave him a quick grin. "Although I

enjoyed hearing about your exploits on the polo field even more. Especially the part where you fell off your horse.''

"I hope that tale didn't totally destroy my credibility with you.''

"Well," she murmured provocatively, "your romantic image is a bit tarnished around the edges. You'll have to apply some polish to restore it to its former state.''

He lifted their entwined hands and brushed his mouth across the back of her hand. "I'll see what I can do.''

Ruthlessly ignoring the streaks of fire that shot from her hand to her elbow to her heart, Maggie followed Adam's lead and fell into an easy bantering dialogue for the rest of the ride. All the while, she was blazingly conscious of the warm, strong fingers nesting hers.

A part of her thrilled to his touch.

To her considerable surprise, a small part of her also resented it.

She'd always kept her relationship with her boss strictly professional, which hadn't been difficult at first. Adam Ridgeway could be somewhat daunting when he chose to. If Maggie had been the dauntable kind, she might have wilted like a limp lettuce leaf the first time he turned that icy stare on her. Or rocked back on her heels the first time those chiseled features had relaxed into a genuine smile.

Adam's smile could cause a less sensible, less professional woman than Maggie to weave all kinds of ridiculous fantasies.

Okay, she admitted, so she'd done some weaving. And some fantasizing. So she'd imagined the feel of his hand in hers more and more often lately, and the memory of his after-shave would tease her at the most unexpected moments. In unguarded moments like this, she found herself wondering just when, or if, they'd tear down the barriers that kept them from acknowledging the attraction simmering between them.

Because it wasn't all one-sided. Despite the elegant, sophisticated women Adam escorted. to various diplomatic functions, despite the unshakable air of authority he always displayed on the job, Maggie had sensed his growing awareness of her as a woman.

But being aware of her as a woman and doing something about it were two entirely different matters. Maggie had no idea if he'd felt the same leap of excitement she had at the thought of their spending two weeks together. If his pulse hammered from the feel of her hand in his. Or if he was simply playing his assigned role.

As they sped north along Rock Creek Parkway under a pale winter moon, she reminded herself that she, too, was playing a part. Still, she couldn't help wondering just how far they'd take their respective roles when the limo pulled up at the vice-presidential residence.

After her experience in the ladies' room, she was just beginning to realize just how little privacy the vice president enjoyed. Conducting a romance, even a fake one, under the watchful eyes of half a dozen agents and those all-pervasive cameras was going to take a bit more savoir faire than she'd realized.

So when they stepped out of the limo under the sheltering overhang of the porte cochere and Adam suggested a walk in the moonlight to stretch their legs, Maggie readily agreed. Unless she invited him up to the vice president's bedroom, which she couldn't quite bring herself to do, the only place they could talk privately was the open air.

"Are you sure you'll be warm enough?" he asked, lifting the collar of her angora cloak to frame her cheeks.

With her face cradled in his hands and his blue eyes

gazing down at her like that, Maggie discovered that warm was *not* a problem.

"I'm fine."

"Good."

He pulled on the black wool overcoat he hadn't bothered with in the limo and tucked her gloved hand in his arm. As he led the way toward the rose garden at the west side of the house, Maggie saw Denise Kowalski nod to another agent who'd stepped out of the chase car. The man bundled his collar up against his ears and trudged after them, staying far enough behind to remain out of earshot.

Wonderful. Just what she needed, the first time she was alone with Adam Ridgeway on a star-studded, moonlit night. A chaperon.

Chapter 4

With the Secret Service agent trudging some distance behind them, Maggie and Adam walked side by side through the dappled moonlight. Snow-laden trees shielded them from the distant murmur of traffic still moving along Massachusetts Avenue. Their footsteps echoed softly on the wet pavement, almost lost in the pounding of Maggie's pulse.

She was vividly, stunningly aware of Adam's nearness. Of the way he slowed his long stride to match hers. Of the warmth of his body where he kept her hand tucked against his side.

"You did well tonight," Adam said quietly. "Very well."

Her small laugh puffed out in a cloud of white vapor. "I almost blew it on the Pan-American Monetary Stabilization Plan. Thanks for rescuing me."

"My pleasure, Madam Vice President."

With a confidence that told Maggie he knew his way around, Adam led her to a brick path cutting through a winter white garden. Concentric rings of severely pruned rosebushes poked through the blanket of snow, like ghostly dwarfs standing sentinel around the small arched arbor at the center of the garden. Despite the bright moonlight streaming through the latticework, Maggie soon discovered that the airy bower provided an illusion of privacy. She ran a gloved finger along a wooden slat, causing a soft shower of white, and tried not to wonder just how many times Adam had escorted Taylor Grant to this same little arbor.

Their Secret Service escort halted at the perimeter of the garden. Hunching his shoulders against the cold, he stomped his feet once or twice and turned slowly to survey the surrounding area. As if to take advantage of their privacy, Adam's shadow merged with Maggie's from behind, and then his arms slid around her waist. He pulled her back against his chest, and she promptly forgot all about their escort.

They were playing a role, Maggie reminded herself once more. This intimate contact with Adam was integral to their mission. Despite her stern reminder, however, she was finding it more and more difficult to separate reality from this enactment of her secret, half-formed fantasies. With a little sigh, she laid her head against his shoulder.

"Did Taylor pass you any information we need to check out?" he asked, his warm breath fanning her ear.

Taylor, Maggie noted. Not the vice president, or even Mrs. Grant.

"She thinks Stoney Armstrong was motivated by something other than a desire to see an old friend when he asked to escort her to the fund-raiser in L.A. tomorrow night. He wasn't particularly pleased when she told him no."

Adam tightened his arms, drawing her closer into his warmth. "What does she think was behind his call?"

"She wasn't sure, but suggested we talk to his agent and his hairstylist."

"His hairstylist?"

Maggie turned in his arms. Mindful of the cameras that swept the grounds continuously, she flattened her palms against the fine wool worsted of his lapels. The steamy vapor of her breath mingled intimately with his as she tilted her head back to look up at him.

"Evidently Stoney's stylist has more input into his career than his agent."

Adam's hand tunneled under the collar of her cape to cradle her neck. "We'll check it out."

His caressing smile made Maggie's heart thump painfully against her bodysuit. When it came to role-playing, she thought, Adam Ridgeway could give Stoney Armstrong a run for his money at the box office.

"Anything else?"

Maggie stared up at the face just inches from her own. The bright moonlight reflecting off the snow cast his lean, aristocratic features into sharp relief. Cameras or no cameras, she felt the impact of his presence to the tips of her toes. Forcing herself to concentrate on her mission, she relayed what the vice president had told her about the other men who'd appeared so briefly in her personal life.

"Mrs. Grant hasn't seen Peter Donovan, her former campaign manager, in over three years. He and his new wife received invitations to the inaugural ball but didn't make it. Donovan had just had surgery, I think."

"An emergency appendectomy," Adam confirmed. "What about the treasury secretary?"

"Mrs. Grant meets frequently with James Elliot. Whenever the president calls a cabinet meeting. Or when Elliot needs to talk to her separately on Treasury business."

The hand cradling her head brought her mouth to within

inches of his. Anyone watching would see two people in an intimate embrace, but only Maggie knew just how intimate it was. She'd never realized how well she and Adam would fit together.

"And?" he prompted, his warm breath feathering her cheeks.

She could do this. She could keep her voice calm and her mind focused on the mission with her hips nestled against his and his mouth a whisper from hers.

"She can't believe the secretary is behind this threat. Besides being one of the president's closest friends, he's a good man, according to Mrs. Grant. The crazy weekend they spent together was just that—a moment out of time that neither one expected to happen and neither wants to repeat. James reconciled with his wife shortly after that, and they seem—"

She broke off as his lips traced across her cheek.

"Keep talking," he murmured.

Right. Uh-huh. She was supposed to talk while Adam planted explosive little kisses on her face and her heart was jackhammering in her chest.

"You said my romantic image needed polishing, remember?" he said, angling her face up for a slow, sensual exploration. "I'll polish while you tell me what else Taylor had to say."

There it was again. That friendly little *Taylor*.

"That's about it," Maggie got out. "Anything new from your end?"

"Not much. Jake's checking out a classified program Donovan's company, Digicon, is trying to sell the Pentagon. He's heard rumors that the program is a last-ditch effort to keep the company from going under."

"Mmm?"

Carefully filing away that bit of information for future

reference, Maggie focused on more immediate aspects of her mission. Like the heat that burned just under her skin when Adam trailed a soft kiss toward the corner of her mouth. And the cold that was creeping up under the back hem of her cloak.

"Adam?"

He raised his head. "Yes?"

"Just how much polishing are you planning to do tonight?"

"Quite a bit."

"Then you'd better do it quickly." Her lips curved into a quicksilver grin. "My front is all toasty from snuggling up to you like this, but my backside is freezing."

His blue eyes glinted. "Let's see what we can do to warm you up."

Maggie had been kissed by a respectable number of men in her thirty-two years. Some had exhibited more enthusiasm than finesse. A few had demonstrated very skilled techniques. More than one had raised her body temperature by a number of degrees. But none had ignited the instantaneous combustion that Adam did.

At the crush of his mouth on hers, heat speared through Maggie's stomach. Tiny white-hot flickers of desire darted along her nerves, setting them on fire. In those first, explosive seconds, she decided that Adam's kiss was all she had dreamed it would be. Hard. Demanding. Consuming.

Then she stopped thinking altogether. Wrapping her arms around his neck, she did some polishing of her own.

When they finally broke contact, Adam's image had been restored to its full glory and Maggie could barely find the strength to drag air into her starved lungs.

His eyes raked her face, their blue depths gleaming with

a fierce light that thrilled her for all of the two or three seconds he allowed it to show.

"Warm enough now?"

"Roasting," she answered truthfully.

He started to reply, but at that moment a loud, reverberating thump shattered the stillness of the night.

They sprang apart.

Adam whirled toward the sound, his hand diving under the flap of his overcoat.

Maggie jumped to one side to get an unobstructed view around him. She reached instinctively for her weapon, then grimaced when she remembered she wasn't armed. Muttering a rather un-vice-presidential oath under her breath, she peered across the moonlit rose garden.

Pinned by their combined glares, the Secret Service agent standing guard at the entrance to the rose garden paused, one foot lifted high in the air.

"Er, sorry…"

Shamefaced, he lowered his foot to the ground.

Guilt flooded through Maggie as she straightened. The poor man had obviously been trying to stomp some warmth into his chilled feet. While she and Adam were polishing away, he must have been freezing.

"We'd better go inside," she murmured.

"I'll take you back to the house, but I won't come in. Not tonight."

Try as she might, Maggie couldn't tell whether the reluctance in Adam's voice was real, or part of this charade of theirs. Her reluctance, on the other hand, was very real. "I'll see you at the airport tomorrow, then."

He brushed a thumb across her mouth, which was still tender from his kiss. Although his touch and his posture were those of an attentive lover, his message held a hint of grim reality.

"You'll see me before that, if you need me. We've rigged a communications center in the British embassy, right across the street. It's well within range of the transmitter in your ring. I'll hear every sound, every breath you take throughout the night."

Maggie swallowed as an unforeseen aspect of this tight communications net suddenly occurred to her. Good Lord, what if she snored in her sleep?

If the memory of Adam's searing kiss wasn't enough to keep her tossing and turning, that daunting thought was. Her own romantic image might need serious polishing come morning, if she treated Adam to a chorus of snores and snuffles.

Tucking her hand in his arm, they strolled back toward the house. Just before they stepped into the pool of light cast by the glowing brass lanterns, Adam pulled her to a halt.

"Here, you'd better take this."

Keeping her body between his and the watchful eyes of the Secret Service man, he slipped a small, handkerchief-wrapped package into the pocket of her cloak.

"What is it? Something from Special Devices?"

Maybe they'd come up with some kind of a weapon for her, after all.

"No," Adam replied, escorting her to the front door. "Something from me."

As she watched the taillights of his car disappear down the long, winding driveway, Maggie felt strangely bereft. She folded her right hand over her left, taking comfort from the feel of the heavy band under her glove.

When the last crunch of tires on snowy pavement faded, she said good-night to her foot-stomping watchdog, went inside and climbed the curving staircase to the second floor.

The soft click of the bedroom door brought Lillian Roth

awake. Jerking upright in a chintz-covered armchair, the dresser ran a hand through her fuzzy gray hair. Fatigue etched her face before it settled into its habitual severe lines.

"You shouldn't have waited up," Maggie protested, shrugging out of the cape.

Lillian pushed herself to her feet. "I always wait up for Mrs. Grant. Well, how did it go?"

"It went…"

A kaleidoscope of colorful images flashed through Maggie's mind. The Kennedy Center's brilliant red-and-gold opera house. The huge ruby winking in the decoration pinned to the Indian ambassador's sash. A moonlit, winter white garden, and Adam's face hovering inches from hers.

"…very well," she finished softly.

"Humph." Lillian reached for the cape lying across the back of a chair.

"I'll take care of that," Maggie said. Whatever Adam had tucked in her pocket, she wanted to check it out herself. "Why don't you go to bed? I can undress myself."

"Mrs. Grant always—"

"Lillian."

The small woman squared her shoulders. In the quiet of the sitting room, two strong wills collided.

"Perhaps you intend to sleep in that corset you're strapped into?"

Maggie conceded defeat. "No, I don't."

"I'll get your gown and robe."

The expression in Lillian's black eyes as she sailed toward the huge walk-in closet wasn't exactly smug, but it was pretty darn close to it.

By the time she returned with a lemony silk nightdress and robe, Maggie had stashed Adam's package under her pillow and loosened as many of the back buttons on the velvet tunic as she could reach. Turning, she waited while

Lillian undid the rest. When the Velcro fastening on the bodysuit gave way, she heaved a sigh of relief.

Only later, when the big house had settled down to an uneven, creaking slumber and Maggie was finally alone, did she pull the package from its hiding place under the pillow. With infinite care, she unwrapped the folds of Adam's crisp, starched handkerchief.

Two bags of cashews and a souvenir box of Godiva chocolates stamped with the seal of the Indian embassy tumbled onto the sheet.

Maggie gave a gasp of delight. Lifting her hand, she murmured into the ring, "Thunder, this is Chameleon. Do you read me?"

"Loud and clear."

"You doll! Thanks for the emergency rations. I owe you one."

After a pause so slight Maggie thought she might have imagined it, his reply drifted through the stillness. "I'll let you know when I'm ready to collect."

"Time to get up."

Maggie opened one eye. She peered at Lillian, then squinted past her at the curtained windows.

"It's still dark out," she protested, pulling the covers up around her ears.

"Mrs. Grant always runs early."

"This early?"

"This early," Lillian confirmed unsympathetically.

Intel had briefed Maggie about the vice president's morning jog, of course, but they'd left out one or two key points. Like the fact that it was apparently accomplished in cold, dank darkness.

"I've laid out some running clothes in the bathroom. Breakfast will be ready by the time you get back."

Breakfast!

The thought of food gave Maggie the impetus she needed to crawl out of her warm cocoon. Frigid air washed over her body, raising goose bumps on every patch of exposed skin. She shivered as the silk of her nightdress cooled and new bumps rose. Although she'd much admired this frothy confection of pale yellow silk and gossamer lace last night, Maggie now heartily wished the vice president's tastes ran to warm flannel pajamas. Pulling on the matching lemon robe, she glanced at the small gold carriage clock on the bedside table.

Five-twenty—a.m.

If she'd slept a full hour last night, she'd be surprised. The knot of tension caused by concentrating so fiercely on her role had taken forever to seep out of Maggie's system. The tension generated by a certain dark-haired special envoy had refused to seep, however. Instead, her inner agitation had coiled tighter and tighter every time she felt the weight of the ring on her finger. It was as though Adam were with her in the darkness. Which he was.

With every restless toss, she remembered the touch of his mouth on hers. Every turn brought back the scent of his expensive after-shave. And every time her stomach grumbled about its less-than-satisfied state, she snuck another chocolate from the foil-covered box.

As she hurried to the bathroom, Maggie smiled at the memory of those luscious vanilla creams and melt-in-your-mouth caramels. Somehow, that little box of candies symbolized more than anything else the subtle shift that had occurred last night in her relationship with Adam Ridgeway.

Over the past three years, they'd shared some desperate hours and days and weeks. They'd grown close, as only members of a small, tightly knit organization can. But until last night, they hadn't allowed themselves to step through the invisible wall that separated OMEGA's cool, authoritative director from his operatives. Maggie had always maintained her independence, and Adam had always kept his distance.

Right now, that wall didn't seem quite as high. Or as impenetrable. And after last night, the distance between them had shortened considerably. Twisting the gold ring around on her finger, she smiled and turned on the taps full blast.

She returned to the bedroom a short while later dressed in blue metallic spandex thermal leggings, a matching long-sleeved top, and comfortable Reeboks. Lillian eyed her critically, then held up an oversize gold-and-blue UCLA sweatshirt.

"I found this in the closet. It should be long enough to disguise your hips."

"Thanks," Maggie said dryly.

"Remember, Mrs. Grant usually does ten minutes of warm-up exercises before her run. Leg bends, calf stretches and twists. Then it's twice around Observatory Circle and back through the grounds."

As she tugged the sweatshirt over her head, Maggie did a rapid mental calculation of the circumference of the seventy-three acres that comprised the observatory grounds. She multiplied that by two, translated the distance into miles, and bit back a groan at the result.

Six miles. At least. Good grief!

Of necessity, OMEGA agents kept in top physical shape, but they had all developed their own individualized conditioning programs. Given a choice, Maggie would have far preferred her own regime of high-impact aerobics in a nice warm spa to slogging six miles in the icy, predawn air.

"By the way," Lillian let drop as she headed for the

door, "the agent who usually jogs with Mrs. Grant won the Boston Marathon a couple of years ago."

This time Maggie didn't even try to hold back her groan.

Lillian's mouth softened into something suspiciously close to a smile.

"But that particular individual is in L.A.," she continued, "working the advance for her—for your trip. The other agents drew straws to see who has to run with you this morning. The loser's waiting downstairs. He's a few pounds overweight, and very slow."

Giving silent thanks for small blessings, Maggie made her way down the curving staircase. Okay, she told herself, it was only six miles. She could do this. She could run six miles in the service of her country.

Four and a half miles later, she was seriously questioning both her sanity and her dedication to her country.

Frigid air lanced into her lungs with every labored breath. Her heart slammed painfully against her ribs. Her legs felt like overcooked spaghetti and threatened to collapse with every step.

The slap of her sneakers against the wet pavement grew more and more erratic as Maggie struggled to pump her way up yet another damned incline. The rolling hills that had appeared so picturesque when she drove through the naval observatory complex yesterday afternoon now loomed in front of her like mountain peaks. Her only consolation was that the poor agent chugging along behind her couldn't hear the sound of her labored breath over his own heaving gasps.

At least the gloomy darkness had given way to a drizzly dawn. Headlights sliced through a soupy gray mist as military and civilian workers arrived for work at the various scientific facilities scattered around the extensive grounds.

The civilians gave a cheerful wave, obviously used to seeing the vice president on her early-morning run. The military snapped to attention and saluted. Hoping her grimace would pass for a smile, Maggie returned their greetings.

When the two-story building that housed the nautical almanac office loomed out of the mist, Maggie sagged with relief. Thank God. Only a half circuit of the perimeter to go! Dragging in another lungful of cold air, she concentrated fiercely on placing one foot in front of the other once. Twice. Three times. Counting seemed to help, she discovered.

Sixty-two steps took her across the broad expanse of parking lot beside the almanac office.

Another thirty-seven brought her to the path that paralleled Massachusetts Avenue.

Five more paces, and she was shielded from the wind by the tall pines, thick on her right, thinner on her left, where the path edged almost to the wrought-iron fence. Her lungs on fire, her calves cramping, Maggie following the curving asphalt trail.

At one hundred and three steps past the west gate, the distinctive conical turret of the vice president's mansion poked into view above the tops of the snow-laden pines. She almost sobbed in relief.

At exactly one hundred and twenty-six paces, the shot rang out.

With a startled ''Umph,'' Maggie hit the ground.

Chapter 5

In a small room on the fourth floor of the British embassy, less than a half block away, Adam froze.

He tore his gaze from the bank of flickering monitors and stared down at the face of his watch, as if expecting an instant replay of the single sharp report—and of Maggie's surprised grunt. Then he exploded into action.

Racing for the door, he snarled an order at the stunned communications technician. "Call Jaguar! Tell him Chameleon's down."

He ripped open the door and raced into the deserted hallway, cursing himself every step of the way. How could he have underestimated the threat? How could he have been so damned cold, so analytical, about the security on the grounds of the naval observatory? He shouldn't have trusted that abstract analysis. Not with Maggie.

His heart battering against his ribs, he crashed through the door to the stairs. The stairwell was empty, as Adam had known it would be. He'd pulled a few strings for this mission. Without a single question, the British ambassador had cleared the entire fourth floor of the embassy for OMEGA's use. It had proven an ideal site for an observation post. Only the broad expanse of Massachusetts Avenue, a screen of pines and a rolling lawn separated it from the vice-presidential mansion and the surrounding grounds.

Even more to the point, the embassy was close enough for OMEGA to tap into the Secret Service's own surveillance system. Adam had tracked Maggie from the moment she emerged from her bedroom this morning. Infrared cameras so sensitive that they picked up even the trickle of sweat rolling down her cheek had recorded her jog through the predawn gloom. With the aid of the concealed transmitter in her ring, Adam had heard her every gasp—and every increasingly acerbic comment she muttered under her breath as she jogged up yet another hill.

As he barreled down the stairs, Adam replayed over and over in his mind those moments when she'd entered the home stretch. There, in those few yards where the pines branched over the path and obscured the camera's angle, she'd disappeared from view for a few seconds. Christ! A few seconds, and he—

"Get…off…me! Puh-leez!"

Maggie's voice jerked Adam to a halt. His chest heaving, he stared down at his watch.

"Are you…all right?"

He didn't recognize the panting male voice, but guessed immediately it was the agent who'd trailed Maggie during her run.

"I'm…fine."

"Are…you…sure, ma'am?"

She sucked in a rasping breath. "I'm sure."

"But you…went down!" The man was still huffing.

"That bus, when it backfired...I thought it was a shot. And you went down."

"I thought...it was a shot, too. That's why I went down." Chagrin, and the faintest trace of rueful laughter, crept into her voice. "I guess I'm a little jumpy this morning."

Alone in the empty stairwell, Adam closed his eyes. His throat was so damn tight he couldn't breathe, cold sweat was running down his back, and Maggie was laughing. Laughing! With great physical effort, Adam unclenched his jaw and headed back to the control room.

Joe Samuels, OMEGA's senior communications technician, stood with one big hand fisted around a radio mike.

"She okay?"

"She's okay. It wasn't a gunshot. A bus backfired."

The grim expression on Joe's face eased, and his brown eyes lost their fierce glitter. "A bus!"

"A bus."

The black man shook his head as tension drained visibly from his big body. "Well, with Chameleon, you never know."

"No, you don't," Adam replied, an edge to his voice that he couldn't quite suppress.

Joe's brows lifted in surprise at the director's acid tone, but he refrained from commenting.

"Get Jaguar on the net, would you? I'll give him a quick update before I go upstairs to the heliport."

Nodding, Joe reseated himself at the communications console. An acknowledged expert in satellite transmissions, he'd been actively recruited by half a dozen major corporations when he left military service a few years ago. He could have named his own salary, strolled into work wearing tailored suits and vests and jetted across continents in sleek corporate aircraft. Instead, he'd joined the OMEGA team at about the same time Maggie had.

Adam was well aware of the bond between them. During long, tense days and nights in the control center, the technician worked his electronic magic to keep her plugged into whichever field agent she was controlling at the time. When Chameleon was in the field, Joe always arranged the duty schedules so that he manned the control center himself.

Adam suspected that their friendship might have been tested a bit lately, however. To Joe's disgust, his twins had developed a passion for Maggie's repulsive house pet. The boys begged to keep the reptile whenever she left town. They delighted in Terence's unique repertoire of tricks, particularly his ability to take out a fly halfway across a room with his yard-long tongue. Joe had been visibly relieved when Maggie informed him she'd drafted her father for iguana duty this time.

While he waited for Jaguar to come on-line, Adam forced himself to relax his rigid muscles. Gradually the tension gripping his gut eased. In its place came a different and even more unsettling sensation.

For the first time in a long, long time, he'd reacted without thinking. Sheer animal instinct had sent him crashing out into the hallway. The last time he reacted like that had been in a dark alley outside a Hong Kong hotel. Eight years ago. Just before the night had erupted in a blinding explosion, and he'd dived for cover.

When he'd heard Maggie's surprised cry a few moments ago, Adam had felt the same as he had when the world blew up all around him.

With a wry grimace, he acknowledged that her cry had irrevocably, irretrievably shattered the detachment he'd forced himself to maintain all these years as OMEGA's director. The distance he'd kept between himself and Maggie Sinclair had narrowed to a single heartbeat. To the sound of a bus backfiring.

Adam refused to deny the truth any longer. He wanted her. With a need so fierce, so raw, it consumed him.

Thirty minutes, he thought, dragging in a slow breath. Thirty minutes until he met her at Andrews Air Force Base for the flight to California. Thirty minutes, and Adam wouldn't have to watch her from a half block away over these damned monitors. When they met at the airport, he promised himself, the "relationship" between the vice president of the United States and the president's special envoy would enter a new and very intimate stage.

"Thirty minutes!"

Sweat-drenched, her lungs on fire and her legs wobbling like overstretched rubber bands, Maggie stared at Lillian in disbelief.

"I thought our plane wasn't scheduled to leave until nine!"

"The White House command post called a few moments ago. There's another snowstorm moving in. The pilot would like to get off before the front hits, if you can make it. I told them you could."

The dresser jerked her mop of frizzy gray curls toward the bathroom. "You have seven minutes to shower and do your makeup. Your breakfast tray and travel clothes will be waiting for you when you get out. We leave the house at exactly oh-seven-twenty."

"Were you ever in the Marines, by any chance?" Maggie tossed over her shoulder as she forced her vociferously protesting legs to carry her toward the bathroom.

Lillian snorted. "Before I came to work for Mrs. Grant, I ran a preschool. I'd like to see any platoon of Marines handle that. You'd better get it in gear."

Maggie got it in gear.

She sagged against the shower tiles for two precious minutes, letting the steaming-hot water soak into her aching muscles, then soaped and shampooed with record-breaking speed. Thankfully, the vice president's short, stylish shag took all of ninety seconds to blow-dry. A slather of concealing foundation, a quick application of mascara and mauve eye shadow, a slash of lipstick, and she was out of the bathroom.

The sight of the VP's breakfast tray, with its single granola bar on a gold-rimmed china plate and its crystal goblet filled with a greenish liquid, stopped Maggie in her tracks.

"What's in that glass?" she asked suspiciously.

"Guava juice," Lillian replied, bustling forward with a creamy wool pantsuit over one arm.

"*Guava* juice?" Maggie groaned. "Why couldn't your boss be a grease-loving biscuits-and-gravy Texan instead of a California health nut?"

Her mouth pursing, the older woman laid the pantsuit on the bed. She lifted the Kevlar bodysuit and dangled it in one hand.

"Maybe if you drank more guava juice and ate fewer biscuits," she said, with patently false sweetness, "you wouldn't need this."

Grinning, Maggie acknowledged the hit. That would teach her to criticize Mrs. Grant to Lillian Roth! Intelligence hadn't understated the bond of affection between the two women.

"Drink your juice," Lillian instructed. "We have exactly fifteen minutes to get you suited up and out of here."

Fourteen minutes later, Maggie and Lillian descended the curving central staircase. After a hurried last-minute update by a staffer on the short speech she was to give tonight in

L.A., she said goodbye to the various members of the staff who drifted out to wish the vice president an enjoyable vacation.

A car waited under the portico to take her and her small party to the naval observatory helipad. Gray, drizzly mist closed around the vehicle, almost obscuring the grounds, as they drove the short distance. Like an impatient mosquito, a navy-and-white-painted helicopter squatted on its circular pad, its rotor blades whirring.

Maggie, Lillian and Denise Kowalski, who would accompany the vice president to California, had no sooner strapped themselves in than the chopper lifted off, banked sharply and headed east. Maggie had flown out of Andrews Air Force Base in Maryland, just across the Potomac from Washington, many times. She settled back against the padded seat to enjoy the short flight and grab the first few moments of relative calm since Lillian had rousted her out of bed two hours ago.

"Have you seen this morning's *Post?*" the sandy-haired agent asked, raising her voice to be heard over the thump of the rotor blades.

"No."

Denise held out a folded section of Washington's leading newspaper. "They did a whole center spread on your appearance at last night's benefit."

"Really?"

Just in time, Maggie bit back the observation that she'd never thought of herself as centerfold material.

"The special envoy looks rather distinguished in black and white, doesn't he?" the agent commented mildly.

He looked more than distinguished, Maggie thought. He looked devastating. Her stomach gave a little lurch when she saw the enlarged close-up shot of her and Adam. Or rather Taylor Grant and Adam. The photographer had caught them just as she emerged from the limo. Adam was holding his out his hand to help her out. Her face was in profile, but his was captured in precise detail. If Maggie hadn't remembered just in time that he was playing a role, the expression in his eyes as he looked down at her, or at Taylor—whoever!—would have caused a total meltdown of her synthetic corset. She stared at the picture, mesmerized, for several long minutes before studying the accompanying article.

The reporter covering the glittering gala had evidently found the VP and her escort far more titillating than the event itself. The story included several more shots of Maggie/Taylor and Adam, as well as a gossipy little side note about the fact that the wealthy, sophisticated special envoy was accompanying the vice president to her private retreat for two weeks. Judging by the way his eyes devoured the lovely Mrs. Grant, the reporter oozed, it should be a most enjoyable vacation for all parties involved.

Maggie might have agreed with her, but for the fact that sometime during this supposed vacation she hoped to lure a killer into the open.

She spent the rest of the short trip leafing through the thick *Post,* although she couldn't help sneaking repeated glances at the folded section in her lap. As she studied the shot of them getting out of the limo, the curious niggle of resentment she'd felt when Adam first took her hand last night returned.

Her lips twisted as she identified the feeling for what it was. Jealousy. Weirdly enough, she was jealous of herself.

She'd wanted Adam to look at *her* like that, to touch *her,* for so long. Almost as much as she'd wanted to touch him. But he'd held himself back, just as she had. Neither of them had been ready to acknowledge the attraction that sizzled between them, as electric and charged as a sultry summer night just before a storm. Neither had wanted to upset the delicate balance between their professional responsibilities and their personal needs.

Now they hovered in some kind of in-between state. That shattering kiss in the snow-swept garden, not to mention those sinful chocolates, had destroyed that balance forever. When this mission was over, when they stopped playing these assigned roles, they'd have to find a new level, a new balance. What that balance would be, she had no idea, but for the first time since joining OMEGA she was more excited about concluding an operation than about conducting it.

Adam's helicopter landed at Andrews Air Force Base a few moments before the vice president's.

Home to the fleet of presidential aircraft and the crews who flew and maintained them, Andrews was well equipped to handle the entourages that normally traveled with their distinguished passengers. Although the various craft used by the chief executive and his deputy were always parked in a secure area a safe distance from the rest of the flight-line activity, a well-appointed VIP lounge was only a short drive away.

Yanking open the helo's door, a blue-suited crew chief gestured toward a waiting sedan. "There's hot coffee in the lounge, sir, if you'd like to wait there. The driver will take you over."

Ducking under the whirring rotor blades, Adam shook his head. "I'm fine. I'll wait by the plane." Turning up the collar of his tan camel-hair overcoat, he walked to the Gulfstream jet warming up on the parking apron.

When discharging the duties of her office, the vice president usually traveled aboard Air Force Two, a huge, specially equipped 747 crammed with communications gear and fitted with several compartments for the media and assorted staff members who traveled with their boss. For this trip—a combination of party business and personal pleasure that didn't require her normal entourage—she'd fly aboard a smaller, more economical plane.

Cold wind whipped Adam's hair as he waited beside the sleek white-painted Gulfstream. Around him, crew members performed a last-minute visual check of the aircraft while a portable power cart slowly revved up the twin Rolls-Royce turbofan engines. Having flown jet fighters during his long-ago stint in the navy, Adam had maintained his flight proficiency over the years. At any other time, he would have observed the takeoff preparations with a keen eye, and his hands would have itched to take the stick. Today, the fists he'd shoved into the pockets of his overcoat remained tightly clenched.

During the short flight to Andrews, reality had set in. The raw male need that had surged through him when he finally admitted that he wanted Maggie had given way to an even fiercer need. The need to protect her.

She was at risk, as she'd never been before. Like a sacrificial goat staked out at the end of a tether, she was offering herself as a target for an assassin. Adam couldn't believe he'd allowed himself to consider, even for a moment, unleashing his desire. He couldn't allow himself or her to be distracted from their deadly mission during the days ahead.

But when this mission was over...

By the time he heard the distant *whump* of rotor blades, he had himself well in control again. Narrowing his eyes against the drizzle, he searched the dense gray haze. A few seconds later, a blue-and-white chopper broke through the mist and hovered above the runway. It drifted down until its skids touched lightly. Then the copilot jumped out to open the passenger-compartment door.

Maggie climbed out first. She smiled her thanks at the helmeted copilot and darted out from under the turning rotor blades. The downwash from the blades ruffled her auburn hair and whirled the skirts of her cream-colored wool coat around her calves.

Although Adam was expecting it, her likeness to Taylor Grant still generated a small shock. The resemblance didn't have anything to do with the wine-colored hair or the jawline that Field Dress had molded so exactly, he decided as he watched her cross the wet tarmac. It was a matter of style. An inner vitality. A shimmering essence that the two women had in common.

But the mischievous gleam that filled Maggie's eyes as she returned the greetings of the crew members who snapped to attention was hers alone. She knew very well that her less-than-precise rendition of a military salute would make Adam grimace inwardly. Which it did. After this mission, he promised himself, he'd teach her just how to bend that elbow. Among other things.

"Good morning."

Taylor's voice carried over the whine of the Gulfstream's engines and the whir of the helo's blades. This was Chameleon at her finest, Adam thought in silent admiration. No one in OMEGA could come close to matching Maggie's skill at pulling a deep-cover identity around her like an invisible cloak.

"Good morning," he replied, taking her outstretched hands in both of his.

In the periphery of his vision, he saw the news team from the White House pool who'd braved the cold to cover the VP's departure recording their greeting.

So did Maggie. Suddenly ridiculously self-conscious, she

smiled up at Adam. She felt like a teenager about to go out on a closely chaperoned date, for Pete's sake!

"Are you sure you want to exchange two weeks of Washington's cold, snowy weather for California's cold, snowy weather?" she asked, tilting her head in a coquettish gesture while the cameras whirred.

"I'm sure. Come on, let's get you aboard before your...nose freezes."

She bit back a grin as he passed her hand to the steward who was waiting to help her aboard.

Shrugging out of her wool coat, Maggie handed it to the hovering attendant. She could get used to this pampering, she thought, if not to the idea of being constantly under surveillance. The interior of the plane was like none she'd ever seen before, all gleaming oak, polished brass and plush blue upholstery.

She had no trouble identifying her seat. A slipcover embroidered with the vice president's seal draped a huge armchair, one of two in a private forward compartment. While she strapped herself in, Adam took the seat opposite her. She shifted her feet under the smooth oak table to make room for his long legs.

Lillian and Denise settled themselves in the rear compartment, along with several other Secret Service agents, who'd coordinated the final details of the L.A. visit. Even before the hatch had closed, Denise had bent over an outspread map and begun a review of the security along the route from the airport to the hotel.

Within moments, the pilot's voice came over the intercom, welcoming them aboard and detailing the flight times and refueling stop. After a smooth, swift roll down the runway, they were airborne. Immediately dense, impenetrable mist surrounded the plane and cut off any view of the capital. The aircraft climbed steeply, and eventually leveled out at twenty thousand feet.

"Would you care for juice, Mrs. Grant?"

Maggie repressed a shudder at the sight of the grayish liquid filling the decanter on the steward's tray. It wasn't guava juice, obviously, and that had been bad enough.

"No, thank you. I'm fine."

"And you, sir?"

"Coffee, please. Black."

Maggie's mouth watered as the aroma of fresh-brewed coffee filled the compartment.

"Mrs. Grant doesn't care for them, sir, but I have an assortment of rolls and Danish for the other passengers. Or I can prepare eggs and bacon in the galley, if you'd like."

Carefully avoiding Maggie's eyes, Adam shook his head. "No, in deference to Mrs. Grant, I'll skip the bacon and eggs. Just bring me a Danish."

Maggie kicked him under the table.

"And some rolls."

"Very good, sir."

As soon as the door closed behind the steward, Maggie fiddled with the intercom switch on the communications console beside her seat. The low hum of voices from the cockpit was cut off.

"Can we talk?" she asked, couching her question in a playful tone, in case the cabin contained listening systems she wasn't aware of.

"We can," he replied, relaxing. "Joe went over the communications wiring diagram of the plane last night, and our people did a sweep this morning. This cabin is secure."

Maggie sagged back against her seat. "Thank God. I never realized how nerve-racking it is to live in an electronic fishbowl every day of your life." She eyed the steaming mug in front of him. "Are you going to drink that coffee?"

"No, you are. Go ahead. I'll listen for the steward."

Cradling the cup in both hands, she inhaled the fragrant aroma before taking a hearty gulp. Her eyes closed in sheer delight as she savored the hot, rich brew.

"Ahh…"

"Better than guava juice?"

She opened one eye to find Adam watching her. "You heard that, did you?"

"I did."

Maggie refused to ask what else he'd heard. Sometime during her restless night, she'd decided that if she snored, she didn't want to know about it.

His voice took on an edge. "I also heard the bus backfire this morning."

She took another sip of coffee. "Talk about your basic motivational techniques! I wasn't sure I could get up that last hill, but after a near-miss by a killer bus, I didn't have any difficulty making it to cover."

"I'm glad you find the incident so amusing."

The acid in his words surprised her. "Didn't you?"

"Not particularly. It just demonstrated how vulnerable you are. How vulnerable the vice president is."

Maggie set the mug down carefully. "So do we have anything more on our list of potential assassins?"

"Nothing on the treasury secretary. Other than his one brief fling with Mrs. Grant during a rocky period in his marriage, Elliot's squeaky-clean. Before being confirmed by the Senate, he went through a background screening that revealed everything from his personal finances to his taste in food."

"Let's not talk about food! What about his finances?"

"He built a personal fortune speculating on the market,

but over the years converted his riskier ventures to T-bonds."

She frowned. "T-bonds? Isn't it a conflict of interest for him to hold treasury bonds in his current position?"

"It would be, if he hadn't placed them in a blind trust, administered by his lawyers and the board of directors of First Bank."

"First Bank?" Something nagged at the back of Maggie's mind, but she couldn't quite place it. "Isn't that the one headquartered in Miami?"

"With branches all through Central and South America."

She frowned, searching her memory. "I've heard something about First Bank recently."

Adam waited for her to continue. When she didn't, a smile tugged at his mouth. "First Bank helped draft the president's Pan-American Monetary Stabilization Plan."

"Oh. Right."

She was going to have to read up on that darn plan, Maggie thought. Stretching out her legs, she leaned back in the buttery-soft leather armchair. Her feet bumped Adam's under the oak table, then found a nest between them.

"Well, so much for James Elliot. What about the others?"

"Jaguar's digging into the contract Digicon, Donovan's firm, is pressing on the Pentagon. He should have something today."

"That leaves the gorgeous hunk of muscle-bound beefcake," she murmured, then caught Adam's cool look. "According to Mrs. Grant. And just about every female over the age of thirty," she added under her breath.

"Evidently Stoney Armstrong's public doesn't consider him quite as gorgeous as it used to. His last five movies were box-office bombs. The word is that he's washed-up in the industry. The exact phrasing, I believe, was that his sex appeal has gone south.''

"Did we get that from his agent?"

"His agent's en route to Poland to consult with an international starlet he's just taken on as a client." Adam paused, his eyes gleaming. "This information came from Armstrong's hairstylist."

"Someone got to him already? That was quick work."

"It took a near act of God, but Doc managed a late-evening appointment with the man."

Maggie choked back a laugh. "Doc? Our Doc had his hair styled?"

Dr. David Jensen was one of OMEGA's most skilled agents. In his civilian cover, he headed the engineering department of a major L.A. defense firm. Brilliant, analytical and cool under fire, he was also as conservative as they came. Maggie would give anything to see him with his short brown locks dressed by an avant-garde Hollywood hair designer.

"The things we do in service to our country," she commented, shaking her head.

"In this case, Doc's sacrifice paid off. Armstrong's stylist also let drop that the star attributes the downward spiral in his career to the fact that Taylor dumped him. As long as he was in her orbit, they shared the limelight. When she moved on, the spotlight followed her, and left him standing in the shadows."

A knock on the door heralded the arrival of the steward with more coffee and a basket of sweet rolls.

Maggie eyed the basket greedily and could barely wait for the steward to pour Adam's coffee and leave. This bundle of yummies would have to hold her until the banquet this evening. She needed all the calories she could ingest to maintain the intense concentration necessary for her various roles as vice president, former lover of an over-the-hill sex symbol, and present companion to the special envoy.

When Stoney Armstrong stepped out of the crowd gathered in the hotel lobby to greet the vice president a few hours later, Maggie realized immediately that Doc had received some faulty information. Whatever else had gone south, it wasn't the star's sex appeal.

Tanned, tawny-haired, and in possession of an incredible assortment of bulging muscles under a red knit shirt that stretched across massive shoulders, he grinned at Maggie.

"Hiya, Taylor—uh, Madam Vice President."

Since he carried no weapon in his hands and there was no way he could conceal anything under his body-hugging knit shirt, she responded with a cautious smile.

"Hello, Stoney."

At which point he sidestepped the ever-present Denise, brushed past Adam and swept an astonished Maggie into a back-bending, bone-crushing embrace.

A barrage of flashes exploded throughout the lobby. Dimly Maggie heard waves of astonished titters sweep through the crowd. Cameras whirred, and news crews climbed over each other for a better shot.

When he set her upright some moments later, Maggie was breathless, flushed, and almost as shaken as when the bus had backfired this morning.

Chapter 6

A million-dollar smile beamed down at her. "You're looking great, Taylor. Really great."

"You too, Stoney," Maggie returned, easing out of his hold.

"I like you with a little flesh on your bones."

"Thanks."

At her dry response, Stoney flashed another one of his trademark grins, all white teeth and crinkly eyes.

"What say I sneak you away from all this political hoopla for a few hours tonight? Like I used to, when you were governor?"

"What say you don't?" Adam's cool voice cut through the babble of the crowd. "The lady will be with me tonight."

Another barrage of blinding flashes went off as the two men faced each other. Talk about your basic headline-grabber, Maggie thought wryly. The vice president's former and current romantic interests squaring off in the lobby of

L.A.'s Century Plaza Hotel. The media were going to play this one for all it was worth. With a flash of insight, she realized that Adam had once more stepped into the breach and diverted attention from her.

Stoney's sun-bleached brows lifted. "Who are you?"

"Adam Ridgeway. Who are you?"

The onetime movie idol blinked, clearly taken aback at the question. "Me? Hey, I'm—"

He caught himself, then gave a bark of laughter. "You almost got me there, Ridgeway."

Grinning good-naturedly, he stuck out a paw the size of a catcher's mitt. Adam took it, a sardonic gleam in his blue eyes.

The media went wild.

The scene had all the drama of a daytime soap, and then some. Two men shook hands in a glare of flashing lights. When this shot hit the newspapers, Maggie thought, every woman in the country would envy Taylor Grant. Imagine being forced to choose between your basic sun-bronzed, superbly muscled Greek god and a dark-haired aristocrat whose eyes held a glint of danger.

When Stoney had milked the scene for all it was worth, Maggie knew it was time to move on.

"Will I see you at the banquet tonight?" she asked.

"Sure. But—" he glanced at Adam "—I kind of hoped we'd have a chance to talk. Privately."

"Maybe after the banquet," she suggested easily. "I'll be tied up until then."

"Yeah. Okay. After dinner."

Maggie spent a long afternoon listening to the California Council of Mayors present their list of grievances against the heavy-handed federal bureaucracy. Fortunately, all she was required to do was nod occasionally and, at the end of the session, promise that their complaints about programs mandated by Congress without accompanying funds to implement them would be looked into.

By the time she and Adam and the ever-vigilant Denise took the elevator to the penthouse suite, the long night, the transcontinental flight and the packed day had drained even Maggie's considerable store of energy. Or maybe it was the lack of sustenance, she thought, collapsing onto one of the sleek white leather couches scattered about the suite.

Sunlight streamed through the two-story wall of glass that overlooked the city, for once miraculously clear of smog, and bathed Maggie in a warm glow. After Washington's snowy cold, L.A.'s balmy, unseasonable seventy degrees felt heavenly. Feeling an uncharacteristic lassitude, she slipped off her shoes, propped her stockinged feet on a glass coffee table the size of a football field and heaved a huge sigh.

"We've got an hour until the banquet," Adam replied, his eyes on her face. "Why don't you relax for a while? I'll go next door to check in with my office, then shower and change. Shall I join you for a drink before we go downstairs?"

"That would be nice," Maggie replied.

"The hotel left a basket of delicacies in my suite. Shall I bring it with me, and we can explore it together?"

"By all means."

The hotel had left a basket in the vice president's suite, as well. To Maggie's infinite disappointment, it had contained only fruit and fancy glass jars of what looked and tasted like dry oats.

Buoyed by the thought of both food and time alone with Adam, Maggie pushed herself off the sofa and headed for the bedroom.

* * *

A half hour later, Lillian zipped up the back of a stunning flame-colored gown in floating layers of chiffon, then stood back to survey her charge. Her keen black eyes took in every detail, from the dramatic upsweep of her short hair to the tips of her strappy sandals, dyed to match the gown.

"You'll do."

Coming from Lillian, that was high praise indeed. Maggie smiled as she peered into the mirror to make sure her matte makeup fully covered the gel-like adhesive bone on her nose and chin.

"Thanks, Lillian. I couldn't pull this off without you."

"After twenty-four hours in your company, I'm beginning to suspect you could pull off this or any number of other improbable capers."

Maggie grinned. "Capers? We refer to them as missions."

"Whatever. I'll be right across the hall. Call me when you get back from the banquet."

"Don't wait up. I can manage. Besides," she added to forestall the inevitable protest, "I may have a visitor after the banquet, remember?"

If things got tense when Stoney Armstrong showed up, Maggie didn't want the older woman in the line of fire.

Lillian gave one of her patented sniffs. "You're going to have more than one visitor tonight, missy. I don't imagine the special envoy is going to leave you alone with Stoney."

Maggie lifted a brow. "We'll see how the situation develops. I'm used to operating independently on a mission, you know."

"Who's talking about your mission?"

Lillian gave the bedroom a final inspection, then left Maggie to mull that one over. She was still thinking about it when she walked into the huge, white-carpeted living room some time later.

Denise Kowalski rose at her entry. Attired in the full-length black satin skirt that Maggie recognized as her uniform for formal functions, the sandy-haired agent was all brisk efficiency as she ran through the security arrangements for the banquet. When Denise finished, she stood and moved to the door.

"I've got to go downstairs for the final walk-though. We're using locals to help screen the guests as they arrive. I want to make sure they know how to operate the hand scanners."

"Fine."

"This entire floor's secure," Denise stated earnestly, as if needing to justify her brief absence. "There are two post-standers at the elevators, and one at each of the stairwells. If you need them, just call." She nodded toward the hot line that linked the vice president's suite with the command post across the hall. "Or hit the panic button beside the bed."

"I know the routine," Maggie said, smiling.

The other woman grinned sheepishly. "Yes, ma'am, I guess you do."

Maggie studied the agent thoughtfully as she gathered her things and left. She was good. Darn good. From the moment their plane touched down at Los Angeles International, she'd been the vice president's second shadow. During the trip in from the airport, she'd directed the motorcade via the radio strapped to the inside of her wrist like a general marshaling his forces. What was more, she'd been prepared to take Stoney Armstrong down when he stepped out of the crowd in the lobby, and no doubt would have done so if Maggie hadn't acknowledged him.

According to the background brief OMEGA had prepared on Denise Kowalski, the woman had almost fifteen years with the Secret Service. She had joined the service at a time when female agents were a rarity, and had worked her way up the ranks. One divorce along the way. No children. Who could manage children and a career that demanded months on the road? Maggie wondered. Or the eighteen-hour days? Or a job that required instant willingness to take a bullet intended for someone else?

Denise would be one hell of an addition to the OMEGA team, Maggie decided. She made a mental note to speak to Adam about it when he joined her.

At the thought of their coming tête-à-tête, Maggie wrapped her arms across her chest. A shiver of anticipation whispered down her spine. They hadn't had a moment alone together since stepping off the plane. In his position as the president's special envoy, Adam commanded almost as much attention as the vice president had. Lobbyists and party hopefuls had clustered around him at every opportunity, bending his ear, asking his advice.

For the next thirty minutes, at least, Maggie would have his complete and undivided attention.

They needed to strategize, she reminded herself. To coordinate their plans for an evening that would include an intimate dinner with two hundred party faithful and a possible assassin in the person of a tanned, handsome movie star.

Although...

After her admittedly brief meeting with Stoney Armstrong this afternoon, Maggie found it difficult to believe he was the one who'd made that call. She'd met her share of desperate men, and a few whose utter lack of remorse for their assorted crimes chilled her. But when she looked up into Stoney's eyes after that mind-bending, back-bending kiss this afternoon, she hadn't seen a killer.

Then again, she reminded herself, Stoney Armstrong was an actor. A good one.

Her brow furrowed in thought, Maggie wandered through

the living room toward the wide flagstone terrace outside the glass wall. A balmy breeze warmed by the offshore Japanese currents lifted her layers of chiffon and rustled the palms scattered around the terrace. Drawn by the glow of lights, she crossed to the waist-high stone balustrade that circled the terrace.

The sight that greeted her made her gasp in stunned delight. Far below her, adorned in glittering gold diamonds, was the city of angels. Los Angeles by day might consist of palm trees and smog, towering skyscrapers and crumbling, thirties-era stucco cottages. But by night, from the perspective of the fortieth floor, it was a dreamscape of sparkling, iridescent lights. Thoroughly enchanted, Maggie leaned her elbows on the wide stone railing and drank in the incredible sight.

The buzz of the telephone sent a rush of pleasure though her veins. That had to be Adam. With his basket of goodies. She went back inside and caught the phone on the third ring.

"Yes?"

"This is Special Agent Harrison, Mrs. Grant. A Mr. Stoney Armstrong just stepped off the elevator. He'd like to speak to you."

Maggie didn't hesitate. "Of course."

In the blink of an eye, her excitement sharpened, changed focus. The woman whose senses had tingled at the thought of a private tête-à-tête with Adam transitioned instantly into the skilled, highly trained agent. Her mind racing with various ways to handle this unexpected contact with a prime suspect, Maggie lifted her left hand.

"Thunder? Thunder, do you read me?"

When he didn't respond, Maggie guessed Adam was still in the shower. As soon as he got out, he'd pick up on her conversation with Stoney and join her—if the circumstances required it. Actually, she thought, it might be better if Adam didn't appear on the scene. She'd be able to draw Stoney out far more easily without another man present, especially one he might consider a rival.

Quickly she dimmed the lights and retrieved the small gold lipstick Special Devices had included in her bag of tricks for this mission. As she tucked the tiny stun gun in the bodice of her gown, she wondered briefly if it was powerful enough to take down a man of Stoney Armstrong's massive proportions, as Special Devices had claimed.

If not, and if necessary, she'd bring Stoney down herself. He'd be unarmed, she knew. He couldn't have passed through the highly sophisticated security screens with a weapon on his person. She'd handled bigger men than him in the past.

When a knock sounded on the door to her suite a few moments later, she was ready, both mentally and physically, to face a possible killer.

If Stoney Armstrong harbored any deadly intent toward Taylor Grant, he didn't show it. His tanned cheeks creased in his famous studio grin that, for all its beefcake quality, was guaranteed to stir any woman's hormones. Perfect white teeth gleamed, and his Armani tux gaped open to reveal a broad expanse of muscled, white-shirted chest as he leaned one arm negligently against the doorjamb.

"Hello, Taylor."

"Hello, Stoney."

"I'm a little early."

"So I noticed. Come in."

He strolled into the penthouse, looking around with unabashed interest. The glass wall drew him like a magnet. Shoving his hands in his pockets, he strolled out onto the terrace.

"It's something, isn't it?" he murmured, his eyes on the endless sweep of lights against a now-velvet sky.

"It is," Maggie agreed.

His mouth twisted. "Hard to believe a thin crust is all that separates the glitter and glamour from the tar pits underneath."

His subtle reference to the La Brea tar pit, the famous archaeological site in the center of the city, wasn't lost on Maggie.

"You sound as though a few saber-toothed tigers might have crawled out of the sludge," she commented softly.

If OMEGA's information was correct, those predators were circling Stoney Armstrong even now, about to close in for the kill.

His broad shoulders lifted. "Hey, this is Tinseltown. Saber-toothed tigers do power lunches every Tuesday and Friday at Campanile."

Turning his back on the dazzling vista, he leaned his hips against the rail.

"God, you look great, Taylor. Sort of sleek and well fed, like a cat or a horse or something."

Stoney did a lot better in a tender scene when he used a script, Maggie thought sardonically.

He leaned against the railing, ankles crossed, hands in his pockets. With the breeze ruffling his gold hair and his tux gaping open to reveal a couple of acres of broad chest, he looked pretty well fed himself.

He cocked his head, studying her face. "It can't be all those raisins and sunflower seeds you put away that gave you such a glow. Is it this guy Ridgeway?"

When Maggie didn't answer, his smile twisted a bit.

"I saw some pictures of you two in the afternoon edition of the *Times*. Christ, I wish I had your publicist. Those were great shots. Especially the one where you were getting out of the limo.''

Maggie had rather liked that one herself.

''I thought maybe they were posed,'' he said, ''like the ones you used to do for me, but...''

''But?''

''But after seeing you two together, I guess not.'' He paused, his eyes on her face. ''You used to look at me like that, Taylor, and not just for the cameras. What happened to us? We used to be so good together.''

Maggie gave silent thanks for Taylor Grant's frankness about her relationship with this man. ''What we had was good, Stoney. Very good. But it wasn't enough for either one of us.''

''I know, I know. But, hey, we've both changed a lot since then. Our needs have changed. I mean, when we were together, you were governor and I was being courted by all the big studios.''

''It wasn't our professional life that got in the way.''

He raked a hand through his hair, destroying its casual artistry. ''Yeah, I know. You were still hurting from your husband's death, and I was paying alimony to two ex-wives. You didn't want emotional ties, any more than I did. But that was then.''

''And now?''

The tanned skin at the corners of his eyes crinkled as he gave her a rueful grin. ''And now you've got this guy Ridgeway prowling around you like a hungry panther, and I'm paying alimony to three ex-wives.''

No wonder Taylor had enjoyed this man's company so much during their brief time together, Maggie thought. For all his absorption with himself, Stoney had a disarming charm when he chose to exert it.

''We could be good together again, Taylor.''

"What we had was right for that moment, that time," Maggie said softly, echoing the vice president's own words. "But not for now. Not for the future."

"Why not? Just think about it. You might decide to go for top billing in the next election. You'd make a hell of a president. Together we'd make an unbeatable team. Just think of the publicity if I hit the campaign trail with you. Hey, look at the press Barbra Streisand got when she campaigned for Clinton."

Maggie bit the inside of her lower lip, not wanting to be the one to break it to Stoney that he possessed neither the star power nor the political acumen of a Barbra Streisand.

"Taylor…"

He closed the small distance between them. Maggie kept her smile in place as he leaned forward, planting both hands on the balustrade on either side of her, but her mind coldly registered his vulnerabilities. With his legs spread like that, he'd left himself wide open to a quick knee to the groin. His outstretched arms gave her room to swing her hand at the side of his neck or to shove a fisted thumb into the bridge of his nose.

When she looked up into his eyes, however, Maggie knew she wouldn't need to exploit those vulnerabilities. In three years of living on the knife-edge of danger, she'd learned to trust her instincts, and every one of those instincts told her this man was no killer.

"Stoney…" she began.

"I want you, Taylor."

Water dripped from Adam's hair and rolled down his back as he yanked a pair of black dress pants off the hanger on the back of the bathroom door.

"It won't work for us, Stoney. Not now."

Maggie's voice, soft and too damned sympathetic, drifted

out of the watch on the marble counter. His jaw working, Adam tugged the slacks up over still-wet flanks.

"I need you."

Stoney delivered the line with a husky, melodramatic passion that set Adam's teeth on edge. Christ! No wonder the man couldn't get a part in anything except B-grade action flicks.

"Give me another chance. Give us a chance."

"It's too late."

"No. I don't believe that. I'll prove it!"

"Stoney, for Pete's sake!"

Maggie hadn't requested backup, Adam reminded himself. She obviously wanted to play this one alone. But her muffled exclamation propelled him out of the bathroom, bare chested and still dripping.

He was halfway to the door connecting their suites when a note of panic entered her voice.

"Stoney! You're too heavy! You're— Watch out!"

Her shrill yelp of terror sent Adam racing for the glass doors leading to the terrace. A knife blade of fear sliced through his gut when he saw Armstrong bent over the stone rail. A single sweep of the terrace showed no sign of Maggie anywhere.

"I...I can't...hold...you!"

Armstrong's agonized cry seared Adam's soul.

He didn't stop to think, didn't allow himself to feel. In a blinding burst of speed, he tore across the terrace and reached over the railing to grab the wrist Stoney held in one huge paw. The instant Adam's right hand clamped around Maggie's wrist, his left swung in a vicious arc. His fist smashed into Armstrong's jaw with the force of a pile driver.

The brawny movie star crumpled without a sound, but Adam didn't even flick him a glance. All his attention, every ounce of his concentration, was focused on the woman who dangled forty stories above the Avenue of the Stars, held only by his bruising lock on her wrist.

"I've got you," he grunted, his neck muscles cording.

Maggie twisted at the end of his arm, her bloodred gown billowing around her flailing legs.

"I…can't…get a foothold!" she gasped.

"You don't need one! Dammit, don't twist like that!" Bent double, Adam kept his left arm anchored around the railing. The rough stone took a strip of flesh off his bare chest as he leaned farther out. "Just grab my arm with your other hand. I'll pull you up."

Maggie's fingers clawed at his, then crept up to fasten around his forearm. With a surge of strength, Adam dragged her up and over the railing. Holding her upright with an iron grip, he raked her with a fierce, searching look.

"Are you all right?"

"I…" She sucked in a huge gulp of air. "I will be. As soon as you…stop crunching my bones."

His adrenaline raging, Adam ignored her attempt to shake loose of his hold. "What in hell happened? Didn't you anticipate his attack?"

"Attack? He didn't attack me."

"He pushed you off a rooftop!"

"Adam, he didn't push me! He was just trying to make love to me. We sort of…overbalanced."

She stopped tugging at his iron hold on her wrist and managed a shaky grin. "I guess you could say he swept me off my feet."

It was the grin that did it. That exasperating, infuriating lift of her lips. For the second time in less than twenty-four hours, Maggie was laughing while fear pumped through Adam's veins.

With a low sound that in anyone else might have been

mistaken for a snarl, he wrapped her manacled wrist behind her back. A single flex of his muscles brought her body slamming against his. His other hand buried itself in her hair.

"You're forgetting your role. I'm the only man who's going to make love to you during this mission."

Maggie's eyes widened. She stared up at Adam, stunned as much by his unexpected force as by the way he held her banded against his chest. His black hair fell across his forehead, damp and tangled and untamed. His eyes glittered with a savage intensity. The muscles of his neck and shoulders gleamed wet and naked and powerful in the dim light.

He was close, so close, to unleashing the power she'd always sensed behind the steel curtain of his discipline. The realization sent a thrill through every fiber of Maggie's being. But at that moment, she wasn't quite sure whether the thrill she felt was one of triumph, or anticipation, or uncertainty.

"Adam…" she began, her voice husky.

She stopped, not knowing whether she wanted to soothe this potent, powerful, unfamiliar male or push him past his last restraint.

They hovered on the edge, each knowing that the next word, the next breath, could send them over.

To Maggie's intense disappointment, the next breath was Stoney's.

Groaning, the star pushed himself up on all fours, then lifted a hand to flex his jaw.

"Damn, Ridgeway," he muttered. "I hope to hell you didn't break my caps."

Chapter 7

Still banded against Adam's body, Maggie didn't see the look he sent the aggrieved star. But it was enough to keep the man on his knees.

"If you touch her again, Armstrong, I'll break more than your caps."

Stoney blinked, as startled by the controlled savagery in his voice as Maggie herself had been a moment ago.

"Hey, man, I get the picture."

"You'd better."

When Adam stepped away, Maggie felt the loss in every inch of her body. She also saw the blood smearing his bare chest for the first time.

"Adam, you're hurt!"

"It's just a scrape," he replied brusquely, yanking the star to his feet. "Go call Kowalski. I'll entertain your friend here until she arrives."

Denise and two other security agents came rushing into

the suite a few moments later. The senior agent turned ashen when she saw the front of Maggie's gown.

"Are you all right, Mrs. Grant?"

Glancing down, Maggie discovered that Adam's blood had darkened the flame red chiffon to a deep wine. "I'm fine. I just fell on the terrace. Well, off the terrace, but…"

Denise paled even more. "You fell off the terrace?"

"Stoney, er, got a little carried away. We overbalanced, and Adam came to the rescue." She gestured toward the glass wall, and the two figures on the terrace.

Denise turned, her eyes rounding at the sight of the president's special envoy, his naked chest streaked with blood, his slacks riding low on lean hips.

With a less-than-gentle shove, Adam propelled Stoney through the open sliding glass doors, into the suite. The two agents with Denise leaped forward to grab the star's arms.

Indignant, he tried to shake them off. "Hey, watch it!"

"Get him out of here," Adam ordered.

"Take Mr. Armstrong downstairs to interrogation," Denise instructed the others. "I want a full statement in my hands as soon as you get it out of him. And, Harrison—"

"Yes, ma'am?"

"Keep him away from the media."

"Yes, ma'am."

The senior agent pulled herself together as she swept the room. Her keen gaze took in the open connecting door between the suites before returning to Adam. Maggie caught a flicker of something that might have been feminine awareness or even admiration in Denise's eyes as they skimmed his lean torso, but it disappeared immediately when she caught the icy expression on his face.

"Where were you?"

Both women stiffened at the whipcrack in Adam's voice. Denise because she'd never heard it before, Maggie because she'd heard it several times. The furious man who'd slammed her up against his chest was gone. In his place was the Adam Ridgeway Maggie knew all too well.

"Downstairs," the agent responded tightly. "Conducting a final walk-through."

"Just what kind of security screens have you set up, Kowalski? How did Armstrong get past your men?"

Maggie stepped into the fray. "Hold it, Adam. Stoney didn't get past them. I told them to send him up."

Two equally accusing faces swung toward her. Adam's could have been chiseled from ice, but Denise's was folded into a frown.

"Was that wise, Mrs. Grant? After Armstrong's stunt in the lobby this afternoon?"

"I thought so," she replied coolly.

Adam didn't say a word, but Maggie could see he was *not* pleased. She fought back a small surge of irritation. She wasn't used to justifying or explaining her actions in the middle of an operation. To anyone.

As quickly as the irritation flared, Maggie suppressed it. Adam was her partner on this mission. She owed him an explanation of Stoney's presence in her suite, but she couldn't give it in front of Denise.

"We'll conduct a postmortem after the banquet," she told the agent with crisp authority. "Right now, I need you to go across the hall and get Lillian."

Denise firmed her lips, then reached for the phone. "I'll call her."

"I'd prefer you go get her. I don't want her hearing about this over the phone and becoming all upset. You know how overprotective she is."

It was a feeble excuse, and they all knew it, but Denise dropped the receiver back into its cradle.

"Fine. I'll go get Lillian. And we'll conduct a *thorough* postmortem after the banquet."

The door shut behind her, and a small, tense silence descended.

Adam was the first to break it, his tone frigid. "I think we need to review our mission parameters."

"I agree."

"This is supposed to be a team effort, remember?"

Maggie's jaw tightened, but she kept her voice level. "I tried to contact you after I told Security to send Stoney up."

"After? It didn't occur to you to contact me before you told them to send him up?"

"No, it didn't. I saw a target of opportunity, and I took it."

"Try coordinating your targets with me next time."

The stinging rejoinder lifted Maggie's chin. "I don't operate that way. I won't operate that way."

His eyes narrowed dangerously. Maggie had never seen that particular expression in them before—not directed at her, anyway. But she didn't back down. Her gaze locked with his, unwavering, determined. There was more at stake here than operating procedures, or even her job. Far more. She knew it. Adam knew it.

"You shouldn't have tried to handle this situation alone," he said, spacing his words. "It was too dangerous."

"I'm trained to handle dangerous situations. You trained me yourself. You and Jaguar."

A muscle ticked in the side of his jaw. "As best I recall, your training didn't include rappelling down a forty-story building without a rope."

"No," she tossed back, "but it included damn near everything else."

Which was true. As the first OMEGA operative recruited from outside the ranks of the government, Maggie had run the gamut of a battery of field tests and survival courses. She'd come through them all, disgruntled on occasion and cursing a blue streak after a memorable encounter with a snake Jaguar had slipped inside her boot, but she'd come through.

"Look, Adam, you know as well as I do, this job isn't just a matter of training. I follow my instincts in the field. I always have."

"I wondered when we were going to come around to that sixth sense of yours." He stepped toward her, his mouth hard. "I'll admit it's gotten you out of more tight spots than I care to think about, but—"

"But what?" she asked him challengingly.

"But even instincts can fail in certain situations."

He was so close, she could scent the tincture of blood and sweat that pearled his body. So still, she could see the pinpoints of blue steel in his eyes. So coiled, she could feel the tension escalating between them with every breath.

The heady, frightening feeling of hovering on the edge returned full force. Maggie had caught a brief glimpse of another Adam behind the all-but-impenetrable wall of his discipline. A part of her wanted to poke and probe and test that discipline further, to take him over the edge, and herself with him. Another part held her back. She knew this wasn't the time or the place. Denise would return with Lillian at any moment.

The time would come, though. Soon. She sensed it with everything that was female in her. With instincts more powerful, more primitive, than any she brought to her job.

Something of what she was thinking must have shown on her face. Adam took another step closer, his eyes locked with hers.

"What does your sixth sense tell you now, Maggie? About *this* situation?"

She hesitated a moment too long. The sound of a door slamming across the hall cut through the heavy stillness between them.

"It tells me we'll have to finish our discussion later," she said, torn between relief and regret.

"We'll finish it," Adam promised. "We'll definitely finish it."

The murmur of voices in the hall grew louder. With a last glance at her face, he started to turn away.

"Thunder?"

"Yes?"

She chewed on her lower lip for a second. "I'm sorry you were wounded in the line of duty."

Driven as much by the overwhelming need to touch him as by the urge to dull the hard edge of anger between them, Maggie reached out to brush her fingertips over the swirl of dark hair that arrowed his chest. Avoiding the raw, reddened patch of scraped flesh, she stroked his skin. Lightly. Soothingly.

He'd been wounded before, she discovered. Her fingers traced the ridge of an old, jagged scar that followed the line of his collarbone and passed over a puckered circle on his shoulder that could only have been caused by a bullet.

"Thank you," she said, dragging her gaze back to his face. "For hauling me back onto the terrace."

His hand closed over hers, capturing it against his heated skin. Under her flattened palm, Maggie felt the steady drumming of his heart.

"You're welcome." The sharp lines bracketing his mouth eased. "Just try to keep both feet on the ground from here on out."

It was too late for that, she thought. Far too late for that.

He'd almost lost her.

Adam stood unmoving while a shocked Lillian painted

his chest with iodine, then covered the scrape with a white bandage. She brushed aside his quiet thanks and left to hurry Maggie into a fresh gown, tut-tutting all the while, in her own inimitable fashion.

With a damp cloth, Adam removed the ravages the stone railing had done to his dress pants. His hands were steady as he slipped on his white shirt, but the damned gold studs just wouldn't seem to fit the tiny openings. Clenching his jaw, Adam forced the last stud into place. Throughout it all, his mind followed a single narrow track.

He'd almost lost her.

This morning he'd finally admitted to himself how much he wanted Maggie, and tonight he'd almost lost her.

Before he possessed her—as much as it would be possible to possess someone like Chameleon—he'd almost lost her.

The raw need he'd acknowledged less than ten hours ago didn't begin to compare with the ache that sliced through him now. Seeing Maggie half a breath away from death had effectively stripped him of any illusion that he could control his need for her.

Two weeks, and this mission would be complete, he reminded himself. Two weeks until he could satisfy the gnawing hunger he didn't, couldn't, deny any longer. For the first time, Adam doubted his own endurance.

Grimacing at the tug of the bandage on his chest hair, he pulled on his black dinner jacket and left the bathroom. He stopped short at the sight of the towering, beribboned basket resting majestically on a glass-topped sofa table.

He'd take it to Maggie after the banquet. At least one of them wouldn't go to bed hungry tonight.

He was halfway to the door when his watch began to vibrate gently against his wrist.

"Thunder here."

"This is Jaguar, Chief. Thought you might want to know we finally cornered Stoney Armstrong's agent."

"And?"

"And he passed on the interesting information that his client floated an eight-figure 'loan' just a week ago. Seems Armstrong decided to produce and star in his own film. The funds went through half a dozen holding companies, but we finally traced them to First Bank."

Adam went still. "First Bank?"

"Yeah. Ready for the kicker?"

"I'm ready."

"Armstrong refused the loan when he discovered that First Bank was putting up the cash. Seems he'd heard some rumors about the institution and didn't want his name connected to it."

"What kind of rumors?"

"Nothing specific, but the agent hinted strongly that it might be doing business with some questionable characters in Central America. Said Armstrong didn't want anything to do with it."

The fact that the brawny star had a few scruples buried under those bulging muscles didn't particularly impress Adam.

"Put a team on First Bank, Jaguar. I want to know the source of every dollar it takes in, and every possible connection between the bank and the vice president."

"I've already got it working. Will get back to you as soon as I have anything."

"Fine. Anything else?"

"No."

Adam flicked a glance at the dial of his watch. "I'd better sign off. The vice president is waiting."

Jaguar chuckled. "How's Chameleon holding up in this role?"

The memory of Maggie's shaky grin after her brush with oblivion filled Adam's mind.

"Better than I am," he replied grimly.

The banquet went off without a hitch.

Stoney Armstrong failed to make an appearance, which didn't surprise Adam. From the determined set to Denise Kowalski's chin, he guessed the agent wasn't about to release the star until she was fully satisfied with his statement.

Maggie, stunning in a two-piece turquoise silk sheath beaded in silver, charmed the men seated on either side of her. From his place across the round table, Adam watched as she picked at the elaborate chef's salad she'd been served. Every so often, her eyes strayed to the succulent rack of lamb on her neighbor's plate.

Remembering the cellophane-wrapped basket in his suite, Adam smiled. The thought of feeding Maggie, bite by bite, the various delicacies snaked through his mind. Sudden, erotic images of what could be done with red beluga caviar and soft Brie made his hand clench around the stem of his wineglass. He kept his smile easy and his conversation with the women seated on either side of him lively, but he couldn't keep his body from tightening whenever he looked at the woman separated from him by a wide expanse of white linen. Adam knew that each lingering glance he gave Maggie added more grist to the rumor mills about the vice president's latest romantic interest.

He also knew that he'd long since stopped playing a role.

When the banquet finally ended, they made their way slowly through the crowded ballroom. Denise and her squad cleared the way, and Adam followed a step or two behind Maggie as they both greeted various guests. As much as it was possible in this press, he kept her body between his and the agent in front of her.

She was incredible, he thought, watching her work the crowd. The people who caught her ear didn't notice that she listened far more than she spoke, or that she waited for them to drop clues about their personal agendas before she gave a noncommittal response.

His gaze traveled from the auburn curls feathering her neck, down the slender back now encased in turquoise silk, to the swell of her hips. The modest slit in the back of her long skirt parted with each step, revealing a tantalizing glimpse of shapely calf. Maintaining her role had to be a tremendous physical and emotional strain, but she didn't allow any sign of it to show in her demeanor or her carriage.

Until they reached the elevator.

When Denise turned to issue a last-minute instruction to the task force leader, Maggie slumped back against the brass rail for a second or two. Adam caught the way her shoulders sagged and her eyelids fluttered shut. With a wry inner smile, Adam abandoned his plans to feed her in erotic, exotic ways.

As it turned out, Denise Kowalski had her own plans for them for the rest of the evening. After a quick but thorough security check, she joined Maggie and Adam in the sitting room.

"We still have to do that postmortem, Mrs. Grant."

Maggie glanced at the clock on the white-painted mantel. "It's almost 3:00 a.m., Washington time. Why don't we get together in the morning, before we leave for the cabin?"

"It's best if we go over what happened while the details are still fresh in your mind," the agent insisted politely but firmly. "Mr. Armstrong's statement, and his subsequent polygraph, substantiate your belief that he didn't intend you bodily harm, but I need to hear exactly what happened. You could have been killed.''

''I know,'' Maggie replied, with a gleam in her eyes that Adam recognized instantly. ''I was the one about to add a new, indelible splash of color to the Avenue of the Stars, remember?''

She realized her mistake almost as soon as the words were out of her mouth. The flippant tone and gallows humor were far more characteristic of Maggie Sinclair than of Taylor Grant.

Denise frowned, and Maggie recovered without missing a beat. Curving her mouth into Taylor's distinctive smile, she tossed her beaded bag down on the sofa.

''Look, I know you're just trying to do your job. I guess I'm a little tired.''

A touch of reserve entered the agent's voice. ''I'm sorry to badger you this late, but I'm charged with protecting you. I can't do it without your cooperation.''

With one hand tucked casually in his pants pocket, Adam eyed the two women. Denise Kowalski was every bit as strong willed and determined as Maggie when it came to her job. She wasn't about to back down, any more than Chameleon had earlier.

Maggie gave in with good grace, recognizing a pro when she saw one. ''You're right, of course. Why don't we sit down?''

''Would you join us, please?'' Denise asked Adam. ''I'd like your input, as well.''

''I didn't intend to leave. Mrs. Grant and I have a few matters of our own to discuss when you're though.''

Ignoring Maggie's quick sideways glance, he joined her on the buttery-soft sofa.

The Secret Service officer was too well trained to allow any expression to cross her face. But as she moved forward to take the seat opposite them, she slanted a quick look at the open connecting door.

The brass carriage clock on the mantel had chimed twice by the time Agent Kowalski finally called a halt to the questions.

"Well, I guess that's it." She rubbed a hand across her forehead, then rose. "I'll tell the folks downstairs to release Armstrong. We'll keep someone on him for a while, with orders to get real nasty, real quick, if he tries to, uh, approach you again."

"He won't," Maggie asserted.

"No, he won't," Adam promised.

The agent glanced from Maggie's confident face to Adam's implacable one. "I guess not. I'll see you in the morning."

When the door closed behind her, Maggie heaved a sigh. Letting her head loll back against the leather, she plopped her stockinged feet on the brass-and-glass table.

"That's one tough woman."

"She reminds me of someone else I know," Adam commented dryly.

"She does, doesn't she?" Maggie's hair made a bright splash of color against the white leather as she turned to face him. "I think we should recruit her for OMEGA after this mission."

"I may have to consider it. If you pull any more stunts like you did with Armstrong, I'll have an opening for an agent."

A gleam of reluctant laughter entered her violet-tinted eyes. "Okay, so maybe dangling above the Avenue of the Stars was a bit extreme," she conceded.

"It was. Even for you."

"Even for me. But at least it convinced me that Armstrong's not our man. I don't have anything to base it on, except the fact that Stoney didn't let go—and the sixth sense you took me to task for earlier.''

"As much as it pains me to admit it, your instincts were right. Again.''

She sat up straight. "Really?''

"Jaguar called just before we went downstairs to the banquet.''

With a succinct economy of detail, Adam filled her in on the details of Jake's call.

"First Bank, huh? Stoney turned down a loan from First Bank because he thinks they might be laundering dirty money?''

"Evidently he was afraid a connection with them might…tarnish his image.''

She grinned. "There's a lot of that going around lately.''

A small silence settled between them. Reluctant to break it, Maggie slumped back against the soft leather. She and Adam still had matters left to resolve, not the least of which was exactly how she would operate for the next two weeks. But she couldn't seem to summon up the energy or the intensity that had driven her earlier.

"If we eliminate Armstrong, that leaves only two names on the list of possible suspects,'' Adam said after a moment.

"Digicon's CEO, and the president's best buddy.''

"Peter Donovan, and James Elliot.''

"Jaguar hasn't dug up anything on either?''

He shook his head. "Not yet.''

The clock on the mantel ticked off a few measures of companionable silence, broken only when Maggie gave a huge, hastily smothered yawn.

"Sorry,'' she murmured.

Adam's gaze rested on her face for a long moment, and

then he pushed himself to his feet and held out one hand to pull her up beside him.

Maggie put her hand in his. Despite the weariness that had dragged over her like a net, a sensual awareness feathered along her nerves at the firmness of his hold. She'd felt Adam's strength twice tonight. Once when he'd hauled her up to the terrace. Once when he'd hauled her up against his chest.

"You'd better get some sleep," he told her.

She hesitated, knowing she was playing with fire. "We didn't finish what we started, out there on the terrace."

"We'll finish tomorrow," he said slowly. "When we get to the cabin."

Tomorrow, she told herself. Tomorrow, they'd be at Taylor's isolated mountain retreat. Tomorrow, Maggie would be rested, in control of herself once more. There wouldn't be as many people hovering around her. Only Denise and a small Secret Service team. Lillian. The caretaker who lived at the ranch. And Adam.

Tomorrow, she and Adam would sort through roles and missions. Tomorrow, they'd finish what they'd started tonight.

"Good night," she said softly.

"Good night, Chameleon."

Leaving the door open behind him, Adam walked through the sitting room of his own suite. With every step, his body issued a fierce, unrelenting protest. But as much as he wanted to, he wouldn't allow himself to turn around, walk back through the door and tumble Maggie down onto that soft white leather.

She needed sleep. That much was obvious from the faint shadows under her eyes. From the droop of her shoulders under the beaded silk. She needed rest. A few hours' relief from the strain of her role.

And Adam needed to keep the promise of tomorrow in proper perspective. If he could.

Halfway across the sitting room, the glint of cellophane caught his eye. He halted with one hand lifted to tug at the ends of his black tie, and surveyed the towering collection of champagne, caviar, imported biscuits and cheeses. Somehow he suspected that those damned cheeses were going to figure in his dreams tonight.

Scooping up the basket, he walked back into the adjoining suite. The thick white carpet muffled his footsteps as he approached the bedroom door.

"You'd better eat something before—"

He stopped short on the threshold, transfixed by the sight of Maggie twisted sideways, struggling with the straps of her body shield.

She'd shed the beaded gown, and she wore only the thin Kevlar corset, a lacy garter belt that held up sheer nylon stockings, and the skimpiest pair of panties Adam had ever seen. No more than a thin strip of aqua silk, they brushed the tops of her full, rounded bottom and narrowed to a thin strip between her legs. In the process, they exposed far more flesh than they covered.

When she glanced up, Adam saw that she'd removed her violet-tinted contacts. Those were Maggie's brown eyes, he saw with a rush of fierce satisfaction. That was her body that beckoned to him.

Another woman might have flushed or stammered or at least acknowledged the sudden, leaping tension of the moment. Maggie gave him a wry grin.

"Remind me to tell Field Dress what I think of this blasted contraption when we get back. It was supposedly designed for easy removal, but I'm stuck."

"So I see. Need some help?"

"Yes, I..."

She straightened, and the last Velcro fastening gave with a snicker of sound. The body shield slipped downward, exposing a half bra of aqua and lace. Maggie bit her lip.

"No, I guess I don't."

Across the broad expanse of white carpet, their eyes met. For a long moment, neither moved. Neither spoke. Then her gaze dropped to the cellophane-covered basket in his arms, and she gave a whoop of delight.

"Adam! Is that food? Real food?"

"It is."

Snatching up a robe, she threw it on. "Thank God! I'm starving! I didn't know how I was going to get any sleep with my stomach rumbling like this."

Her forehead furrowed as she crossed the room, yanking at the sash of the robe.

"I got sloppy with Denise tonight, and I know it's just because I'm tired. And hungry. What's in the basket?"

"Caviar."

"Yecch!"

"And Brie."

Her face brightened, and she reached for the bundle of goodies. "Great! I love Brie. Especially warm, when it's so soft and creamy, you can spread it on all kinds of stuff."

Adam's jaw clenched. He'd spent over a decade in service to his country. He'd done some things he might have been decorated for if they hadn't been cloaked in secrecy. Some things he might have been shot for if the wrong people had caught up with him. But handing that basket over to Maggie was the toughest act he'd ever had to perform in his personal or professional life.

"Eat up," he told her, "then get some sleep. You can't afford to get sloppy. With anyone."

''Mmm...'' she mumbled, busy delving into the assorted treasures.

Tomorrow, Adam promised himself as he walked back to his suite. Tomorrow, this hard, pounding ache would ease. They'd be at the cabin. There'd be fewer people around. He could put a little distance between himself and Maggie, yet still keep her under close surveillance.

By tomorrow, he'd have himself under control.

Chapter 8

The vice-presidential party arrived at the white-painted twenties-era frame house tucked high in the Sierra Nevada late the next evening.

Too late for Maggie and Adam to finish the ''discussion'' they'd begun on the terrace of the Century Plaza's penthouse suite. Too late for more than a cursory look around the rustic hideaway. Too late for anything other than a quick cup of hot soup in front of a low, banked fire and a weary good-night. The trip that shouldn't have taken more than a few hours had spun out for more than twelve.

The short flight from L.A. to Sacramento had gone smoothly enough. They landed in the capital city in time for a late lunch at one of Taylor's favorite restaurants. Maggie basked in the reflection of the former governor's popularity with the restaurant staff and managed a cheerful smile when she was served a glutinous green mass in the shape of a crescent with unidentifiable objects jiggling inside it. She was still too stuffed from her late-night raid on

Adam's treasure trove of goodies to give his ham and cheese on sourdough more than a passing glance.

It was only after they lifted off in the specially configured twin-engine Sikorsky helicopter for the final leg of their trip that the problems began. The pilot, a veteran of the Gulf War, countered most of the sudden up-and downdrafts over the foothills with unerring skill. But when the aircraft approached the higher peaks, the ride took on a roller-coaster character.

At one violent thrust to the right, Maggie grabbed the armrests with both hands. Behind her, Denise sucked in a quick breath. Even the redoubtable Lillian gasped.

"Feels like we've run into some convective air turbulence," Adam commented.

"We've certainly run into something," Maggie muttered.

He stretched his long legs out beside hers, unperturbed by the violent pitch and yaw of the craft. Having seen him at the controls of various aircraft a number of times, Maggie wasn't surprised at his calm. Adam could handle a stick with the best of them. He knew what to expect. She, on the other hand, was bitterly regretting even the few bites of green stuff she'd managed to swallow at lunch.

"This kind of turbulence is common when flying at low levels over mountains." He scanned the tilting horizon outside the window. "From the looks of those clouds up ahead, we're going to lose visibility soon."

"Great."

He smiled at her drawled comment. "I suspect we'll have to turn back."

Sure enough, a few moments later the pilot came back to inform her that regulations required him to return to base. He couldn't risk flying blind, with only instruments to guide him through the mountains, while ferrying a code-level VIP.

On the ground in Sacramento, they waited over an hour for the front to clear. When the weather reports grew increasingly grim, Maggie was given the choice between remaining overnight in the capital city and driving up to the cabin in a convoy of four-wheel-drive vehicles. In blessed ignorance of the state of the roads leading to Taylor Grant's mountain retreat, she chose the drive.

At first, she thoroughly enjoyed her first journey into the High Sierras. Despite the lowering clouds, the scenery consisted of spectacular displays of light and shadow. White snow and gray, misty lakes provided dramatic backdrops for dark green ponderosa pine and blue-tinted Douglas firs.

When the convoy of vehicles turned off the interstate onto a narrow two-lane state road, Maggie spied deer tracks in the snow. Chipmunks darted along the branches arching over the road and scattered showers of white on the passing vehicles. Every so often the woods thinned, and she'd catch a glimpse of an ice-covered waterfall hanging like a silvery tassel in the distance.

As they climbed to the higher elevations, however, the two-lane highway gave way to a corkscrew gravel road that twisted and turned back on itself repeatedly. Fog and swirling snow slowed their progress even more, until the four-vehicle convoy was creeping along at barely five miles per hour.

It occurred to Maggie that one of those blind curves would make an excellent spot for an ambush. With the vehicles slowed to a crawl, a sniper perched in a nearby tree would have no difficulty picking off his target. As a result, she spent most of the endless trip alternately searching the gray snowscape ahead and wondering why in hell Taylor Grant would choose such an inaccessible spot for her personal retreat.

As soon as she saw the cabin, she understood. The small

white frame structure nestled on the side of a steep slope in a Christmas-card-perfect setting. Surrounded by snow-draped pines and a split-rail fence, its windows spilled golden, welcoming light into the night. The scent of a wood fire greeted Maggie as soon as she stepped out of the Land Rover. While Adam went back to help sort and unload the bags, she stood for a moment in the crisp air. The profound quiet of the night surrounded her. Deliberately she willed the knotted muscles in the back of her neck to relax.

Boots crunched the path behind her. Lillian appeared at her elbow, looking much like a pint-size snowman in a puffy down-filled coat, with a fuzzy beret pulled over her springy curls.

"Feels good to be home," she said, sniffing the air.

"Mmm…"

"Too bad it's too late for you to jog down to the lake."

"Yes, isn't it?"

Maggie was *not* looking forward to running anywhere in this thin mountain air, much less down a steep mountain path to the tiny lake she knew crouched in the valley below, then back up again. Running was bad enough at sea level. At an elevation of nine thousand feet, a jog like that would be sheer torture. She had several excuses in mind to justify a change in the vice president's routine, including a desire for long, *slow* walks with a certain special envoy.

Mindful of the agents milling around behind them, Lillian shot her a look heavy with significance.

"You'll just have to wait until morning to trek down to the lake, even though you say you never feel at home until you've seen your tree. The one with the initials."

Biting back a sigh, Maggie resigned herself to the inevitable. "I don't. If the snow doesn't obscure the path, I'll go down in the—"

"Grrr-oo-of!"

She broke off with a startled gasp as the mounded snow-bank on her left suddenly erupted. In a blur of white, a shaggy creature sprang out of the snow and planted itself in front of her. Its shaggy coat hung in thick, uncombed ropes, and only the upright stub of a tail told Maggie which end was which. The thing looked like a well-used floor mop, only this mop had to weigh at least a hundred pounds and was making very unfriendly noises.

"Radizwell! Get back, you idiot!" Lillian swatted the woolly head with her purse. "It's too late to play games tonight. Go on! Shoo!"

The creature stood its ground, growling deep in its throat at the woman garbed in its mistress's clothes.

Maggie had been briefed that the livestock kept on Taylor's small ranch included several horses, a flock of sheep that grazed the high alpine meadows in spring, and a breed of sheepdog she'd never heard of before. According to intelligence, the komondor had been introduced into Europe by the Magyars when they invaded Hungary in the ninth century. The animal was ideal for the rugged Hungarian mountains. Its huge size and thick, corded coat enabled it to withstand the harshest winter climates, and at the same time protected it from the fangs of the predators that preyed on the flocks.

Maggie could understand how the creature in front of her would intimidate a bear or a wolf or a fox. It certainly intimidated her. Unfortunately, intel had stressed that Taylor Grant never went anywhere around the ranch without this beast at her side. Maggie knew she had to win him over, and fast.

Dragging in a deep breath, she crouched down on one heel and held out a hand. "Come here, Radizwell. Come here, boy."

Another growl issued from deep under those layers of ropelike wool.

Maggie set her jaw. If she could convince a bug-eyed iguana to respond—occasionally—to her commands, she could win over this escapee from a mattress factory.

"Here, Radizwell. Come here."

A warning rumble sounded deep in its throat.

Despite the almost overpowering urge to draw her arm back, Maggie kept her hand extended. "Here, boy."

One huge paw inched forward. A black nose poked out of the shaggy layers. The creature sniffed, growled again, then edged closer.

From the corner of one eye, Maggie saw the front door open and a jacketed figure step out onto the porch. She guessed it was Hank McGowan, the caretaker. Of all the dossiers she'd studied for this mission, his had fascinated her the most. An ex-con who owed Taylor both his life and his livelihood, he'd made this isolated ranch his home.

Before Maggie could give her full attention to McGowan, however, the showdown between her and Radizwell had to be decided. One way or another.

"Come here, boy."

A cold nose nudged her palm. Understanding his confusion, she let the dog sniff her for a few moments. When he didn't amputate any of her fingers, she lifted her hand and gave his feltlike coat a cautious pat. That proved to be a mistake.

Radizwell instantly moved forward to make a closer inspection. His massive head butted into her chest with the force of a Mack truck. Maggie lost her precarious balance and toppled backward.

Adam and the caretaker arrived at the same moment from opposite directions to find her on her back in the snow, with a hundred pounds of dog straddling her body. Thankfully, its growls had given way to a low rumble as his wet nose moved over her cheeks and chin. She managed a laughing protest to cover what she knew was the dog's uncharacteristic behavior.

"Radizwell, you idiot. Get off me!"

Shaking his head in disgust, the caretaker burrowed a hand under layers of wool to find a collar.

"I penned him up when they radioed that you were on the last mile stretch. Guess I should have put a lock on the shed."

He bent forward to haul the dog back, and Maggie saw his face clearly for the first time. Although the dossier she'd studied had prepared her somewhat, his battered features shocked her nonetheless. They added grim emphasis to his checkered past.

Henry "Hank" McGowan. Forty-three. Divorced. One-time foreman of a huge commercial sheep ranch outside Sacramento. Convicted murderer, whose death sentence had been commuted to life imprisonment by the then-governor, Taylor Grant.

His conviction had been overturned when new evidence proved he hadn't tracked down and shot the drunk who'd battered him senseless with a tire jack after an argument over a game of pool. McGowan had drifted after that, unable to find work despite his exoneration, until Taylor hired him to act as stockman and caretaker.

In his last security review, McGowan had stated flatly that he owed Taylor Grant his life. He'd give it willingly to shield the vice president from any hurt, any harm.

Right now, that consisted of hauling a hundred pounds of suspicious sheepdog off her prone body.

"For heaven's sake, lock him in the shearing shed tonight," Lillian said tartly. "You know how excited the idiot gets whenever we come home. The last time he just about stripped the paint off the porch, marking his territory for the new agents who came with Mrs. Grant.''

To Maggie's relief, the dog allowed himself to be led away before he felt compelled to mark anything for this stranger in Taylor's clothes.

"There's a pot of vegetable stew on the stove," McGowan tossed over one shoulder. "If anyone's hungry."

If anyone was hungry! At this point, even veggies simmering in a rich, hearty broth sounded good to Maggie. She grabbed the hand Adam extended and scrambled up. Dusting the snow from her bottom, she gave him a grin.

"I certainly seem to be taking more than my share of falls lately."

"So I've noticed. Do you think you can make it to the cabin upright, or shall I carry you?"

Now there was an intriguing invitation.

"I can make it," she said, regret and laughter threading her voice. "Come on, let me show you the homestead, such as it is."

The vice president's home had been featured in a five-page spread in *Western Living* magazine, but not even that glossy layout had prepared Maggie for the stunning interior. Only a woman of Taylor Grant's style and confidence could pull off this blend of rustic and antique, polished mahogany and shining oak, plank floors and scattered floral rugs.

Most of the cabin's downstairs interior walls had been demolished, leaving only an open living-dining area, a small kitchen, and the bedroom Lillian occupied. A huge stone fireplace in the living room was the focus of a collection of comfortable dude-ranch-style furniture. A magnificent Chippendale dining room table with eight chairs dominated the dining area. Interspersed throughout were bronze pieces sculpted by Taylor's deceased husband, Oriental vases filled with dried flowers, framed Western art, and the occasional mounted trophy, including a huge moose head beside the door that served as a hat rack.

While Maggie showed Adam around, using the impromptu tour as an excuse to familiarize herself with the downstairs, Lillian went upstairs to direct the placement of the luggage. Denise dragged off her gloves and conferred with the agent who'd been sent to the cabin several days ago as part of the advance team. After a thorough walk-through of the entire cabin, she joined Maggie and Adam at the stone fireplace. Politely declining a mug of the steaming stew, she gave a brief report.

"The cabin and the grounds are secure, Mrs. Grant. We've activated the command center in the barn."

According to intelligence, the Secret Service had converted the barn behind the cabin into a well-equipped bunkhouse and a high-tech command-and-control center—at a cost of several million dollars. Idly Maggie wondered whether the horses were going to enjoy the central heat and exercise room when the Secret Service finally vacated the premises.

"If you don't need me any more tonight, I'll get the team settled. Dunliff will stand the first shift."

"All right. It's been a long day. Get some rest, Denise."

"You too," the agent responded.

Although Denise kept her face carefully neutral when she wished Adam a courteous good-night, Maggie caught the quick speculative look the other woman gave him.

A few moments later, Lillian came downstairs. "You're all unpacked, Mrs. Grant."

"Thank you."

"I think I'll turn in, too. It takes me a while to reacclimate to the altitude."

"Don't you want some stew? It's delicious."

Surprisingly, it was. Maggie might have awarded the rich

stew her own personal blue ribbon, if it had contained just a chunk or two of beef or lamb or even chicken.

"No, thank you."

When Lillian retired to her room, the agent on duty discreetly left Maggie and Adam alone. More or less. Hidden cameras swept the downstairs continuously, allowing the occupants only the illusion of privacy.

Upstairs, Maggie knew, was a different matter. Upstairs there were only two small rooms, each with its own bath. Upstairs, Mrs. Grant had insisted on privacy for herself and her guests. Which meant Maggie and Adam didn't have to take their assigned roles as lovers any farther than the first stair. At this moment, Maggie wasn't sure whether she was more relieved or disappointed.

This complex role they were playing had become so confused, so blurred, she'd stopped trying to sort out what was real and what wasn't. Since last night, when she'd felt Adam's arms locked around her and his naked chest beneath her splayed hands, she'd hungered for a repeat performance.

Not that she'd either experience it or allow it. The rational part of her mind told her they wouldn't, couldn't, complicate their mission further by setting a spark to the fire building between them. But when she thought of that small, private nest upstairs, her fingers itched for a match.

Not an hour later, she tiptoed across the darkened hall and ignited a flame that almost consumed them both.

The soft scratching on the wooden door to his room brought Adam instantly awake. He didn't move, didn't alter the rhythm of his breathing, but his every sense went on full alert.

The door creaked open.

"Adam? It's me. Taylor. Are you awake?"

Maggie's use of her assumed identity in this supposedly secure part of the house tripped warning alarms in every part of Adam's nervous system. He rolled over, the sheets rustling beneath him, and followed her lead.

"I'm awake."

She stepped out of the shadows and moved toward the wide double bed that took up most of the floor space. Bright moonlight streamed through the windows, illuminating the fluid lines of her body. She wore only a silky gown, and without the constraining Kevlar her breasts were lush and full. Nipples peaked from the cold pushed at the thin gown.

Adam felt his stomach muscles go washboard-stiff. Forcing himself to focus on the reason behind her unexpected visit, he rose up on one elbow. The old-fashioned hickory-rail bedstead bit into his bare back as he propped a shoulder against it.

"I couldn't sleep," she whispered, her feet gliding across the oak plank floor.

She stopped beside the bed, so near that Adam could see the tiny beads of moisture pearled on her shoulders. Her hair was spiked with water, as though she'd hurriedly passed a towel over it once or twice.

As if in answer to his unspoken question, she ran a hand through her damp waves. "I took a hot bath. To help me relax. It didn't work."

His mouth curved. "I tried a cold shower. It didn't work for me, either." He raised an arm, lifting the covers, not sure where this was going, but following her lead. "Maybe we can help each other relax."

She hesitated, shifting from one bare foot to the other. "I know we promised to take this slow and easy, to use these two weeks to get to know each other, but…"

"Come to bed, Taylor."

"I need you to hold me, Adam. Please, just hold me for a little while."

She slid in beside him, her gown a slither of damp silk against his skin. He dragged the covers over them both.

Her body felt clammy through the gown where it touched his, which was just about everywhere. Wrapping an arm around her waist, Adam brought her closer into his heat. She burrowed against him and tucked her icy feet between his. Her head rested on his shoulder. Her mouth was only an inch from his.

They fit together as if cast from molds. Male and female. Man and woman. Adam and Maggie. Thunder and Chameleon, he amended immediately.

"I was thinking about what happened last night," she said softly, "and I started to shake."

That didn't help him much. A lot had happened last night. He didn't know if she was referring to Stoney's unexpected appearance, her near-fall, or the sharp difference of opinion they'd had over procedures. A difference that had yet to be resolved.

"I guess I experienced a delayed reaction to the fall," she murmured, her breath feathering his cheek. "It happened so fast, I didn't have time to be frightened last night. But now...now I shake every time I remember how... how..."

She shivered and pressed closer. Adam pulled the downy covers up higher around her shoulders, almost burying her head in their warmth.

"There's a bug in my room." The words were hardly more than a flutter of air against his ear. "I was so terrified, so helpless," she continued, a shade more loudly. "And then you reached for me and pulled me to safety."

The covers shook as she shuddered again.

"It's okay, Taylor. It's okay." His lips moved against her cheek. *"I thought you swept the room yourself."*

"I did. Either I missed this one, or someone planted it while I was downstairs scarfing up vegetable stew." She gave a tremulous sigh. "Oh, Adam, I could have pulled you over that railing with me. I could have killed us both."

"No way. I wasn't about to let go of either you or that stone rail. *Where did you find it?"*

"Above the bathtub." Her hand inched up to rest lightly on the bandage on his chest. "I'm so sorry you were hurt. You should have had a doctor take a look at this."

"It's only a scrape. *Where above the tub?"*

"Behind the wallpaper. When I ran hot water into the tub, steam dampened the paper. All but this one small patch. Are you sure you're all right?"

"I'm fine, darling. *Did you neutralize it?"*

"No. I didn't want to tip off whoever was listening. There's probably one in here, too." She nuzzled his neck. "I'm glad you're here, Adam. I'm glad you came with me."

"I'm glad, too. We both have too many pressures on us in Washington. *I'm sure there is."*

The knowledge that someone had planted devices in these supposedly secure rooms churned in Adam's mind, vying for precedence with the signals his skin was telegraphing to his brain at each touch of Maggie's body against his.

No one could have gotten into the cabin undetected. Despite its isolated location, the ranch bristled with the latest in security systems. Which meant that whoever had planted the bug had ready access to the grounds.

The caretaker, Hank McGowan? He certainly had access, although his loyalty and devotion to Taylor Grant supposedly went soul-deep.

Lillian Roth?

A member of the Secret Service advance team?

Denise Kowalski herself, when she'd done her walk-through of the cabin?

Which one of them, if any, was in league with the man who'd made that chilling call to Taylor? And why?

Suddenly the threat to Maggie became staggeringly immediate. Instead of narrowing, their short list of suspects had exploded. The sense of danger closing in rushed through Adam, and his arms tightened reflexively around her waist.

She took the gesture as a continuation of their roles, and snuggled into him. "Just think," she murmured. "Two weeks to learn about each other. Two weeks for each of us to discover what pleasures the other."

Her movement ground her hip against his groin. In spite of himself, Adam hardened. The dappled moonlight and soft shadows in the room blurred, merged into a swirling, red-tinted mist.

"I don't think it's going to take two weeks for us to get to know each other," he said, his voice low.

She tilted her head back to glance up at him from her nest of covers, a question in her shadowed eyes. "Why not?"

"Now that I have you in my arms, I don't think I can let you go."

He angled his body, allowing it to press hers deeper into the sheets. His hands tunneled into her still-damp hair. The muscles in his upper arms corded as he angled her face up to his.

He shouldn't do this. His mind posted a last, desperate caution. Deliberately Adam ignored the warning. Lowering his head, he covered her mouth with his. It was warm and full and made for his kiss.

After a moment of startled surprise, Maggie pushed her arms out of the enfolding covers and wrapped them around his neck, returning his kiss with a sensual explosion of passion. Her mouth opened under his, inviting, welcoming, discovering.

With an inarticulate sound, Adam plunged inside, tasting her, claiming her. Teeth and tongues and chins met. Exploration became exploitation.

Maggie couldn't be a passive player, in this or in any part of life. Her arms tightened around his neck, and she arched under him, lifting her body to his in a glory of need. She felt his rock hardness against her stomach, and a shaft of heat shot from her belly to her loins. Without conscious thought, she wiggled, rubbing her breasts against his chest. The tips stiffened to aching points. She shifted again, wanting friction. Wanting his touch.

As though he'd read her mind, Adam dragged a hand down and shaped her breast. His fingers kneaded her flesh. His thumb brushed over the taut nipple. Maggie gave a small, involuntary gasp.

"Adam!"

The breathless passion in her voice drew him back from the precipice. The very real possibility that someone else had heard her gasp his name acted on Adam like a sluice of cold water. He dragged his mouth from hers, his breath harsh and ragged. Resolve coiled like cold steel in his gut.

When he made love to Maggie, which he now intended to do as soon as he got her away from this cabin, it sure as hell wouldn't be with anyone listening or watching. There would be just the two of them, their bodies as tight with desire as they were now. But he'd be the only one to hear her groans of pleasure. No one else would see the splendor of her body. Would observe her responses to his kiss and his touch and his possession. Would watch while he drowned in the river of passion flowing in this vital woman.

He eased his lower body away from hers. "I'm sorry, Taylor."

The sound of another woman's name on Adam's lips slowly penetrated the haze of desire that heated Maggie's mind and body. Like a cold mist seeping under the door, reality crept back. It swirled around her feet and, inch by inch, worked its way along her raw, burning nerves, dousing their fires.

His body was heavy on hers. Hard and heavy. Yet when he looked down at her, she wondered who he saw—her, or Taylor Grant.

"I shouldn't have done that," he said softly. "I'm sorry. We both agreed to take this slow and easy."

Adam's withdrawal stunned Maggie...and shamed her. For the first time since joining OMEGA, she'd lost sight of her mission. In his arms, she'd forgotten her role. When it came to cool detachment in the performance of duty, she wasn't anywhere near Adam's league.

It took everything she had to slip back into Taylor's skin. "You don't have to take all the blame," she murmured throatily. "Or the credit. I was the one who asked to be held, remember?"

She pushed herself out of his arms. One bare foot hit the icy floor, and then the other.

"We've got time. Time to savor each other. Time to get to know each other." She struggled to pull herself together and grasped at the straw Lillian had offered earlier. "Why don't you come with me in the morning? We'll walk down to the lake, see the sunrise together."

"Taylor..."

"I want whatever it is that's between us to be right, Adam."

His eyes met hers. His seeming detachment was gone, and in its place was a blazing certainty that went a long way toward soothing Maggie's confused emotions.

"It's right," he growled. "Whatever it is, it's right."

Chapter 9

A distinctive aroma jerked Maggie out of a restless doze. She lifted her head, sniffing the cold air like a curious raccoon.

Bacon! Someone was cooking bacon!

She squinted at the dim light filtering through the closed shutters. Not even dawn yet, and someone was cooking bacon!

A crazy hope surged through her. Maybe Adam hadn't been able to sleep, any more than she had. Maybe he'd decided to take her up on her offer to see the sunrise, and was cooking himself breakfast while he waited for her. Maybe she could snatch a bite before the tantalizing scent lured everyone else out of bed, as well.

The thought of food, real food, galvanized Maggie into action. Throwing off the covers, she dashed into the bathroom and ran water into the old-fashioned porcelain sink. She washed quickly and, remembering Taylor's comment that she'd didn't bother with makeup in the mountains, slathered on only enough foundation needed to cover the artificial bone.

Returning to the bedroom, she tugged on a pair of thin thermal long johns. The lightweight silky fabric molded to her body like a second skin. Maggie wished she'd been issued subzero-tested undergarments like these for the hellish winter survival course OMEGA had put her through. They would have been far more comfortable for a trek over the Rockies than the bulky garments she'd had to wear.

Twisting and bending, she managed to strap the Kevlar bodysuit in place, then pulled on a white turtleneck and pleated brown flannel slacks. The palm-size derringer and spare ammunition clip Maggie had found in the bedside table fit nicely in the roomy pants pocket. Relieved to be armed again, if only with this small .22, she rummaged in the chest of drawers for an extra pair of wool socks. The thick socks warmed her toes and made the boots she found in the closet fit more comfortably.

The vice president might wear a smaller dress size, Maggie thought with a dart of satisfaction, but her feet were bigger. As ridiculous as it was, the realization that Taylor wasn't quite perfect helped restore Maggie's balance—a balance that had been badly shaken by those few moments in Adam's arms last night.

Grinning, she paused with her hand on the cut-glass doorknob. Okay, so she'd almost lost it for those breathless, endless, glorious moments. So she'd come within a hair of jumping the man's bones. So he'd been the one to pull back, not her.

It was right. He'd said it. She felt it. Whatever this was between them, it was right.

His parting words had lessened the shock of her loss of control, but they'd also kept her tossing all night. His words, and the utter conviction that she and Adam would make love. Soon. Maggie felt it in every bone in her body.

But they wouldn't do it in another woman's bed. What was more, she darn well wasn't going to be wearing another woman's skin. She wanted to hear Adam murmur *her* name in his deep, husky voice. She wanted to feel his hands in her hair. Dammit, she wanted him. Fiercely. Urgently. With a hunger that defied all logic, all caution, all concerns over their respective positions in OMEGA.

All she had to do was stay alive long enough to discover who among the various people at the cabin had planted that bug. Learn if that person was in league with a possible assassin. And track said assassin down. Then she could satisfy her hunger.

Another succulent aroma wafted through the thin wood, and Maggie twisted the doorknob. If she couldn't satisfy one hunger for a while longer, maybe, just maybe, she could satisfy another. Chasing the mouth-watering scent, she went downstairs.

A tired-eyed agent pushed himself out of an armchair beside the fire in the living room. In her rush to get to the kitchen, Maggie had forgotten all about the post-stander. No doubt the agent had heard her tiptoe across the hall to Adam's room last night. In spite of herself, heat crept up her neck. Good grief, she felt like a coed who'd been caught sneaking out of a boy's dorm room. No wonder Taylor's list of romantic liaisons had been so brief! The woman had no privacy at all. Bugs in her bathroom. Agents standing guard in her living room. Armed escorts on all her evenings out.

Summoning a smile, Maggie nodded to the man. "Good morning."

"Good morning, Mrs. Grant. You're up early."

"Yes, I wanted to catch the sunrise."

"Should be a gorgeous one." He lifted an arm to work at a kink in his neck. "The snow stopped around midnight, just after I came on shift."

"Mmm…"

Maggie was trying to think of some excuse to keep him from accompanying her into the kitchen when he supplied it himself.

"If you're going out, I'd better get suited up and let Agent Kowalski know."

"Fine."

He moved toward the front door, snagging a ski jacket from the convenient moose-antler rack. "Just buzz when you're ready to go."

Maggie hurried toward the kitchen, praying fervently that the person rattling pans on the top of the stove was Adam.

It wasn't.

Years of field experience enabled her to mask her intense disappointment when the figure at the stove turned. Resolutely Maggie ignored the thick slabs of bacon sizzling in a sea of grease and smiled a greeting.

"Good morning, Hank."

"Mornin', Taylor."

She barely kept herself from lifting a brow at his casual use of the vice president's first name. Either Mrs. Grant didn't bother any more with protocol than with makeup while in the mountains, or this was a test.

Maggie had nothing to fall back on in this moment but her instincts. And the memory of the charismatic smile Taylor had given her when she invited Maggie to call her by her first name. She guessed that the vice president didn't stand on ceremony with the man she'd rescued from death row. Nor was he likely to be intimidated by a position or a title.

In the well-lit kitchen, his rugged features appeared even

more startling than they had when Maggie first glimpsed them last night. The drunk who'd wielded that tire jack had done so with a vengeance.

McGowan jerked his head toward a carafe sitting on the oak plank table that took up most of the small kitchen. "Coffee's on the warmer. Hotcakes are just about done."

He turned back to the stove, and Maggie pulled out one of the ridgepole chairs. Pouring the rich black brew into an enameled mug, she propped her elbows on the table and studied McGowan. He looked almost as formidable from the rear as he did from the front.

Brown hair, long and shaggy and obviously cut by his own hand, brushed the collar of his blue work shirt. The well-washed fabric stretched tight across wiry shoulders. Rolled-up sleeves revealed thick hair matting his forearms, one of which bore a tattoo of a snarling, upright bear. His scuffed boots had been scraped clean of all dirt, but looking at their stained surface, Maggie didn't doubt he wore them for every chore, including cleaning out the stables.

He walked over to the table and placed a heaping platter in front of her.

"Buckwheat hotcakes. Like you like them. No butter. No syrup."

"Thank you." She managed to infuse a creditable touch of enthusiasm into her tone. "They look wonderful."

"Figured your...friend might want something more substantial. Biscuits and bacon do for him?"

The hesitation was so slight, most people might have missed it, but Maggie's training as a linguist had sensitized her to the slightest nuances of speech.

"Biscuits and bacon will be fine," she replied casually.

McGowan nodded and returned to the stove. Her eyes thoughtful, Maggie forked a bite of the heavy pancake.

Did the caretaker resent Adam Ridgeway's presence in

Taylor's cabin, not to mention her life? Had his supposed devotion ripened into something deeper? And darker? Had he been corrupted into planting that bug in her room, or had he done it for his own purposes? His closed face gave her no clue.

After a moment, he tossed the spatula into the sink and leaned his hips against it. Folding his arms, he raised a brow in query.

"You want the snowmobiles?"

Maggie chewed slowly to cover her sudden uncertainty. Did she want the snowmobiles? Would Taylor want them?

"You don't need them," he added on a gruff note, watching her. "I cleared the path down to the lake with the snowblower before I started breakfast. Knew you'd want to go down there first thing."

The lake. Evidently everyone was aware of Taylor's little ritual of walking down to the lake to find her tree, whatever and wherever that was.

Before Maggie could reply, the kitchen door opened. The lump of buckwheat lodged halfway down her throat.

After last night, she should have anticipated Adam's impact on her traitorous body. She should have expected her empty stomach to do a close approximation of a triple flip. Her thighs to clench under the table. Her palms to dampen. But she darn well hadn't expected her throat to close around a clump of dough and almost choke her to death. She took a hasty swallow of coffee to ease its passage.

Damn! Adam Ridgeway in black tie and tails was enough to make any woman whip around for a second, or even third, look. But Adam in well-worn jeans and a green plaid shirt that hugged his broad shoulders was something else again.

He wore the clothes with a casual familiarity that said they were old friends and not just trotted out for a weekend in the woods. He hadn't shaved, and a dark stubble shadowed his chin and cheeks. Seeing him like this, Maggie felt her mental image of this man alter subtly, like a house shifting on its foundations—until she caught the expression in his blue eyes as he returned the caretaker's look. That was vintage Thunder. Cool. Assessing. In control.

"We didn't get a chance to meet last night," he said, crossing the small kitchen. "I'm Adam Ridgeway."

A scarred hand took his. "Hank McGowan."

Their hands dropped, and the two men measured each other.

"I understand from Taylor you run the place."

A wiry shoulder lifted. "She runs it. I keep it together while she's away."

"It's a big place for one man to handle."

"A crew comes up in the spring. To help with lambing, then later with the shearing. The rest of the time, we manage." He flicked Maggie a sideways glance. "Me and the hound."

"You met him last night," Maggie interjected, although she knew Adam wouldn't need a reminder. Even if they hadn't been briefed on what to expect at the cabin, the first encounter with that strange-looking creature would have stayed in anyone's mind.

"So I did. Radizwell, isn't it?"

"Actually," she replied, dredging through her memory for details, "his registered name is Radizwell, Marioffski's Silver Stand."

McGowan's lips twisted. "Damnedest name for a sheepdog I ever heard. You going to take him down to the lake with you?"

"Of course. You know very well that I couldn't get away without him, even if I wanted to."

His battered features relaxed into what was probably

meant as a smile. "True. Biscuits and bacon are on the stove, Ridgeway."

Politeness demanded that Taylor share the table with her guest while he ate. Adam, bless him, took pity on Maggie.

"I'm not hungry right now. I'll just have a cup of coffee and tuck a couple of those biscuits in my pocket for later. A walk down to the lake should help me work up an appetite."

"Suit yourself."

"You'd better take more than a couple," Maggie suggested blandly. "It's a long walk."

When the huge, shaggy sheepdog bounded through the snow toward her, Maggie saw at once that he was still suspicious of her. Her hands froze on the zipper of her hot-pink ski jacket as he circled her a few times, sniffing warily.

Before he issued any of the rumbling growls that had raised the hairs on the back of her neck last night, however, Adam dug into the pocket of his blue ski jacket and offered the dog a bacon-stuffed biscuit.

"Here, boy."

Maggie bit back her instinctive protest as she watched, and the delicacy disappeared in a single gulp. The animal, now Adam's friend for life, cavorted like an animated overgrown dust mop, then took off for the trees.

Muttering under her breath, Maggie zipped up her jacket, tugged a matching knit band over her ears and trudged after him. Adam followed her, and the ever-present Secret Service agent trailed behind.

The path to the lake was steep, snow-covered in spots, and treacherous. It pitched downward from the side of the cabin, wound around tall oaks and silver-barked poplars, then twisted through a stand of Douglas fir. On her own, Maggie would have been lost within minutes. Luckily, the komondor knew exactly where they were headed. Every so often he stopped and looked back, his massive head tilted. At least Maggie assumed it was his head. With that impenetrable, shaggy coat, he could very well have been treating her to a calculated display of doggy disdain. Or waiting for Adam to offer another biscuit as an incentive. Ha! There was no way the creature was getting any more of those biscuits, Maggie vowed.

Although cold, the air was dry and incredibly sharp. The snow, a foot or more deep along the slopes, thinned as they descended to the tiny lake set in its nest of trees. Maggie was huffing from the strenuous walk by the time they left the path to circle the shoreline. Her silky thermal undershirt stuck to her shoulder blades, and the Kevlar shield trapped a nasty little trickle of perspiration in the small of her back.

Well aware that wet clothes led to hypothermia, which could kill far more swiftly than exposure or starvation, she slowed her pace and strolled along the shore beside Adam as though they were, in fact, just out to enjoy the spectacular sight of the sun burnishing the surrounding peaks. In the process, she searched the trees ringing the lake.

Maggie had no idea which was Taylor's special tree—until a lone twisted oak on a narrow spit of land snared her gaze. Lightning had split its trunk nearly in half, but the tree had defied the elements. Alone and proud, it lifted its bare branches to the golden light now spilling over the snowcapped peaks. Sure enough, Radizwell raced out onto the narrow strip and bounded around the twisted oak. His earsplitting barks echoed in the early-morning stillness like booming cannon fire.

"He probably thinks he's going to get another treat," Maggie muttered.

"Isn't he?"

"If you give away another one of those biscuits, that shaggy Hungarian won't be the only one howling."

He sent her an amused look. "You get a little testy when you're hungry, don't you?"

"Very!" she warned. "Remember that."

"I will," he promised, his eyes glinting.

The agent patrolled the shore while Maggie and Adam walked out onto the spit for a few moments of much-needed privacy. They had to contact headquarters. Relay the latest developments to Jaguar. Formulate a game plan for communicating in an insecure environment. None of which could be done in a house wired from rooftop to wood-plank floor.

Despite the urgency of their mission, however, the initials carved into the weathered trunk tugged at Maggie's concentration. Pulling off a glove, she traced the deep grooves.

"*T* and *H*. Taylor and Harold."

"Hal," Adam reminded her, leaning a forearm against the tree. His breath mingled with hers, soft clouds of white vapor in the sharp mountain air. "She called him Hal."

Maggie nodded. "Hal."

With the tip of one finger, she followed the smooth cut. It had been blunted a bit over the years, but had withstood the test of time.

"Did you know him?" she asked.

"I met him once, just before he died. He was a good man, and a gifted sculptor. I have a bronze of his at home."

The glint of gold on Maggie's finger caught her gaze. "They must have loved each other very much," she said softly. "The words inside this ring make me want to cry. *Now, and forever.*"

When Adam didn't reply, she squinted up at him, her eyes narrowed against the now-dazzling sunlight reflected off the lake's frozen surface.

"Don't you believe in forever?"

Unaware that she was doing so, Maggie held her breath as she waited for his answer. There was so much she didn't know about this man, she acknowledged with a stab of uncertainty. He kept his thoughts to himself. His past was shrouded in mystery. Their only contact was through OMEGA and their work together.

Only recently had she finally acknowledged how much she wanted him. Yet now, staring into eyes deepened to midnight by the dark blue of his ski jacket, she realized with shattering clarity that wanting wasn't enough. Physical gratification wouldn't begin to satisfy the need this man generated in her.

In that moment, with the sun cutting through the distant peaks and their breath entwined on the cold, clear air, Maggie knew she wanted more. She wanted the forever Taylor had never had. With this man. With Adam.

"I believe in a lot of things, Maggie, my own," he said softly, in answer to her question. "Several of which I intend to discuss with you very soon."

My own.

She liked the sound of that. A lot. Suddenly very soon couldn't come fast enough for Maggie.

"It seems as though the list of things we have to discuss with each other is getting longer by the hour," she replied, her smile answering the promise in his eyes. "Right now, though, I guess we'd better contact Jaguar."

They moved to a boulder at the end of the spit. While Maggie brushed the snow off its flat surface, Adam punched the necessary codes into the transceiver built into his watch.

To the agent on the shore behind them, it must have appeared as though they were enjoying the panoramic vista of an ice-crusted lake skirted by towering dark green firs. Shoulder to shoulder, Maggie and Adam shared the rock and waited for headquarters to acknowledge the signal. He kept his arm tucked against her body to muffle the sound of Jake's voice.

"Jaguar here. Been wondering where you were."

"I couldn't check in this morning. Chameleon discovered a hidden device in her room. We had to assume there was one in mine, as well."

Through the crystal-clear transmission, Maggie could hear the frown in Jaguar's voice. "What kind of device?"

"One that our scanners didn't pick up when we swept the rooms last night. Or someone planted while we were downstairs."

"Can you describe it?"

Maggie bent her elbows across her knees and leaned forward. Keeping her voice low, she spoke into the transmitter. "About an inch square. Wafer-thin. Blue-gray in color, made of a composite material I've never seen before. It looks like plastic, but it's a lot more porous, almost like a honeycomb."

"That doesn't fit any of the designs I know. I'll have the lab check it out."

"Tell them to dig deep. This might be the first break we've had on this mission."

A hint of excitement had crept into her voice. She'd had plenty of time to think through this unexpected turn of events during the long hours of the night…after she'd left Adam's bed.

"Tell the lab to talk to the Secret Service's technical division. Those guys have access to the latest materials."

"You think the Secret Service planted a bug in the vice president's bedroom without her knowledge or approval?"

"I don't know," Maggie confessed. "But if they did, the order had to come from high up in their chain."

"Like from the secretary of the treasury himself," Jaguar drawled.

"Exactly."

"Slip someone into Digicon's labs, as well," Adam instructed. "I'm willing to bet they're using this composite material in the work they're doing for NASA."

"I'd say that's a pretty good bet," Jaguar commented. "By the way, you might want to know that we've confirmed Stoney Armstrong's suspicions about First Bank."

"First Bank is laundering drug money?"

"Laundering it, dry-cleaning it, and serving it up starched and folded. It took our auditors some time, but they finally uncovered a blind account that traced back to a dummy corporation fronted by a major cartel."

"Tell them they did good work."

"They didn't do it all on their own. We got some inside information. From a source tracking it from the other end."

"Is the source reliable?"

"Ask Chameleon," Jake drawled. "She had dinner with him when he was in Washington a few weeks ago."

"Luis!" Maggie exclaimed. "*That's* where I heard about First Bank! I knew it was in connection with something other than the president's inter-monetary whatever."

Adam's black brows snapped together. The idea of Maggie having dinner with the smooth, oversexed Colonel Luis Esteban, chief of Cartozan security, didn't sit particularly well with him.

"What's Esteban's interest in First Bank?"

"His government's trying to unfreeze the assets of the drug lord Jaguar and I helped take down last year. Evidently First was holding some."

"And?"

Maggie shrugged. "Cartoza's a small country. They were getting the runaround from some bureaucrat or another. I made a few calls to one or two of my contacts and hinted at high-level government interest on our side.''

"How high?"

Her eyes gleamed. ''I more or less left it to their imagination.''

Adam frowned. There were too many references to First Bank cropping up for simple coincidence. First, there was the president's plan for stabilizing the Latin-American economies, which the bank had helped draft. Then Stoney Armstrong. Now Maggie and her smarmy Latin colonel. There was a connection. There had to be.

''Is that team of auditors still in place?'' he asked Jaguar sharply.

''I was going to pull them out today.''

''Keep them there. Have them examine every transaction, every wire transfer, for the last two years. See if Digicon does any business with them.''

''Roger.''

''And have them look into any blind trusts that may have been set up to handle accounts for persons currently in public office.''

''Like the secretary of the treasury?''

''Like the secretary of the treasury. Get back to me immediately if they turn anything up. Anything at all. There's a link here that we're missing. Something that ties it all together.''

''Will do.''

Adam signed off. Rising, he shoved his hands into his back pockets and frowned at the lake.

''What do you think it could be?'' Maggie asked. ''This link?''

''I don't know. But it's there. I'm sure of it.''

She regarded him with a solemn air. ''Careful, Thunder. Your sixth sense is showing.''

Adam turned, and felt his heart twist.

Maggie shone through the facade of her disguise. His Maggie. Irrepressible. Irresistible. Her eyes alight with the mischievous glow that snared his soul.

Surrendering to the inevitable, he reached for her. At that moment, he didn't care who was watching. Who was listening. He had to kiss her.

"Mmm…" she murmured a few moments later. "Nice. See what happens when you let yourself go and operate solely on instinct?"

"I've been operating on instincts where you're concerned for a long time," he said dryly. "You defy all logic or rational approach."

Laughter filled her eyes. "I'll take that as a compliment."

Adam caught her chin in his hand. Tilting her face to his, he warmed himself in her vibrant glow. "It was intended as one."

"Hmm… I think this is something else we have to add to our list of topics to discuss. Soon."

"*Very* soon."

Her breath caught. "Adam…"

He would always remember that moment beside the lake and wonder what she might have said—if the distant throb of an engine hadn't snagged her attention. If the agent on the shore hadn't turned, his head cocked toward the humming sound. If the dog hadn't risen up off its haunches and swung its massive body around.

Adam lifted his head and searched the tree line.

"It sounds like a snowmobile," Maggie murmured, a frown sketching her forehead. She listened for a moment, then stiffened in his arms. "It's not coming from the direction of the cabin."

"No, it's not. Come on, let's get off this unprotected spit."

Tension, sudden and electric, arced between them. The dog picked up on it immediately, or perhaps sensed the danger on his own. He growled, deep in his throat, and pushed ahead of them onto the pebbled shore. His huge paws had just hit the snow when the first snowmobile burst out of the screen of trees.

It darted forward, a blue beetle whizzing across the snow on short skis. A second followed, then a third. The white-suited driver in the lead vehicle lifted his arm, and a burst of automatic gunfire cut the Secret Service agent down where he stood.

Maggie and Adam dived for cover. In a movement so ingrained, so instinctive, that they could have been synchronized swimmers, they rolled across the snow. On the first roll, Maggie had freed Taylor's puny little weapon from her pants pocket. On the second, Adam's far heavier and more powerful gun was blazing.

The first attacker came at them, spewing bullets and snow as he swerved to avoid the counterfire. Maggie left him to Adam and concentrated on the second, who was circling behind them. She got off one shot, and then a shaggy white shape hurtled through the air.

An agonized scream rose over the sound of gunfire and roaring engines, only to be cut off by a savage snarl.

Chapter 10

Adam saw at once that they were outgunned and outmaneuvered.

Their Secret Service escort lay writhing in the snow, blood pumping from a hit to the stomach. They couldn't reach him without running along a stretch of open, exposed shoreline. The downed man's only hope of survival was for them to keep the attackers focused on their primary target. And her only hope was escape.

Obviously Maggie reached the same conclusion at exactly the same moment. She thrust herself upward, leaving the shelter of the shallow depression her body had made in the snow.

"Cover me!"

"No! Get down! Dammit, Maggie—"

Since she was already plowing across the snow, Adam had no choice. Cursing viciously, he rose on one knee. His blue steel Heckler & Koch spit a stream of fire at a white-suited figure zigzagging through the trees on a gleaming blue snowmobile. The driver jerked, and a sudden blotch of red blossomed on his shoulder. The hit was too high, only a flesh wound, but the assailant fell back, out of range, before Adam could get another clear shot.

Cursing again, he swung around.

Radizwell had knocked the second figure sideways, out of his seat. The riderless vehicle had skidded forward for another fifty or so yards before running up a high drift at an angle and tilting over. Screaming and thrashing, the driver flailed his arms in an effort to protect his face from the dog's savage assault. Adam didn't dare risk a shot from where he knelt. The sheepdog's massive body all but covered the downed man.

The third attacker circled through the Douglas firs, spraying automatic rifle fire in wild arcs as he tried to handle both his vehicle and his weapon. Adam couldn't get a clear line of fire through the screen of trees. In frustration, he raised his arm and squeezed off a shot. An overhanging branch snapped, dumping a shower of white just as the figure passed under it. For a few precious seconds, the automatic went silent.

Those seconds were all Maggie needed. Plunging through the knee-high snow, she reached the overturned snowmobile. At that point, she had to choose between charging forward another fifty yards to retrieve the Uzi the driver had lost when Radizwell hit him and snatching at their only chance of escape. The sound of rifle fire behind her decided the matter. She couldn't hope to reach the weapon before the other two attackers cut her—or Adam—down.

Grunting with effort, she heaved the sputtering snowmobile upright. Bullets stitched a line in the snowbank just above her head as she threw herself onto the seat and grappled frantically with the controls. The vehicle jerked forward, almost tumbling her backward. She grabbed at the handles for balance, then leaned low and gunned the engine.

The few moments it took her to reach Adam would repeat themselves in her nightmares for the rest of her life. He knelt on one knee, arm extended, pistol sited at a target darting through the trees. His black hair and blue ski jacket stood out against the dazzling whiteness of the snow and made him a perfect target. He was trying to draw the attackers' fire, Maggie knew. Away from her.

At the sound of the snowmobile coming at him from an angle, Adam swung around. For a heart-stopping moment, his weapon was trained directly on Maggie. It jerked in his hand. A sharp crack split the air.

Glancing over her shoulder, she saw that the figure struggling to escape Radizwell had made it to his knees. Adam's shot sent him diving facedown in the snow for cover. The dog promptly landed on his back.

Maggie reached Adam half a heartbeat later. Throttling back on the controls, she slowed a fraction. As soon as she felt his weight hit the seat behind her, she rammed the machine into full power. His arm wrapped around her waist like an iron band, cutting off her air. She barely noticed. She hadn't drawn a full breath since the first shot. Opening the throttle all the way, she aimed for the tree line.

The chase that followed could have come right out of a movie. A horror movie. Using every evasive tactic she'd been taught, and a few she invented along the way, Maggie dodged under low-hanging boughs, swerved around granite outcroppings and sailed over snowbanks. At one point, she took a turn too close. Prickly pine needles lashed her face, momentarily blinding her. The snowmobile swerved, tilted, righted itself.

''There!'' Adam shouted in her ear, pointing over her shoulder.

She squinted through the involuntary tears caused by the sting of the needles. Following the line of his arm, she saw a wall of serrated granite slabs thrusting out of the snow to their left. To her blurred eyes, the gray-blue mass looked impenetrable.

"Take it hard and fast! Right through the notch!"

"What notch? I can't see!"

He twisted on the seat behind her, shoving his weapon into his jacket. Then he reached forward, an arm on either side of her, and took the controls. Maggie felt a craven urge to close her streaming eyes completely as the sheet of granite loomed in front of their hurtling vehicle.

Just when it seemed they were about to hit the wall, Adam threw his weight to one side and took her with him. The vehicle tilted at an impossible angle. Its left ski lifted, scraped stone. The engine revved louder and louder as the right ski dug into the snow. The vehicle hung suspended for what seemed like two or three lifetimes, then shot through the narrow opening.

Maggie would have shouted in joyous relief, if her blurred vision hadn't cleared just enough to see what lay on the other side of the wall. A ravine. A big ravine. About the size of the Grand Canyon. At its widest point.

Adam's hands froze on the controls for half an instant, then twisted violently. The engine screamed into full power.

"Hang on!"

As if she had any choice!

Maggie didn't hesitate at all this time. She scrunched her eyes shut and didn't open them until a bone-jarring jolt told her they'd landed on the far side. When she saw the steep, tree-covered slope ahead, she was sorry she'd opened them at all.

Branches slashed at their faces, tore at their bodies, as they whipped down the incline in a series of snaking turns.

Her heart jackhammered against her ribs with each zig. Her kidneys slammed sideways on every zag. All the while she strained to hear behind her, listening for sounds of pursuit over the scream of their engine and the roar of her blood in her ears.

At the bottom of the slope, Adam yanked on the controls and slewed the machine to a halt. He shoved himself off, backward, and immediately sank to his knees in the snow.

''You take it from here.''

''No way!''

''Get moving.''

''No!''

Above his whiskered chin and cold-reddened cheeks, Adam's eyes flashed icy blue fire. ''That's an order, Chameleon. Move!''

''I'm the field agent on this mission. I'm not dividing my forces, or what little firepower I have!''

''Dammit—''

''I'm not leaving you. Get on the vehicle!''

Every second wasted in argument could be their last. She knew it. He knew it.

His jaw working, Adam threw a leg over the rear of the snowmobile.

They finally slowed to a stop at the crest of a wooded rise. Maggie kept the snowmobile idling, afraid to shut it off completely, in case they had to make a quick getaway. Eyes narrowed against the sun's glare, bodies tense, they listened and searched the woods below for signs of pursuit. Maggie was the first to pick up the rise and fall of engines in the distance.

''There's at least…two of them,'' she panted. ''Maybe three…if…Radizwell didn't have the S.O.B. for lunch.''

Adam angled his head, listening intently. "They're following the ravine. Looking for a place to cross."

He shoved back his sleeve. The flat gold watch nestled among the dark hairs of his wrist glinted in the morning sun.

"Jaguar, this is Thunder. Do you read me?"

Their breath puffed out in white clouds, rapid and ragged, while they waited for a response.

"I read you. Go ahead, Thunder."

"We've run into a little unfriendly fire. How close is the backup team?"

"Twenty minutes by helicopter," Jake snapped instantly. "Give me your coordinates."

Anticipating the need, Adam had already dug a small rectangular case out of his pocket. Not much bigger than a package of chewing gum, the digital compass received signals from the Navstar Global Positioning System. Navstar had proved its capabilities during the Gulf War by guiding tank commanders across the vast, featureless Saudi deserts. Its current constellation of twenty-four orbiting satellites could pinpoint time to within one-millionth of a second, velocity to within a fraction of a mile per hour, and location to within a few feet.

"Latitude, three-nine degrees, six—"

He broke off as the distant sounds died. Maggie inched the throttles back as far as she dared to quiet the noise of their own engine and concentrated all her energies on listening.

"Six minutes," Adam continued. "Longitude, one-two-oh degrees—"

A sudden burst of horsepower cut him off once more. He stiffened, the tendons in his neck standing out like cords as he swiveled in the direction of the sounds.

"They got across!"

Engines revved. Grew louder.

"They're coming straight at us!" he snarled. "How the hell did they double back and find our tracks so quickly?"

Maggie turned a startled face to his, as stunned as he. Then her eyes dropped to the gold watch.

"Maybe they didn't find our tracks! Maybe they're homing in on the satellite signal!"

Adam didn't waste time in further speculation. The satellite signals were supposed to be secure. Scrambled. They'd never been broken or intercepted before. But an individual who knew how to bypass the sophisticated electronic filters in the White House switchboard might well have broken into a supposedly secure satellite system.

"Six-one, Jaguar! Six-one!"

With that emergency signal telling Jake to stand by until further contact, Adam abruptly terminated the transmission.

They managed to shake their pursuers once again.

The sounds of the distant motors fell away as Maggie steered an erratic course, up one slope, down another. Dodging fallen trees and low-hanging branches, she headed for a line of low, ragged peaks to her right. From the angle of the sun, she calculated they were headed due east, away from the cabin. Given the topography, however, she couldn't circle back. She had to follow where the mountains led.

Her face was stinging with cold and her numbed fingers were locked on the throttles when the machine under her began to sputter and miss. Maggie glanced down at the dash, trying to find the fuel gauge. She tore one gloved hand loose and rubbed it across the snow-covered indicator. Sure enough, the red bar danced at the bottom of the frost-encrusted gauge, almost out of sight.

Not two minutes later, the engine died. The snowmobile

skidded a few feet farther up the slope, slowed to a crawl, stopped, then began a backward slide. Adam dug his boots in and brought them to a halt.

For a few seconds, neither of them moved. They remained silent. Listening. Searching the trees behind them.

Somewhere below them, their attackers were equally silent. Listening. Searching the trees above them.

"They're waiting," Adam said, his voice low. "For us to signal again."

"Bastards."

"They won't have used as much fuel as we did riding double. They'll catch us easily."

"Who?" Maggie muttered angrily. Her mission had just exploded in her face, and she was furious with herself for not having anticipated it. "Who are 'they'? How did we go from a narrow list of suspects to a whole damned strike team?"

"Whoever knew you were going to be at the lake this morning," Adam tossed back.

From the rigid set to his jaw, Maggie saw that he was no happier about this unexpected turn of events than she.

"Everyone knew," she snapped. "It was some kind of a ritual with Taylor."

"And if they didn't know, we told them," Adam added, disgust lacing his voice. "Last night, in my bedroom."

Maggie struggled to rein in her anger. "We're no longer dealing with a lone assassin here. This individual has a whole organization behind him. Obviously we need to reassess our mission parameters."

"Obviously." Adam pushed himself off the snowmobile and drew in a steadying breath. "Right now, though, our first priority has to be cover. If they don't pick us up soon, they'll call in air support and continue the search from the air."

"Denise and her people will have heard the shots and found their downed man by now. They'll be searching, too—assuming one of them wasn't behind the attack in the first place," Maggie finished heavily.

"I don't think we can assume anything at this point. I suggest we burrow in until dark. The chances of them picking us up at night after we signal Jaguar will be slimmer. Marginally slimmer, admittedly, but slimmer."

Nodding, she clambered off the snowmobile and surveyed the now-useless vehicle.

"I guess we'd better see what we can salvage from this hummer."

While Adam used the butt of his pistol to break off pieces of one of the small mirrors mounted on the handles, Maggie pried open the storage compartment. Inside, she found a pitiful cache of survival equipment—one metallic solar blanket, so thin it folded into a plastic pouch the size of a candy bar, a small tool kit, and a spare pair of goggles. Evidently their attackers hadn't planned on a prolonged stay in the wilderness.

Adam knelt on one knee to bundle their small cache of equipment in a piece of fender he'd broken off. "You'd better take that off," he said, nodding to indicate her bright pink jacket. "I'll wrap it up with the rest of this gear."

Maggie didn't need to be told that the vivid color made too visible a target. Her shiver when she tugged off the thick layer of down wasn't due to the chill air.

Adam removed his own jacket, as well, but didn't offer it to her out of any misguided sense of male gallantry. He knew as well as she that the exertion of walking through the snow would work up a sweat, which had to be allowed to evaporate, or it would freeze their clothes to their bodies.

They left the vehicle buried under a nest of branches. As she trudged up the slope, trailing a screen of branches to cover their tracks, Maggie repeated to herself over and over the principle her instructors had drilled into her during survival training. Stay dry. In the jungle. In the Arctic. Stay dry. Foot rot from wet boots while slogging through swamps was as dangerous as frostbite from sweat-dampened undergarments in cold climates.

With that in mind, she tugged the hem of her turtleneck out of her waistband to let air circulate. Adam did the same with his plaid flannel shirt. Maggie saw that he wore the same style of high-tech long johns she did—under his shirt, at least. She didn't see how anything would fit under those snug jeans.

As they neared the crest, the trees thinned, as did the snow. Bare, windswept slabs of granite made the going easier, but also made Maggie feel far too vulnerable. The skin between her shoulder blades just above the bulletproof corset itched as though a big round circle had been painted on it.

Once over the top of the ridge, they scouted for a spot that would protect them from both the elements and searching eyes while they decided on their game plan.

"There," she panted, out of breath from the steep climb. "Under that tree."

The conifer she pointed to was at least sixty feet tall and shaped much like a pointed stake. Its branches grew wide at the bottom to catch the sun and narrowed dramatically toward the top. Laden with snow, the lower limbs drooped to the ground. They'd provide both concealment and natural insulation.

Maggie and Adam scrambled down the slope, brushing away their tracks as best they could. Squatting, he peered under the sagging branches.

"Perfect. I'll tunnel us in. You gather some branches."

She smiled wryly at his ingrained habit of assuming command, but decided not to take issue with it. In this instance, it didn't matter who dug and who gathered, as long as the tasks got done, and fast. Besides, she didn't have enough breath right now to argue.

Using the fender from the snowmobile, Adam knelt on one knee and set to work scooping a shallow trench in the snow under the drooping limbs. He worked quickly, but took great care not to disturb the thick layer of white coating the branches.

When Maggie came back with the first armload of pine branches, she stopped abruptly a few feet away. Adam had shed his plaid shirt to keep it dry. His thermal undershirt showed damp patches, attesting to the strenuous effort physical labor required at this elevation. It also attested to his superb physical condition. The silky white fabric clung to his body with a loving attention to detail that made Maggie's mouth go dry.

His upper torso might have been sculpted by Michelangelo. Broad and well toned at the shoulders, narrow and lean at the waist, he was basic, elemental male. When he bent forward, his jeans rode low on narrow hips. A curl of dark hair at the small of his back drew Maggie's fascinated gaze. With each scoop, his muscles rippled with a primitive, utterly beautiful poetry.

At the sight, something wrenched inside her, and she knew she'd never view Adam the same way again. The image of the cool aristocrat that she'd carried for so long in her mind and her heart shattered.

"Want me to dig the rest?" she asked, dumping the prickly pine branches beside the entrance.

"No, I'm all right. We'll need more branches to line the interior walls, though."

She nodded, stooping to check his progress. "Better not make the opening too narrow," she advised him with a wry smile. "As Lillian is so fond of pointing out, I'm not quite a perfect size eight."

Adam rested an arm on the bent fender and watched her retrace her footsteps in the snow. A tantalizing snatch of conversation he'd overheard between her and Lillian the night of the Kennedy Center benefit came back to him. Maggie had protested then that she wasn't a perfect anything, and he'd silently agreed. He hadn't changed his opinion. If anything, the past few days had reinforced it.

Fiercely independent didn't begin to describe this woman. Her adamant refusal to follow his orders today came as close to insubordination as he'd ever allowed an OMEGA operative. Only her acid reminder that she was the field commander on this mission had stopped him from shredding her to pieces on the spot. That, and the fact that Maggie Sinclair wasn't particularly shreddable.

But Adam knew he'd never erase from his mind his stunned fury when she'd sprung up out of the snow and dashed for the snowmobile. Or his sudden, swamping fear. He'd expected a bullet to slam into her body at any second. To see her thrown back by the force of a hit. He'd kept his mind focused and his hand steady as he provided covering fire, but a silent litany had reverberated through him with every step she took.

No more talk.

No more waiting.

No more denying the raw need that gripped him. And her.

That same refrain echoed in his mind now as he bent to scoop fenderful after fenderful of snow out of the shallow trench.

No more talk.

No more waiting.

If they lived through this day, neither of them would ever be the same. Soon had become now.

While he dug, Maggie rounded up enough pine branches to construct a thick, springy mat that would keep them off the snow. More feathery branches provided insulation for the walls Adam built up around the depression. Above these walls the sagging tree limbs formed a natural sloping ceiling.

Within a remarkably short time, their hidden lair was complete. While Adam crawled inside to spread the lightweight solar blanket over the springy mat, Maggie gathered their meager gear.

She handed him the items one by one, still panting a little from her foraging trips. Pine needles stuck to her white turtleneck, which in turn stuck to her back and shoulders.

Adam got to his feet and dusted the snow from his knees, frowning as he took in the damp hair curling around her face.

"You crawl inside. I'll brush the rest of the tracks and seal the entrance."

Maggie nodded and dropped to her knees.

"Strip off as much as you can. I'll help you with the body shield when I'm done here, so you can get out of those damp long johns."

She paused halfway through the narrow tunnel. Bottom wiggling, she backed out again.

"Let's just review the situation here. We're in the middle of nowhere. Two, possibly three stalkers are searching for us as we speak. We don't know who sent them, we can't contact headquarters for help, and we have no idea at this moment how long we're going to be stranded here."

"That about sums it up."

"Not quite."

She eyed his chest, which was damp from exertion. Her

fingers dug into her thighs with the need to stroke its broad planes. Dry them. Curl into their warmth.

Lifting her gaze to his face, she grinned. It wasn't much of a grin, more a grimace than an expression of mirth, but it was the best Maggie could do at the moment.

"If we crawl into that hole and get naked together, I'm not going to be held responsible for my actions."

He smiled at her then. Not the smooth, easy smile he'd given "Taylor" the past few days. Not the cool half smile he allowed himself on occasion at OMEGA headquarters. This was a slow, satisfied, devastatingly predatory twist of his lips.

"Maggie, my darling, when we get naked together, responsibility is the last thing I want from you."

At her start of surprise, his smile lost its razor's edge. "Go on, get inside. You know as well as I do that the next few minutes could make the difference between life and death."

Chapter 11

Mind racing, heart pumping, Maggie crawled through the narrow tunnel.

Okay. All right. It was a matter of survival. Hers and his. They had to strip off. They had to stay dry. In the Arctic. In the jungle.

She was a professional. She'd been trained for situations like this. It was a matter of survival.

Yet when she entered the chamber Adam had carved for them under the spreading boughs of the majestic fir, her chaotic thoughts centered on a different kind of survival. The kind that had to do with the continuation of the species.

Her blood rushed through her veins, bringing with it a heat that added to the moisture dewing her neck. Breathing hard, she made herself sit back on her heels. While she waited for her pulse to slow, she admired the fruits of their labors.

Both the size and the warmth of this subterranean nest surprised her. The tree's massive trunk formed a solid, rounded back wall. Mounded snow defined the rest of the area. Overhead, drooping, snow-laden branches slanted down at an angle from the base of the tree to the outer walls. The fragrant pine boughs Maggie had gathered lined the interior walls and made a thick mat for the floor, adding an extra layer of insulation.

Amazing. They'd constructed a tight, neat lean-to using nature's own materials, with no tools or modern implements except a fiberglass fender scoop. Adam had spread the thin Mylar blanket over the mat, but Maggie knew they could have survived without it.

Survival.

The pulse that had slowed a fraction leaped into action again.

It was a matter of survival.

And, as Adam had said, the next few minutes could make the difference between life and death.

Settling cross-legged on the shifting mat, she pulled off her gloves. Carefully she placed her weapon atop her folded pink ski jacket to keep it both dry and close at hand, then went to work on her bootlaces. Within moments, her brown pants hung from one of the overhead branches. She was just reaching for the hem of her white turtleneck when Adam backed into the chamber.

Suddenly the pine-scented nest didn't seem nearly as spacious as it had a moment ago.

Maggie edged over to make room for him. The springy mat shifted under her and tipped her sideways. Her elbow dug into his thigh. His shoulder thumped her chest. It took a bit of doing, but they finally maneuvered themselves back into sitting positions. He laid his weapon next to hers and glanced around the interior. A half smile curved his lips as he surveyed his work.

''The hole seemed a lot bigger when I was digging it. It's kind of tight in here.''

''At least it'll be warm.''

He nodded, eyeing the mounded walls. ''When the snow sets, this cave will be as well insulated as any house. Better than most.''

Maggie believed him. She already felt the extra heat his presence generated in the small chamber. He'd brought a musky warmth into the dim interior, which combined with hers to drive off the chill. The trapped air warmed perceptibly around them while he unlaced his boots. And when his hand went to the zipper of his jeans, Maggie could have sworn the temperature shot up another dozen degrees or so.

It was a matter of survival. It was…

Hastily she dragged her turtleneck over her head.

Matter-of-factly he shoved the well-worn denim down over his hips. He rose up on one knee to drape his pants over the limb beside her top.

To Maggie's intense relief and equally intense disappointment, he did wear high-tech long johns under those snug jeans. But where her bottoms covered her from waist to ankle, his came only to midthigh, like running or biking shorts. They might have been meant for his warmth, but they contributed greatly to hers.

If his upper torso had been sculpted by Michelangelo, his lower body was by the same unknown Greek artist who'd created the statue of Hercules she'd once seen in a museum in Athens. All long lines and corded sinews. Sleek. Powerful. Well muscled. And bulging in places that sent a shaft of heat spearing straight through Maggie.

''Are your socks wet?''

She dragged her gaze up to his face. ''My socks?''

''Your socks. Are they wet?''

''No.''

"Good. You'd better keep them on, along with the thermal underwear. But the body shield needs to come off. Bend over."

Maggie bit her lip.

"You're damp under the Kevlar. You need to dry off. It's a matter of—"

"I know. A matter of survival."

Pushing herself to her knees, she twisted to one side. The rasp of Velcro echoed through the nest. Once. Twice. When the corset fell away, she felt strangely naked. Without the constraining shield, her breasts regained their fuller, firmer shape. Beneath the thin covering of her undershirt, her nipples puckered with the cold. Or the heat. At this point, she couldn't have said which.

The damp, silky underwear molded to every line of her chest as faithfully as it did to Adam's. Maggie felt an instinctive urge, as old as woman herself, to hunch her shoulders and hide herself.

Immediately, another, even older urge flowed through her. The need to claim her man. Her mate. Her forever.

They might have only this hour together. Only these few moments. Yet Maggie knew they would last her a lifetime. Slowly she straightened her shoulders. Sitting back on her heels, she met Adam's eyes. The blue fire in them ignited the flames licking at her blood.

His gaze drifted from her face to her throat. Her breasts. Her stomach. Involuntarily her thighs clenched.

A muscle ticked in the side of his jaw, shadowed with the night's growth.

"Do you have any idea how beautiful you are?"

A momentary doubt shivered through her as she remembered the artificial bone that shaped her nose and chin. The violet contacts. The auburn hair. Who did he see? Who did he find beautiful? She had to know.

"Who, Adam? Me, or Taylor? Who do you see?"

In answer, he smiled and lifted a hand to curve her cheek. "I see you, Maggie. A woman of incredible courage and vibrant, glowing life."

That pretty well satisfied her doubts, but she had no objection when Adam expanded a bit.

"I see the same woman who sailed out of my office swathed from head to foot in a black nun's habit. I see the high-class hooker who took off for France in a slithery shoestring halter that kept me awake for a solid week."

She tilted her head into his hand. "A week, huh?"

"At least."

"Who else? Who else do you see?"

His thumb brushed her lower lip. "I see the woman who infuriates me on occasion, and intrigues me at all times. Who makes me want to lock my office door and throw her down on that damned conference table she always perches on."

Maggie's brows shot up. "Really?"

"Really."

"Hmm…"

The idea that he'd harbored a few fantasies about her thrilled Maggie to her core. Almost as much as the thumb rubbing across her lip. Incredible, what a single touch could do.

"Adam?"

"Yes?"

"Do you have any idea how many times I've imagined…us? Together? Alone?"

His hand curled around the back of her neck, urging her closer. Branches shifted. Mylar crinkled. They were chest to chest. Mouth to mouth.

"No. Tell me."

"A few."

"Only a few?" He kissed her right eyelid.

"Okay, more than a few. A dozen."

"Only a dozen?" He kissed her left eyelid.

She smiled up at him. "A hundred or two."

"And?"

"And never, ever, in any one of those thousands of times, did I picture us making love underground. In a nest of pine needles. Fully clothed. Well, one of us fully clothed."

"Maggie, my darling, I've pictured us underground and aboveground and on the ground."

Laughter welled inside her. "All that was going on behind your Mr. In Control, always-so-cool exterior?"

"All that, and more."

"Well, well…"

He kissed her mouth then, and brought her down with him. Legs entangled, she sprawled across his chest. Hungrily she explored his mouth with her tongue and teeth. His unshaven chin rasped against hers. The tiny, stinging sensation sent a rush of liquid warmth to Maggie's belly. Her hand slithered down his chest, and she discovered that clothes were no impediment to a determined woman. He filled her fist, rock-hard, ridged, sheathed in satiny softness.

His hand tugged up the hem of her shirt and found her breast. It swelled in his hold, the nipple throbbing with an ache that matched the one between her legs. An ache that grew with every kiss, every thrust of his thigh between hers.

Time and space dissolved. Merged. Melted into two bodies and one need. When she couldn't bear their separateness any longer, she lifted slightly and arched her pelvis against his hardness.

His hands stilled her hips. "Wait, Maggie. Wait."

"No. No more waiting."

"Not this way."

"Why not?"

His eyes glinted with regret. "Because, sweetheart, even my vivid fantasies didn't include making love to you in the snow beside a frozen lake. I didn't bring any protection when I walked out to view the sunrise with you."

Nonplussed, Maggie stared at him helplessly.

With a surge of his powerful body, he rolled her over. "Let me love you in a way that's safe. In a way that will still give us pleasure."

His hand found the convenient opening in the bottoms of her long johns. The wayward thought shot through Maggie that the manufacturers of winter survival wear knew what they were doing. A person didn't have to undress to perform any vital function. And taking Adam into her body was becoming more vital by the second.

He slid a finger inside her welcoming wetness, then another. His thumb pressed the hard core at her center. Gasping, she arched under him.

The scent of crushed pine needles, sharp and pungent, rose around her. Maggie knew she would never again walk through a forest or touch a Christmas wreath or open a bottle of kitchen cleaner without thinking of this man and this moment. Then his mouth came down on hers, and Maggie forgot about kitchen cleaners and walks and everything else.

Their breathing grew more labored. Their bodies hardened. As his hands and his mouth worked their magic, wave after wave of sensation washed through Maggie, drawing her closer to the edge.

With infinite skill, he primed her.

With infinite need, she caught his face between her hands. Panting, breathless, she could only gasp her desperate desire.

"Adam. Listen to me. We're in the middle of nowhere.

On our own. We may never make it out of here alive. This could be the only moment we ever have."

"Maggie…"

"This could be our once. Our forever. I don't want protection. Not from you. I want you."

They fit together the way she'd always known they would. Female and male. Woman and man. Maggie and Adam.

He rose up and thrust into her. She lifted her hips and thrust against him.

He filled her, full and powerful and hard and urgent. She took him into her, wrapping her body and heart and soul around him.

Mylar twisted around their legs. Branches poked at backs and knees and elbows and bottoms. Maggie didn't feel any of it. Her entire being was focused on Adam.

When he reached down between their bodies and rubbed her tight, aching core, she climaxed in an explosion of white light and red, searing pleasure. She arched under him, groaning, flexing her muscles in an instinctive need to take him with her.

The violent movement dislodged a clump of snow from the branch overhead. It landed on Adam's shoulder, slid down to Maggie's chest.

Her eyes opened in shock, and she laughed.

Adam groaned at the sound and surged into her a final time.

Afterward, long afterward, they exchanged the clothes that clung to their slick bodies for the dry ones hanging over their heads. With a rustle of boughs, Adam propped his back against the tree trunk, stretched out his legs and brought Maggie into his lap. She laid her head against his shoulder, sighing.

"How much time do we have?"

Adam smiled at the reluctant question. He wasn't in any more of a hurry than Maggie to leave this small den. Resting his chin on the top of her head, he drew her closer into his warmth. The scaly bark of the tree trunk bit into his back through the flannel shirt, but he barely noticed. With one hand, he reached out to check his gold watch.

"It's not even ten. We have a long time to wait before we contact Jaguar and call in an extraction team."

She shifted a little. "Let's talk about that."

"What is there to talk about? As soon as the sun goes down, we go up on the net. We evade any searchers until the team arrives. They can have you—can have us out in fifteen minutes."

Adam cursed his slip, and Maggie didn't miss it. She twisted around in his arms.

"You're not going, are you?"

"No."

"Neither am I."

"The hell you're not."

One wine-colored brow arched, and Adam moderated his tone. "As you said yourself, our mission parameters have changed. Drastically. We're not trying to lure a lone assassin out in the open any longer. We're facing a strike team."

"And I'm their target."

Her words triggered a staggering suspicion in Adam. With great effort, he kept his face impassive. Before he said anything to Maggie, he needed to think this through.

She mistook his sudden silence for disagreement. Pushing herself out of his arms, she got to her knees. "I'm the only one who can bring them into the open, Adam. I'm the only one who can—"

A long, rolling growl filled the air, cutting Maggie off in midsentence. She clamped a hand across her stomach.

"Good grief. Sorry 'bout that."

Adam forced a smile. "Sounds like the natives are getting restless."

She sent him a sheepish grin. "Well, hungry, anyway."

Deliberately Adam decided to take advantage of the diversion her growling stomach offered. They had a few more hours. He needed the time to think. To absorb the gut-wrenching implications of her blithe comment. Maggie was right. He knew it with a cold, chilling certainty. She was the bait. She was the one they were after. Not Taylor Grant. Her.

Whoever had targeted the vice president could have hit without warning. Yet the assassin had signaled his intent with that anonymous phone call. He'd issued a threat he must have known would activate an elaborate screen of defenses.

Somehow, some way, that call had led to the attack on Maggie. Not Taylor. Maggie.

Adam didn't know why or who or how, and at this moment he didn't care. His only concern was to keep Maggie alive until they could unravel this increasingly bizarre situation.

They had a few more hours. A few precious hours. He needed to think.

"Maybe it's time to break out the emergency rations," he suggested evenly.

"Rations?" She swept their small pile of supplies with a quick glance. "What rations?"

He reached for his blue ski jacket.

"Adam!" She scrambled up on her knees, her face alight. "I forgot all about your stash of biscuits! And bacon!"

He fished around in the deep pocket, then withdrew his hand and flipped the jacket over to reach the other.

The eager anticipation in her eyes gave way to a look of comic dismay. "Oh, God, I hope they didn't fall out of your pocket when we did that wheelie through the pass. We were standing on our heads."

"No, here they are."

He drew out a napkin-wrapped bundle, and Maggie scuttled closer while he unwrapped the edges of the cloth. When the treasure was uncovered, it turned out to be little more than a handful of crumbled dough and bits of bacon, gray with cold, congealed grease.

The unappetizing sight didn't deter Maggie at all. She pinched a bite between thumb and forefinger and popped it into her mouth. Closing her eyes, she savored the tiny morsel.

He had to smile at her beatific expression. "Good?"

"Mmm...wonderful!"

Eyes closed, head back, she wiped her tongue around her lips in search of stray crumbs.

Adam's fist clenched on the napkin. Their small nest wasn't quite a penthouse suite, and the pile of crumbs in his hand hadn't come from a beribboned basket of imported delicacies. Yet the same primitive urge that had swept him in L.A. crashed through him once again. Now, as then, he wanted to feed her. Bit by bit. Bite by bite.

But here, in this tiny snow cave, with danger all around them, the swamping, driving urge intensified a hundredfold. Subtly, swiftly, it shifted from erotic to primordial.

It was a matter of survival. Of responding to the basic instincts that drove all species. This woman was his mate. Adam wanted to feed her, and protect her, and love her. The realization that he might be able to accomplish only two out of the three made his stomach twist. That, and the knowledge that Maggie didn't want protection.

Of any sort.

His gaze roamed her upturned face, and Adam knew he'd love her differently if she did. He'd still want her with a need so raw it consumed him. He'd still lose himself in her laughing eyes. Without the fierce independence that made her Maggie, however, he'd love her with a different need.

Somehow he suspected that need wouldn't be anywhere near as powerful as the one that drove him now.

Uncurling his fingers, he found a fair-size sliver of cold bacon.

"Open your mouth."

Her eyes opened instead.

She glanced from his face to the morsel in his fingers, then back to his face.

"Aren't you going to have any?"

"No."

"You didn't have any breakfast. Aren't you hungry?"

"Yes. Very. But not for bacon. Let's feed you, and then we'll feed me."

The small stash of food and their clothes disappeared at approximately the same time.

With the passing hours, the light filtering through the snow-laden branches overhead grew brighter, then gradually dimmed.

They took turns dozing, and risked one trip outside the cave for a quick surveillance and an even quicker trip behind some bushes. After the warmth of the air trapped in the small cave, the outside seemed twice as cold. Maggie eyed the shadows drifting across the slopes as the sun played hide-and-seek among the tall peaks. They'd have to leave their small nest soon.

Her teeth were chattering by the time they'd blocked the entrance up again. She sat cross-legged on the Mylar mat and tucked her hands into her armpits to warm her fingertips.

"What time is it?"

Adam shoved back his sleeve. "Almost four. It should be dark in an hour."

"We'll have to leave then."

"We will."

She was silent for a moment, marshaling her thoughts. The muted growl that filled the small cavern took them both by surprise.

Maggie's red brows snapped together as she frowned down at her stomach.

"We cleaned out our entire supply of emergency rations," Adam reminded her. "You'll have to wait until we get back to—"

Another low growl rumbled through the air.

Maggie shook her head. "It's not me this time," she whispered.

Nodding, Adam reached for his pistol.

Maggie had hers in hand, as well, when they heard the scratching in the snow at the entrance to the tunnel.

Adam's jaw hardened. "Get dressed," he hissed. "Fast. Put on as many layers as you can."

As quickly and quietly as possible, Maggie scrambled into her clothes. Not for warmth. If a wild animal was digging at the entrance to their lair, she'd need the layers for protection against fangs and claws. And if the predator was of the two-legged variety, she didn't want to face him in her underwear.

Zipping her jacket up to her chin, she handed Adam his. While he pulled it on, she kept her pistol leveled at the entrance. Automatically they positioned themselves at either side of the tunnel entrance, out of the line of fire.

Another low, hair-raising growl convinced her their uninvited guest was close to gaining entry. Her finger tightened on the trigger.

The snow shifted. A black nose poked through the white. Sniffed. Pushed farther. More snow crumbled, and a muzzle covered in thick ropes of snowy fur appeared.

Radizwell!

Maggie sagged against the wall in relief, but had the presence of mind not to speak. The animal might not be alone out there. He might well have led a strike team right to them. Or a rescue team.

When he finally gained entrance, they discovered he hadn't led anyone to them at all. Apparently he'd come in search of Adam. And more bacon. The reproachful look the dog turned on Maggie when he discovered the empty, grease-stained napkin filled her with instant guilt.

Chapter 12

With the komondor's arrival, the air in the small cave became suffocatingly warm and decidedly aromatic. Crushed pine needles couldn't begin to compete with the aroma drifting from his ropes of uncombed fur, or his doggy breath. Nor could Maggie or Adam move without crawling over or under or around the animal.

She nodded when Adam suggested that the dog's arrival necessitated a change in plans. With less than an hour of daylight left, they couldn't take the chance that someone might pick up the dog's tracks and follow them here. They should scout out a better defensive position until they could call in the extraction team.

Maggie crawled out of the snow cave with mixed emotions. As much as she hated to leave their private nest, she needed air. Adam followed a moment later. Keeping to the shelter of the towering conifer, they breathed in the sharp, clean scent of snow and pines. Radizwell hunkered down on Adam's other side, pointedly ignoring her. Maggie suspected that he still hadn't quite accepted this stranger in Taylor's clothes. Or forgiven her for the empty, bacon-scented napkin.

They stood still and silent for long moments, searching the slopes above and below. Nothing moved. No sounds disturbed the quiet except the distant, raucous call of a hawk wheeling overhead and Radizwell's steady panting. The sun slowly slipped toward the high peaks, deepening the shadows cast by the towering trees and bathing the snow in a soft purple light.

"We'll have to head farther east," Adam murmured after a few moments. "Just in case they picked up Radizwell's tracks and are heading this way."

He pointed toward a jagged ridge a short distance away. "Let's try for those rocks. Even if the wrong people lock on to our signal, it will be harder to see us up there at night. We can hold them off until the extraction team gets here."

Maggie drew in a deep breath. "I don't think we should hold them off. We should try to pull them in."

He swung around to face her. "We've already talked about this."

"We started to," she said evenly, "but my growling stomach interrupted us. As I recall, we got sidetracked by a few cold biscuits and bacon bits."

A small smile tugged at his mouth. "So we did."

As much as she wanted to, Maggie didn't let herself be drawn in by the softening in his face or the glint in his eyes. She'd known this confrontation with Adam would come, and she was ready for it.

Keeping her tone brisk and businesslike, she reiterated the conclusions they'd reached in the cave.

"Look, we both agree the scope of the mission has changed somewhat."

"Somewhat?"

"Okay, a lot. But my basic role in the operation hasn't changed at all. I'm still the bait."

"You were the bait when we thought we were dealing with a single assassin. Now we know that individual has a whole team backing him up."

"That's just it, Adam. I'm still the one they want. I'm still—"

She stopped abruptly, frowning.

"I'm still the one they want," she said slowly. "The one *he* wants."

Adam stiffened, and in his eyes Maggie saw an echo of the same suspicion that was forming in the pit of her stomach like a cold, heavy weight.

"He wants me." She articulated each word with careful precision, not wanting to believe them, even as she said them. "He wants me. Not Taylor Grant. Me."

He didn't answer. Didn't say a word, and his silence hammered at Maggie like a crowbar striking against a metal wall.

"You think so, too, don't you? Don't you?"

"I admit the idea occurred to me. But—"

"But nothing! This unknown assassin knew how to bypass the White House phone system. Which meant he probably could have circumvented the personal security system and gotten to the vice president any time he wanted. But he didn't really want her, did he? He wanted me. I've been the target all along."

She stared at Adam, stunned. "That's it, isn't it, Adam? You know it as well as I do. He wants me."

A muscle ticked in his jaw. "All right, Maggie. Let's say you're right. Let's say he wants you. Who is *he?*"

She shook her head. "I don't know. Whoever made that call."

"Who? Who made it?"

"I don't know."

Snow crunched under his boot as he took a step toward her. "Think! Who wants you dead?"

"I don't know!"

Radizwell picked up on the tension arcing through the air between them. He whined far back in his throat and padded forward to nudge a jeans-clad hip. Adam ignored him, his attention focused on the woman before him.

"Who, Maggie? Who wants to get to you?"

She flung out a gloved hand. "Any one of a dozen men, and a few women, all of whom are behind bars now!"

"Why?" The single syllable had the force of a whip, sharp and stinging.

"Because they're behind bars!"

Adam's eyes were blue ice behind his black lashes. His breath came fast and hard on the cold air. "Not good enough. Try again. Think! Why would any of those people want you dead?"

"Because..." She wet her lips. "Because I know something I'm not supposed to know. Or I saw something I wasn't supposed to see. Or heard something I wasn't supposed to hear."

The shadows obscured his face now. Maggie couldn't see his eyes, but she felt them. Narrowed. Intent. Searing.

"What? What did you see or hear? What could you know that you're not supposed to?"

"I don't know, dammit! I don't know!"

The sharp frustration in her voice sliced through the tension-filled air like a blade. Radizwell gave a low growl, unsure of the source of their conflict, but obviously unhappy about it. He edged closer to Adam. If it came to choosing teams, Maggie thought in a wild aside, the dog had already chosen his.

"What I don't understand is, why here?" she said, bringing herself under control. "Why not in D.C.? Or anywhere else? Why set this trap, using me as bait? Luring me in like this. Or—" She stopped, her eyes widening. "Or out!"

"Out, how?"

"Out of my civilian cover. My God, Adam. Maybe that's it. Maybe someone staged this elaborate charade to draw me out, because he couldn't get to me any other way. He couldn't get to Chameleon."

The flat, hard expression on Adam's face might have signaled disbelief, or denial, or a combination of both.

"It's possible," she insisted. "No one outside OMEGA knows our real identities. Hell, only a handful within the agency have access to that information."

"You're saying someone set this whole thing up? Just on the chance you'd be tagged to double for the vice president?"

"It's possible," she repeated stubbornly.

"For God's sake, do you have any idea how remote that possibility is?"

"Not that remote," she snapped. "I'm here, aren't I?"

That stopped him. He went completely still, his arms at his sides, his hands curled into fists. His face could have been carved out of ice.

"If that's the case," he said finally, "this all boils down to a question of who knew you might double for the vice president. Who, Maggie?"

"No one," she protested. "No one knew, except the president, and the vice president. Lillian. Jaguar. The OMEGA team. And—"

She stopped, swallowing hard.

"And the director of OMEGA," Adam said slowly.

She didn't breathe, didn't blink. It seemed to Maggie that her body had lost all capacity to move. Her brain had certainly lost all ability to function. It had gone numb and completely blank. The white, silent woods seemed to close in, until her world became a single, shadowed face.

"Why, Maggie?" he asked softly, bringing them full circle. "Why would any of those people want you dead?"

She struggled for an answer. Any answer. One that would satisfy him, and her. The silence spun out, second by cold, crystalline second.

A hundred chaotic thoughts tumbled through Maggie's numbed mind. A thousand shattering emotions fought for preeminence in her heart. Could Adam have brought her to this isolated spot for some desperate reason of his own? What did she know of him? What did any of the OMEGA agents know of him? His past was shrouded in secrecy. Even now, he led a double life that few knew about. He'd always kept himself so remote. His feelings so shuttered.

Until today. Until he'd held her in his arms and she'd taken him into her body. When he'd looked down into her eyes. There had been no shutters on his soul then.

Her riotous emotions stilled. The confusion dulling her mind faded. She didn't need to know the secrets in Adam's past. She didn't care about his present double life. If she was ever going to trust her instincts, it had to be now.

Adam didn't, couldn't, want her dead.

She'd stake her life on it.

Drawing on everything that was in her heart, she summoned a valiant grin. "Well, I think it's safe to cross the OMEGA team off our ever-expanding list of suspects. I put my life in their hands every time I walk out the door. And I know the director of OMEGA wouldn't set me up like this."

He didn't respond for long, agonizing moments. "Do you?" he said at last.

The cool, even tone was so quintessentially Adam that Maggie didn't know whether to laugh or to cry. She did neither. Instead, she folded her arms across her chest and nodded.

"I do. Although he's tried to take my head off on several memorable occasions in the past three years, he's in love with me. He hasn't admitted it yet. He may not even realize it yet. But he is. What's more, I love him. With all my heart and soul."

If anyone had told Maggie that she'd finally articulate her feelings to Adam while standing knee-deep in snow, with cold nipping at her nose and a team of killers searching for her, she would've checked their medication levels. Of all the times and all the places to have the "discussion" she and Adam had delayed for so long!

Not that it was much of a discussion, she realized belatedly. So far, the exchange had been entirely too one-sided.

"You can jump in here anytime," she invited sweetly.

With a sound that was half laugh, half groan, Adam swept her into his arms. He locked his fists behind her back, holding her against his chest. The deepening shadows didn't obscure his eyes now. Now they blazed down at her with a fierce emotion that warmed Maggie's nose and toes and all parts in between.

"I am. I do. I know."

"Come again?" she asked, breathless.

"I am in love with you. I do realize it. I know you love me, too."

"Well, well, well…"

Her smug, satisfied grin made Adam want to pick her up and carry her back to the snow cave. Hell, it made him want to throw her down in the snow right here, rip off her various layers and lose himself in her fire. He had to satisfy himself with a shattering kiss.

They were both breathing fast and hard when he pulled back. It took some effort, but Adam put her out of his arms.

"We'll finish this interesting discussion when we get out of here."

Her mischievous smile almost shattered the remnants of his control. "It's finished. At least as far as I'm concerned. You are. You do. You know. What more is there to say?"

"Maggie…"

"All we have to decide now is what to do about it."

"Correction. Right now we have to get you out of here. We can decide about it—about us—after we get you to a safe haven."

Her teasing smile faded a bit. "I can't operate out of a safe haven. I'm a field operative."

He bent to pick up their small store of supplies. "It's too dangerous in the field. I'm calling you in."

She winced at his use of the euphemism every OMEGA agent dreaded hearing. He was calling her in. Out of the cold. Ordering her to abandon her cover and her mission.

Maggie shook her head. "Not yet, Adam. You can't terminate this mission yet. We won't find the answer in a safe haven. The answer's here, in the field."

He didn't reply. He didn't have to. They both knew she was right. Maggie saw his jaw work. He wanted to find whoever was behind this scheme as much as, or more than, she.

"I can't go in," she said softly, firmly. "Not yet. You wouldn't have any respect for me if I did. You wouldn't…" She circled a hand in the air. "You wouldn't see me the same way, ever again. As an agent, or as a woman. You wouldn't love me the same way."

Her uncanny echo of his earlier thoughts pierced Adam's wall of resistance. He would love her. He would always love her. But he would love her differently if she wasn't the Maggie who stood nose to nose with him, in the middle of nowhere, with no food, little firepower, and a killer on her trail, yet refused point-blank to run for cover.

Still, he made one last effort. "Do you think I'll ever see you the same way again after those hours in the snow cave? As a woman, or as an agent?"

"Good Lord, I hope not!"

Her startled exclamation wrung a smile out of him. Maggie pounced on it like a cat after a ball of catnip.

"Whatever else happens," she said softly, "we'll always have those hours in the snow cave."

"Maggie..."

"And the memory of those bits of bacon."

She cocked her head, inviting him to capitulate, giving him the means to.

"And don't forget the feel of pine needles," she murmured wickedly. "Prickling us in places few people have ever felt pine needles prickle before. And the interesting way we found to melt that handful of snow. And..."

"All right, Maggie. All right." His jaw clenched. "Suppose you tell me how you think we should handle this situation."

She wasn't the type to crow. "We keep it simple," she said briskly. "I'm the lure. We use me to bait a trap, then spring it."

"We stake you out like a skinned rabbit and wait for the hungry predators to arrive, is that it?"

"That's not quite what I had in mind," she drawled.

"So tell me."

"We have to assume they'll lock on to our signal when we contact Jaguar, right?"

"Right."

"So instead of trying to evade them while we wait for the extraction team to arrive, we let them find us. Or think they have. We draw them in and pin them down until the team gets here.''

Thankfully, Adam didn't point out the obvious. He knew as well as Maggie that they didn't have enough firepower to keep attackers armed with automatic weapons and night-vision equipment pinned down. Which meant they had to use the terrain to their maximum advantage. And use their wits.

''We can do it, Adam.''

''We can try it,'' he said slowly, reluctantly.

Yes! Maggie wanted to shout her relief, but one look at his face warned her he was not happy about this. At all. Wisely she kept silent while he scanned the darkening horizon.

''That ridge won't work. We'd lose them in the rocks and boulders.''

''We'd better head down to lower ground.'' Shoving her hands in her pockets, she turned to scan the steep slope. ''What we need is a canyon or crevice of some kind.''

What they found was a shack.

Or rather Radizwell found it.

Maggie and Adam had only gone a few yards down the slope, angling through the trees to avoid detection and make the descent easier, when the komondor decided they were heading in the wrong direction. He stopped, and a low whine alerted Adam to the fact that the animal wasn't following.

''Come on, boy. Come on.''

The dog backed up a few steps, rumbling a low sound deep in his throat.

''Heel!''

Even Radizwell recognized the voice of authority. Belly

to the ground, he slunk across the snow, whining pitifully all the way.

Adam's dark brows slashed together. "What? What are you trying to tell us?"

Taking courage from the more moderate tone, the shaggy beast leaped up and bounded down the slope a few feet in the opposite direction. He skidded to a halt in the snow, turned back to face them, then let loose with a deep, rolling thunderclap bark.

"Good grief!" Maggie exclaimed. "Who needs a satellite transmission? Anyone within a five-mile radius can lock on to that."

It was an exaggeration, but only a slight one.

Adam quieted the animal with a slicing gesture of command. Radizwell snapped his jaws shut and plopped back on his massive haunches, as if sitting at attention.

"Obviously he wants us to follow him," Adam commented. "Since he appears to know these mountains better than we do, I suggest we see where he leads us."

He led them on what Maggie suspected was a merry chase. The moment he saw them start in his direction, Radizwell whirled and raced down the slope at a steep angle. He dodged around trees and over snow-covered fallen logs with surprising agility. Just before they lost sight of him completely, he skidded to a halt and waited for them to catch up.

When they were almost up with him, he jumped up and took off again. After the third or fourth relay, Maggie was huffing from the exertion and Adam's breath was coming in short, sharp pants. The sun had slipped behind the peaks now, and the shadows had deepened to long purple streaks across the tree-covered hillside. Overhead, a few early stars glowed in an indigo sky. Maggie caught a glimpse of a pale moon floating between the tips of the pines.

Although it was difficult to judge distance with their visibility obscured by the towering trees, an occasional clearing gave them some idea of progress. Maggie guessed they were three-quarters of the way down the slope when she had to stop to catch her breath. The dog padded back, not even winded.

She eyed him with mounting suspicion. "You don't suppose…this is his way…of getting back at me, do you?"

Adam propped a foot up on a half-submerged boulder. Leaning an elbow across his knee, he drew in several long breaths. "For what?"

"For scarfing…up all the biscuits…and bacon."

"Could be."

Maggie groaned. "I knew it!"

"Come on. Let's keep moving. We're almost at the bottom of the slope."

The ground began to level out a little while later. To Maggie's relief, the trees thinned, then ended abruptly. A few more steps brought them to the edge of a flat expanse of snow, about the width of a football field and twice as long. A narrow, ice-encrusted stream cut a crooked path across the field, dividing it almost in half. On the far side of the field, tree-studded slopes rose to touch the dark sky.

As soon as he saw the open space, Radizwell charged forward. Just in time, Adam grabbed a fistful of his ropy fur and hauled him back. The dog growled a low protest, but stood beside Adam while he and Maggie surveyed the still, flat area.

"It's an alpine meadow," Adam murmured after a moment. "I would imagine some of Taylor's sheep graze here in the summer. Which means…"

He glanced down at the sheepdog at his side.

"Is there a shelter here, boy? A shepherd's hut? Is that where you're taking us?"

Maggie hunched her shoulders and huddled closer to Adam. Excitement shot through her.

"That would work. A hut would work. It would make a perfect trap."

"I'm only guessing there's anything here at all, Maggie."

"It's a good guess. Radizwell brought us here for a reason. Besides, my feet are freezing and we're both sweating. Before we set our trap, we should dry off and thaw out. Or thaw out and dry off."

She jerked her chin toward the eager animal. "Let him go. Let's see where he heads."

He headed straight across the meadow toward the trees on the other side. His white coat made him difficult to follow against the sea of snow. Maggie squinted, watching carefully to track the shadow flying with astounding speed across the open space. For a big, klutzy-looking guy, the Hungarian could sure move.

Weapon drawn, she crouched beside Adam in the shelter of a dead pine and watched the dog's unerring progress. On the far side of the open space, Radizwell skidded to a stop, just short of the tree line. Lining up on a dark patch among the trees, he gave a deep, basso profundo bark.

The sound echoed from the surrounding peaks and rolled back at them. Maggie stayed absolutely still beside Adam's rigid form. Nothing moved on the other side of the meadow. No one answered Radizwell's call.

"Do you see anything?" she hissed.

"No."

They waited a while longer. The komondor padded back and forth in front of the dark tree line, then stretched out in the snow. He laid his head down on his paws, waiting.

A snicker of metal brought her head jerking around. Moonlight gleamed on the blue steel of the weapon in Adam's hand.

"Here, take my weapon."

"Why? What are you—?"

He grabbed her derringer and slapped the heavier, more powerful pistol into her hand.

"Cover me!"

"No! Adam, wait!"

It was Maggie's nightmare scene from this morning in reverse. This time it was Adam who plowed across an open, unprotected space and Maggie who dropped to one knee, weapon raised.

Her heart crashed against her ribs as she watched his progress, and the acrid taste of fear rose in her throat. At any moment, she expected to hear gunfire shatter the stillness. To see Adam's body jackknife through the air.

When he made it to the tree line on the far side, she almost sobbed in relief. Then reaction set in. By the time he returned, Radizwell plunging in circles at his side, she was so furious she was ready to shoot him herself.

Chapter 13

Maggie stormed through the ankle-high snow, the P7 gripped in her gloved hand.

"Don't ever do that to me again!"

Her vehemence sent Adam's brows winging. "Do what?"

"Go charging off like that! Without coordinating with me first!"

"The way you did this morning at the lake, you mean?"

In the face of that piece of calm logic, Maggie fell back on an age-old, irrefutable argument. "That was different!"

"Of course."

She stomped up to him, still furious. "Listen to me, Thunder. I love you. I do *not* want you dead. I do *not* want to see your body splattered across a snowy field. I have *plans* for that body!"

Evidently the dog did *not* like the threatening tone she directed toward Adam. With a deep warning growl, he placed himself between Maggie and his good buddy.

She glared at the huge lump of uncombed wool, then at the man surveying her with a cool glint in his eyes. The intensity of her fury surprised Maggie herself. In a back corner of her mind, she realized she'd just had a taste of what Adam must have gone through all these years as OMEGA's director. It was a hell of a lot harder to stand back and watch someone you loved run headlong toward danger and possible death than to make the charge yourself. For the first time, she understood his icy anger during the debriefs after some of her more…adventurous missions. Still, she wasn't quite ready to forgive him for the fear that had twisted through her body like barbed wire.

Adam handed her the derringer and took the P7 in exchange. "Remind me to ask about these plans of yours when we get out of here."

"They'll probably change—several times—before then," she muttered.

"I wouldn't be surprised. Mine are changing by the minute. Would you like to know what I found under the trees?"

She checked the safety on the .22 and shoved it into her pants pocket. "Yes."

"A small shack, just as we guessed."

"Good."

"Well stocked with blankets and fuel."

Maggie stomped over to pick up their small bundle of gear. "Good."

"And food," he added with a small smile.

She swung around. "Food?"

"I thought that might get your attention."

"What kind of food?"

"There's a whole metal locker full of canned goods. Pork and beans. Beef stew. Chicken and dumplings."

"Chicken and dumplings, huh?"

Adam's smile edged into one of his rare grins. It lifted

his fine, chiseled mouth and crinkled the skin at the corners of his eyes. The last of Maggie's uncharacteristic anger melted as he stepped forward and brushed a knuckle down her cheek.

"I can see that one of my main tasks in the future will be keeping your stomach full."

"Among other things."

"First things first. Come on. Let's get you fed."

Hunching her shoulders, Maggie plowed through the snow beside him.

The shack was small and airless and dark. While Adam kept watch outside, Maggie explored its single room cautiously. She didn't dare use the matches she found in a waterproof tin container to light the oil lamp left on the single table, but then, she didn't really need to.

Adam left the door cracked just enough to let in a sliver of moonlight and allow him a clear view of the open meadow.

"The food and other supplies are in the metal locker in the corner," he told her.

When she opened the locker, the first items Maggie reached for were musty, folded blankets. Passing one to Adam, she pulled another one out for her own use and tossed it on the narrow cot built into one wall. Then she stacked half a dozen cans on the table and rooted for a can opener. She could open the cans without one, but she'd rather not trudge out in the snow to find a sharpened stick if she didn't have to. Luckily, the middle shelf yielded an old-fashioned, rusted opener and several large spoons.

As hungry as she was, Maggie was too well trained to attack the food without taking care of other, more urgent needs first. Perching on the narrow cot, she tugged off her boots. Her lightweight waterproof footgear had keep most of the moisture out, but her toes were numb with cold, and she didn't want to risk frostbite.

While she massaged warmth into her stockinged feet, Radizwell made himself right at home. He took a couple of circuits of the small room, sniffing out scents left by various visitors since the last time he'd been there. When he poked his nose into a stack of long-handled tools in one corner, sudden mayhem erupted. His stub of a tail shot straight up, he let loose with a woof that made Maggie jump clear off the cot, and a half-dozen tiny furry creatures darted out from among the tools. Squeaking and squealing, they scattered in all directions, with Radizwell pouncing joyfully after them. His resounding barks bounced off the hut's walls.

"For God's sake, shut him up!" Adam ordered from his post at the door.

"Right. Shut him up."

Maggie planted herself in the middle of the shack to wait for the dog's next pass and jumped half out of her skin when one of the tiny squeaking creatures ran across her foot. Praying it hadn't taken a detour up her pant leg, she braced herself as the dog skidded to a halt. Or tried to. His momentum carried him smack into her. Once again, Maggie found herself flat on her back, with a hundred or more pounds of belligerent komondor straddling her. Doggy breath bathed her face as he growled his displeasure.

"Look, pal," she growled back, "I don't like you any more than you appear to like me. But let's declare a truce, okay? I don't want to waste what little ammunition I have on you."

Adam deserted his post long enough to drag the dog off her. "Maybe if you offered to share the chicken and dumplings with him, you two might just strike up a friendship," he suggested dryly.

Maggie scrambled up. "Ha! What makes you think I want to be friends with an ugly, overgrown floor mop?"

"This from the woman who keeps a bug-eyed reptile for a pet?" Adam shook his head and resumed his post.

Holding out her pant leg, Maggie gave her foot a vigorous shake. When nothing more than a small clump of snow hit the floor, she sighed in relief.

Despite the glare she sent the unrepentant dog, she could no more let him go hungry than she could the frantic mama wood mouse who'd scurried back into the stack of tools after rounding up her tiny charges. Opening the different cans, Maggie dumped the contents of three of them into a metal bowl she'd scavenged from the locker.

"Come on, hound. You can eat this outside and pull guard duty at the same time."

Radizwell didn't move. Sitting on his haunches like an upright bale of unprocessed cotton, he looked from the bowl in her hand to Adam for guidance. Maggie shook her head. When males bonded, they bonded.

At Adam's signal, the dog graciously condescended to allow Maggie to feed him. Padding to the door, he stepped outside. She set the bowl down in the snow, took a quick glance around the serene moonscape, then ducked back inside. The knowledge that the moonscape wouldn't stay serene for long added impetus to her actions.

In short order, she handed Adam an open can and a spoon, dropped a cold, soggy dumpling behind the stack of tools and wrapped the blanket around her legs and feet to warm them. Shuffling across the hut, open can in hand, she joined Adam at the door.

"I'll stand watch. You go dry off."

"I'm not wet."

They shared a few moments of silent companionship while they ate, both wrapped in thought. Maggie tried to ignore the insidious, creeping realization that these quiet moments with Adam might be their last, but the cold reality of their situation intruded.

In a few minutes, they'd lure an unknown number of killers to this isolated spot and try to hold them off until the Jaguar's extraction team arrived. With a total of eight rounds of ammunition between them. Adam had expended all but two of the rounds in his nine-round Heckler & Koch during the firefight at the lake. Maggie had exactly six left for Taylor's .22, including the one in the chamber and five in the spare clip she'd tucked in her pocket this morning.

God, had it only been this morning? She tipped her head against the doorframe, thinking how much her life had changed since then. Her gaze slid to Adam's lean, shadowed face. Whatever happened, she'd have those hours in the snow cave. Whatever happened, she'd have the memory of his blue eyes smiling down at her when he'd taken her in his arms and said he was, he did, he knew.

"Adam?"

"Yes?"

"How long do you think we have?"

His eyes lingered on her lips, then lifted. In their depths, Maggie caught a glimpse of raw, masculine need, overlaid with regret.

"Not long enough."

She sighed. "That's what I thought you'd say."

"They could be following the dog's tracks and be heading this way right now. We have to contact Jaguar."

"I know."

He curled a hand under her chin, lifting her face. "Tomorrow, Maggie. We'll have tomorrow. And forever."

"If we don't…thank you for today."

His cheeks creased. "You're welcome."

Maggie dipped her chin to kiss the warm skin of his

palm. Closing her eyes, she savored his taste and his touch and his scent. Then she sighed again and moved away. With the blanket swaddled around her lower body, she began to pace the small hut.

"Okay, let's review the situation here. We need to contact headquarters to let Jaguar know our coordinates. As soon as we do, there's a distinct possibility the unfriendlies, whoever they are, will glom on to the signal."

"If they haven't already picked up our tracks," Adam reminded her.

"When they arrive on the scene, it's up to us to make sure they don't leave until the counterstrike team can get here."

Maggie felt adrenaline begin to pump through her veins in anticipation of the action ahead. She'd been in tight situations before. Not quite as snug as this one, perhaps, but pretty darn close.

Blanket swishing at her ankles, she strode across the small room and yanked open the metal locker. The rectangular red container she pulled out was heavy and full.

"All right. We have eight rounds of ammunition and one gallon of gasoline to hold off a possible army of bad guys armed with automatic weapons, high-powered night scopes, and every destructive device known to man." She grinned at Adam. "I've done more with less. How about you?"

He shoved his shoulders off the doorframe. "A lot more with a lot less. Let's get to work."

Pillaging the metal locker, they found the makings for crude flash bombs. While Maggie poured the gasoline into the bottles, Adam tore strips from his blanket to stuff in the neck as wicks. Carefully dividing the matches, he gave half to Maggie and tucked the other half in his pocket, along with the jagged pieces of mirror he'd smashed from the snowmobile.

Leaving Radizwell to stand sentry at the hut, they disappeared into the surrounding woods. Working silently, quickly, they gathered fallen limbs and dry timber. Within moments, they'd scattered the debris in a seemingly random pattern around the hut. After placing a few of the gasoline-filled bottles for maximium detonation, they doused the wood with the remaining fuel. A single careful shot could detonate the ring of fire.

After that they separated, Maggie going left, Adam right, searching for just the right tree to climb to put the hut in a cross fire and make the best use of their remaining flash bombs. The temperature had dropped significantly, but Maggie didn't notice. Her heart thumped with the realization that their time was running out. She zigzagged through the trees to find exactly the one she wanted.

Its thick trunk provided excellent cover and a full complement of stair-stepping branches. An easy climb took her a good thirty feet up. Using both hands and her body for leverage, she bent back a couple of obscuring limbs to give her a clear line of fire to the hut. With so few rounds of ammunition, she'd need it.

Her breath was coming in short, puffy gasps by the time she got back to the shack.

"You set?" Adam asked tersely.

"As set as I'll ever be. Let's get Jaguar on the net."

Maggie gave a small puff of surprise when he gripped her upper arms, his hands like steel cuffs.

"Listen to me, Chameleon. It's not too late. You can climb the ridge behind the hut. Take cover in the rocks until the extraction team arrives."

"And just what do you plan to do while I'm taking cover?"

He gave her a small shake. "You're the one they're after, not me. I can stay here. Talk to them. Delay them."

"After that scene beside the lake, do you think they're going to stop for a friendly chat? You took at least one of them down, remember?"

"Dammit, Maggie..."

"Chameleon."

"What?"

"You called me Chameleon a moment ago. That's who I am, Thunder. That's who I have to be. I am not running for cover, and I'm sure as hell not leaving you to face the fire alone. Any more than you'd leave me."

His fingers bit into her arms. Maggie could feel their tensile strength through the thick down of her ski jacket. Under its day's growth of dark beard, his jaw worked.

"Thunder," she said softly, "kiss me. Hard. Then get Jaguar up on the net."

He kissed her. Hard.

Then he dug in his pocket for the handheld navigational device. While waiting for the readings to display on the liquid crystal screen, he shoved his sleeve back and activated the satellite transceiver.

"Jaguar, this is Thun—"

Jake's voice jumped out of the gold watch. "I read you! You okay?"

"We are."

"Both of you?"

"Both of us."

"Give me your coordinates."

Adam rapped out the reading from his GPS unit.

Jake was silent a moment, then came back on the net. "The extraction team's in the air. Twenty minutes away. Cowboy's leading them in."

"Cowboy?"

Maggie felt a rush of wild relief. She and the lanky Wyoming rancher had worked together before. The last time, they'd repelled an attack similar to this one, led by a scar-faced Soviet major. After Adam, Nate Sloan was Maggie's number one pick for a partner in a firefight. The knowledge that he was leading the counterstrike team gave her a surge of hope.

"Tell Cowboy to hover behind the ridge line due east of us," she instructed Jaguar. "I don't want him to scare away our game. We'll call him in when we've sprung the trap."

"Roger. You two sure took your time getting back to me. I've been having to hold off the entire Secret Service single-handedly."

"What do you mean?"

"Special Agent Kowalski's demanded half the federal government and most of the state of California to search the Sierras for you two. I convinced the president to hold her off until I heard from you, but she's mad. Hopping mad. Someone's attacked her charge, and she's taking it real personal. She doesn't understand why we've kept word of the attack quiet, and she doesn't like it." He paused. "Either that, or she's putting on one hell of an act."

"What do you mean?" Adam asked sharply.

"The lab confirmed that the listening device Chameleon found in the VP's bedroom is manufactured by Digicon—for the Secret Service. The Presidential Protective Unit personnel are the only ones using it."

Adam muttered a vicious curse. "Digicon and the Secret Service. Peter Donovan and James Elliot. Even if Kowalski planted the bug, we still don't know who the hell's behind this."

"We will soon," Maggie promised, her mouth grim.

Adam nodded. "Look, Jaguar, we've got to get into position. Tell Cowboy to wait for my signal. I'll bring him in."

"Roger. Good hunting, Chief."

"Thanks.

"And, Chameleon?"

"Yes?"

"When you catch that polecat you're baiting the trap for, I'll skin him and tan the hide for you. I remember how much you disliked gutting your catch during survival training."

"I don't think I'll have a problem with this one," Maggie replied, grinning crookedly.

Adam dropped his sleeve down over the gold watch. For a few moments, the only sounds in the small shack were their rapid breathing and the faint thump of the sheepdog's paw on the snow as he scratched himself.

"You ready, Chameleon?"

"I'm ready."

His gaze, blue and piercing, raked her face a final time. Maggie ached to touch him once more, to carry the feel of his bristly cheek with her into the night, but she didn't lift her hand. The time for touching was past.

He nodded, as if acknowledging her unspoken resolve. "Let's get moving before our company arrives."

"Too late. It's already here."

Maggie and Adam spun around as a bulky figure in a sheepskin coat kicked the door back on its hinges.

"Don't!" McGowan shouted. "Don't reach for it! I'll shoot her, Ridgeway, I swear!"

Adam froze in a low crouch, his hand halfway to the weapon holstered at the small of his back.

For long seconds, no one moved. No one breathed. McGowan kept his rifle leveled squarely on the center of Maggie's chest. She didn't dare go for her gun, and she knew Adam wouldn't go for his. Not with the caretaker's weapon pointed at her.

"There's an oil lamp on the table, Ridgeway. Matches

beside it. Light it. And keep your hands where I can see them, or she's dead.''

Adam straightened slowly. As though she were inside his head, Maggie could hear the thoughts that raced through his mind. With light, they could see McGowan's eyes. A person's eyes always signaled his intent before his body did. With light, they could anticipate. Coordinate. Take him down.

Moving with infinite care, Adam crossed to the small table. Metal rattled, a match scraped against the side of the box, a flame flared, low and flickering at first, and then steady as the wick caught.

In the lantern's glow, Maggie saw McGowan clearly for the first time. Above the rifle, his battered face was frightening in its implacable intensity. Not a single spark of life showed in his gray eyes. They were flat. Cold. A convicted murderer's eyes.

The click of claws on wood jerked Maggie's attention from the caretaker's face to the shape behind him. To her fury, Radizwell ambled into the hut and hunkered down, as if settling in to enjoy the show.

''Some guard dog you are, you stupid—''

With great effort, she bit back one of the more descriptive terms she'd learned from her father's roughneck crews. It was a mistake to let McGowan see how furious she was, and she knew damn well it was unfair to blame Radizwell. The sheepdog wouldn't view Hank McGowan as an enemy. Hell, the thumping they'd heard a few seconds ago was probably his stump of a tail whapping against the snow in an ecstatic welcome. Still, there were two hides she wouldn't have minded tanning at this moment.

''Who are you?''

McGowan's low snarl brought her eyes snapping back to his face.

"What?"

"Who the hell are you?"

The dog picked up the savagery of his tone and tilted his head, as if confused by this confrontation between humans he knew and trusted.

"Never mind," McGowan continued. "I don't care who you are. Just tell me what you've done with Taylor."

Maggie's mind raced with the possibility that this man wasn't the one they'd tried to bait the trap for. Slowly, carefully, she shook her head.

"I haven't done anything with the vice president."

His mouth curled. "I'd just as soon shoot you as look at you, lady. If Taylor's hurt, you're dead anyway. Where is she?"

"I can't tell you. You have to trust—"

"The first shot goes into her knee, Ridgeway." His eyes never left Maggie's face. "The second into her right lung. How many will it take? How many do I have to pump into her until you tell me?"

As it turned out, the first shot didn't go through Maggie's knee. It came through the open door and went right through McGowan's shoulder. Blood sprayed, splattering Adam as he leaped for the man.

It was the second shot that hit her. The rifle in McGowan's scarred hands bucked. A deafening crack split the air, and Maggie slammed into the back wall of the hut.

Chapter 14

In the curious way time has, it always seems to move in the most infinitesimal increments at moments of greatest pain.

When Adam lunged forward to knock the rifle aside, he felt as though he were diving through a thick pool of sludge. Slowly. So slowly. Too slowly.

His mind recorded every minute sensation. He felt warm blood splatter his face. Saw McGowan's finger pull back on the trigger in an involuntary reaction to the bullet that ripped through him. Heard the roar as the rifle barrel jerked. Tasted the acrid tang of gunpowder and fear as Maggie crashed back against the wall.

Like a remote-controlled robot, Adam followed through with his actions. He shoved the barrel aside. Digging a shoulder into McGowan's middle, he took him down. He rolled sideways, away from the caretaker, and was on his feet again in a single motion. Through it all, every nerve, every fibrous filament, every neuron, screamed a single message in a thousand different variations.

Maggie was hit. Maggie was down. Maggie was shot.

Only after he'd yanked the rifle out of McGowan's slackened hold and spun around did another stream of messages begin to penetrate his mind.

She was down, but not dead. She was hit, but not bloodied. She was shot, but not wounded.

She'd been thrown against the wall and crumpled to the floor, but her eyes were wide and startled, not glazed with pain. A look of utter stupefaction crossed her face, then gave way to one of sputtering panic.

As Adam raced toward her, he heard a hiccuping wheeze and identified the sound instantly. He'd seen enough demonstrations of protective body armor to recognize that choking, sucking gasp. The force of the hit had knocked the air out of her lungs. She was so stunned that her paralyzed muscles couldn't draw more in.

He couldn't help her breathe. She had to force her lungs to work on her own. But he could sure as hell protect her from the two white-suited figures who came bursting through the open door at that precise moment.

Shoving Maggie flat on the floor, Adam covered her body with his. He twisted around, his finger curling on the rifle's trigger as he lined up on the lead attacker.

The figure in white arctic gear and goggles ignored him, however. Legs spread, arms extended in a classic law-enforcement stance, he covered the sprawled McGowan.

Or rather *she* did.

Adam recognized Denise Kowalski's voice the instant she belted out a fierce order to the downed man.

"Don't move! Don't even breathe!"

Keeping her eyes and her weapon trained on McGowan,

she shouted over her shoulder, "Ridgeway! Is she hit? Is the vice president hit?"

Before Adam could answer, a savage snarl ripped through the hut. From the corner of his eye, he saw Radizwell rear back, his massive hindquarters bunching as he prepared to launch himself at this latest threat.

The second agent swung his weapon toward the dog.

"No! Don't shoot! Down, Radizwell! Down!"

At the lash of command in Adam's voice, the sheepdog halted in midthrust. Confused, uncertain, he quivered with the need to act. Under his mask of ropy fur, black gums curled back. Bloodcurdling growls rolled out of his throat like waves, rising and falling in steady crescendos.

In the midst of all the clamor, Maggie's feeble cry almost went unheard.

"Adam! Get...off...me!"

At the sound of her voice, the two agents froze. Then Denise transferred her weapon to her right hand and shoved her goggles up with her left. Keeping the gun trained on McGowan, she risked a quick look at the far end of the hut.

Adam pushed himself onto one knee. With infinite care, he rolled the wheezing Maggie onto her side. She immediately drew up into a fetal position, her knees to her chin and her arms wrapped around her middle.

Relief crashed through Adam when he saw where she cradled herself. The bullet had struck low, below her breastbone. A higher hit might have broken her sternum or smashed a couple ribs.

"Herrera!" Denise snapped. "Get out your medical kit. The vice president's been hit."

"She's wearing a body shield," Adam said. "I think she's okay."

Maggie's awful wheezing eased. "Okay. I'm...okay."

Slowly, her face scrunched with pain, she straightened

her legs. Adam slid an arm under her back and helped her to her feet. Her knees wobbled, involuntary tears streaked her cheeks, and she kept her arms crossed over her waist, but she was standing.

With everything in him, Adam fought the desperate urge to crush her against his chest. Added pressure was the last thing she wanted or needed now. She'd have a bruise the size of Rhode Island on her stomach as it was.

Incredibly, she gave a shaky grin and tapped a finger against her middle. "What do you know! It…worked."

After their hours together in the snow cave, Adam had been sure he couldn't love this woman more. He'd been wrong. Then, her passion and her laughter had fed his soul. Now, her courage stole it completely. As long as he lived, he would remember that small grin and the way she gathered herself together to shake off the effects of a bullet to the stomach.

A grunt of pain behind them brought both Maggie and Adam swinging around. The caretaker pushed against the floor with one boot, bright red blood staining his worn sheepskin jacket as he dragged himself upright.

"I told you not to move, McGowan," Denise warned.

He sagged against the wall, and he sent her a contemptuous look. "What are you going to do? Shoot me?"

"I'm considering it. And this time I won't shoot to wound."

"Too bad you took down the wrong man, Kowalski."

"I got the right one. The one holding a gun on the vice president."

His lips curled in a sneer. "Are you blind or just stupid, woman?"

"Neither. Nor am I lying in a pool of blood."

Pain added a rasp to McGowan's gravelly voice. "She's not the vice president."

"Sure. And I'm not—"

"That woman is not Taylor Grant."

His utter conviction got through to Denise. Adam saw the first flicker of doubt in her eyes as she threw a quick look at Maggie.

"Come on," McGowan jeered, wincing a little with the effort. "I know you're new to Taylor's detail. But even you must have picked up on the dog's reaction to her last night. She's good, whoever she is, damn good. But she's not Taylor Grant."

The agent's mouth thinned. "Herrera! Search this man for weapons."

She kept her gun leveled on the caretaker's head while the second agent opened the sheepskin and patted him down.

"He's clean."

"Keep him covered."

The agent swiveled on his heels to look up at her. "Shouldn't I patch that hole first?"

"In a minute."

"But—"

"He'll live!"

Her sharp retort wrung a half smile, half grimace from the wounded man. "You're one hard female, Kowalski."

"Remember that, the next time you pull a weapon on one of my—" She stopped abruptly. "On one of my charges," she finished slowly.

Maggie heard the hitch of uncertainty in Denise's voice. Well, the agent might have her doubts, but Maggie had a few of her own, as well. Hanging on to Adam's arm with one hand, she casually slipped the other into her pants pocket. Her palm curled around the derringer.

"Did you—?"

She had to stop and drag in a slow breath. Pain rippled

through her at even that slight movement of her diaphragm, but Maggie gritted her teeth and finished. "Did you plant a listening device in my bedroom, Denise?"

The agent stiffened.

"Did you?"

Denise didn't respond for long moments. When she did, her brown eyes were flat and hard. "Yes."

Maggie felt Adam's muscles tense under her tight grip. "Why?" she asked sharply.

"Because it was ordered by the vice president," Denise replied with careful deliberation. "Who isn't you, apparently."

A sudden silence descended, broken a moment later by McGowan's snort of derision.

"Taylor wouldn't allow any bugs upstairs. She doesn't even like the cameras downstairs. That cabin is the only place in her whole crazy world she has any privacy. She'd never authorize you to peep into her bedroom."

"Well, she did." Denise bit the words out, her eyes on Maggie.

"Did she, Kowalski?" Quiet menace laced Adam's voice. "Did she personally order it?"

Denise dragged her gaze from Maggie to the man beside her. She frowned, obviously debating whether to reply. "The order came down through channels," she said at last.

"What channels?" Adam rapped out.

"Secret Service channels. What the hell's going—?"

"Who issued the order?"

Despite the ache in her middle, Maggie almost smiled at the stubborn, angry look that settled on Denise's face. She'd had the same reaction herself, on occasion, to being grilled by OMEGA's director.

"Dammit, what's—?"

"Who, Kowalski? I want an answer! Now!"

Denise responded through clenched teeth. "The order came from the secretary."

"The secretary of the treasury?"

"The secretary of the treasury. Personally. Direct to me. He told me..." Her jaw tightened. "He told me the vice president had authorized it."

"Bingo," Maggie whispered.

Adam's eyes met hers. A muscle twitched in one side of his jaw. The president's friend, he thought. The highest financial officer in the nation. The bastard.

"We may know who," he said, his jaw tight, "but we still don't know why."

"We will," Maggie swore. "We'll get the last piece of the puzzle if we have to..."

A coldly furious female intruded on their private exchange. "If one of you doesn't explain in the next ten seconds what this is all about, I'm going to take action. Very drastic action."

"Better tell her, Ridgeway," McGowan drawled. "If you don't, she'll shoot to wound, and get her rocks off watching you bleed to death."

"Oh, for—" Shoving her hood back, Denise raked a hand through her short sandy hair. "Stuff a bandage in his wound or in his mouth, Herrera. I don't care which. Now tell me—" she glared at Maggie "—just who you are and what the hell's going on here."

Maggie opened her mouth, then closed it with a snap. Slicing a hand through the air for quiet, she cocked her head and listened intently.

In the stillness that descended, she heard the echo of a faint, wavering roar. Her fingers dug into Adam's arm as she whipped around to face Denise.

"Is more—" She gasped as the violent movement

wrenched at her middle, then shook her head, as if denying all pain. "Is more of your team on the way?"

Frowning, Denise responded to the urgency in Maggie's voice. "No. There's only Herrera and me. The president wouldn't authorize a full-scale search," she added stiffly.

"So you came on your own?"

Her chin jutted out. "So we came on our own. You are— you *were* my responsibility. We tracked McGowan from the moment he left the cabin."

"Hell," the caretaker muttered in profound disgust. "I'm getting sloppy. Tracked down and gunned down by a female."

Denise ignored him, her sharp gaze focused on Maggie's face. "What do you hear?"

"Snowmobiles," she murmured, moving closer to the door to listen.

"Do you think it's the team that hit you this morning and took down my man?"

"Probably."

"I owe them."

A ghost of a grin sketched across Maggie's mouth. "Me too."

"Listen to me, Kowalski," Adam cut in. "The vice president is safe. She's at Camp David, working on some highly sensitive treaty negotiations. But before she left, she received a death threat, a particularly nasty one, which is why my agent is doubling for her."

"Agent?"

"That's also why the president wouldn't authorize you to institute a search," Adam continued ruthlessly. "We told him not to."

Denise blinked once or twice at the news that the president apparently took orders from the tall, commanding man in front of her.

"Why no search?" she asked, doubt in her eyes, but still tenacious.

"Because we didn't want the wrong people walking into the trap we've set. We want the team that hit us and your man this morning. Badly. And the individual behind them. Are you with us?" Adam asked in a steely voice. "You have to decide. Now."

Maggie saw at once that she wasn't the only one who'd learned to trust her instincts. Denise flicked another look from her to Adam, then back again. Squaring her shoulders, she nodded.

"Tell me about this trap."

"I'll tell you as soon as I call in our reinforcements," Adam said, shoving back his sleeve. "From the sound of it, we're going to need them."

At Cowboy's laconic assurance that he was barely a good spit away and closing fast, the tension in the hut ratcheted up several more notches.

Working silently and swiftly, the small team readied for action. At Denise's terse order, Herrera divided up their extra weapons and ammunition. While Maggie showed the two agents the placement of their rudimentary defenses, Adam propped a shoulder under McGowan and took him into the shelter of the trees. Radizwell trotted at their heels, rumbling deep in his throat until Adam's low command stilled him.

"Christ," McGowan muttered. "He never obeys me like that. Or anyone else, Taylor included. Last time she was home, she threatened to skin him and use him for a throw rug."

"It's all in the tone."

"Yeah, I guess so."

His lips white with pain, McGowan was still for a moment. The distant rise and fall of engines grew louder with each labored breath. "You'd better give me my rifle."

Without speaking, Adam eased his support from under the caretaker's shoulder.

"I didn't mean to pull that trigger," McGowan stated flatly. "Not when I did, anyway."

"I know."

"I would have, though. I would've shot you both if I thought you'd harmed Taylor."

The whine of the engines pulled at Adam. He needed to coordinate a final approach for Cowboy. To check the disposition of his meager forces. To make sure Maggie was secure. But the bleak expression in the caretaker's eyes held him for another second.

"You love her that much?"

A flicker of pain crossed McGowan's face, one that had nothing to do with his wound.

"About as much as you love that woman, I reckon," McGowan said quietly. His gaze drifted to Maggie, a slender shadow against the snow. "They're a lot alike, aren't they? Her and Taylor?"

"Many ways. And nothing alike in others." Adam started back to the hut. "I'll send Herrera out with your rifle."

"Ridgeway?"

"Yes?"

"Good luck. Take care of your woman."

A wry smile tugged at Adam's lips. "She prefers to take care of herself."

It was over almost before it began.

Scant moments after the hut's occupants took position in the trees surrounding the hut, a wave of dim shapes burst into the open meadow. They raced across the snow, throwing up waves of white behind their skis. The first few were halfway across when a Cobra gunship lifted above the dark peaks directly behind them.

Maggie couldn't see the chopper, since it flew without lights, but she heard it. The steady *whump-whump-whump* of its rotor blades drowned the sound of the approaching snowmobiles.

When they caught the sound of the chopper behind them, the attackers swerved crazily. Gunfire erupted, and streaming tracers lit the night sky. The cacophony of noise intensified with the appearance of a second gunship, then a third.

The choppers circled the swarming vehicles like heavenly herders trying to corral stampeding mechanized cattle. Blinding searchlights turned night into day. One of the 50 mm cannons bristling from the nose of the lead gunship boomed, and a fountain of snow arched into the sky.

One after another, the buzzing snowmobiles stopped. Their white-suited drivers jumped off, hands held high, while the giant black moths circled overhead.

Only two mounted attackers escaped the roundup. The first dodged across the snow and headed for the trees behind the hut. The second followed in his tracks, almost riding up the other's rear skis.

From her high perch, Maggie took careful aim. She wasn't about to let even one of these scum get away. As soon as the second vehicle entered the ring outlined in the snow by the scattered brush, neither one of them was coming out. No one in their right mind would drive a gasoline-powered snowmobile though the flames about to erupt.

Her finger tightened on the trigger just as a white shape flew out of the trees. Maggie's shot ignited a flash bomb at the same moment Radizwell crashed into the lead driver, knocking him off his churning vehicle.

Flames shot into the sky and raced around the ring of

gasoline-soaked brush. Two drivers and one savage, snarling komondor were trapped inside a circle of fire. Horrified, Maggie saw the second driver jump off his snowmobile. Lifting his automatic rifle, he spun toward the dog and his thrashing victim.

In a smooth, lightning-fast movement, Maggie braced her wrist against the limb, took aim and fired. With a sharp crack, the driver's weapon flew out of his hand. When another warning shot threw up a clump of snow just in front of him, he dropped to his knees. Rocking back and forth, he clutched his injured hand to his chest.

Maggie had shimmied halfway down the tree when she caught sight of a dark figure running toward the wall of flames. Bending his arm in front of his face, he disappeared into the fire.

"Adam!" Her instinctive cry was lost in the fire's roar.

By the time Maggie leaped through the fiery wall and joined him, Adam had the injured driver covered, and Radizwell had terrorized and almost tenderized the other. Adam held the straining animal with one hand while the man scuttled backward, crablike.

"I don't know!" he shouted.

"Talk, or I let him loose!" Adam snarled, as fearsome as the creature at his side.

"I told you, I don't know who hired us!"

Adam relaxed his grip enough for Radizwell to leap for the man's boot. Clamping his massive jaws around it, he shook his head. The driver screamed as his whole body lifted with each shake, then thumped back down in the snow.

"Call him off! I swear, I don't know!"

Maggie skidded to a halt beside Adam. She watched the man's frantic gyrations with great satisfaction.

"Have him chew on his face for a while," she suggested,

loudly enough to be heard over the growls and cries. "It will improve his looks, if nothing else."

Evidently Radizwell had reached the same conclusion. He spit out the boot and lunged forward. The man screamed and threw up an arm. At the last moment, Adam buried a fist in the woolly ruff and hauled the dog back.

"You've got five seconds. Then I let him go."

"I don't know," the man sobbed. "Our instructions come to a post office box, unsigned. The money's deposited in an account at the bank."

Adam stiffened. "Which bank?"

"What?"

"Which bank?"

"First Bank. In Miami."

The three choppers settled on the snow like hens nesting for the night. In the blinding glare of their powerful searchlights, a heavily armed counterstrike team rounded up the band of attackers and stripped them down to search for weapons.

A tall, lanky figure left the circle of activity and plowed through the snow toward the ring of fire.

"Thunder? Chameleon?"

"Here!" Maggie shouted.

Leaping over dwindling flames, Cowboy came to an abrupt halt. He pushed his Denver Broncos ball cap to the back of his head, surveying the scene.

A white-suited figure with his hands behind his head stumbled forward in front of Maggie, who covered him with the puniest excuse for a weapon Cowboy had ever seen. Adam knelt in the snow to retrieve a semiautomatic. And a mound of shaggy white perched atop the stomach of a downed attacker, fangs bared. A series of spine-tingling growls rolled toward Cowboy, and he didn't make the mistake of moving any closer.

He shook his head in mingled amusement and relief. "Here I bring the cavalry chargin' to the rescue, and you didn't even need us. You've got your own..." He jerked his chin toward the still-growling creature. "What *is* that thing, anyway?"

"A Hungarian dust mop," Maggie said.

"A Hungarian sheepdog," Adam corrected.

The Hungarian in question snarled menacingly.

"Not exactly a hospitable sort, is he?"

Maggie shook her head emphatically. "No."

"Yes," Adam countered. "Once he gets acquainted with you."

"Well, we'll have to get acquainted some other time. My orders are to get you back to Sacramento immediately. Jaguar's got a plane standing by to fly us to D.C."

"Why the rush?" Maggie asked.

She was as anxious as he to bring down the final curtain on this mission, but she'd thought—hoped—she and Adam would have at least an hour or two at the cabin to clean up and finish one or more of the several interesting discussions they'd started in the past few days.

"Jaguar radioed just before we landed. The vice president's completed those treaty negotiations faster than she or anyone else thought possible. She's flying in from Camp David, and insists on resuming her public persona. Death threat or no death threat, she wants to be at the press conference tomorrow when the president announces the treaty. He's calling you in."

Chapter 15

As it turned out, the entire ragged band flew back to Sacramento with Maggie and Adam.

A grim-faced Denise Kowalski insisted on accompanying her "charge" back to D.C. Hank McGowan set his jaw and refused to be taken to a hospital. He wanted to see with his own eyes that Taylor was safe. A medic with the counterstrike team packed and patched his wound on the spot.

To Maggie's disgust, even the dog got into the act. He whined pathetically when Adam climbed aboard the chopper and refused to remove his massive body from a skid. Forced to choose between ordering the pilot to lift off with a hundred pounds of komondor on one track and taking the creature aboard, Adam had opened the side hatch. With a thunderous woof that had half a dozen well-armed counterstrike agents swinging around, weapons leveled, Radizwell leaped into the cabin.

With his odoriferous presence, the air in the helicopter took on a distinct aroma. After a day of strenuous physical activity followed by a night that had raised Maggie's nervous-tension levels well beyond the stage of a discreet, ladylike dew, she wanted nothing more than a bath, a good meal and Adam, not necessarily in that order. For a few more hours, though, she had to maintain her role.

With unerring skill, the chopper pilot put his craft down a few yards from the gleaming 747 that waited for them, engines whining. The media, alerted to the vice president's departure by the presence of Air Force Two, crowded at the edge of the ramp. Realizing that this might be her last public appearance as the vice president of the United States, Maggie gave them a grin and a wave as she walked to the aircraft. Luckily, the night was too dark and the photographers were too far away to record the precise details of Taylor Grant's less-than-immaculate appearance, much less the blackened hole in the front of her ski jacket left by a 44-40 rifle shell.

The diminutive martinet who waited for her inside the 747 saw it at once, however. Lillian's black eyes rounded as she gaped at Maggie's middle.

"Good heavens! Are you all right?"

"I'm fine."

Her face folding into lines of tight disapproval, the dresser scowled at Denise, who entered the plane behind Adam. "You told me she'd been attacked down at the lake. But you didn't tell me she was hit."

"She wasn't," Denise said wearily, dragging a hand through her sandy hair. "Not down at the lake. McGowan put a bullet through her, or tried to."

"Hank?" Lillian's gray eyebrows flew up. "Hank shot the vice president?"

The uniformed stewards ranged around the huge cabin listened with wide-eyed astonishment. All the crew knew was that a call from the president had cut short the vice president's scheduled vacation. And that an "accident" of some sort had occurred just prior to their departure from the cabin for Sacramento.

"It was a mistake," Denise said, confirming the story. "One McGowan's already paid for," she added. "I put a bullet through his shoulder."

"Good heavens!" Lillian repeated faintly.

"She's a damn hard woman," the caretaker stated, panting. He leaned a forearm against the bulkhead to catch his breath. The effort of climbing the stairs had pearled his face with sweat and darkened a spot on the shoulder of the jacket he'd borrowed from Herrera. He'd insisted on coming along, but it had obviously cost him.

The arrival of Cowboy, Herrera and an enthusiastically sniffing Radizwell snapped Lillian into action. In her best drill-sergeant manner, she took charge.

"I've laid out clean clothes in your stateroom, Mrs. Grant. I knew you'd want to shower and change as soon as we took off. Hank, you come with me. I'll look at that shoulder. Steward! Take this animal to the aft compartment. He stinks!"

"The understatement of the year," Maggie murmured.

Unfortunately, Radizwell refused to be separated from his pal, Adam. Maggie suspected the delicious aromas wafting from the galley had something to do with his fierce, growling stance. The hound wanted his share.

So did she. As her nose picked up the mouth-watering scents, her bruised stomach sent out a series of growls very close to Radizwell's in volume and intensity. Suddenly Maggie realized she could fulfill all three of her most immediate needs and still maintain her role.

"Why don't you come with me, Adam?" she suggested. Keeping her tone light, for the stewards' sake, she nodded toward the forward compartment. "You said you needed to contact your people to let them know about our change of plans. You can use my office while I shower and change. Then we can have a bite to eat.''

''Fine.''

''We'll serve as soon as we're airborne,'' the head steward added helpfully. ''We've prepared a vegetable quiche for Mrs. Grant, but perhaps you'd prefer a steak, sir?''

''Steak,'' Adam replied, his eyes glinting. ''Definitely the steak.''

In the privacy of the well-appointed bathroom, Maggie made free use of various sundries kept on hand for the vice president. It was amazing how much a toothbrush and the prospect of soothing, perfumed lotion after a hot shower could revitalize a woman.

The prospect of the hot shower itself was even more revitalizing. Eagerly Maggie shed her boots and socks, along with the turtleneck and brown pleated pants, now a great deal the worse for their wear. Her movements slowed a bit when it came to removing the bodysuit.

Wincing, she twisted to one side to reach the Velcro straps. Her stomach muscles screamed a protest as the supporting shield fell away. Using both hands, she lifted the hem of her thermal undershirt, then froze. Her jaw dropping, she surveyed the effects of the rifle shell in the bathroom mirror.

A bruise the size of a dinner plate painted her middle in various shades of green and purple, with touches of yellow and blue thrown in for dramatic emphasis. She gulped at the dramatic colorama, then tugged the shirt over her head and bent to push off the bottoms. An involuntary ''Ooooch'' escaped her when she tried to straighten up.

Realizing that she might have to adjust the scope of her plans for the next few hours or so, Maggie padded to the

glass-enclosed shower. Under her bare feet, the floor vi-
brated with the power of the 747's huge engines. While she
waited for the water to heat, Maggie let her appreciative
gaze roam the wood-paneled bath.

Air Force Two was a model of efficient luxury. It had to
be. It served as a second home for the vice president on
her frequent trips around the globe. Just as her predecessors
had, Taylor Grant represented the president at everything
from weddings to funerals of various heads of state. This
duty required extensive traveling, so much so that Mrs.
Bush had once quipped that the vice president's seal should
read Have Funeral, Will Travel.

Maggie smiled at the thought and stepped into the
shower. With a groan of pleasure, she lifted her face to the
pulsing jets and let the hot water sluice down her body.
Sighing in sybaritic gratification, she dropped her arms to
her sides while heat needled her shoulders and breasts.

She was still standing in a boneless, motionless lump
when the shower door opened.

"The steward just served your dinner," Adam said, his
face grave. "Having experienced firsthand how testy you
get when you're hungry, I thought I'd better let you know
immediately."

"Thank you," Maggie replied, equally grave, as though
she weren't standing before him completely naked.

Through the mist of the escaping steam, she saw that
he'd taken advantage of the selection of sundries in one of
the other bathrooms, as well. The dark bristles shadowing
his cheeks and chin were gone, and he'd made an attempt
to tame his black hair. He'd scrounged up a clean white
shirt, but wore the same snug jeans and ski boots.

Adam appeared just as interested in her state of dress, or
undress, as she was in his. In a slow sweep, his gaze traveled from her face to neck to her breasts. Maggie felt her

nipples harden under his intimate inspection, and a twist of love at the sudden pain in his eyes when he saw her stomach.

"Remind me to give the chief of Field Dress a superior performance bonus when this is over," he said fiercely. "A big one."

Maggie was too busy enjoying the blaze of emotion on his face to spare more than a passing thought for the pudgy, frizzy-haired genius who'd produced her torturous corset. A fiery warmth that had nothing to do with the water steaming up the shower enclosure coursed through her belly, and her muscles contracted involuntarily. Maggie ignored the stabbing ache in her middle and focused instead on the ache building a little lower.

Lifting his gaze to hers, he smiled. His eyes held a tender softness in their blue depths that Maggie had never seen before. One that intensified the liquid heat gathering low in her belly.

"Do you want to eat now, or later?"

"Now," she told him with a grin. "And later."

As she watched Adam strip off his clothes, Maggie thought she'd melt from the sizzling combination of hot water and spiraling desire and disappear down the shower drain in a rivulet of need. From a snow cave to a 747, she thought. From under the ground to a mile above it. From an attack beside a frozen lake to a ring of fire beside a deserted shack. Out of all the missions she'd ever been on, she knew this one would always remain vividly emblazoned in her mind.

And when Adam stepped inside and closed the shower door behind him, Maggie knew the expression in his eyes would always—always!—remain imprinted in her heart.

Water streamed over his broad shoulders and down his

chest as he buried his hands in her wet hair. Tilting her face to his, he smiled down at her.

"I love you, Chameleon. In all your guises. But I love you in this one most."

His use of her code name gave Maggie a little dart of pleasure, then one of pain. Her personal relationship with Adam was so inextricably bound to her professional one. Yet she knew in her heart that couldn't continue. They'd stepped through the barriers that separated them, and there was no stepping back. Not now. Not ever.

"I love you, too," she whispered, sliding her palms up the planes of his water-slick chest. "In all your guises. Special envoy. Director. Code name Thunder. Plain ol' Adam Ridgeway. But I love you in this one the most."

She wrapped her arms around his neck and brought his mouth down to hers. He tasted of warm, rich brandy. Of smoky fire. Of Adam.

Rising up on her toes, she brought her body into his. She managed to contain her startled gasp when her bruised tummy connected with his, but he didn't miss the tiny, involuntary flinch. Sliding his hands down the curve of her waist, he grasped her hips gently and pushed her away.

She murmured an inarticulate protest.

Guiding her gently, he rotated her slick body until she faced the wall. "Like this, my darling," he whispered in her ear. "Like this. I don't want to hurt you."

Maggie discovered that "this" wasn't bad, after all. In fact, she thought on a gasp of pure pleasure, "this" was wonderful. Adam's broad chest felt solid and strong and sleek against her back. The way he reached around to mold her breasts with both hands sent waves of sensation washing through her. The touch of her bare bottom against his belly was even more electrifying. Hard and rampant and fully erect, he pressed against her.

Bracing her palms on the shower tiles, Maggie arched her back. Her head twisted, and he bent to take her mouth. While his tongue and hers met in a slow, sensual dance, his hands played with her nipples. With each tug and twist, fire streaked from Maggie's breasts to her belly. With each nip of his teeth against her lower lip, she felt the sting of need in her loins.

When his hands left her breasts to brush with a feather-light touch down her middle, her pelvis arched to meet them. Her head fell back against his shoulder as he parted her folds and opened her to his touch and the pelting of the pulsing water. Maggie gasped at the exquisite sensation.

"Adam! I don't think— I can't hold— Oh!"

"Don't think," he growled in her ear. "Don't hold back. Let me love you, Maggie. Let me feed your soul, as you feed mine."

When her soul had been fed, twice, and Adam's at least once, they decided it was time to feed their bodies. While he used one of the fluffy towels monogrammed with the vice president's seal to dry himself, Maggie pulled on a thick, sinfully soft terry robe.

Plopping herself down on a vanity stool, she treated herself to a spectacular view of Adam's lean flanks and tight white buns as she towel-dried her hair.

"Mmm... Nice." Her fingers curled into the towel. "Maybe that steak could wait a few more minutes."

"The steak might, but Radizwell probably won't. I left him sniffing around the office. If we don't get back in there, he's liable to—"

"Adam!" Sheer panic sliced through Maggie. Throwing the towel aside, she jumped off the stool. "You didn't leave that animal in the same room with my steak, did you?"

The terry-cloth robe flapped against her legs as she

rushed through the paneled bedroom and threw open the door to the office.

"I'm going to shoot him!"

Hands on hips, Maggie glared at the shaggy creature stretched out contentedly beside the litter of dishes he'd pushed off the table onto the floor, all of which were licked clean. Sublimely indifferent to her anger, Radizwell raised his head, thumped his tail at Adam a couple of times, then yawned and laid his head back down.

"I'll shoot him!" Maggie snarled again. "I'll skin him. I'll—"

"Strange," Adam murmured. "McGowan said Taylor threatened to do the same."

"It's not strange," Maggie fumed. "It's natural. It's possible. It's very likely, in fact, that someone will do so in the very near future. Why Taylor would keep this obnoxious, smelly, greedy beast is beyond me."

"Probably for the same reasons you keep a bug-eyed reptile with a yard-long tongue."

"Terence," Maggie pronounced with lofty dignity, "has class."

Adam laughed and lifted her in his arms. Taking care not to bump her stomach, he carried her to the wide leather sofa at the far end of the office.

"It's not funny," she muttered. "That…that Hungarian ate my steak!"

"My steak, remember? Don't pout, Maggie. I'll order another one. I seem to have worked up quite an appetite."

The head steward delivered Adam's second dinner some time later.

By then, Maggie had retreated once more to the bedroom to finish dressing. She couldn't bear the thought of strapping the body shield on over her sore stomach again, and she left it on the dressing stool.

To her surprise, the pantsuit Lillian had laid out fit perfectly even without the tight corset. A size eight, no less! She smoothed her hands over trim hips covered in a soft, pale yellow wool and admired her silhouette in the mirror. Biting her lip, Maggie debated whether she should forgo her half of Adam's second steak, after all.

Nah! Not this time!

She flipped off the lights, casting a last look over her shoulder at her reflection in the mirror.

Maybe next time, though.

They had just polished off their meal when Cowboy rapped on the door. Poking his sun-streaked blond head inside the office, Nate Sloan gave them a lazy grin.

"You two finished chowin' down yet?"

"We're finished," Adam replied.

"About time!"

Nate strolled into the office with his graceful, long-legged gait. Radizwell lifted his head lazily, issued a halfhearted growl, then thumped it back down again. A juicy steak appeared to have the same mellowing effect on his temperament as it did on hers, Maggie thought in amusement.

"Jaguar's been trying to raise you for the last half hour," Cowboy said casually. "Forget to put your transceiver back on, Chief?"

Adam glanced down at his wrist, which was bare except for its dusting of dark hair. "Apparently."

Maggie remembered last seeing the thin gold watch tossed on the bathroom carpet, along with Adam's clothes.

"Jaguar said he could wait, so I decided not to interrupt your…meal."

"I'll go get the transceiver," Adam said, unperturbed.

Maggie, on the other hand, wavered between a grin and

a ridiculous blush at Nate's knowing look. She struggled with both while he sprawled with his customary loose-limbed ease in the leather chair opposite her and regarded her with a twinkle in his hazel eyes.

"We were all taking bets on which way this mission would go, you know."

"Is that right?"

"We figured you and the chief would find a way to patch up your differences or come back ready to use each other for target practice on the firing range. Looks like you did some patchin'."

Maggie tucked her legs under her and rested her hand on her ankle. The glint of gold on her ring finger caught her eye. She smiled, realizing that she and Adam would have their forever, after all.

"I'm not sure I'd call it patching," she said, her smile easing into the grin she'd struggled against the moment before. "And we still have a few significant differences to work out. But we will work them out, one way or another."

Nate's eyes gleamed. "He's a good man, Maggie. One of the best."

"*The* best," she replied.

"Hellfire, woman, it took you long enough to recognize that fact."

"I recognized it a long time ago. I just wasn't ready to do anything about it."

"Why not?"

Her smile slipped a bit, but she answered easily enough. "He's my boss, Nate. He's had to maintain a distance, an objectivity, just as I've had to keep my personal feelings separate from my professional ones."

"And now?"

"Now? Now I couldn't separate them if I tried."

"So what are you going to do about it?"

She hesitated, not quite ready to put into words the decision she'd come to in the shower, but Nate already knew the answer to his question.

"You're going to leave OMEGA."

Maggie nodded. "I have to. Wherever our relationship goes, I have to leave OMEGA. Neither one of us can operate the way we have been. Not anymore."

"Adam might have something to say about that."

A gleam of laughter crept into Maggie's eyes. "I'm sure he will. He usually has a long list of items to discuss with me when I return from a mission."

She stretched, feeling immeasurably relieved now that she'd taken the first step.

"There's nothing to discuss about this particular matter, though. You know Adam's needed more at OMEGA than I am. He has the president's ear. He moves in the kind of circles necessary to carry off his double role as special envoy and director of OMEGA. He's the best man for his job. The only man."

"So what will you do?"

"I don't know." She glanced around the wood-paneled compartment. "Maybe I'll run for office. I could get used to traveling like this. And there are a few issues I'd like to tackle."

"Such as?"

"Such as the distribution by gender of toilets in public places."

Nate gave her a look of blank astonishment. "Come again?"

"You don't think all those long lines outside women's rest rooms are a violation of the First Amendment? Or whichever amendment guarantees us life, liberty, and the pursuit of happiness?"

"Maggie, darlin', I can't say I've ever given women's rest rooms much thought."

"Neither has anyone else," she said sweetly. "That's going to change."

Nate was still chuckling when Adam came back into the office a few moments later. His blue eyes gleamed with a suppressed excitement that didn't fool Maggie for an instant. For once, Adam Ridgeway's cool control had slipped.

"What?" she asked, sitting up. "What is it?"

"I just talked to Jaguar. We've got it, Maggie. We've got the 'why.'"

"We do?"

She scrambled out of the leather chair.

Detouring around a half acre of prone sheepdog, she joined Adam at the vice president's desk. Her eyes widened as she scanned the notes he'd scribbled during his conversation with Jaguar.

"Adam! You were right! First Bank is managing James Elliot's blind trust during his term as secretary of the treasury. That might be the connection."

"They're managing more than a blind trust. Elliot has several accounts with them." Adam smiled grimly. "Accounts he failed to disclose during his background investigation and his Senate confirmation hearing. Accounts that received large electronic deposits from offshore banks."

"Good grief! Drug dollars?"

"It's possible, and very likely. We'll have to dig deeper for absolute proof. The mere fact that he failed to disclose the accounts will cost him his office, however."

Maggie shook her head. "But what does all this have to do with me? I don't have any involvement with First Bank. Why did he go to such desperate—?"

She broke off, her eyes widening. "Luis Esteban! Those phone calls I made for him, hinting at high-level government interest in First Bank! My God, Elliot must gotten wind of the calls and thought I was on to something.''

"He thought a nameless, faceless special agent with the code name Chameleon was on to something. He had to flush her out. One way or another.''

Chapter 16

"We're here to see the president. I believe he's expecting us."

The White House usher looked a little startled at Adam's cool announcement. A dubious expression flitted across his face as he took in the gaggle of people ranged behind the special envoy.

Maggie couldn't blame the poor man. They constituted a pretty intimidating crew.

After flying through the night, Air Force Two had landed at Andrews Air Force Base just as a weak January sun washed D.C. in a gray dawn. The entire entourage had piled out of the plane and driven straight into the city. Adam couldn't have shaken any one of them if he tried.

Maggie, of course, wanted to be in on the kill.

Cowboy had come along for backup.

Denise Kowalski refused to abandon her post.

Hank McGowan wanted to make sure Taylor was all right.

gave Maggie a sympathetic smile. "I understand I wasn't the target, after all. It was you all the time."

"We think so."

"Perhaps we should have reversed our roles. Instead of pouring out my most intimate secrets to a stranger, I could've spent a couple of weeks in the mountains with Adam, acting as your double."

"I *don't* think so."

Taylor blinked at the drawled response, and Maggie saw that her message had been received. No one, not even the vice president of the United States, was going to be spending any weeks with Adam Ridgeway. In the mountains or anywhere else.

Except Maggie.

Smiling, she took a sip of her mocha coffee while Taylor greeted the rest of the entourage. She gave Lillian a quick hug, then gasped aloud.

"Radizwell!"

Maggie swung around to see the sheepdog calmly lowering his leg. Having marked his territory to his satisfaction on the delicate hand-painted eighteenth-century wallpaper, he moved on to explore the rest of the office.

Taylor's violet eyes squeezed shut. "I'm going to skin that animal," she said through gritted teeth. "I'm going to skin him and tan him and use him as a throw rug."

Shaking her head in disgust, she summoned the dog. "Come here! Here, boy."

The komondor ignored her.

Adam snapped his fingers once.

Radizwell obediently plodded to Adam's side and settled back on his haunches with a satisfied air. He'd seen his duty, and he'd done it.

Taylor's auburn brows shot up, but before she could comment, the door to the inner office opened.

The chief of staff stepped out, his eyes widening as he looked from Taylor to Maggie, then back again.

"Madam Vice President...er, Madams Vice President, the president will see you now. And you, of course, Mr. Special Envoy. He's asked the secretary of the treasury to join you in a few moments, as you requested."

Adam stood aside to allow the women to precede him. Taylor took one step, then stopped and stood aside for Maggie. "This is your show. You have the honors."

Nodding graciously, Maggie sailed into the Oval Office.

After the gut-wrenching tension and chilling events of the past few days, Maggie would have expected the moment the perpetrator was finally unmasked to be one of high drama.

Instead, James Elliot's face turned ashen the moment he stepped into the Oval Office and saw her standing beside Taylor. When a shaken president confronted his longtime friend with evidence of his failure to disclose ties to a bank with links to a Central American drug cartel, Elliot seemed to collapse in on himself, like a hot-air balloon when the air inside the silk bag cools.

Under Adam's relentless questioning, Elliot admitted everything, including his desperate attempt to silence the woman known only as Chameleon.

Maggie's nails bit into her palms when the man who had wanted to kill her wouldn't even look at her.

"She had to die," he whispered, in a remorseless confession to the president. "That was the best solution. The only solution. I didn't know how much she knew. Just the tiny scrap of information linking First Bank to the frozen assets of the Cartozan drug lord was enough to bring my whole world tumbling down if she followed up on it. She had to die."

"Get him out of here," the president said in disgust.

A grim-faced Denise Kowalski was given the distinction of arresting her own boss. She walked into the Oval Office, flashed Elliot her badge and advised him of his rights. With Buck Evans on one side and Denise on the other, the former secretary of the treasury departed.

For long moments, no one moved. Then the president shoved a hand in the pocket of his charcoal gray slacks and walked over to the tall windows facing south. He stared at the stark obelisk of the Washington Monument rising out of the mists drifting off the tidal basin.

"Christ! Jimmy Elliot!"

His shoulders slumped, and the indefatigable energy that characterized both him and his administration seemed to evaporate.

Adam's eyes met those of the vice president. She gave a slight nod, then addressed the man at the window with remarkable calm.

"You have a press conference in ten minutes, Mr. President. Do you want to go over the treaty provisions a final time, or do you feel comfortable with them?"

The president squared his shoulders. Turning, he gave his deputy a tight smile.

"No, the brief you sent me from Camp David was excellent." He paused, and then his smile eased into one of genuine warmth. "I still can't believe you pulled this treaty off. Good work, Taylor. Whatever the hell bad choices I might have made, when I picked you, I picked a winner."

"I'll remind you of that when you get ready to announce your support for your successor," she replied, laughing.

"You do that!"

Walking across the room, he held out his hand to Maggie. "I'm sorry you had to go through this torturous charade."

"I'm not. The assignment had its finer moments. Besides," she continued smoothly, ignoring Adam's raised brows, "it was all in the line of duty.

"A duty I understand you do extremely well. The director has told me that you're good. Damn good. One of the best."

"*The* best," Adam said coolly.

Maggie flashed him a startled look. His eerie echo of her exact words to Cowboy surprised her, until she remembered the transmitter in her ring. Adam must have heard the entire conversation, including the part about her decision to leave OMEGA!

From the steely expression in his eyes, she knew that this mission's postbrief was going to make all her others seem tame by comparison.

"We'll have to talk about that later," the president said, with a smile for Maggie. "Right now, I have a press conference to conduct. Adam, if you'll stay just a moment, please?"

Some moments later, Maggie stood in the wings beside Adam and Taylor Grant as a composed and forceful chief executive strode to the podium in the White House briefing room. His back straight, he glanced around the packed auditorium. Ignoring the clear Plexiglas TelePrompTer in front of the podium, he addressed the assembled group directly.

"I called this press conference to announce a historic treaty, one that constitutes the first positive step toward eliminating a scourge that hangs over our world."

He paused, his jaw squaring. "But before I give you the details on this treaty, I have another, less pleasant duty to perform. I regret to say that a few moments ago I was forced to request the immediate resignation of James Elliot, my treasury secretary, for reasons I'm not yet at liberty to discuss."

A wave of startled exclamations filled the room. The president waited for them to die down before continuing.

"I can tell you, however, that I've already selected his replacement. Ladies and gentlemen, it gives me great pleasure to introduce my nominee for secretary of the treasury, Adam Ridgeway."

Stunned, Maggie lifted her eyes to the man beside her. She heard the spatter of applause that quickly rolled into thunder. And the hum of excited comments from the audience. And Taylor's warm congratulations. But none of them registered. All that penetrated her whirling mind was the glint in Adam's eyes as he tipped her chin.

"We'll talk about this, among other things, when we get back to headquarters," he promised.

"Our list of items to discuss is getting pretty long," she replied breathlessly.

He kissed her, hard and fast and thoroughly, then strode out to join the president at the podium.

Dazed, Maggie listened to his brief acceptance and the easy way he fielded the storm of questions from the media.

A welter of emotions coursed through her. She couldn't imagine OMEGA without Adam Ridgeway as director. He'd guided the organization and its tight cadre of agents and technicians for so long, with such unerring skill. In her mind, Adam *was* OMEGA.

At the same time, Maggie swelled with pride. She couldn't think of anyone more qualified for a cabinet post than this man.

And she wouldn't have been human if a thrill of excitement hadn't darted through her veins. Adam's promotion meant she didn't have to leave OMEGA. He wouldn't be her boss any longer. What he would be was something they would discuss as soon as they got back to the headquarters. Anticipation and joy leaped through her.

Knowing Adam would be mobbed by the media even after the treaty announcement to follow, Maggie decided to slip away. She wanted to be out of Taylor's skin and in her own when she and Adam met again. For once, Chameleon wanted no guises, no cover, nothing to hide her from the man she loved.

Her pulse thrumming, she turned to leave.

Taylor stopped her with a hand on her arm. "I didn't thank you. For being me when I was the target. Even though it was you... Well, you know what I mean."

Maggie's quicksilver grin blossomed. "It gets confusing, doesn't it? Half the time I wasn't even sure just who the heck I was."

The other woman's eyes gleamed. "It doesn't appear Adam had that problem."

"No, I guess he didn't."

"He'll make an excellent secretary of the treasury. And I think you'd make an excellent special envoy."

For the second time in less than ten minutes, Maggie was dumbfounded. "Me?"

"You. We don't have enough women with your rather unique qualifications in leadership positions. I'll talk to the president about it."

"While you're at it," Maggie replied, still astounded but regrouping fast, "you might mention establishing a commission to—"

She stopped, too anxious to get back to headquarters to take the time to explain the public potty proclamation she'd issued at the Kennedy Center.

"Never mind, I'll talk to you about it later. Right now I have to change back into me. I want to be wearing my own skin when I claim my forever."

A smile feathered Taylor's lips. "Your forever? That's nice."

"It's from your ring."

At her blank look, Maggie held up her hand. "The inscription in your wedding ring. *Now, and forever.*"

"What are you talking about? There's no inscription in my ring."

Chapter 17

On the outside, the elegant Federal-style town house on a quiet side street just off Massachusetts Avenue appeared no different than its neighbors. Neatly banked snow edged the brick steps leading to its black-painted door. A brass knocker in the shape of an eagle gleamed in the cold afternoon sunlight. The bronze plaque that identified the structure as home to the offices of the president's special envoy was small and discreet, drawing the attention of few passersby.

Inside, however, the town house hummed with an activity level that would have astounded even the most jaded observer of the Washington political scene.

Raking fingers through hair newly restored to its original glossy chestnut color, Maggie stepped out of the third-floor crew room into a control center crackling with noise. Joe Samuels's banks of electronic boxes buzzed and beeped and blipped continually as the harried senior communications technician fielded a steady stream of transmissions from all corners of the globe. Word of the president's startling announcement had been beamed to OMEGA agents in the field, and they wanted to know the details. All the details.

"Roger, Cyrene," Joe said into the transmitter. "It's true. The confirmation hearings are scheduled for next week. There are going to be some changes around here."

His dark eyes caught Maggie's. "A lot of changes," he added, grinning.

Maggie shook her head at his knowing grin. She'd only been back from the White House a little over two hours. Most of that time had been spent with Jaguar in a closed-door mission debrief, the rest in a fever of anticipation in the crew room, working frantically to restore herself to her natural state.

She hadn't had time to discuss with anyone, let alone the still-absent Adam, any of the several urgent items on her list. Yet OMEGA's global network had already spread the word. There were going to be some changes around here. A lot of them.

Joe answered another beep, then nodded to Maggie over his bank of equipment. "Chief's on the way back from the White House, Chameleon. Be here in fifteen minutes. Think he'll have any news for us?"

Maggie sidestepped Joe's less-than-subtle probe to discover what she knew, if anything, about Adam's replacement. The idea that she might actually be named to head OMEGA was too fantastic to consider. Besides, she had more important matters to take care of right now.

"I don't know," she replied, heading for the elevator. "I'll let you know as soon as I hear anything for sure."

She took the specially shielded high-speed elevator to the underground lab and bearded the chief of Special Devices in his den.

"I need that special lubricant, Harry. Right away."